MRS RUSHWORTH

MRS RUSHWORTH

a novel by

Victor Gordon

ANDRE DEUTSCH

First published in Great Britain 1989 by
André Deutsch Limited
105-106 Great Russell Street London WC1B 3LJ

British Library Cataloguing in Publication Data

Gordon, Victor
Mrs Rushworth.
I. Title
823′.914[F]

ISBN 0 233 98358 9

Phototypeset by Falcon Graphic Art Ltd
Wallington, Surrey
Printed in Great Britain by
Billing and Sons Limited, Worcester

OVERTURE

By way of epilogue to Mansfield Park *and prologue to the present work*

If generosity, or what often passes for that elusive virtue, is sometimes reciprocated by ingratitude, it may also be inspired by nothing more amiable than the hope that a liberal act will erase a mean one. Such cause and effect were both apparent in the dispositions which followed the desertion of Mr Rushworth by his bride, Maria Bertram, and the subsequent desertion of Maria by her admirer, Mr Crawford. Sir Thomas Bertram, despite his better judgement, having given his daughter in marriage to, or as it turned out *against*, a man whose only claim to good sense was the enjoyment of £12,000 a year, was perfectly capable of apprehending that family support and affection alone could undo the damage which family teaching and family ambition had largely created. Instead he gave her money. He settled an ample allowance on his elder daughter subject, of course, to her never darkening his portal again, by which magnanimous act he simultaneously saved himself from the prickings of conscience, absolved Mansfield Park and its example of all possible blame, and protected a considerable part of Northamptonshire from the risk of moral contamination.

3

Mr Henry Crawford, more spoilt than spoiling, was equally eager to purchase freedom from the obligations he had assumed in pique, bravado and disappointment after Fanny Price had rejected his hand for the second time.

That both gentlemen paid rather over the odds for their respective evasions was thanks to Mrs Norris. The negotiation of Maria's allowance had been her last contribution to the family weal before her own departure from Mansfield. Sir Thomas's anxiety to speed his sister-in-law on her way had added £100 to the £750 per annum which he believed would secure his daughter's comfort.

Mr Crawford was also responsive to Mrs Norris's disinterested persuasion. While approving society's view that Mrs Rushworth alone should bear the censure for their joint misconduct, he was quick to appreciate that the military interlude which now suggested itself as a suitable and patriotic outlet for his energies might be jeopardised if, as Mrs Norris solicitously suggested, his recent behaviour were scrutinised too carefully by the regiment in which he was to purchase a commission. In the event, the acceptance of his services by the 15th Hussars cost somewhat less than the withdrawal of his services from Maria, since in the latter case he had to forfeit one of the Crawford farms in addition to a lump sum.

Thus Maria Rushworth, beautiful, reckless, and divorced, found herself in the social wilderness with only her money and her aunt to console her. They were of little avail. At first, she allowed Mrs Norris to order her whole existence, giving personal opinions only in contexts which involved the vindication of her own conduct or the vilification of Mr Rushworth's, Mr Crawford's, or Sir Thomas's. Her aunt encouraged her to believe that she was wholly blameless and that everyone else was guilty. So emphatic and repeated were her animadversions that, as the months wore by, they began to lose their power to evoke response. Occasionally, spurred by some devious contumely or responding to fresh charges, Maria would become animated again, but only to revert to listlessness and torpor as soon as the new line of thought led back, as it inevitably did, to the extenuations and exculpations they had so frequently rehearsed. Still Mrs Norris persevered; there was, in all conscience, little enough to talk about as they journeyed through the country on the extended tour she had prescribed before they should settle down in the decent obscurity upon which Sir Thomas insisted.

'So it has come to this,' she began one morning, putting down the newspaper, 'your brother and cousin are married. Fanny has become Mrs Edmund Bertram. I knew it would happen. The moment that girl set foot in our house ten years ago, she determined to capture Edmund, and now she has succeeded. How often did I warn Sir Thomas that she was not to be trusted, coming from where she did. But he would never understand who and what she really was. He insisted on treating her almost – though not quite (I saw to that) – like his own flesh and blood, and look at the result! Would that she had stayed in Portsmouth where she belonged. Of course, my dearest Maria, I must bear part of the responsibility, I am first to admit that. It was my original idea that we should try to help Fanny. Mine was the generous impulse, though goodness knows I could ill afford it, to relieve my poor younger sister of the burden of Fanny's maintenance and education. Ah, if only I could have foreseen the outcome. But that is ever the way: selflessness goes unremarked, unrewarded, while single-minded, self-seeking ambition carries all and everyone before it. Your own misfortunes, my dearest, are attributable to Fanny. It was her obstinate, arrogant, and ungrateful refusal of Mr Crawford (an offer she was in duty bound to accept in view of her uncle's clearly expressed wishes) which was the real cause of that misguided young

5

gentleman's subsequent behaviour towards you. In effect, you and I are paying for Fanny's selfishness.'

Mrs Norris paused. It was on the tip of her tongue to add that before refusing him, Fanny had designedly set her cap at Henry Crawford and by so doing had diverted his affections from Maria herself. Perceiving, however, that this argument was far from complimentary to her favourite, she hastily continued (Maria herself vouchsafing no remark) with a line of thought which took her to the safe, familiar ground of self-congratulation.

'Of course, it is money she is marrying, not Edmund. Fanny came to us without a penny and can never forget it. Now she will be dowered by Sir Thomas and before she is finished she will be mistress of Mansfield Park – for, mark my words, your brother Tom will never reach thirty. Edmund will inherit both title and estate, and Fanny Price will be the next Lady Bertram. Whatever next? Not that I worry on my own account. Money and titles mean nothing to me, and never have. I am constantly astonished at the way some people will stop at nothing to acquire them. In Fanny's case, however, she will have to put up with less than her full pound of flesh. At least I have the satisfaction of knowing that you are adequately provided for, my dearest. Thank goodness I arranged your allowance, and had it very substantially increased, before your cousin achieved total power over Sir Thomas. At least something was salvaged from the wreck. She shall never get her greedy little hands on your money, not while I have anything to say about it.'

Intelligence of the forthcoming marriage elicited no immediate response in Maria. All at Mansfield were collectively attainted by their failure to stand by her in her misfortune, yet she realised that neither Edmund nor Fanny possessed the will to resist Sir Thomas, on her behalf, even had they so wished. She had never particularly liked

– or disliked – her cousin, regarding her first as a timid and sickly dependant, latterly as a harmless though
insipid embodiment of the deadly virtues. Even in her
present bitterness, however, Maria found it difficult to
accept Mrs Norris's accusations. Sympathy for the social
transgressor and subterfuge for personal gain both seemed
outside Fanny's compass. Edmund himself, while revealing
an unsuspected streak of nonconformity in his long flirtation
with Mary Crawford, had reverted to the path of impeccable
respectability following his ordination. He was cut out to be
one of those clergymen for whom Mary Magdalene was an
embarrassment, and for whom good Samaritans and prodigal
sons – (or sisters) – offered no lessons which were consistent
with the maintenance of ecclesiastical dignity.

Had she been in the habit of looking truthfully into her
own mind, Maria might have realised that this family marriage,
and the happiness it implied, added jealousy to the remorse
and isolation which were her daily lot. As it was, she merely
saw that unless she affected indifference, Mrs Norris would
revert to the marriage constantly, so she determined to say
and think as little about the subject as possible.

Try as she might, however, her thoughts returned regularly to Mansfield Park, her childhood and youth. Certain
scenes, etched as it were on her memory – the rehearsals
for those ill-fated theatricals, her father's terrible return from
Antigua, the visit to Sotherton – came to her again and
again; others lurked secretly until, unbidden, they surfaced,
sometimes rubbing salt into her wounds, sometimes balm.
One such involved an episode soon after Fanny's arrival at
Mansfield. Just fourteen, Maria was alone in the schoolroom
pretending to work but really day-dreaming about romance,
matrimony and London. The sound of weeping invaded her
dream and distracted her from the most promising dalliance.
That funny little cousin of hers must be crying on the attic

7

stairs. She tried to go back to her reverie but the sobbing continued. Reluctantly but with quite good grace for a fourteen-year-old bidding fair to become a duchess, she opened the door and tiptoed, so as not to alarm the pale pinched ten-year-old, towards the staircase. At that moment she heard a new voice.

'My dear little cousin, what can be the matter? Are you ill? Is anyone angry with you? Have you had a quarrel with Maria or Julia? Or do you not understand your lessons? Can I help you with them?' Maria was surprised at the gentleness of her brother's voice – he never spoke to his sisters like that (but never had cause to either). Fanny blew her nose and began to stop crying. Maria softly returned to the contemplation of ducal coronets.

Remembered now after all those years, the incident helped to reconcile Maria to the marriage. It reminded that while she may have been outwardly reserved to her cousin, inwardly she was quite well disposed towards her. Fanny was not among those she owed a special debt of guilt and therefore not one of those whom she now had to resent. As to Edmund, well, he had staked his claim on Fanny's affections soon enough. Maria did not think him capable of what she would call happiness but she supposed the couple would find contentment in a minor key.

She came to this realisation on a solitary walk soon after they had reached a new resting place on their Grand Tour. In front of her was the gleaming bow window of some local tradesman, on either side attractive, newish houses, and just down the road baths, opened a few years before, which formed the chief attraction of the little town, and had recommended it to Mrs Norris. Maria could not remember the name of the place but it seemed pleasant enough. A closer look at the shop in front of her showed that it belonged to a Mr Hollies and that his principal activity was the letting and sale of local property. On impulse she opened the door and asked to speak to the proprietor.

'I am thinking of settling here for a spell,' she told him, 'and require a small, furnished residence. Have you anything which would suit two single ladies?'

Mr Hollies was sure he could oblige. What style would the ladies be living in? Would they be entertaining very much? How much garden would they require? And how large a staff?

Maria cut short his questions. There would be no entertaining and a minimum of staff. All they required was something warm, comfortable, and reasonably secluded. Maria spoke in the most offhand manner Mr Hollies had ever encountered in his professional life; it was as if she were not at all interested in where she lived. Yet there was nothing to suggest that the enquiry was idle.

'I have four properties on my books which I believe would suit you admirably, madam.' He took some papers from a drawer. 'First there is Spa Villa, a most delightful abode; then there is Sycamore Cottage, charmingly secluded yet close to church and shops; or Copenhagen Lodge, completed in the year of the great victory and lived in by one family ever since; or Hamlet House, somewhat larger than the other three, and with a small park. I am sure that any of these four would be perfect for you, madam, and I shall be most happy personally to conduct you round the properties so that you may see which suits your needs particularly.'

'That will not be necessary.' Again she cut him short. 'Your professional word that each would suit is quite enough. Should you be wrong we shall merely leave.' She glanced at the carefully written details he had placed before her. The three smaller houses seemed very similar.

'Let us take Copenhagen Lodge.' Mr Crawford's commission in the army had given her a marked bias in favour of the Royal Navy.

'Certainly, madam. I can have it prepared for your reception within a week if you so wish.'

With something between a nod of assent and a shrug of indifference, she gave him to understand that the date she took possession of Copenhagen Lodge could be left to Mr Hollies.

'May I enquire you name, madam?'

'Mrs Rushworth. You will find me at the Crown Hotel.'

Mr Hollies bowed and began his standard speech about being honoured to do business with so distinguished a client, never guessing in what particular Maria was indeed celebrated. But his client was already at the door.

'By the by,' she said, 'what is this village called?'

'Why Leamington, madam, Leamington Priors.' He looked in astonishment at the departing figure, and thought that he had never seen a lovelier face nor a sadder expression. Now, if she had been in mourning . . .

'Or Leamington *Spa*, madam, as some of us now think it should be called. Copenhagen Lodge is most conveniently placed for the— ' But she was gone.

Mrs Norris was as surprised as Mr Hollies when she heard what Maria had done, but not nearly as pleased. It was no plan of hers that Maria should make important decisions, and even minor decisions were expected to be made in full consultation with herself.

'Impossible, Maria, I have no wish to bury myself in this – this Leamington.'

'Where else then, aunt? London and Brighton, Bath and Bristol are all impossible. Likewise our home county, or Mr Crawford's Norfolk, or Mr Yates's Wiltshire (for my sister and I have no wish to see each other at present).

10

Would you have us go to Mrs Price's Portsmouth, perchance?'

'Of course not, but there still remains much of England. We should look around first and decide on a place which will suit us both.'

'Oh, what does it matter where we live? One place is as good as another. Or as bad.'

'But my dear child, we would find many towns more lively and fashionable than this. True it would be difficult to go to London or Brighton, but we do not have to cut ourselves off from the possibility of any diversion at all, I hope. Hastings or Eastbourne, now— '

'Next year; sometime; perhaps. But not now. We have been moving from one place to another for two years, and I, for one, must stop. Travel changes nothing. If anything it makes matters worse. No post-chaise or stage-coach can convey me from my past. I now realise that I must live with it, and I propose to try living with it in Leamington. You must do as you please.'

This speech was the second surprise of the day. Not only was it the firmest expression of opinion which Maria had made since the collapse of her affair with Crawford, it was also her first serious essay in self-examination. As such it marked a change in relations between the two women. Mrs Norris would still dominate, but Maria began to sense the authority which financial and mental independence could confer.

'Really, Maria, I think you must allow me to know best. I abhor travelling myself but I apprehend that you, above all, need the stimulus of new scenes and new experiences. I consider it my duty to make you understand this, and to accompany you. Through no fault of your own, misfortunes have been heaped upon your head; to settle down here and now, in a place you know nothing about, would be

11

purest folly, and probably lead to enduring distress. Not that I mind about myself. As a hapless widow I have long ceased to have any ideas of personal gratification, but in *your* interest I must insist that we continue the journey I have planned so carefully. Our arrival in York, for instance, coincides with a visit of Mr Kean at the Theatre Royal and I have a passion to see him.'

'You may go to York, but I stay here in Leamington.'

Mrs Norris could usually compel those weaker, poorer, or gentler than herself into bending to her wishes, and in small matters her determination could very often win the consent of those who were richer or stronger than herself, but she lacked that firmness of purpose and soundness of principle which prevail in matters of serious moment. At root, she was infinitely flexible in her views, seeking only to maximise her self-esteem in any situation which presented itself. Faced with Maria's intransigence, she soon began to see merit in prolonging the stay at Leamington – a rented house, for example, would be cheaper than the hotel. Before the week was out, having taken Maria's hint and visited Mr Hollies herself, she had dropped all opposition to the scheme, and begun to treat it as if it were her own. Whether Mr Hollies was relieved to find that the second of his lady clients was prepared to take a more normal interest in the Copenhagen Lodge letting is open to conjecture.

'I have inspected the house twice now and think it may serve our purpose adequately. Certain alterations, naturally, will have to be made. The curtains in the drawing-room must be replaced and the pictures are a disgrace. Wishy-washy things by a Mr Turner, obviously knocked down at auction as a job lot suitable for provincials. I have instructed Hollies to procure engravings of Warwickshire country seats instead. And some of the furniture is so frail and delicate – though new – that it will surely break as soon as the servants touch it. I

12

told Hollies we could take no responsibility for such shoddy stuff and that he must either replace it or reduce the rent. And talking of rent, do you know what the man was asking? A full £50 per annum. Naturally, I told him that was out of the question and offered £25. We agreed on £37 10s to be paid six-monthly in arrears. As for the spare room, that will have to be redecorated entirely, at the owner's expense.'

'What do we want a spare room for, aunt?'

'Oh, I must have a spare room for a friend. I always have had a spare room for a friend, however much it might cost me. Goodness knows I have barely enough for my own needs but I hope I have not come to such a pass, since poor Norris's departure, that I can never offer hospitality to a friend.'

Mrs Norris proceeded to exercise her talents for household management with selfless energy, exemplary thrift, and perspicacious attention to detail. As a result, the two ladies moved into Copenhagen Lodge within six weeks instead of one. The extra time had been profitably employed in antagonising Mr Hollies, establishing acrimonious relationships with the local tradespeople, and rejecting excellent cooks and housemaids in favour of a Mrs Dollery and her niece, previously considered unemployable but now persuaded that their true vocation was to serve Mrs Norris at half the going rate.

Edmund Bertram and Fanny Price were married, meanwhile, at Thornton Lacey church. It was a beautiful and solemn occasion. Lady Bertram had a nice little nap during the bishop's address.

BOOK ONE

Chapter One

All too soon after Quatre-Bras and Waterloo, the pleasures of war gave way to the horrors of peace. Twenty-two years of conflict with Napoleon had been an economic godsend to landowners, merchants, and industrialists; had united the kingdom more effectively than the Act of Union; had even improved living standards for the poor. Bonaparte's defeat, however, was followed by an economic depression which quickly embraced the whole victorious country. The worst sufferers were the urban masses – thrown out of work or, if still employed, forced to accept reduced wages at a time when prices were rising steeply. Yet the journeymen and small factory owners, the craftsmen, the farmers, the shopkeepers, and, by degrees, the upper-middle and upper classes all, however unequally, began to feel the pinch. To maintain their way of life, the latter increasingly resorted to mortgages and borrowings, often at usurious rates, as a result of which bankers and financial entrepreneurs – Jacob Rothschild being the archetype – greatly increased their power, and more gradually their status, in the country. While the upper class instinct for survival decreed acceptance, with reluctant alacrity, of this new blood, the lower class instinct for survival had no such lifeline. Together with what remained of the peasantry and small yeomanry, the landless workers, now half the population and including some 300,000 soldiers demobilised without gratuity (or medal) for saving their country, were overwhelmed by one single fact of life, the cost of bread. Hunger and despair rapidly split the country back into two nations.

The family at Mansfield Park, though more concerned with the price of cake than that of bread, was no exception to the rule. Sir Thomas's affairs in Antigua again took a turn for the worse and his farming interests at home, along with those of all landowners who had increased their wheat acreages during the war, were adversely affected by the slump in agricultural prices. He passionately advocated duties on imported wheat of up to five pounds a quarter, but though he sat in a House of Commons which spent a disproportionate amount of its time debating and amending the Corn Laws, the paradox of wheat prices being too low for the wheat-growers and bread prices being too high for the breadwinners continued for a quarter of a century.

One daughter's adultery and the other's elopement, however, had a restraining, sobering influence on the rest of the family. Prudent extravagance prevailed at Mansfield Park rather than the self-gratifying folly which, led by the Court, overtook fashionable society. Tom Bertram, for example, lived only a little beyond his means, and even when he had at last thrown off the debilitation of his long illness, never returned wholeheartedly to his former pursuits. Lady Bertram, for her part, expected no additional comforts to those she already enjoyed, though she allowed herself to indulge Susan Price in a way she had never indulged Susan's sister and predecessor, Fanny. Similarly, Mrs Edmund Bertram exercised dutiful thrift in the tasteful improvements she ordered to the parsonage at Thornton Lacey, and in the arrangements she made as to servants, carriage, and furnishings – permitting herself only what was expected, indeed demanded, of a baronet's daughter-in-law.

Sir Thomas, however, did not always appreciate his good fortune in having so few extra demands upon his purse.

'I could sometimes wish that we still had your aunt's example,' he confided one day to Edmund and Fanny. 'If we could have the benefit of Mrs Norris's frugality while dispensing with the delights of her company, the future well-being of the estate would be assured.'

Edmund considered for some moments before replying, 'I believe my aunt to be an exceedingly worthy person and have no inclination, either as nephew or as clergyman, to criticise her in any respect. Her zeal for economy and her self-denial are lessons for us all. Nevertheless, one cannot help remembering that her charity not only began at but was confined to home, and one fears, sir, that her return to Mansfield, whatever its non-material gains, would prove an added burden rather than a financial saving to the estate.'

Sir Thomas had no serious wish for Mrs Norris's return to the family circle, and was resolved that should she ever take up residence in the White House, and he allowed she had the right, she should do so on a very different footing from before as regards the Park; however, time and distance were beginning to lend a measure of enchantment to her austerities.

'We must be thankful, sir, that at least Maria has Aunt Norris's guiding hand in these difficult times,' said Fanny.

For over two years following the scandal, Maria's name had not been uttered by the family. All intercourse with the erring daughter had been conducted through Sir Thomas's lawyers even after the penitent Julia, now Mrs Yates, had been readmitted to the fold. Arrangements for the dispatch of certain personal belongings to Leamington, however, had made it necessary for Maria's continued existence to be acknowledged, and the acknowledgement had not, strange to relate, produced the vapours in Lady Bertram, apoplexy in Sir Thomas, or fainting fits in

Fanny. About that time, true, the latter had begun to experience occasional bouts of giddiness but these were due to conjugal rights rather than cousinly wrongs, and it was Fanny, her prestige further strengthened by the promise of Sir Thomas's first grandchild, who most frequently alluded to Maria.

'Mrs Rushworth is adequately provided for, I think.'

'Oh more than adequately, sir; most generously,' said Fanny.

'Even without Mrs Norris she could manage very comfortably on half of what I allow her. A single woman with no dependants.'

'Do you not suppose, sir, that she may in some measure at least have to support my aunt?' enquired Edmund.

'Very possibly, but Mrs Norris has her own £600 a year, to say nothing of what she must have put by while she lived at Mansfield. Between them they must have nearer two thousand than one per annum, assuming one includes the liberal – however tainted – settlement from Crawford.'

'The expenses of removing to Copenhagen Lodge may have been very heavy,' said Fanny.

'I hardly think so. The house is small and furnished, the rental modest. The removal can scarcely have cost them £50 and the running costs cannot exceed £150 per annum.'

'If indeed that, sir. When I think how little Fanny and I need with our much wider responsibilities (both current and expected), it is difficult to perceive where their far greater resources will be deployed. Not that their money will avail them aught; no income, however large, can purchase a clear conscience.'

'Very true, Edmund, your self-denial does you credit.

Yet it remains unfortunate, to say the least, that the guilty should enjoy easy circumstances at the expense of the innocent. For the circumstances at Copenhagen Lodge must surely be easier than those at Mansfield Park as long as our present inadequate and iniquitous Corn Law continues. Besides, if it were not for Maria, I could make better provision for you.'

'Oh do not consider us,' cried Fanny. 'We only hope that our own economies will help beloved Mansfield through these troublesome days. We all have to suffer it seems . . .'

At this Fanny broke off, bit her lip, and began to cry quietly but bravely. The two men exchanged understanding glances: tears were only to be expected of someone in Fanny's condition. The immediate cause, it transpired, was her brother rather than her baby, however. The thought of innocent people suffering had reminded her that Lieutenant William Price R.N. was shortly to lose his ship and be put on half pay. He was due to visit Thornton Lacey as soon as Fanny had recovered from her confinement, but the pleasure which his lengthy stay promised was clouded by doubts about his future.

Edmund tried to comfort his wife, and Sir Thomas made his departure, but the subject of their conversation was by no means terminated. The incongruity of Maria's relative wealth and the family's reduced circumstances, the moral and legal impossibility of reversing the said situation, and the lack of true thrift in his own household became increasing preoccupations with Sir Thomas, invariably ventilated on his visits to the parsonage.

In due course, Fanny was delivered of a small and sickly son. Named after his Uncle William, he surprised the doctors by living nearly three months. The grandfather took Billy Bertram's death almost as much to heart as the parents.

21

Edmund decided that the iniquity of fathers being visited upon children, as promised in Exodus 20, subsumed the iniquity of aunts being visited upon nephews. In short, the new family tragedy was a consequence of the old family scandal.

Chapter Two

Back in 1814 the publication of *Mansfield Park* had made some small stir in London but none in the provinces where *Waverley*, another anonymous work, became the rage. It was not until a few months after Fanny's ill-fated confinement that the book came into the hands of Maria and her aunt. On one of her regular visits to the new library in Leamington, Mrs Norris had chanced upon it, quickly divined its subject, and purchased all three volumes of the only copy in the shop. Soon read, it made a profound impression on both women and was better understood by Maria than by Mrs Norris. Both agreed that it was a prejudiced, proud, and unpersuasive account of the affair, lacking equally in sense of propriety and sensibility of understanding.

'The author, whoever he may be, has no understanding of what took place or why,' declared Mrs Norris, 'although some of the facts are superficially correct. He seems absolutely unaware, for example, of Fanny's consistent policy of insinuating herself into Sir Thomas's good graces at the expense of her cousins.'

'Yet in certain ways he – or she, for I suspect a female hand – is perceptive about Fanny. It must indeed have been strange and difficult for her at first. There is some truth in the early part of the book; Edmund was always kinder to our little cousin than the rest of us.'

'A sentimental, mawkish kindness perhaps, but the real solicitude, though I say it myself, was mine. It was I and I alone who brought Fanny to Mansfield. But of course I receive no credit for that. Not that I care: by my age one has ceased to expect any just appreciation of what one does for others.'

'The author is less than generous about you – about all of us except Edmund and Fanny (and even they are not depicted as very appealing characters). But he does at least show your force of character, aunt. In a way you emerge as the strongest person in the story.'

Mrs Norris was somewhat mollified. In reading the book she had noted with approval the central part ascribed to her and the prominence often given to her views, but had largely missed, or misunderstood, the author's defamatory asides.

'Yes, it has some merit, I suppose. That only makes it the more perverse that you are allowed none of the virtues, except your good looks, and Fanny, with her false humility, her sanctimonious humbug, and her overweening ambition is depicted as a paragon.'

'As to Fanny, I always thought her a timid little creature. She was poor company, with nothing to say for herself, and no sense of humour. Yet, to be fair, she had good taste and sound judgement in some things. Fanny was the first to appreciate the worthlessness of Rushworth, and she was never deceived by Crawford. Her views on conduct are pious and conventional in the extreme but they are sincerely held.'

'Is it not more than coincidence that she is so closely in accord with Sir Thomas?'

'No doubt his example has helped to mould her character, but I suspect that she would have been much the same whatever her upbringing. In short she is dull by nature not by design.'

Mrs Norris began to reiterate her charges against Fanny without having pondered Maria's view, but her niece broke in and changed the subject.

'Where I take exception to the author is in her description of Julia and myself. She looks sympathetically at the childish Fanny and explains her fears with womanly insight, but she treats us with unmitigated and uncomprehending severity from the start. We are presented as vain, selfish, unprincipled minxes – our characters fully formed by the ages of twelve and thirteen respectively. In reality I suspect we were normal children, high spirited and self-centred at times, but nothing worse. The only kind thing she says about us in the whole book is that we had "no positive ill nature". In my opinion the ill nature is on the side of the author.'

'I cannot recall the book giving any instances of your being cruel to Fanny.'

'No, for there were none, except that we had an unspoken agreement to leave her with Edmund (whom she liked best) as much as possible. We regarded her as my brother's preserve. As far as I can remember, Julia and I, who were almost of an age, treated Fanny very much as we would have treated a younger sister. But, as I say, even if we were on occasion thoughtless (as we must have been), we were but children ourselves. The author shows no sympathy for our youthfulness and no understanding of how ill-judged, in many respects, was our preparation for the world. We are depicted as mature, vain and wicked from the start.'

'Ill-judged?' broke in Mrs Norris. 'How can you say that? You had every advantage: the best instructors, a sensible balance between formal education and the artistic accomplishments expected of a lady, a curriculum sanctioned by your father and supervised by myself. Few people are more fortunate.'

'Aunt, I attach little blame to you. My father's wishes were correctly interpreted and faithfully implemented, but – and I have often thought about this during these last years – my father's ambitions for us, and the training we were given to further those ambitions, led naturally, almost inevitably, to the events described at the end of this book. Mansfield Park is the true villain of the piece, not the daughter of the house.'

'I cannot accept that argument, Maria.'

'Let me explain farther. Julia and I were prepared exclusively for advantageous matrimony. Our book work, our music and painting, our social training were all fashioned for the acquisition of suitable, that is to say rich, husbands. Marriage was almost a religion at Mansfield Park. Allowing us considerable freedom in small things, my father expected unquestioning obedience in any matter he considered impor-tant. From an early age I knew I would have no real choice in the selection of a husband. Oh yes, there was always the chance that I might happen to fall in love with someone who was also "suitable". Without that hope, life would have been intolerable, for all its comfort. Rushworth was precisely the kind of person I was brought up to marry. He was the most eligible young man in our neighbourhood, so I did what was required of me and consented to the betrothal. It was foolish and cowardly, but all my upbringing pushed me into the match. No one, least of all my father, considered what kind of a person Rushworth might be. That was unimportant. All that mattered was that he had twelve thousand a year and would add lustre to the house of Bertram. Do you see what I mean?'

'No. It was your decision to marry him and to do so with almost precipitate haste. I grant that the older generation indulged, as it always does, in a little match-making, but it was perfectly understood that the final decision was with the young people themselves.'

'In theory, no doubt, but in practice that final decision had been made in the schoolroom. And if it had not been Rushworth, it would only have been someone else very like him. I did not understand what was happening at the time and I do not fully understand it now, but I am sure it wasn't I who married him – it was the dutiful daughter of Mansfield Park. It is a great pity the book misses that point (and most unfair).'

'And was it the dutiful daughter of Mansfield Park who – who . . .'

'Who looked elsewhere for the connubial obligations which her husband could not . . .' Maria coloured. Apart from Mr Rushworth himself, Henry Crawford was the only person who realised that her marriage had been consummated by proxy. She continued hastily. 'Who absconded with Crawford? I suppose not. That was a prisoner trying to escape. She escaped into another prison, true, but not such a degrading one as marriage to Rushworth. Anyone reading that book with an impartial mind would understand. They would also see that Fanny and Edmund are an ill-matched pair. Edmund would have done better with Mary Crawford. She might have made something of him. How depressing it all is! I cannot believe that *Mansfield Park* will enjoy much success, however, since the author is clearly a most disenchanted person. Hardly a single character is portrayed in a sympathetic light; even Fanny is depicted as being pious, moralising, and obstinate to excess. I suspect that the author – who on earth can it be? – is just as disillusioned with the world's behaviour as I am.'

'The book will doubtless achieve the failure it deserves,' agreed Mrs Norris, 'yet however unattractive the characters and inaccurate the reporting, I had rather that it were not read in Leamington. Should any further copies find their way to the library I shall purchase them all, or have Mrs Dollery do so, no matter what the cost to me personally. By the by,

26

the price demanded is a disgraceful seven shillings and sixpence for each volume, so I have reimbursed myself twenty
two shillings and sixpence from the money you gave me yesterday. It is but a small price to pay for a good name.'

'Do as you please. I have no interest in my name, good
or bad.' Maria picked up the third volume thoughtfully. 'Yet
I own I am puzzled about the identity of the author and the
source of his (or her) information.'

'I collect there were a number of newspaper reports
about – about your "matrimonial fracas" as they called it at the
time. It was in the newspapers almost before we heard about
it at Mansfield, for instance, and as the book admits, the first
Fanny heard about it was a report she read in Portsmouth. Is
it not probable that some Grub Street hack has reconstructed
the rest of the story?'

'But how? We were not consulted.'

'Your scandalmonger is deft at eliciting confidential information from the unwary. Fanny, Edmund, Tom, the Price
family – all of them could have helped unwittingly. And Mary
Crawford, what a source of information she would make!'

'Or my mother, yes. But the style of the book is not
that of a Grub Street hack. Like it or not, one cannot
but remark distinction in the writing. Besides a mere journalist would hardly have won the confidence of Fanny and
Edmund. The last thing they would have wanted to do was
talk about the scandal.'

'Yet once it was in the papers . . .'

'The facts and events reported are accurate, but over
and over again the author's explanation of our behaviour
or motives is quite one-sided. It sounds like Fanny speaking,
yet Fanny could never have written about us all like that.'

'You say the facts are true, but — '

'Substantially true, yes, but selectively so, of course. Any
fact to one's advantage is omitted. The author of *Mansfield*

Park is horribly clever at giving harmless actions the most sinister connotations.'

'Well, if he is not a journalist he must be a skilled and experienced writer of some sort. The libel reads like a novel. I wash my hands of the authorship and only hope the book is accepted as fiction.'

As Mrs Norris's nice, clean hands stretched for the scissors, she was struck by a new idea: 'Should we not take the publisher to court, Maria?'

'And stir it all just when people are beginning to forget? Beside, all the more damaging facts have already been published in the papers. The book says nothing worse than what has been public knowledge since Fanny's father found that column of innuendo and gossip in the *Morning Post*, as reported in the book itself. We had best leave ill alone.'

A pause ensued. Maria took up her work listlessly while Mrs Norris considered the new light thrown upon her niece's short-lived marriage. It had never occurred to her that Maria might have had legitimate grounds for an annulment. Too late now to invoke canon law but there was time to spare for shocked enjoyment of Mr Rushworth's marital shortcomings. They offered justification for Maria's contempt, mitigation for her infidelity, and hours of spiteful, scandalised, genteel diversion so long as Maria would countenance the subject.

'Although Mr Norris and I were denied the felicity of issue,' she mused circumspectly, 'that was not because my husband neglected his conjugal rights. In the early days of our union, he was perhaps too mindful of them, even declaring on one occasion that duty and inclination seldom coincided so forcefully in the clergyman's daily lot – a personal compliment which succeeded in its purpose despite my having a sick headache at the time and despite his having had his way as recently as the previous month. Happily his prayers and mine were subsequently answered, and he was granted the precious gift of continency. But if Mr Rushworth never – was unable – my dearest, in that case you were never married at all in the eyes of the church and could have procured a dissolution, with honour to yourself and shame to your husband.'

'So it would seem. I wish I had known at the time. My education was sadly lacking until completed, in more ways than one, by Mr Crawford.'

'Poor Mr Rushworth,' said Mrs Norris complacently. 'I always knew there was something not quite manly about him. The book suggests as much, now I come to think of it.'

Thenceforth Mrs Norris kept a wary eye on the library, visiting it almost daily and gaining some small reputation as a bookworm. For several weeks no copy of *Mansfield Park* appeared on the shelves, but the fateful day arrived when a further supply of three complete sets answered Mrs Norris's enquiring look. The problem of abstracting all nine volumes without exciting attention immediately began to exercise her. If she bought the whole consignment, questions might be asked by the garrulous sisters who ran the library, and another batch of copies would most certainly be ordered. The place was practically empty, moreover, which meant that any purchase made would bring literary comment from the Misses Clissold. The stratagem hit upon by Mrs Norris was to buy one copy of *Mansfield Park* together with two other works, both by Lord Byron. Inevitably it was *The Corsair*, and, more particularly, *The Bride of Abydos* which became the subject of the librarians' approving but slightly shocked comment, and by the time Mrs Norris was back at Copenhagen Lodge neither lady would have been able to name the third purchase.

The second part of the plan was to send Maria to the library – where she was to all intents and purposes unknown – and that was equally successful. By mid-morning two of the three copies were safely under

29

lock and key. Mrs Norris then dispatched the cook on a similar errand.

'Mrs Dollery, please go and fetch me a book called *Mansfield Park* from the library. I saw it there this morning. *Mansfield Park*, can you remember that? Here are the twenty-two shillings and sixpence which the three volumes will cost.'

'Yes ma'am.'

'Thank you. What is the name of the book?'

'. . . Mans . . . Field . . . er, place?'

'No, not place, Mrs Dollery, *park*. *Mansfield Park*. Don't say place on any account. Remember it must be *park*.'

Mrs Dollery departed with the word 'park' ringing in her ears and when she reached the library forgot the Mansfield bit.

'I know it's "something Park", beginning with an M. Mmm – something – Park,' she told Miss Clissold. 'Oh dear, the mistress will be that cross if I don't get it right.'

Miss Clissold could think of no book or author which fitted 'Mum – something – Park' and consulted Miss Betty Clissold.

'M . . . Mmmm . . . Ummm I know, Mungo Park. The explorer. That must be it!' Just to make sure the librarians consulted their catalogue and found there were no other Parks prefaced by an M. Indeed no other Parks were listed at all. Accordingly, Mrs Dollery returned to Copenhagen Lodge proudly bearing *Travels in the Interior of Africa*.

Mrs Norris was exasperated; the more so as by now the library was closed for the day. She told Mrs Dollery she was a fool and that the wasted money would be deducted from her wages. Mrs Dollery, whose weekly wage was just nine shillings, suggested that she might return the next day and ask the librarian to exchange the books but Mrs Norris, fearful of attracting unnecessary attention to the transaction, would not countenance it.

'I have no intention of putting Miss Clissold to any such inconvenience on account of your incapacity. It was your stupidity, and you must pay for it. I shall deduct the twenty-two shillings and sixpence from your wages at the rate of half a crown per week for the next nine weeks. And may that be a lesson to you. No, you may leave the book here. I may as well read it, I suppose.'

Mrs Dollery looked appealingly at Maria. The forfeiture of so large a part of her already low wages would mean severe hardship. Maria, however, had a book in her hands and appeared to be paying little or no attention to the dispute.

On the following day Mrs Norris reached the library early but found that someone had been there before her. The final copy of *Mansfield Park* was no longer on its shelf. Had she felt safe in asking its whereabouts, she would have learned that it was in the back room where Miss Clissold had spent an incurious half hour with it the evening before, it being her professional custom to read the first and last chapter of as many books as possible. Fear of drawing attention to *Mansfield Park* prevented Mrs Norris from asking about the book and so allowed it to pass into Leamington's literary life.

While Mrs Norris was at the library a curious thing happened in Copenhagen Lodge. Mrs Dollery found two sovereigns in the attic where she slept. She dutifully took the coins to Maria, asking whether either of the ladies had missed so large a sum. Maria showed no particular interest but said that no money was lost so far as she

31

knew. The coins had probably been lying unnoticed for years. She advised Mrs Dollery to keep the money. As the cook left, Maria added, 'I may mention the matter to Mrs Norris but there will be no call for you to allude to it yourself.'

Chapter Three

The ladies of Copenhagen Lodge realised that their attempt to prevent all distribution of *Mansfield Park* in Leamington was now doomed to failure. What might have been a practicable policy had the Miss Clissolds procured fewer copies became the very opposite as soon as one copy escaped into general circulation. At first all went well. Reading just the opening and closing chapters – and only to find out whether the ending was happy or unhappy – the librarian saw no connection between her good customer Mrs Norris and the affairs of the Bertram family. She could recommend the elevating story of a poor relation's rise to wealth and happiness, however, and over the months copies of *Mansfield Park* found their way into several hands.

The Fanthorpes of New Priory had noticed young Mrs Rushworth's arrival in Leamington with mixed feelings. Lady Fanthorpe and her daughter, considering the newcomer dangerously beautiful, dismissed her as unfashionable and commonplace; Sir Guy and his son Paul, though denying that she had any charms for them, maintained she had breeding. Maria's clear determination to play no part in local society spared the Fanthorpe household an extra source of friction, rather to the regret of father and son who were slaves to the fair sex. Time, marriage, and self-indulgence had done little to temper Sir Guy's ardour which varied from gallantry to coarseness according to the social status of the object admired. He was somewhat more fastidious than Mr Paul who, at the tender age of twenty-three made no secret of the fact that for the time being he was more interested in quantity than quality where women were concerned. This was one of the few areas of discord between a father and son whose compatibility of outlook was otherwise an object lesson. Paternal solicitude urged the merits of a superior mistress, preferably a ballerina; filial inexperience inclined to experimentation with a succession of chambermaids, professional ladies, and complaisant married gentlewomen. Lady Fanthorpe pretended to know nothing about this preoccupation, and at the same time tried to thwart it.

'There an't many fish in the sea as good as that Mrs Rushworth,' declared the observant young man. 'For two pins I might set my cap at her.'

Lady Fanthorpe was the first at New Priory to read *Mansfield Park* and one of the first in Leamington to put two and two together. Before mentioning her discovery she gave the book to her daughter. Henrietta Fanthorpe agreed that Mrs Rushworth and Mrs Norris of Copenhagen Lodge were two and the same as Mrs Rushworth and Mrs Norris of *Mansfield Park*. Clearly there could be no question of social intercourse between the two families; indeed the mere presence of an undeclared divorcée was an affront to Leamington. Such persons should seek the anonymity of brash, new Birmingham rather than the intimacy of a genteel, up-and-coming spa. Both ladies were jealous of Leamington's moral welfare, for however retiring Maria might now appear there was no knowing how long that phase would last, and if she chose she could have all the gentlemen in the area at her feet. Lady Fanthorpe was still a handsome woman and Henrietta by no means unprepossessing, but they could not compare with Maria, and they knew it. Accordingly they began to talk.

33

It took relatively little time for hints of scandal and copies of *Mansfield Park* to reach all the people who mattered in Leamington and a good many who did not. The book was lengthy (if scandal can ever be lengthy) but was soon mastered by enough gentlefolk to make sure that its drift was soon acquired by the remainder. Within weeks it had filtered down to the professional classes, tradespeople, and even the domestics.

At first, Mrs Norris ascribed the extra attention and penetrating looks she began to receive to the impact of her personality. She was rudely disabused, however, when she overheard – as intended – a conversation at the baths between Lady Fanthorpe and Mrs Whybrow.

'Thank you so much, dear Lady Fanthorpe, for telling me about that new book. I have been unable to stop reading it. Such goings on! And all completely true, I understand; not really a novel at all.'

'If it be fiction, Mrs Whybrow, it is but thinly disguised. Of the main facts there can be no disputing, else the protagonists, particularly that aunt – Mrs Morris or whatever she was called – must surely have taken legal action.'

'And the married daughter, did she really run off with that reprehensible young man?'

'Indubitably. I recall the occasion well for I was in London at the time, some three years ago. The newspapers were full of it; naturally they had to withhold the real names, just calling them Mrs. R., Mr. C., and so forth, but there can be no doubt they are the same people. Oh, it was quite a nine days' wonder, I assure you.'

'By drawing our attention to such behaviour, the author has done us all a service. For all we know that wicked "Mrs. R." may be posing as a respectable person while seeking to prey on married men. Forewarned is forearmed.'

Having made certain in their own minds that Leamington's unwelcome guests had been socially undone, Lady Fanthorpe and her daughter set off on their annual visit to relations in the West Country, confident that no mischief would befall.

Mrs Norris was more disturbed by this development than Maria, to whom she repeated the conversation word for word, urging immediate departure.

'I don't care for my own reputation and never have, but I cannot stand idly by while you are slandered, my dearest. We must depart at once.'

'I see no necessity. Unless we change our names we are as likely to be discovered in any other place as in this.'

'But we cannot go on living here, Maria, amid this shame and gossip. Wherever I go now I meet with strange looks: my own feelings have long ceased to matter, but I will not tolerate the dishonour and indignity it casts on you.'

'Dishonour? Indignity? Shame? My dear aunt, I have been foolish and impulsive no doubt; I have offended against society's rules, and am paying the penalty. The world will never forgive me for leaving a very rich man. But I am not in the least ashamed. I grant it was unwise of me to carry out my family's wishes and marry Rushworth, and unworldly of me to run away with Crawford instead of accepting him as a secret lover which is what the social code prescribes, the Court endorses, and half London practises. But to my mind there is more dishonour in secrecy and hypocrisy than ever there is in open and unambiguous behaviour.'

'That has always been exactly my opinion,' returned Mrs Norris. 'I care not what others may say just so long as my own conduct is correct by my own standards. Virtue is its own reward. Accordingly, if the fashionable world seeks to ostracise me then I, in turn, ostracise the fashionable world and hold it self-condemned. To thine own self be true. Norris was exactly the same and I am perfectly aware that it was his uncompromising honesty which kept him from advancement in a church whose increasing venality he did not hesitate to reprobate. The positive ill-will of Lady Fanthorpe and the better classes of Leamington is, however, another matter. It would be intolerable to have her and them shunning our company – shunning it as a matter of principle, I mean: it goes without saying that one would never sink to seeking their good opinion or courting their hospitality – and impugning our respectability. Therefore I think we had best move on. After all, we have been here the better part of a year and the change of scene would do us both good.'

'You must do as you think fit, my dear aunt, but I am resolved to stay here at least for the time being. I have never met Lady Fanthorpe, probably never shall, and certainly have no wish to do so. Her tittle-tattle does not worry me in the least.'

At this point the door was opened by Mrs Dollery.

'Mr Paul Fanthorpe,' she announced, standing to one side.

Before aunt or niece could respond a most agreeable and well turned out young man strode confidently into the room.

Chapter Four

'Mrs Norris, Mrs Rushworth – I crave forgiveness for what must seem an unwarrantable intrusion on your privacy. Informality is a besetting sin of the age and we Fanthorpes, I fear, are very up to the mark. My father desired me but to leave his card. Ascertaining from the excellent Mrs Dollery that you were both at home, however, I could not resist the temptation of presenting it in person.'

He smiled, bowed, and placed Sir Guy's card on the table beside Mrs Norris.

Maria was about to dismiss him with the curtest of civilities when she became aware that he was gazing at her. His look contained a once familiar blend of appraisal and admiration but was more challenging than anything she had been accustomed to at Mansfield Park. It was consistent with, but not proof of, lack of respect. She felt herself colouring and for a moment looked down demurely, but it immediately occurred to her that primness was one of the characteristics she had always found most tedious in Fanny Price. She therefore returned his gaze, looked him up and down with assurance, and made him the first to look away.

'We are pleased to make your acquaintance,' said Mrs Norris guardedly. 'Pray give our compliments to Sir Guy and Lady Fanthorpe.'

Despite the young man's attempt at a brazen approach, Maria did not altogether dislike what she saw. He was well-built and vigorous, and seemed the more so to eyes which had seen no personable young gentlemen in close proximity for nearly three years. Though better looking than Henry Crawford, he was more like her former lover than her former husband. She sensed, however, that he lacked Crawford's wit and that while he might subscribe to the manners – and no doubt to the morals – of London, there was an agrestic simplicity lurking below his sophistication. He spoke of the weather, of Leamington, of gardens – the words toppling over each other as if carefully prepared but in danger of being forgotten. The family, he declared, would be delighted if Mrs Norris and Mrs Rushworth would honour New Priory with their presence at tea the following day.

Mrs Norris was the least surprised and the first to recover. She began to reason that the conversation over-heard between Lady Fanthorpe and Mrs Whybrow could bear a different construction from that which she had at first given it (though what the new one might be she need

37

not, for the moment, decide), and that the cold-shouldering and strange looks of the village might, as she had originally believed, be no more than a reluctant comment on her non-gullibility in household management. The years of virtual exile from society had given her a private longing for any audience likely to be more receptive to her voice and views than Maria, provided only it had reasonable claim to gentility.

'Sir, you are too kind. Now let me see . . . of course, this is a busy time of year but, now I come to think of it, we have no compelling engagements tomorrow afternoon. We shall be only too pleased' (turning to her niece for confirmation).

Maria acquiesced gravely, but wanted time to think. 'You must excuse me,' she said, and left the room.

'Mrs Rushworth is a martyr to migraine,' said Mrs Norris hurriedly. 'Yet it is very probable she will recover in an hour. We seldom go into company since – her illness and – loss, but I keep telling her that she cannot remain for ever in seclusion. For myself I am no lover of society. The company of a few, very particular friends is all I require, but Maria is young, meeting new people must do her good. Besides I feel that of all our new acquaintance in Leamington, it is the Fanthorpes – if I may say so without hauteur – with whom my niece, in view of her connections, may have the most in common. That remains to be seen. I am the most retiring and least pushful of companions, but unless I communicate with you by noon tomorrow, we shall be most happy to join you for tea at, shall we say, six o'clock?'

Neither as a pretty child nor as a beautiful young woman had Maria been so fortunate as to reward admiration (seldom stinted) from the opposite sex with that instinctive disfavour which is a sign of true virtue. She invariably reacted with

38

heartfelt warmth and so gained, in some quarters, a reputation for heartless vanity. At first she had taken it for granted that Mr Rushworth's admiration was genuine, but as her wedding approached, she concluded it was more to do with his own self-esteem: while adorning Sotherton her good looks would endow him with the credit which his abilities denied. Nevertheless her natural inclinations might still have overcome growing disrespect, and allowed her to apply Lady Bertram's dictum 'attach your gentleman first and fall in love with him afterwards,' had Mr Rushworth's initial ardours been less easy to contain. With a little encouragement her husband would have succeeded in his marital duties at the second or third attempt, but in the event it was Mr Crawford who fanned her warm vivacity into a dangerous and reprehensible fire. Under adversity that fire had been suppressed, as decorum required, but by no means forgotten or extinguished. At three and twenty she was more than ready to be fallen in love with again. Thus Mrs Norris, prepared to do battle over the unexpected invitation, found her surprisingly co-operative. Token resistance only was put forward and soon they found themselves discussing, with near animation, what clothes they should wear the following day.

The only doubt in Mrs Norris's mind concerned Sir Guy Fanthorpe's card. Why had her son not presented Lady Fanthorpe's? The question hardly seemed important enough to mention to Maria. As for the possibility of Sir Guy having read *Mansfield Park*, she dismissed it. Baronets never read novels.

During her brief reign as a London beauty, Maria had bought several gowns at the height of the immodest fashion then prevailing in the capital. Worn once, if worn at all, they had languished in drawers and boxes ever since. One of them, she was convinced, had brought Crawford to his moment of decision, finally inducing him to give up his pursuit of Fanny

Price and take up with herself. That decision had brought a short period of shadowed happiness followed by endless winter, but she felt no hostility to the garment itself; at least it had freed her from Rushworth. She tried it on. It still fitted well, though she was thinner now. Was it only three years since she had invited all men to gaze at her and imagine what little they could not see? Were Leamington and London on the same planet? She laughed for the first time since she and Crawford had parted, but her days of mischief-making were over and she dressed for the visit as if for church.

Fortified by a good dinner, and with but one bottle of claret apiece, the gentlemen were benignly sober when the ladies arrived. They had agreed to comport themselves with propriety on this first encounter in order to win Maria's confidence, not but what young Paul Fanthorpe had been impatient to dispense with the preliminaries. He argued that the avowal of admiration, the allure of rank, the prospect of a liberal establishment, and the threat of exposure were keys to Maria's affections; his father on the other hand, though responsible by precept for his son's view, counselled initial caution. The daughter of a fellow baronet, albeit the fallen daughter, should at first be treated with the respect due to her father, poor fellow, if only for tactical reasons. To assume she would behave like an actress might only force her – if she had any remaining pride or scruple – to act like a nun.

When the ladies were announced, Sir Guy's first duty was to apologise for the absence of his wife and daughter. Without telling the lie direct he implied that Lady and Miss Fanthorpe were all eagerness to meet Mrs Norris and Mrs Rushworth and that only quite unforeseen circumstances prevented them from being present. He made his rather vague excuses with such a frank, confident, and gentlemanly air that they were perforce accepted, but he confirmed Mrs Norris's speculation about the visiting card.

Tea was served and all the formalities most punctiliously observed.

'And how do you like Leamington, Mrs Norris?'

'We like it very well, sir. It is charmingly conceived and the waters themselves, whatever they want in palatability, surpass those of Cheltenham and even Bath, in their therapeutic qualities. My niece's health has markedly improved.'

'I am delighted that you should so feel after but a short stay. My grandfather, the late Sir Ralph, always ascribed his longevity to our waters, while my own father's abstinence from them – in favour, I confess, of somewhat stronger waters – has often been blamed for his premature demise.'

'I hear that Malvern in your neighbouring county is also developing its mineral springs. Are they in any way comparable with yours, Sir Guy?'

'No indeed, ma'am. Malvern water's wretched stuff, if not downright dangerous. Friend of mine went there for curative treatment, came back in a hearse.'

The talk turned to Leamington's shops and other amenities (the library was not mentioned as if by tacit consent), and thence to local places of interest. An expedition to Kenilworth Castle was courteously suggested and graciously accepted. Neither gentleman gave proof positive that he had read *Mansfield Park* nor did either lady try to find out, except by listening carefully for concealed meanings. Mrs Norris, at first the more wary of the two, was soon convinced that they were the most guileless and gallant father and son that ever hunted with the South Warwickshire, and mercifully unbookish. Maria let her aunt do most of the talking.

'Kenilworth, of course, was given to the worthless Leicester by Queen Elizabeth,' said good Sir Guy. 'Always

41

a dangerous family, the Dudleys, but at least the Fanthorpe who married into it fared better than Amy Robsart. Ah, if ever an innocent woman was sacrificed to ambition and hypocrisy it was Amy, Countess of Leicester . . .'

Did he just glance at Maria? And did she for a second frown with quickened interest or feel a tingle in her cheek? If so, Mrs Norris did not notice.

'Pray remind us of the story, Sir Guy. Amy Robsart now, did she not marry secretly? Such a mistake.'

'Leicester concealed the marriage from the queen, ma'am, after he became her favourite; and no one else dared tell her. The poor girl was hidden away at Kenilworth and eventually murdered. Her only crime was matrimony, and even that she was forced into by her father. The Robsarts were gentry but Robert Dudley represented a great marriage. They say she loved another.'

'At least that could not happen today, Father.'

'I would not be too sure, my boy. Society has ways of murdering people without taking their lives. But enough of this misanthropy: Kenilworth is now a most delightful and happily ghost-free ruin, and it shall be our pleasure, ladies, to show you all its beauties. Meanwhile, the evening sun is warm and our gardens await your inspection. We even have a ruin of our own. It was designed by William Kent and completed in the year of Trafalgar . . .'

The gardens of New Priory were all that money and fashion could provide, and the gentlemen were all that condescension and complaisance could require.

Mrs Rushworth and Maria returned to Copenhagen Lodge not at all displeased with their first venture into Leamington society.

'Well, when the cat's away, the mice can play, and they don't get much chance these days,' was how Sir Guy summed up the evening over his next bottle. 'That's the most beautiful woman I've seen in twenty years. If I were a little younger I'd set her up before you could say Jack Robinson, cat or no cat. Cold as ice on the surface, warm as brandy underneath – and yours for the taking m'boy, provided you play your cards carefully.'

Paul Fanthorpe agreed with his father, and was as nearly in love as he could be without qualifying his promiscuous admiration for others of the sex. Maria was indeed the loveliest of his ladies and had she not been tainted with scandal he might well have courted her honourably (providing only that she was worth a nominal thousand a year). Clearly that was out of the question for the Fanthorpe son and heir. Therefore the correct and decent alternative was to offer her his protection; he could give her the brilliant delights of Brighton, or perhaps – why not – Paris, without embarrassment to her or risk to himself – and at the same time rescue her from the clutches of both her past and her aunt. Seen in this light, it was his duty to intervene, and he prepared himself for the Kenilworth trip like some latter day Sir Launcelot about to rescue a damsel in distress (synonymous, in his terms, to compromising a gentlewoman).

Chapter Five

When they had been an hour in the grounds of Kenilworth, Sir Guy contrived to detach Mrs Norris and lead her over to the castle wall where he discoursed knowledgeably on inner and outer baileys. She paid only slight heed to his words but enjoyed them thoroughly because they came from the lips of a baronet and were addressed to her alone. It was like old times.

It was like old times for Maria too, to have a personable young man answering her every remark with some form of compliment. She could see that his initial admiration was maturing along predictable lines and, for the first time, began to wonder whether the life sentence society normally prescribes for her offence might be commuted to no more than temporary exile. Of course, it was much too early for such thoughts, but Paul Fanthorpe's assiduity and excitement told her that something was in the wind. In the event, the answer to her speculation came sooner than she expected, for he suddenly began, by way of confession, to declare himself.

'Dear Mrs Rushworth, you cannot be unaware of my regard for you since I am entirely lacking in those arts of concealment and subterfuge which are sometimes deemed proper. To be true to one's own impulses and to express them frankly is the only form of conduct I respect, and I had rather be misunderstood by the world than be disloyal to my own beliefs. Yet in one respect – as regards yourself – I have fallen short of that standard of integrity to which I aspire, and ere I say another word, I have a grave admission to make. Madam, before I met you I had the misfortune to read a book which contained a slanderous account of your marriage. It was largely to offer my friendship, my support, my protection that I presented myself at your house last week. Yet I was so impressed by your composure at that first interview, so transported by your beauty, that I feared my sympathy would seem mere impertinence. As my attachment grows, however, continued silence is becoming a barrier and a deceit. Know, therefore that I am cognizant of the calumnies being mongered about you, that I hold them as naught, but that I shall never again trespass, without your bidding, on a subject which must be infinitely distressing to you.'

Maria was alarmed but managed to hide her discomposure. Her first instinct was to plead ignorance, the next lofty indifference, the third to charge the young man with gross presumption and ill-breeding. Old instincts of deception and self-deception die hard. But she hesitated long enough for her new, painfully acquired policy of resigned candour to prevail.

'If you mean what you seem to mean, I thank you. Your openness does you credit,' she said very softly. 'The subject is painful to me, naturally, but I must be equally frank and tell you that the events described in – in that book are, I regret to say, substantially true.'

'Madam, I shall never believe it. In vain I have struggled: in vain I have told myself there is no smoke without fire, that it is madness to allow my admiration to develop. I cannot believe those libels — '

'It is my duty to disabuse you. The book is all too true in the essentials. I did marry Mr Rushworth and I was unfaithful to him, and I am paying the price.'

'What of it? That is mere commonplace. Half London is unfaithful to the other half every week.'

'Not openly.'

'Then is your crime only that you were "open" where others are furtive, in conduct which is otherwise à la mode?'

'Yes. No. I was very foolish. And wrong too, I suppose. Yet I could not have stayed long with Rushworth. It is in the estimate of my character and intentions that the author of that book is perhaps ungenerous.'

'My view exactly. And is your life to be forever forfeit for one indiscretion? You are young and beautiful – must you accept society's hypocritical condemnation without a fight? Madam – Maria – let me help you. I have fought against it but I love you. I have loved you since before we met – from the moment I read about you in fact. Permit me to bring the light back into those eyes, the laughter to those lips . . .'

Though flattered by his attentions and reassured by his admiration, Maria found she had little interest in Paul

Fanthorpe. He was amiable enough in the style of Mr Yates and other friends of her brother Tom, but his apparent proposal brought no answering warmth. To accept him might be as much of a mistake as accepting Rushworth. Nevertheless, she was touched by his generosity.

'I am deeply sensible of the honour you do me, but for your own sake must urge you to put such thoughts away. Your family, your friends, the world will never forgive you if you take up with me.'

'Fiddlesticks! Oh, there might be some small trouble at first. I own that I had rather you were not so, well, so compromised, but love will conquer all. Do not, I beseech you, consider my position. Any difficulties I encounter will be as nothing to those you are faced with and from which I must – I *shall* – rescue you.'

'You are too generous, but I cannot believe that you have understood how utterly you would be ruined. Your mother would never stand for it, your — '

'Ruined? How so? Was Crawford ruined?'

'Crawford?' Maria coloured. 'But that is different. In any scandal, society blames the woman but exonerates the man, provided only that he does not commit himself irrevocably.'

Fanthorpe looked at the ground. 'I am not necessarily talking about irrevocable commitment. Not at the start anyway.'

'Then what are you talking about, sir, pray?'

It was his turn to colour now. 'I – let us say – well, I suppose I agree with you about society. If I were to marry you now there would indeed be an outcry. Not that I care on my own account. Let them heap coals of fire upon my head. The one reason why I would not advocate the full commitment of matrimony yet is that it would, in practice, be an obstacle to my fulfilling the dearest object of my existence which is to render service to you. Were I, for

46

example, spurned by my family and cut off with a shilling, my obligations to you would, of necessity, go by default, but without the formality of marriage (and it is a mere formality these days) I can give you the affection and protection which you so sorely need. Believe me, I understand what you have been through. Now, if I take a house in, say, Brighton, or anywhere else you fancy — '

'In short, you are inviting me to repeat the error for which I have suffered so much already. So much for your solicitude. Good day to you, sir.'

Mr Fanthorpe laughed. 'Don't play the great lady with me, Maria. Offended dignity don't ring quite true, y'know. Now look, neither of us is a saint, let's be clear about that; but you need my protection and I can afford it. Very well, I cannot promise to make you the next Lady Fanthorpe, much as I might like to, and I certainly can't wave a magic wand to give you back your reputation – but I'll make certain that you are accepted wherever we go – Paris, Brighton, Boulogne – which is more than Crawford did, I'll be bound.'

'What you suggest is as impertinent as it is dishonourable. Take me back to my aunt and to Leamington at once, and hold your tongue, sir.'

They had strayed to the edge of the castle grounds. No one else was in sight. The young man, again laughing, said, 'But it's your aunt and Leamington from which I am going to deliver you. Come, I like a wench who puts up a bit of a struggle.' In an instant he took Maria by the waist, pulled her towards him, and started kissing at her face. She tried to detach herself but found that her arms were pinioned to her sides while her attempted screams were effectively muffled by his immediate proximity. Next she found that the front of her gown was being pulled at, and it struck her that the young gentleman had it in mind there and then to demonstrate that he was a worthy successor to Mr Crawford. The realisation

47

seemed quite to overcome her; at any rate the cries turned to sighs and her legs appeared to sag. However, as Mr Fanthorpe was considerately helping lower her to the soft grass, an accident occurred. The pointed toe of her left boot, jerking upwards, embedded itself in his person, somewhere below the belt but rather above the knee, in what must have been a particularly sensitive or vulnerable place, perhaps an old wound sustained in some manly sport and never completely healed.

The young man leapt into the air with an alto cry and fell back into a bed of nettles. Smoothing her dress, Maria looked down at him with all appropriate sympathy, but as she turned away she seemed to be smiling.

Neither of them felt obliged to mention the incident during the journey back to town. Mrs Norris prattled to Sir Guy with arch deference, not noticing the young people's studied silence or heightened complexions (hers pink, his mauve). Only once did she address her niece and then in a largely rhetorical manner. Their carriage had reached the main road just outside Leamington when it was forced to stop in order to allow a large mail-coach to pass.

'There it goes again, Maria, is it not the bane of our lives? The noise and dust of the Liverpool mail beggars description, and I declare that the traffic on this road gets worse every day. Why should anyone wish to go to Liverpool, I ask myself. If Liverpool were razed to the ground tomorrow, I believe we should all be much better off.'

Maria nodded her indifferent agreement, and frowned. She was concentrating on feeling insulted but had to keep suppressing a mysterious, light-headed gaiety. Mr Fanthorpe, she noticed, had changed colour to an hilarious pale green. The jovial father, however, could not allow Mrs Norris's strictures to pass without comment.

48

'Indeed, we would all be much poorer, madam. It is upon towns like Liverpool that the prosperity of this country largely subsists. It was towns like Liverpool which enabled us to defy the might of France for twenty-two years. Liverpool is now the principal port for trade with our American cousins, exceeding even Bristol in its tonnage. Without Liverpool, you would have no muslin and I no tobacco.'

'Then I shall allow Liverpool's continued existence and condemn it only for the pernicious rise in the cost of muslin and for the discomfort which its coach produces in Leamington. It is not myself I am thinking of but the health and safety of young families in the town, sir.'

For some reason this struck Maria as inordinately funny. A rich brown laugh danced wildly but briefly round the carriage, until trapped in a hastily fumbled handkerchief.

Mrs Norris pointed out that it was no laughing matter. Sir Guy kept his thoughts, if any, to himself.

Back at Copenhagen Lodge, Maria went to her room, confused by behaviour so out of character. Where she should have been outraged by Mr Fanthorpe's attack, she was amused and flattered; instead of weeping, she wanted to dance and sing; rather than shame or anger, she felt relief. It was as if by deserving her contempt he had extinguished her self-contempt.

Since the scandal she had often affected scorn for society and indifference to her fate within it, but secretly she had accepted its condemnation, admitted her guilt, and almost despised herself. For three years she had wanted to be somebody else; suddenly she questioned – doubted – her own iniquity. She began to know in her heart what she had only argued with her head, that other people were as bad as herself, if not a good deal worse. Other people planned their misconduct, hers had been an unconsidered accident. And now a ridiculous Lothario had taken at least some of her fault upon himself. On the other hand, he had also revealed just how far she had fallen. His attempted ravishment the world would blame on her, not him. The notorious Mrs Rushworth. Indeed the world would only be satisfied if she retired to a convent or, better, confirmed its censure by becoming a mistress or courtesan. She would oblige it on neither count. Instead she would try to forgive herself – by starting a new life.

Maria did not, however, understand everything that was going on in her mind as she paced her room re-enacting the afternoon's events. Thoughts came haphazardly, not in rational sequence, nor were they examined for flaws. They left an impression, half articulated, then half forgotten. Logic and intellectual rigour had little part in the Mansfield Park curriculum.

One thing she did understand before resigning herself to a sleepless night: it was time for change.

A sound, dreamless sleep nevertheless followed, and helped to compose her mind. After writing two letters, each at the second or third attempt, she felt calm enough and determined enough to face her aunt.

'You were sensible to stay indoors, Maria, the wind has been appalling. I nearly lost my bonnet twice during my morning constitutional, and the temperature is more like March than August. Nothing seems to have happened except that Mrs Dollery has broken some more cups. Fortunately they are not ours. Has there been any sign of the Fanthorpes? I rather supposed they might call.'

'Mr Paul Fanthorpe will not be calling today, nor any other day. He is very probably in bed.'

'In bed? What capriciousness is this? How can you know? Why should he be in bed? Did he sneeze or cough yesterday? He seemed in perfect health to me, and I am usually allowed to be a fair judge of such matters. In fact, I am always the first to notice if someone is off-colour. It is a question of sensitivity. There was nothing the matter with Paul Fanthorpe yesterday.'

'There is now. If you must know, aunt, he suffered an injury to a part of the person which most gentlemen particularly esteem. I was the agent of that misadventure.'

'My dear! Good gracious – the unwitting agent I am sure. He could hardly hold that against — '

'No. The witting agent. I did it on purpose.'

Maria told Mrs Norris about Fanthorpe's empty compliments, insulting proposition, and amorous assault, deriving some little pleasure from the account. She was already able to look at the episode with enough detachment to see it mainly as a symbol of what she must expect, in one form or another, wherever she was identified with the Maria of *Mansfield Park*. She would always be branded as a fallen woman: permitted quarry of the Regency male; sacrificial victim of female orthodoxy.

'I shall be nobody's game,' she declared, 'nor shall I assume a mantle of false piety. This repulsive but ridiculous affair has opened my eyes to what passes for morality in England. But I cannot fight it singlehanded. For the time being I shall go elsewhere. I shall go to America, by way of Liverpool.'

Once her decision had been made and announced, a degree of agitation returned to Maria: was her bold plan of action just another example of that reckless impetuosity which had been her downfall three years before? No, it was but common sense. English society, she settled, was at once decadent and sanctimonious; it would pursue her wherever she went and punish her the moment she stopped punishing

51

herself. Fanthorpe symbolised the typical male response to her position – eager to enjoy but not to share her fall, happy to use moral or physical force to make her pay for – and add to – her transgression. But was her own sex any more forgiving? Maria sensed that it was above all women – not least those beside whom her own behaviour was pure and innocent – who insisted that their sisters pay the price of folly with usurious interest. America, on the other hand, was surely interested in the future rather than the past. There all were equal and she would be able to make a fresh start (with her financial security providing insurance against serous risk).

'I wouldn't dream of letting you take up residence among those rebels, Maria. It is my duty to dissuade you from this madness.'

'They are no longer rebels, aunt. America has been a sovereign, independent republic these forty years.'

'A totally uncivilised one, you mean.'

'What is so civilised about England? If America lacks our mendacity so much the better.'

'And the people – the riff-raff of Europe; the scum – as the dear duke would have it – of the earth. To say nothing of the savages, who are cannibals I shouldn't wonder.'

'Many of our best families are no better.'

'Besides, what would you do, where would you go?'

'I shall visit the principal cities, I suppose, settle in the one I like best, and perhaps – why not? – take up some occupation.'

'Work? I will not hear of it. Have you no dignity? In any case, what could you do?'

'I could teach music or drawing. Or better still I could act. Yes, I shall go on the stage and fulfil the ambitions so callously thwarted by my father.'

'Go on the stage *professionally*? What would everyone say? Why actresses are no better than — '

'They cannot say anything worse about me than they already have. However, my mind is open on that score. I have sufficient money to support myself and I have little doubt that I shall find a husband if I feel disposed so to do (and provided I am not too particular).'

Unable to quarrel with such a self-evident truth, Mrs Norris snorted as if to imply that marriage to an American was licensed immorality.

'Well, if you go to America, Maria, you go alone. I shall not set foot in that land of traitors. I am quite firm as to that. Nothing will budge me.'

'So be it. That is entirely your decision.'

Mrs Norris's firm stand persisted. It was a full twenty-four hours before she changed her mind and took upon herself the arrangements for their journey. She terminated the Copenhagen Lodge tenancy, gave Mrs Dollery her notice, booked seats in the Liverpool coach, arranged for the early dispatch of their heavy baggage, and did so with such officiousness that the news of their proposed departure soon reached the whole of Leamington.

On their return, Lady Fanthorpe and her daughter were quietly satisfied, little guessing the immediate cause of Maria's flight.

'I do hope Paul recovers in time for my birthday reception,' said Miss Fanthorpe, who was nearly one and twenty. 'He does so enjoy his balls.'

Chapter Six

Sir Thomas Bertram soon learnt about his daughter's plan. Maria had written both to her sister, Julia, and to the family lawyer, and each had immediately communicated with Mansfield Park. The lawyer's letter was primarily concerned with arrangements for Maria's allowance to be paid in America. He foresaw no serious difficulties and suggested a method which Sir Thomas at once confirmed.

It was not quite so easy for the head of the Bertram family to accede to the suggestion set out in Julia's letter. She urged that the family now make up its differences and receive Maria back, at least for a token visit, before her departure.

Julia's letter from Maria had contained a passage which read:

> Pray tell my father that I undertake my exile not as a penitent sinner but as a helpless victim of that double standard which condemns in one sex what it condones in the other. Yet I harbour no especial rancour against my family (except as it upholds that standard) and for my part am now prepared to forgive and forget its lack of support. My removal to America would seem an appropriate time for reconciliation.

After consultation with her accommodating but empty-headed husband, followed by several false starts, Julia tactfully transcribed the passage as follows:

> While not denying her error, my sister asks you to allow that she is also victim of a double standard which condemns in one sex what it condones in the other. She respectfully hopes that this circumstance, combined with her removal to America, makes the present an appropriate time for reconciliation.

Sir Thomas read Julia's letter several times and with mixed feelings. For many years Maria had been his favourite as well as his most beautiful child. Her ardent participation in the Mansfield Park theatricals had led to the first rift in a relationship which, by Sir Thomas's standards, was close, and that in turn had contributed significantly to the Rushworth marriage. At any other time he might have insisted on a much longer engagement before the final union. To that extent he acknowledged a portion of the blame, but when he considered the enormity of her subsequent behaviour and the completeness of the disgrace it had brought upon his name, he felt that he had been punished far too much for a very minor error. Yet, with the passing years, his pain and anger had receded and he could not but notice that the incident had inflicted no lasting damage on his position either in Westminster or Northamptonshire. Unable to make up his own mind, he lost no time in consulting his wife and elder son.

Lady Bertram's indolent benevolence had prevented her from having strong feelings at the time of the scandal. 'Such a pity' was all that she said about it (though she said that several times) – the imaginative exertion of family shame being just as much beyond her range as that of maternal love. She now thought it would be 'Such a nice idea' to see Maria again, and 'A pity to miss the chance of a little chat' before her daughter went off to America. Tom, on the other hand, was robustly in favour of reconciliation, taking the self-insuring view that families should always stick together and that anyway Rushworth was an ass. Susan Price was not directly consulted but let it be known that she agreed with Tom by nodding her head sagaciously. Sir Thomas then sent a servant to the parsonage with Julia's letter and a note informing them that he would ride over the next day.

By the time he joined Edmund and Fanny, Sir Thomas had all but settled the matter. Unless either of them presented insuperable objections, he would allow the reconciliation to take place and publicly acknowledge his daughter once more. The scandal had long since been succeeded by others; Rushworth had sold his estate and moved to another county (where he had promptly been lured into a second marriage);

and Maria was destined for foreign parts. A meeting before her departure could do no harm.

'I agree, sir,' said Edmund. 'We cannot in charity do less than comply with her request. And – there is good biblical precedent for such magnanimity.'

'That is what I expected from you, Edmund. Such, I made certain, would be your view, and it does you credit. And you, my dearest Fanny, will you receive your cousin again?'

He looked across at his new favourite. Despite the summer day her face was pale and she seemed to be feeling chilly. She had by no means recovered from the birth and death of her child, though William's extended visit – reluctantly terminated the week before – had seemed to lift her. Now she had relapsed into her characteristic state of uncomplaining low spirits. Fortitude in adversity must surely be added to prudence, rectitude, and family loyalty in her growing tally of virtues.

'I shall now welcome her as a sister rather than receive her as a cousin.'

'Then I shall write directly. The past is past and cannot be undone, but time is a great healer. I applaud Maria's decision to go abroad, though I do not necessarily endorse her selection of America. That is too lax. One of the Calvinist countries of northern Europe would be more suitable.'

'Rejoice for she that was lost is found,' said Edmund.

'An admirable sentiment and most apt.'

'It is not for us – certainly not for *me* – to judge,' said Fanny quietly, 'yet the fault was never entirely Maria's. Her penitence, for such I take it to be, is the more praiseworthy for its lack of self-extenuation.'

'Her *apparent* lack of self-extenuation; precisely. One senses a commendable change in moral outlook,' added Edmund, handing Julia's letter back to his father. Sir Thomas nodded, but instead of putting the letter in his pocket began to re-read it thoughtfully.

'And yet it must be noted that she is not actually reported to have expressed her penitence in so many words,' he said at length.

'She certainly infers it, sir,' cried Edmund earnestly. 'Besides those are Julia's words, not Maria's.'

'Julia, perhaps, is not the most diligent, nor even the most accurate of correspondents,' said Fanny.

'Very true; but if Maria's letter were full of remorse and contrition, even Julia would surely have mentioned the fact – knowing my principles as she does,' said Sir Thomas. 'Indeed one would expect Julia to take special pains over such a communication since she, above all the family, wishes her sister to return to the fold.'

'I think you may be reading too much between the lines, sir,' pleaded Fanny. 'It is most unfortunate that Julia forgot to forward Maria's own letter. If she had there could have been no doubt or ambiguity.'

'That she did not choose to do so is in itself suspect.'

Edmund frowned. 'Oh come, sir, I have no doubt at all that you are being less than just. Probably there was some small phrase which prompted Julia to withhold the letter, some ill-judged, inappropriate expression. But clearly Maria admits, and by implication regrets, her sin. That should be more than sufficient for a family anxious to heal its wounds.'

'It merely says that she does not deny her error,' persisted Sir Thomas, refreshing his memory from the letter once more, and passing it to Fanny. 'There's nothing about regretting it.'

Edmund shrugged his shoulders. Both men looked expectantly at Fanny.

'What your father says is true *literally*, Edmund. To write "While not denying her error" is not quite the same,

57

for example, as "while confessing her error" and Julia's use of the former clause would be quite compatible with Maria having made no allusion to error at all. Compatible but not at all likely, in my opinion.'

'Nor in mine,' said Edmund. 'You might as well take issue with the suggestion that Maria is a victim of double standards.'

'I expect you are right, Edmund. The error should have been acknowledged unequivocally,' said Sir Thomas, 'but we must assume that it is, as you say, inferred.'

'It is certainly true that Maria has been ostracised and condemned, while the other, equally culpable party has resumed his position in society,' continued Edmund.

'The fact itself cannot be gainsaid; the impropriety of Maria alluding to it should, in the present case, be over-looked,' said Fanny.

'Except in so far as it is offered as a defence of the indefensible. The more I consider it the more I question my daughter's true penitence. That observation about "condemning in one sex what is condoned in the other" smacks more of accusation than confession. It could come straight from that Wollstonecraft woman.'

'And yet Maria has surely suffered enough,' said Fanny.

'We have all suffered,' said Edmund feelingly.

'Again, that is very true, Edmund,' said Sir Thomas. 'We have all suffered and the family has suffered most of all. There is no indication in this letter that the author of our shame appreciates or regrets the dishonour she has heaped upon our hearth and home.'

In the ensuing silence it was Edmund who again took up Julia's letter. At length, and choosing his words with extreme care, he said, 'Julia's epistolary technique leaves something to be desired. Many different shades of feeling, many nuances of meaning, can be elicited from this particular example. For my part, I believe that the simplest exegesis is the right one and that Maria, regretting her folly, is genuinely asking for family forgiveness. As Christians it is our duty to forgive, as relations it should be our pleasure to open our hearts. Accordingly, sir, I urge you – and I'm sure Fanny joins me in this – to accede to her filial request. I would only add that as her father you have an unquestionable right to seek prior assurances as to her true penitence, her loathing of the moral turpitude to which she once sank, her resolve to atone for her fall by leading an exemplary life henceforth, and her full appreciation of the unhappy consequences her misconduct had for the family. But, dearest Fanny, you are looking tired and disturbed. I think you should rest.'

'Excellent idea, I shall write to her at once,' assented Sir Thomas, and rose to depart.

'While I think of it, sir, there's one other matter we ought to discuss,' said Edmund. 'The Mansfield and Thornton Lacey common lands are becoming a disgrace. We should do something about them.'

Sir Thomas only nodded. His mind was on other things. On his return to the large house he composed a suitably condescending letter to Maria giving his consent to their reunion subject only to the conditions advocated by Edmund. It was a stern but very paternal epistle, full of family feeling, and almost entirely free of rebuke or exhortation. He was pleased with it and took a copy for his memoirs.

'I hope my father will not be too harsh towards Maria. She has her pride and will not take kindly to reprobation, however merited. It was surprising, almost perverse, the way Sir Thomas changed his mind and began to doubt his daughter's sincerity,' said Edmund when Fanny next joined him.

'Our advice, after all, was unequivocal.'

'He came here apparently resolved on reconciliation, and then tried to talk himself into a *volte-face*. It is most perplexing.'

'The only possible explanation — ' Fanny stopped as if she had either forgotten what she was going to say or was uncertain how to put it into words.

'A compromise was clearly the best solution which is why I recommended that written assurances should be sought, albeit such assurances are, in my view, supererogatory. But have you some private theory to account for my father's tergiversation, dearest Fanny?'

'No, really Edmund, unless it be . . . well, I think that in recent months he has sought and taken your counsel less often than heretofore.'

'Now you mention it, that may be so. Doubtless he is returning to his former habits of self-reliance. The events of three years ago naturally made him look to me, to us I should say, for support. His more independent attitude now indicates the completeness of his recovery. I welcome it.'

'We cannot but be cheered by his restoration provided wise counsels prevail. A man of his advancing years must necessarily be influenced by those around him.'

'You mean my mother. She is of course the most excellent of women. I am devoted to her. Yet I cannot believe she has the force of character seriously to guide or direct my father.'

'Very true.'

'Then there is brother Tom. He was ill at the time of which we were speaking but he has now been at home for longer than at any period since his adolescence, and he is fully recovered. It would be quite natural for my father to discuss matters with him. Tom has been rash in the past but is greatly changed.'

'I do not question Tom's improvement but whether he should supersede you is another matter.'

'What can we do about it? In the fullness of time Tom must inherit. Meanwhile we must hope that it will be my father who influences Tom rather than the other way about.'

'Your father is the stronger character.'

'I agree. Well, that only leaves Susan. Surely you cannot be concerned about her influence on Sir Thomas?'

'My sister has the sweetest disposition. If she has any influence, it must be for the good. But she is high-spirited and at times quite forceful.'

'There can be no danger in that. Her high spirits lift my parents and prove to Tom that life can be enjoyed without intemperance. I cannot see why you have reservations, Fanny.'

'I was thinking that if anyone has influenced Sir Thomas in connection with Maria it might have been Susan – perhaps unwittingly. She is very content with Mansfield Park as it is now, as she has always known it, in fact, and without realising her interest in the matter might prefer to leave well alone. In short the return of Maria could, possibly, be seen as an unwelcome development by Susan – if only because its consequences are so unpredictable.'

'To some extent Susan may have taken Maria's place, as well as yours, at Mansfield. If Maria were to return that position could, in theory, be threatened. Yet there is no question of a return, merely of reconciliation, together with a brief visit.'

'Even a brief visit might affect her plans – and Tom's intentions.'

Edmund looked startled. 'Pray be a little more explicit, Fanny.'

Fanny hesitated and confusion brought a rare touch of colour to her cheeks. 'If two personable young people are thrown constantly into each other's company, and if there is no serious conflict of character or other impediment, they are likely to become attached to one another, and eventually to start contemplating marriage.'

'So that's what is on your mind. I see. But Tom is a confirmed bachelor. Besides, think of the difference in age.'

'He is not yet thirty; Susan will be twenty in less than three years. The difference in age is much the same as that between your own parents, and less than that of several people we know.'

'You must be mistaken. Much as I like Tom, I cannot – I cannot think he is worthy of your sister. His misspent youth, his – of course, he is greatly improved of recent years.'

'Susan has no doubt heard (or read) that reformed rakes make the best husbands.'

'If you are right, we should do something about this before it's too late.'

'Yes, but what? I find myself thinking about it every night when I cannot go to sleep. Of all people, Edmund, you and I must endorse their union. If we do not, it will be assumed that we wanted Mansfield Park, and all that goes with it, for ourselves.'

'Heaven forfend! It is Tom's by right. I grant that you would be the ideal mistress of the Park, but that is not to be – unless, well, sometimes I have the impression that Tom's long illness weakened him so much that he may predecease my father. Should that come to pass, the baronetcy would, I suppose, enable me to fulfil my ministry the better, but we must cast such thoughts aside, and pray for Tom's health and strength. I could have wished that you had mentioned this prospect somewhat earlier, Fanny.'

'My suspicions were so vague, so difficult to substantiate. I thought it might just be sisterly instinct, for I do so want Susan (and Tom, of course) to be happy. It was only when

I was seeking an explanation for your father's contradictory behaviour that I began to think that my guesses might be correct. And then I began to wonder if Susan would have babies more easily than I . . . '

Whether it was the thought of her own lost child or the prospect of a lovely little nephew, tears came to Fanny's eyes (eyes it must be admitted which were usually a trifle watery). Edmund wondered whether his arguments in favour of family reconciliation had been as forceful as they could have been and resolved, as a good Christian, to pray that they would prove effective.

Next day his prayer was answered. The living at Mansfield at last became vacant thanks to the obliging apoplexy of Dr Grant, the incumbent. Edmund and Fanny accepted this as a sign that their example was needed at home and agreed to remove to Mansfield parsonage without further ado.

Chapter Seven

Her father's letter enraged Maria. She seized pen and paper and poured forth her fury in half a dozen pages of repetitious invective, accusing Sir Thomas of canting hypocrisy and her brother of pharisaical self-interest. Mrs Norris watched silently, resolving that no such reply should ever be dispatched, but she knew Maria too well to interfere straight away. She had lived close to that impulsive temper for twenty years and expected it to abate almost as quickly as it had erupted. In the event, it took a little longer than Mrs Norris had expected, but ultimately the storm gave way to resentful but calm animosity.

'Sir Thomas's letter certainly sounds ungenerous and unbending, but I suspect it is influenced by Fanny. It cannot reflect his true feelings since you were always the child of his heart. Your father is writing what he feels he ought to write.'

'He orders me to go down on my knees and beg forgiveness.'

'For form's sake only.'

'I have no intention of returning home on sufferance – an object of charity condemned to eat humble pie *ad infinitum*. I am as much a Bertram as Tom or Edmund and have as much right at Mansfield Park.'

'That is undeniable. As head of the family, however, your father has certain powers and privileges. These are best complied with for, if flouted, they can be used against you, whatever your claims as a member of the family. For example, your father has made financial provision for you but he retains the option of changing it, and he has complete discretion over the ultimate dispositions he makes. The understanding is that you will be cared for after his death in a manner fitting to your station in life, but if you wilfully antagonise him now, you may find that he will use that as a reason for neglecting his paternal obligations.'

'Are you suggesting that I should submit to humiliation for mercenary reasons?'

That was precisely what Mrs Norris was suggesting, so she said, 'Certainly not. I am merely advocating that your reply should be tempered with caution and tact for the sake of family unity. There is something so distressing about a feud, and it would be most uncharitable to quarrel any further. All too often one member of a family – often somebody with fewer rights than the others – officiously exceeds her position, or usurps authority, or abuses a trust in order to pursue personal interest at the expense of others. My dear Maria, it would be playing into the hands of Fanny to dispatch that letter to your father. I beg you to think again. Here, I have taken the liberty of jotting down a few sentences which I believe would satisfy Sir Thomas without belittling your own position.'

Mrs Norris had been at some pains to find a form of words which would gratify the inflexible old gentleman without forcing Maria into absolute untruths. At the same time she realised that any meeting between the two sides of the family in the present circumstances would be likely to inflame rather than heal the wounds. Accordingly, she persuaded Maria that no personal degradation was involved in expressing regret for embarrassment caused to her father, and she pointed out the extreme inconvenience of visiting Mansfield Park, two days eastward of Leamington, before going to Liverpool, a hundred miles to the north-west. The final version of the letter was as pompous as Sir Thomas could have wished.

Your letter reflects with perfect justice the exemplary principles which always guide your conduct and which you look for in others, especially in your own family. I own that I have fallen very far short of these standards and ask your forgiveness. The unhappy consequences of my conduct as they affect myself are not deserving of your notice and I shall not allude to them here, but as they affect your own honour and standing I cannot overlook them. I detest the thought that my behaviour should bring suffering to, of all people, he who gave me life. In mitigation, I can only promise that henceforth I shall bring you no further distress and that I sincerely regret the pain which my single lapse has caused. That you sanction my proposed tour is a matter of great satisfaction to me. I rejoice that I shall sail with your blessing. My only concern is that it now appears impossible for me to call on you before my departure . . .

When the letter was finished, Mrs Norris was satisfied that it would placate Sir Thomas and produce a spirit of generous relief at Mansfield Park.

'It is a tissue of half truths,' said Maria witheringly, 'almost equally accurate and false.'

'Let us say rather that it is sensible, conciliatory, and not dishonest. Ah, if everyone were equally sensible, conciliatory, and honest the world would be a better place.'

Mrs Norris's assessment of the letter's reception was correct. Latent doubts as to the justice of Maria's banishment were reassuringly allayed, hopes as to her true contrition were satisfied in a way that made her prospects in the after-life look distinctly brighter, and fears that the reconciliation would emotionally disrupt life at Mansfield were removed. Maria's voluntary decision to extent the separation produced a sudden access of goodwill which found expression in the improved financial arrangements Sir Thomas promptly implemented through his gentleman of business, Mr Jefferies.

The baronet's paternal gesture was requited by his daughter's expeditious removal from Leamington.

The Liverpool mail bore them by way of Birmingham into a Staffordshire which gave little sign that it was about to be industrially revolutionised. Though Birmingham was growing apace, the Black Country was still largely green; Wedgwood's Etruria Works were approaching their jubilee but pottery workers were still outnumbered by agricultural labourers in the Five Towns area and the labourers, like the farmers themselves, were restive. Following a cool, dry summer, it was harvest time and the heavens opened. This could only mean a long, hungry winter for most of the people in the richest country on earth.

In some ways the mail-coach reflected the state of the nation. Inside, Maria and Mrs Norris were glad of their travelling rugs as were their fellow, well-to-do passengers.

The outside passengers belonged to another, harsher world, improvising their survival against a succession of hazards, clinging to life as they clung to the coach itself, accepting their lot boisterously or resignedly as the case might be. Only one of them was even noticed by Maria's companions. Drenched to the skin but dressed in clothes which had once been expensive, she was clearly expecting a child, though she wore no wedding ring. What particularly attracted attention was her ashen face, smouldering eyes, and flame-coloured hair, now lashed by wind and rain. Someone inside the coach knew part of her story and, to pass the time, gradually imparted it to the two passengers who had boarded the coach at Leamington. It was as commonplace as her looks were not. At seventeen, seduced by a London beau, she left home and sweetheart for metropolitan delights; at twenty she had reaped the just deserts of her sin when her protector married an heiress and sent her packing. Now she was crawling home to beg forgiveness and, no doubt, to die. For her own sake and that of her child, it would be best that way.

'One only hopes she does not come to her time *en route*,' said a kindly gentleman. 'Conditions at these posting inns are most unsatisfactory and midwives, no doubt, few and far between. Besides, it would inevitably mean delays and I have the most urgent business in Liverpool.'

'It was foolish of her to make the journey in her condition,' said another passenger.

'Preposterous, I quite agree,' interposed Mrs Norris definitively, 'and thoughtless too. I'm surprised the coach authorities allowed it. Think of the inconvenience it could mean to others, especially those who have paid the *inside* fare, to say nothing of the outrage. A fine pass we have come to if respectable people have to rub shoulders with strumpets when they travel. And what possible reason could there be for this woman to have her wretched child in the

67

north? There are perfectly adequate institutions in London, I daresay, where her shame could be cloaked in anonymity. By returning home she shows no consideration for her family, since it merely increases the disgrace. Evidently she is as callous as she is wanton. I have no patience with such people.'

By happy coincidence, the radical view that society should be organised to ensure the greatest good for the greatest number was almost unanimously held inside the Liverpool mail-coach, and Mrs Norris's apt exposition and application of the principle won democratic approval. It was clear that their fellow passenger's selfishness threatened the public weal. That agreed, Mrs Norris organised a game of whist and clean forgot about the inconsiderate woman outside.

Maria played no part in the game or the desultory chatter which lasted till the evening. She rebuffed without qualm one gentleman who tried to be affable, but another – a Mr Randall – with a tinge of regret. He was old enough to be the kind of father she would have liked.

The whole party spent the night at a large, sprawling inn on the Cheshire border. Mrs Norris saw to it that Maria was given the best and most secluded room so that she could retire early without being disturbed. It had a cheerful fire, comfortable chairs and sofa, a turkey carpet, and a large four-poster. Pleading a headache, Maria took only the lightest of refreshment and stayed in her room, while Mrs Norris – enjoying the company as much as her niece misliked it – settled down to a good supper followed by cards, tea and wine.

Rid of her companions, Maria felt in no need of sleep. She looked at the fire and asked it whether she was doing the right thing in going to America. As if to find a reply, she took out her copy of *Mansfield Park* and began to read, starting with the account of her own marriage. She skimmed through the well-thumbed pages until she came to the events leading up to and surrounding her flight: Fanny pining for Edmund in Portsmouth; Edmund courting Mary in London; Mary and Crawford both wooing Fanny only to be rejected; and Maria herself chained to a man she despised, but depicted as a carefree worldling given over to empty gaiety . . . How cleverly the author set the scene so that the climax seemed an act of reckless infamy. No attempt was made to assess her own or Crawford's motives. The misery of a forced, unconsummated marriage was dismissed as a self-inflicted cross which it was her duty to bear; the despair of the twice-rejected Crawford was treated as the petulance of a spoilt child; the mutual solace of two lonely, vulnerable, ill-used people was condemned as depravity.

'No, no, no,' she half-cried, half-whispered, flinging the book across the room, 'it wasn't like that. It was misery and desperation which made us do it, not vice. He needed me. And I him. It saved our lives.'

Maria struck an attitude of helpless, hopeless defiance, but after a few moments began to feel she was overdoing the histrionics. Acting was for theatres, not hotel bedrooms: she pulled herself back to normal with a shrug, and looked around the room sheepishly. Standing in the doorway was the outside-passenger from the coach, with flame-coloured hair, burning eyes, but ash-grey cheeks. Maria, remembering the woman's silent unreturned gaze at one of the stopping places during the day, stared back at her.

Chapter Eight

After the first surprise, angry embarrassment prolonged her speechlessness. To have been approached by such a person was bad enough but to have been surprised in a moment of self-exposure and private grief was much worse. Presumably the woman had come to beg. She would receive nothing. With unquestioning acceptance of their respective positions, Maria reached out for the bell; in a few moments the incident would be closed – and banished from memory. A gesture on the intruder's part stopped her.

A gesture of authority. Those wide-set eyes were not pleading or begging, but giving some sisterly command as of right. Shutting the door she advanced into the room and as the physical gap closed between the two women, so the social chasm seemed also to narrow. Instinctively, Maria jumped to her feet and tried to reassert her position as a baronet's daughter by backing to a safe distance. The stranger appeared not to notice. She sat down and looked about her collectedly, hardly breathing, it seemed, except for a sharp exhalation every now and again.

Maria struggled for words which would send the woman packing. She needed no new appendage. She was already quite miserable enough. Yet the words dissolved into meaningless rote, and it was the other who eventually broke the silence. Taking up a piece of jewellery which Maria had left on a small table, she said, 'This is lovely. It reminds me of something I was once given, or lent — ' She stopped abruptly and there was a long pause during which she seemed to lose all interest in what she had been saying. Her eyes fluttered to a close, and the pause lasted two minutes. Maria held her breath as long as she could.

'But do you need it?' she continued as abruptly as she had left off.

Maria shrugged her shoulders.

'Because I do.' A statement of fact, no more, no less, made – again – with simple but unarguable authority.

'Take it, it is yours,' said Maria, eager to forget her vow. A wave of relief flooded over her as she assured herself that the woman was, after all, just a superior pauper. To give

away a piece of jewellery was neither here nor there compared with giving of herself. For a moment she had sensed
that appalling, emotional demands were going to be made of
her, and that she would be weak enough to respond, but if it
was only a jewel she was after, only cash, in effect, to buy
some partial remission of her fault or to secure parental
forgiveness – she was welcome. In sparing the trinket Maria
would spare herself.

The visitor should now have poured out some hurried
words of thanks, tearfully kissed her patron's reluctant hand,
and stumbled out of the room. Instead she stayed, warming
herself by the fire until a vestige of colour returned to her
cheeks. She seemed also to acquire warmth and strength
from the silent companionship, resentful though it was on
Maria's part. The bracelet sparkled in her hand and after
several moments was clasped impulsively over her heart
where it seemed to compete with rather than complement
her flickering incandescence. Impatient to be rid of her, Maria
found it impossible not to look at the young woman.

'I shall never forget,' said the stranger at length, rising
to go. Even as she did so the colour ebbed from her face
and she had to grasp one of the bed posts for support.
Recovering slightly, she tried to walk on but her legs refused
to carry her and she sank on to her knees, clutching the post.
With a sudden, new foreboding Maria found herself heaving
the woman up on to the bed itself, and hoping against hope
that if she did not utter what she now suspected, the woman
would, after all, recover and go.

The figure on the bed was in no condition to say anything.
It was in the throes of some spasm – perhaps a fit – and
seemed unaware of its surroundings. The breaths now came
in short pants interspersed with sharp moans as she exhaled
all the air from her lungs. But the spasm passed as quickly as
it came, and suddenly she smiled.

71

'Sweet heaven, my time has come. Two weeks too soon.'

'You mean you are . . .? Here?'

'Yes. Leave me. You have been kinder than you intended.'

Maria almost ran to the door, but found she could not bring herself to go without at least a gesture of help.

'I shall tell the landlady and – and have her fetch the local midwife. Don't worry about — '

'No, I forbid it.'

'If you haven't the money, I'll pay.'

'It's not that. I forbid you to tell the landlady. I have done her injury and would prefer, much prefer, to die than accept her help. Besides, she would rather turn me out into the night than deliver a child of mine.' The familiar note of command had a new urgency and Maria did not press the point.

'Then what are you going to do? You cannot have the child alone and unaided.'

'Why not? Millions have done so before; animals do.'

'But people, modern people, are different. You are not a savage, I think.'

'I am a farmer's daughter and I know what to expect. I delivered my first lamb when I was eight, and helped at both my sisters' confinements.'

'What did I say, you fool? Your sisters needed help, and so will you. If you cannot accept the landlady, let me send out for medical assistance without telling her. I will pay.'

'No.'

'But you will probably die.'

'That, I assure you, would be no hardship. I submit the decision to God.'

'And your child will die also. That will be murder.'

'If God is merciful, as the preachers say, he will allow my child to die. Leave me. It is no problem of yours. You have grief enough already.'

Maria was offended. How dare such a woman patronise her betters?

'Very well,' she said, 'kill yourself and your child. As you say, it is no concern of mine.'

Without a further glance at the bed, she swept up her overnight bag and left the room. No matter whether the woman lived or died. Better surely that she did die – better to make an end of it now than prolong a life of degradation and despair. How dare she put Maria into a position like this? The difference in their stations freed her from any kind of obligation, and the gift of that valuable bracelet went far beyond the limits of Christian charity. The gem would either sustain the wretched woman for several weeks, or pay for a decent burial. Seldom could social insolence and moral blackmail have been responded to more bounteously.

Slamming the door behind her, Maria found herself on an ill-lit and deserted landing. She regretted now that fatigue and ungraciousness had made her insist on the quietest room in the inn. There was but one other door in sight and, taking the small lamp on the landing table, she went straight over to it. To her relief the room was empty and, though fireless, contained a made-up bed and washing things. She quickly prepared herself for the night, lay down, closed her eyes, and cleared her mind of everything except her anger.

No sleep came. Time ticked away on her little carriage clock. She remained wide awake although she was dog tired. Why was she holding her breath, straining to catch sounds – any sound – from the other room? What was that? Nothing. The silence was keeping her neighbour's pain a secret. Or was it? Was that another of the involuntary moans? Was the panting coming faster now? No, it was just her imagination. She closed her eyes even tighter, and her ears, and her mind. Still thoughts and fears crowded in unasked. Would she manage to sleep if she went and roused the inn or the innkeeper's wife? Could she do so having promised – having been ordered – not to? Should she tell Mrs Norris then? Or that kindly, paternal gentleman? Why did it matter what the woman wanted or did not want? Others would know better. She was no one, some farmer's daughter, with a little education, dazzled into sin, like thousands of others, like – not altogether unlike – no, the comparison was false. As if she, Maria, could ever sink to this. The only point of similarity was that they were both paying, in their different ways, for falling into temptation. Maria, having lost what the red-haired baggage had never possessed – position, wealth, reputation – was the one to be pitied. What was the transient inconvenience of a confinement to the termination of all those fair and brilliant prospects? After an hour of such pleading, she opened her eyes and looked at the clock. Only ten minutes had passed. She clenched them again, held her breath, and listened.

Another moan reached her ears, this time born of anguish rather than imagination. It came from her own throat. After all she had suffered, this was the final straw. How dare this farmer's daughter impose upon her private misery? By what right did a total stranger demand her support, almost as if they were sisters? They were not even sisters under the skin. One of them had done what she had done only for money; the other had given up £12,000 a year. Beside, what possible use could she be, now that her offer to pay for a doctor or midwife had been so ungraciously declined? She could only make matters worse. If she tried to help, she might have two deaths on her conscience for the rest of her life. It was kinder to let nature take its course, to let God's will be done. By refusing a physician the woman was attempting suicide. That was her affair. No one could blame Maria. Everyone would declare that she had, if anything, done too much. Far too much. Far, far, far too much.

Very well, she would go even farther, she would try once more to make the stupid girl see reason. A few sovereigns should overcome both her objections and the landlady's imagined injuries.

She dragged herself out of bed, half hoping that she would be too late. If mother and child were already dead, it would be because they had refused her help. No censure would attach to her. Yes, that would be the best thing. It was what the girl had wanted. Pray God, He had released her quickly. She tiptoed across the landing, opened the door, and to her dismay saw that all was well. The woman was propped up on the pillows smiling at her. Maria went straight up to the bedside and shook her.

'Confound you! How dare you do this to me? Why should I care what happens to you and your wretched child? Why won't you let me sleep? Haven't I suffered enough already? Be damned to you, woman!' Suddenly the anger dissolved into self-pity and the last few words (fortunately) were lost in tears. Maria buried her face in the other's breast.

When she looked up she saw that the girl was having another of her spasms. This time she was lightly stroking her swollen stomach and seemed to be counting silently.

'Pray excuse my language. Very well. What do you want me to do? I suppose I must try to do something, but I warn you I shan't be any use at all.'

There was no reply.

'I don't know anything about confinements. It's not my fault. Oh why can't you answer instead of smiling and counting in that idiotic way? Look, we can't all be farmers' daughters. You were brought up one way, I another. I can repeat the Kings of England in chronological order with the dates of their accession, and the Roman Emperors down to Severus. Heathen mythology, the metals, semi-metals, and planets, and philosophers also formed part of my studies. I read Latin, I speak French and German but – oh, if only you'd tell me what to do.'

'Fetch a towel and put it under me. The waters are breaking.'

'What waters?'

'I can't explain now. Heat the kettle and find some more water if you can. There may not be enough in the pitcher.'

Maria took a towel and, keeping her head averted, slid it under the woman's rump; next she filled the kettle and set it on the trivet; then she went to the other room and collected more water, towels and, on impulse, sheets and blankets.

'As a matter of fact, I never got very far with German. Tell me what to expect and when.'

'Now that the waters have broken it should be quite soon, but may still be hours. I have a wide pelvis so the birth should be simple. These spasms now – I shall have several more. They hurt but I know how to reduce the pain by breathing and by stroking myself. And gradually I will open up down here.' To Maria's disgust she pulled back her loose clothing, splayed her legs apart, lifted her knees and pointed.

'Don't turn away. You will have to look if you are going to be any help at all.'

Maria gritted her teeth and looked briefly between the girl's legs, without seeing anything.'

'Can you see anything yet? Is there a little hole?'

'No, there's nothing. I wasn't much good at philosophy either.'

'My feet are cold,' whispered the girl.

Maria saw that another of the spasms was beginning. She tucked a blanket round the girl's ankles and put another loosely over her legs. What next? She could think of nothing and stood helplessly, as if rooted to the spot.

'Make up the fire, pour the warm water into a bowl, and refill the kettle. Try and find a sponge or a flannel,' said a weak but confident voice from the bed. 'Then take the things out of my reticule and put them here beside the bed. There should be a pair of scissors. You'll need them to cut the cord.'

'What cord?'

'When the baby is born it will be attached to me by a cord. You cut it and knot it near the baby. Then you knot the bit still attached to me. Don't look so worried, it won't hurt you. It won't even hurt me.'

Maria found the scissors and washed them. For something to do she washed the girl's forehead with cool water and gave her a drink. Silence followed.

'I'm on my way to America,' she said at last. 'In two weeks' time I shall be on the high seas. In two months' time I shall have started a new life. Just as you're starting a new life here. Do you want to know why I'm going to America? It's a long story. It goes back to the time I was learning the Roman Emperors and the Kings of England and all those other stupid facts. You see I was taught everything that had happened and learned nothing that mattered. Crawford used to say I was as Unready as Aethelred. What is it now? You want me to look at you again? Must I? Oh very well.'

Again Maria cast her almost unseeing eyes at the dark, moist, threatening place between the girl's legs. All her senses told her that the baby would emerge thence, accompanied by pain and blood, but she did not want it to be like that. She did not even want to think about it. If she kept on talking it might not happen. Or it might be delayed. Or someone might come. Oh fool that she was not just to go away now. After all, the girl had said she could cope by herself: she was a farmer's daughter, for goodness' sake. Besides no one would ever know except the two of them, and by the time it was all over she would be heading for Liverpool.

77

'Why I'm staying here when I'm sure I cannot be of any use to you, I really do not know. Doesn't it worry you having me here? I've got a long day tomorrow and really should get some sleep. Don't grip my hand like that, it hurts. Here, have some more water. Oh, what shall I do? What would Fanny do in my place? Oh I know, she'd be wonderfully tender and consoling and selfless – and then faint at the first sight of blood. Yes, that would be her all over. She's not hard like Aunt Norris makes out, she's just fainthearted. There's no harm in the girl, but one really isn't at all surprised that her own child was stillborn or whatever. I shouldn't have said that but don't worry. Anyone can see you're a fine strapping woman who is going to have a fine strapping child. Quite different from my sister, as I suppose I have to call her. Here, let me have another look at you. Fanny wouldn't be able to do it without swooning, but I don't mind . . . '

This time Maria took the lamp and peered conscientiously. Sure enough a hole the size and shape of a large walnut had appeared where there had been a mere slit before, and within it, yes, there was something reddish. Could that be the baby?

'Ow,' said the girl, catching her breath.

'There's a hole about so big. You look awful. Is it hurting a great deal?'

Two-way conversation now became impossible. A mixture of panic and excitement caught Maria in its grip. Suddenly she heard someone saying, 'Don't push, for goodness' sake, don't push yet. I'm sure it's coming of its own accord.'

It was her own voice but for the second time that evening she did not recognise it. The hole was now approaching the size of her wrist and the reddish thing was beginning to look like a head. Maria noticed that the towel she had laid on top of the sheet was getting damp and bloodied, so she placed another on top of it and cleaned the woman's legs with a damp cloth.

The hole was larger still and the girl's urge to force it irresistible.

'Don't! Wait!' screamed Maria. 'It's all right without that. I'm sure it is. It – it looks lovely.'

Suddenly everything seemed to stop. It was as if the baby had decided to have nothing to do with the outside world. For several minutes there was no sound or movement. The child hovered between oblivion and reality, the woman between consciousness and instinct.

Then the process started up again without warning. Eyes and mouth wide open, shoulders heaving, the woman gave an explosive thrust, like some giant, all-embracing sneeze. Maria dropped the hand she had been squeezing and looked at the baby's head. There it was, an unmistakable crown, already a third of the way out. She cupped her hands to catch it or break its fall. Fast on the heels of the first great thrust came a second – and the baby now emerged as far as its chin. A third revealed neck and shoulders, and then, with no apparent effort on the mother's part, the rest of the body slid out, guided almost imperceptibly by Maria's hands. When both feet were safely delivered she lifted the child and noticed the cord for the first time. Grabbing the scissors, she cut and knotted it as ordered. The baby took a deep breath (deep, that is, considering its age) and began to cry. Maria quickly gave it to its mother and knotted the other end of the cord. In a flash she understood how navels came about, but what, she wondered, happened to the other end?

The two women smiled at each other for the first time and the baby stopped crying.

'Thank goodness that's over,' said Maria in a business-like way. 'Now we can both – all – get some sleep. I'll just give the baby a little wash and – and – oh bother . . .'

To her chagrin, tears were suddenly running down her face.

'It's not quite over.' The mother looked as if she was about to start pushing again.

'Oh no, you're not having twins?'

'No, it's just the afterbirth. Here . . . wait . . . there.'

Maria saw that the rest of the cord, attached to a sack of innards, had been deposited on the towels. She wrapped the whole mass up in the topmost towel and deposited it on the commode and as she did so a strange elation came over her. Far from being sleepy she felt more awake and alive than she had ever felt before. It was as if she had been born herself, born full grown and aged twenty-three. She cleaned her patient and washed the baby with almost reverential care, wrapping the child in a sheet and blanket, and staunching a discharge of blood from the place it had just vacated with the last clean towel. In a short while, mother and child fell asleep in each other's arms. Maria crept about the room, tidying it and cleaning it as best she could, then with a glance to see that all was well, departed.

As she opened the door of the room across the landing she heard a cock crow. The sky was already lightening. It took a few minutes for her to make up her mind how next to proceed, but once the decision was made she carried it out calmly and purposefully.

She washed, changed her clothes, brushed her hair, and went downstairs to rouse the landlady. The woman was already up, however, supervising the preparation of breakfast. She was surprised to see that the arrogant beauty of the evening before was up and about so early, and even more surprised when summoned into private conversation.

'What is your name, my good woman?'

'Mrs Partridge, ma'am.'

80

Uncharacteristically alert, Maria noticed at once that Mrs Partridge lacked the servile manner and language of professional innkeepers. On impulse, she deferred the main part of her questioning. 'You have not always been an innkeeper's wife, I think, Mrs Partridge?'

'Oh no, ma'am, we were farmers in Northwich. Why, is something wrong?'

'No indeed. What made you exchange the sturdy independence of farming for the bondage, however respectable, of your present situation?'

Mrs Partridge stiffened angrily.

'The times, ma'am. And family reasons. We made a personal choice: it's no one's affair but our own.'

She turned to go, not attempting to hide her affront, but Maria was not in the least abashed.

'Stay, Mrs Partridge – and answer this. Was your decision in any way connected with that unfortunate young woman who is expecting a child?'

Incredulity succeeded anger on Mrs Partridge's face.

'How did you know?'

'From something she said.'

'Would that I had never clapped eyes on that wicked child! She has brought nothing but shame and misery to us all. When I saw her last night I would have turned her out into the rain only my husband forbad it. Said it would lose us the mail-coach contract. Oh, how dare she come here – here of all places?'

'Did she know you had left Northwich and taken an inn? They say she has been up in London these three years.'

'Aye, that's true. Happen she did not know. Betsy would never have told her, even if she'd known where to write to.'

'Betsy? Her mother?'

'Her mother, yes, and my sister.'

'So you are her aunt. That explains — '

'Aunt? No! She is nothing to me now. Less than nothing. Filth. Loved her like a daughter I did, and she would have been my daughter too, had she married my Harry, but she up'd sticks and went off to her ruin. 'Twas through her we lost both son and daughter, everything, for when she left, he left. Set off for Canada and drowned on the way.'

'I – I'm sorry. So very sorry, but I see.'

'And now, at last, she has got her desserts. God is just. May she and her child both die, and the sooner the better.'

'Do you mean that, Mrs Partridge? It won't bring your son back.'

Mrs Partridge avoided her eyes. 'Certainly I mean it, ma'am. I hate her. I have a right to, haven't I? She killed my only boy as surely as if she poisoned him, and broke my sister's heart . . . and – and brought shame on us all. Oh why did she have to come here when we were beginning to forget?'

The landlady thrust out her chin defiantly but two large tears rolled down her honest cheeks. Maria took her hands quietly into her own and waited.

'All right. To answer your question truthfully, ma'am, no. No, I can't let her die. She has done us great harm but I suppose I still love her. Fate has brought her to our door rather than her father's and she will stay here till the child is born. Her time is near. I shall send for the surgeon after breakfast.'

'That will not be necessary. At least, perhaps, yes *do* send for the doctor. She had the baby in my room about an hour ago. I came down to arrange for them to be looked after until they could travel.'

Maria's plan had also been to pay for their board and lodging but now she stayed silent on that subject. Mrs Partridge stared at her in stupefied silence.

'They were both asleep when I left them.'

'But they're – they're all right?'

'Perfectly, so far as I can tell.'

'Praise be to God, how wonderful, praise be . . . ' The woman dropped to her knees and embraced Maria's skirts passionately. 'Angel, angel, angel – may God reward you.'

'Pray control yourself, Mrs Partridge,' said Maria, not at all displeased, 'and stop being so melodramatic. It was nothing really.'

'But how did you do it? And why?'

'I had very little choice in the matter. It was a question of trying to help, or leaving her all by herself. I tried to do that but found I – well, I changed my mind.'

'Why did you not call for assistance? Why didn't you tell me? I could have summoned a doctor.'

'She would not let me; said she had done you terrible injury and that she would rather die than ask your help.'

'Oh, bless her! She could not have known we were here. It was fate. The shock of seeing me last night must have brought the baby forward. Oh bless her, bless them both! Is it a boy or a girl?'

Maria blushed. 'I don't know,' she said. 'It did not seem particularly important. That is to say, I was quite busy with other things at the time. At least . . . in short, I forgot to enquire. You will soon find out I have no doubt, but first, Mrs Partridge, I must have my breakfast. I ate nothing yesterday and have had a busy night of it. I should like a dish of eggs, some good ham, potted beef, muffins and tea. And – yes, why not – a pint of Mosel.'

'Certainly, Mrs Rushworth. You shall have the best the house can provide.'

The remainder of the mail-coach party descended to the dining-room in ones and twos while Maria was making the heartiest meal she had had for years. Several noticed the improvement in her appetite and appearance as compared with the previous day.

'I am relieved to see you looking so much better, my dear,' said Mrs Norris. 'You must have slept particularly well.'

'Thank you, aunt, I passed a tolerable night.'

'My own bed was a disgrace. I didn't sleep a wink and shall complain to the landlady. When one considers the extortionate cost of a room these days, it is absolutely unforgivable — '

'Allow me to have a word with Mrs Partridge on your behalf. I'm sure she will wish to make tangible amends,' said Maria, hastily finishing her wine. She left the room and retraced her steps to the birth chamber. On the stairs she met Mrs Partridge who again embraced her.

'It's a little girl,' she babbled. 'So sweet. A perfect little girl. The image of her mother.'

Maria disengaged herself from the landlady's arms and went on to the room alone. At the door she hesitated before entering. Would it not be better just to disappear into the future rather than expose herself to the gratitude and obligation of what must become a mutually embarrassing, if short-lived relationship? They had met as strangers, had briefly become sisters, and were now strangers again; it was better thus. Yet she longed to see the child just once more.

Bending down, Maria looked through a chink in the door and saw that both were still asleep. She crept in, fleetingly minded (she knew not why) of her parents.

Yes, it was a nice-looking baby and the mother was indeed handsome, but were they different from any other mother and child? Maria tried to persuade herself that they were not. Yet there was something different. It was not the mother and child, Maria realised, but herself: she was quite different: now. It was she who should be grateful to them, not the other way about. On impulse, she took the pendant from her neck – a simple but expensive jewel with the word 'Maria' picked out in diamonds on a gold background – and tied it by its filigree chain loosely round the baby's wrist. Then she left the room happy and, though she did not acknowledge it, humbler than she had ever been before.

In the coach to Liverpool that day Maria was hardly less silent than before, but the improvement in her looks and temper was even more marked than at breakfast. There was colour in her cheeks, animation in her whole demeanour.

'I always say that a good night's rest is better than a dozen doctors,' said Mrs Norris to her neighbour.

'How right you are, dear lady. And talking of doctors, by the by, I see we have lost our red-haired friend in the – ah – *interesting* condition.'

'And an excellent thing too. Thoughtless little slut. She could have seriously inconvenienced us all. Why the coach authorities allowed her to travel like that is a mystery. I shall write to the board of directors and complain. It will be a great nuisance but one has to be public-spirited on these occasions or else other people suffer.'

Elsewhere that day, in an equally public-spirited frame of mind, Sir Thomas Bertram agreed to enclose the common lands at Mansfield and Thornton Lacey. As Edmund pointed out, new agricultural methods had rendered strip-farming obsolete and uneconomic. Village smallholders, accordingly, were no longer able to sell their produce profitably and far too many of them were feeling the pinch. It was Sir Thomas's duty to steer an Enclosure Act through Parliament which would, in time, enable cottagers to seek gainful employment in the thrusting new industrial towns of the East Midlands and at the same time enable the Bertram estate to justify the increased allowance which had been bestowed on the erring elder daughter.

Chapter Nine

All day long the weather improved. As the coach drew into Liverpool, Maria, with budding elation, looked about her brightly and expectantly. She would be here but a few days before embarking for America but she felt eager to respond to the northern town and start her life anew.

Liverpool had overtaken Bristol as the second port of England and jostled with Manchester for the position of second town. It combined architectural elegance (soon to be violated) with commercial zeal. A century of growth based on the slave trade had given way to a new century of growth based on legitimate shipping and industry, though privateering remained an important source of wealth. The harsh hedonism of the slavers had yet to be replaced by the self-advancement, self-doubt, and self-satisfaction of nineteenth century provincial business.

Maria understood little of all this as the coach deposited her at the hotel in Abercrombie Square, but she liked Liverpool instinctively and felt she was already half-way to America. London, with its hierarchies and hypocrisies, seemed to belong to another world, two thousand rather than two hundred miles away. No one knew about her past here, nor would anyone care – the slate was clean. Mrs Norris sensed the same thing but reacted differently. It made her feel a nobody. Liverpool did not realise who she was nor to whom she was connected. It was just a sprawling uncivilised place for birds of passage where she neither knew nor wanted to know a soul: hate at first sight. The strength of her feeling was increased by Maria's unconcealed enthusiasm. How could it be that Maria, so long dependent on her aunt for initiative and companionship, could so easily forget the cold superiority which a baronet's daughter should display in such uncouth surroundings? This inexplicable show of vivacity, though it had not yet found expression in social intercourse, produced a severe headache in Mrs Norris and she retired to bed, while Maria, ever more liberated, decided to take a walk in the late afternoon sunshine.

The hotelkeeper suggested a route which would show her Rodney Street, the Wellington Rooms, the principal shops, the Town Hall, and the theatre. The latter was in Williamson Square, on the edge of an area where it was not safe for unaccompanied ladies to venture after dark, he warned. Maria sallied forth impetuously.

The more she saw of Liverpool the more she liked it, not least, perhaps, because she soon became aware that Liverpool admired her. Every few yards she was quizzed admiringly by gentlemen, and even their ladies seemed to look at her with generous interest. She was not at all displeased by the stir she made, the shop windows she inspected, or the opportunities for diversion which she saw displayed. In particular she lingered at the Theatre Royal, committing to memory the principal offerings of the next few days. By coincidence, Mr Kean, for whom Aunt Norris had been so anxious to visit York, was that very evening playing Sir Giles Overreach in *A New Way to Pay Old Debts*.

'I am delighted to see you share my interest in the drama, Mrs Rushworth. My wife and I never miss a good play and we have admired Mr Kean in all his rôles. His Shylock and his Richard the Third are superb but his Overreach is even better.'

She turned and saw the stout, fatherly gentleman from the mail-coach, accompanied by a good-looking, apple-cheeked lady. He bowed in the most natural way and Maria started to wonder why he had not inspired more interest during the journey. He was clearly a man of some culture and breeding.

'My wife and I have a box for this evening's performance,' he continued. 'It would give us the greatest possible pleasure if Mrs Norris and yourself were to join us.'

'Thank you. That is most amiable of you, sir, but my aunt is indisposed. The journey has fatigued her and she has already retired to her room.'

'I am sorry to hear that, but perhaps a short rest will restore her energies?'

Maria surmised that the combination of rest and Mr Kean would prove very therapeutic. 'There is no likelihood of that, I fear. My aunt has robust health but when she does have one of these migraines she keeps to her bed for at least a day. I would not like to disturb her.'

This was not strictly untrue. Maria could clearly remember one occasion when Mrs Norris had pleaded a headache and withdrawn herself for twenty-four hours.

'Then may I entreat you at least to honour us with your company? But forgive me, I have yet to introduce my wife. Mrs Rushworth – Mrs Randall.' He performed the introduction as if such formalities between lovers of art and drama were unnecessary, but Mrs Randall curtseyed conventionally enough and added her own hospitable entreaties to her husband's.

Maria had not seen Kean. Her short, ill-starred residence in London had coincided with the actor's debut at Drury Lane, but she had never been able to persuade Mr Rushworth to attend the new actor's performances. His very poor showing at the rehearsals for the Mansfield Park production of *Lovers' Vows* had confirmed her husband's indifference to serious drama, though he enjoyed burletta, and had made him distrust Maria's love of – and talent for – acting. He had given way to her so far as to permit two visits to the respectable but old-fashioned Mr Kemble, at Covent Garden, but they had both been bored by the statuesque, declamatory style.

'I shall be delighted to accept your invitation, Mr Randall,' said Maria decisively.

The Randalls accompanied her back to the hotel, volunteering some of the personal particulars she would have been too discreet to solicit. They lived mostly in Liverpool where she had family and he had business connections, but also had houses in the country and in London. Their only son ran the London office of his father's business and would take over in due course. Maria divined that Mrs Randall, related to the powerful Molyneux family, had married somewhat beneath her but that the social disparity had long since been bridged by her husband's affability and success.

An hour later Mr Randall returned and took Maria to his own house for refreshment before the play. They were greeted in the hall by Mrs Randall and told that before their wine they must go upstairs and see her new great-nephew. Maria had never liked or pretended to like babies, but after her recent experience felt obliged to try. The cot, placed in the middle of a pretty room, was being rocked by a nurse and ignored by a man who was standing at the window with his back to the door. Unable to hear their entrance above the baby's crying, the man did not move, but the nurse bobbed respectfully. Mrs Randall made soothing noises and the baby bawled even louder. Maria peered down dutifully and tried to think of something not too insincere to say about the fat, bald, purple-faced child. It was only about three months old but its eyes seemed to dart from one grown-up to another with malevolent intelligence and the thick upper lip above

89

receding double chins seemed to promise indulgence and excess consistent with its present, over-emphatic behaviour. Maria wondered what her hosts would say if they knew she had delivered a baby the night before, but she could not associate the lovely little thing she had brought into the world with the shrieking monster before her, and the cries gradually blotted out thought. The same noise made conversation happily difficult. A smile and an appreciative nod should be enough.

'*Lasciate ogni speranza voi ch'entrate.*' The words were spoken quite softly but the timbre of the voice made them distinct. Maria looked up and found the man who had been standing in the window looking at her from the other side of the cot.

'Fine pair of lungs,' he continued, 'good resonance, and a very impressive range. Did you note that top C just now? Should make a good singer when he grows up. Hideous, of course, but the spit and image of his parents, and a true-born Cheviot if ever there was one. What an ill-favoured family we are, Cousin Kate.'

All the time he spoke he continued to look at Maria but now he turned his attention to Mrs Randall.

'Speak for yourself, Charlie. My grandmother always said the Cheviots were one of the best-looking families in the north of England.'

'Young Figaro here must be the exception which proves the rule.' At this the child, who had seemed to moderate his cries at the sound of another male voice, took a deep breath preparatory to renewed efforts, but the young man seized the infant and, lifting it to arms' length, warned it (in loud, persuasive tenor) to moderate its behaviour since it was on a tree top with the wind blowing and the cradle rocking in imminent danger of breaking boughs and a sudden disastrous descent.

The baby heeded his injunction and even attempted a sickly smile as it was handed back to the nurse. For a moment Maria felt that she too was up in a tree with the wild wind blowing through her hair.

'Perhaps we had better leave you, nurse,' said Mrs Randall.

No further cries were heard till they were half-way down the stairs.

Tall and dark, Charles Cheviot had the dashing indolence of someone who has given and received much enjoyment in his first twenty-five years without exerting himself unduly. He was Mrs Randall's cousin, grandson of her nonagenarian uncle, Mr Cuthbert Cheviot of Seaforth Grange, Northumberland. Until recently he had been the favourite child of a doting mother, but Mrs Cheviot had died unexpectedly, and he was now the black sheep of an embittered father. Born of jealousy, the rift between Charles and Colonel Cheviot had been widened by the young man declining an army career and consorting instead with musicians, poets, painters, foreigners, and even actors. They were no longer on speaking terms.

A little of this was imparted to Maria by Mrs Randall before they were joined by the gentlemen; observation supplied a little more. Mr Cheviot was elegantly dressed yet there was a careless mockery about his attire which prevented him from appearing the complete man of fashion. Maria sensed that his style would hardly be altered by changes in dress. She was not at all displeased to learn that he was the fourth member of their theatre party, although his informal manner and casual acceptance of her own presence there was in marked contrast to the special attentions which the Randalls continued to pay her.

Time passed quickly as refreshments were served and the contents of two decanters were approved. The curtain-raiser would soon be over, but the party showed no sign of moving. Massinger's satire was about to begin. Maria showed her disappointment.

91

'My dear Mrs Rushworth,' said Cheviot, addressing her directly for almost the first time, 'you have missed nothing of any consequence, I assure you.' He strode across to the square piano and played a few chords. 'Permit me to explain what has proceeded so far. Some of the audience have already appeared – gentry in the boxes, the good burghers of Liverpool in the pit, riff-raff from the docks and taverns in the gallery, but the theatre is only half full.' He illustrated the scene, identifying each social class with comic music, ending with a monstrous fanfare:

'And now the manager appears on the stage. He thanks the audience for its courtesy in patronising his humble place of entertainment and begs its indulgence for – what is it, I forget, oh yes – for "Alexis and Celia", his modest and unworthy curtain-raiser. The gallery hisses him off stage and the orchestra strikes up *burlesco e giocoso*. Celia, of course, is Columbine, but which is Alexis, the enamoured shepherd, is he Harlequin or Pierrot? Therein lies the suspense. The story unfolds in mime and acrobatics, tricked out by jugglers and by songs, including "Where the bee sucks there suck I", "When daisies pied", and other improving gems. Eventually all is resolved, Alexis holds Celia in his arms, and the last word goes to Mr John Dryden.' Charles broke into song:

Whilst Alexis lay pressed
In her arms he loved best
With his hands round her neck
And his head on her breast,
He found the fierce pleasure too hasty to stay
And his soul in the tempest just flying away.
When Celia saw this,
With a sigh and a kiss
She cried 'Oh my dear, I am robbed of my bliss'. . .
The youth, though in haste

And breathing his last,
In pity died slowly, while she died more fast . . .
Thus entranced they did lie
Till Alexis did try
To recover new breath, that again he might die.
Then often they died; but the more they did so
The nymph died more quick and the shepherd more slow.

When the song was finished Mr Randall laughed heartily and Mrs Randall's apple cheeks deepened to a charming russet. Maria had listened to the voice rather than the words and had not puzzled out the meaning before the mood of the music changed from pastoral dalliance to melodrama and black menace. The pianist was now commenting on the first act of *A New Way to Pay Old Debts*.

'Sir Giles Overreach, a cruel and rapacious upstart, has acquired his nephew's fortune by villainous treachery, and plans to enhance his position further by forcing his beautiful daughter into marriage with Lord Lovell. Margaret herself is in love with Tom Allworth, friend of Overreach's dispossessed nephew, and consents to a trick against her father which has been concocted by the two young men and is supported by both Lady Allworth and Lord Lovell . . . and if we repair at once to the Theatre Royal, Mrs Rushworth and Mrs Randall will learn the exact nature of that deception and see for themselves the terrible retribution in store for the unspeakable Overreach – as only Mr Kean can reveal it!'

Williamson Square was only a few minutes' walk away. As they approached the theatre they heard sounds of commotion and ironic cheers from a neighbouring tavern. Suddenly the doors of the establishment burst open and a small, dishevelled man, clothed in extremely old-fashioned dress, issued forth with a young woman on either arm. The trio strolled across the road followed by a worried-looking man in formal attire, and by a chorus of vulgar comment from onlookers inside and outside the tavern. At the stage door, the man in fancy dress turned and bowed as if receiving an ovation, lingeringly embraced his companions, and attempted to kick the troubled little man who was hustling them into the theatre. At this the actor – Maria knew at once it was Mr Kean – lost his balance and fell through the entrance. The girls went tumbling after him much to the appreciation of the crowd before the stage door was slammed and locked.

So that was the great Kean? The unedifying spectacle had taken Maria aback rather than shocked her. It seemed that her eventful day must, after all, end in disillusion and anticlimax. However well Kean acted he could have no magic for her now – he must always remain the strutting little drunkard she had just seen. Most probably he would be replaced by an understudy. Mr Randall apologised and offered to postpone the theatre visit, but Cheviot argued that since they were already there they should try at least one act of the play.

Maria took her seat with a heavy heart and suddenly began to feel the sleepless night behind her.

'And which do you prefer,' asked Cheviot, 'comedy or tragedy?'

'Tragedy. It gives more scope for the revelation of character and in doing so makes greater demands on the performer's skill.'

'Ah, a tragedienne *manquée*. Have you ever acted yourself?'

'Alas no. My father would not even countenance private theatricals. Once, some years ago, we started preparing a performance of *Lovers' Vows*, but were not permitted to continue. It led to all sorts of trouble.'

94

'*Lovers' Vows?* With yourself in the part of Agatha, I trust?'

'Yes. How jealous my sister was about that! But looking back, those rehearsals were one of the happiest of times.' She sighed. 'I do enjoy acting, but I have been to the play all too little.'

'Now is the time to begin.'

'Hardly. I am on my way to New York.'

Mr Cheviot received this news with a lift of the eyebrows but no other sign of interest. After a while he said, 'The American stage is inferior to our own as yet, but its possibilities are boundless. All it needs is a Kean.'

'From what little I have seen of him, that is the last thing it needs.'

'Not Kean the man, but Kean the actor.'

'Can you separate the two?'

'I stand corrected, but, lo, the curtain rises.'

The man who had just made a spectacle of himself in the street was no longer playing the part of Sir Giles Overreach. Kean had been replaced and, in spite of herself, Maria was at first disappointed. The new Sir Giles was completely different in stature, bearing, voice and physiognomy, though his dress was similar. Whoever he was, this understudy, he was brilliant, and soon the whole audience was spellbound in horror. There on the stage below was no actor at all, but Overreach himself, the vilest of extortioners about whom some day Mr Massinger would write a play, a play for future generations to act and future actors to use for virtuoso performances. But here the story was unfolding for the first time. Two centuries and more dissolved as one man forged his way to self-destruction, calling down eternal hatred on his name. Mortgaging his own soul this Overreach jeopardised everyone else's and struck terror into every breast. No member of the audience was safe from his heroic, all-corrupting evil – least of all Maria. As the curtain fell, he seemed to be looking at her and her alone; as if she was his next victim; he smiled a triumphant, mortal smile as she fainted.

'What happened?' she asked when Mrs Randall's smelling-salts had revived her.

'Kean the actor,' said Mr Cheviot.

The final scenes were even more thrilling and horrid, the last of all consigning Overreach to Bedlam – and beyond. Even from hell itself he would have fought his way back, but undone widows sat palpably upon his arm, wronged orphans' tears glued sword to scabbard, steel whips scourged his soul as, finally, he crashed to eternal death.

'How he foams,' said one of the other actors unnecessarily.

Impenetrable silence met the final curtain. Death itself was exhausted. After two or three minutes Charles Cheviot broke the spell by shouting 'bravo' and beginning to clap. It was only then that Maria realised she was clinging to his arm and digging her nails into his wrist. She released him at once, too drained to feel embarrassed. The applause began to swell, the curtains parted, and there was Overreach alone, foaming, twitching and writhing like a chicken after strangulation, as he lay spreadeagled on the madhouse floor.

'Massinger described it as a comedy,' said Cheviot when the tumult had at last subsided. 'Why are you all looking so discomforted? Evil has received its just desert; good has prevailed, and everyone except Sir Giles lives happily ever after.'

There was a knock on the door of the box and two flunkeys appeared bearing trays.

'Don't look so miserable,' continued Cheviot. 'Ah, here's something to set you up.' Light refreshments and a flask of brandy were set upon the table, and soon helped to revive the party.

'Is he . . . do you think . . . that is, will Mr Kean be all right?' asked Maria, after drinking more brandy in

96

a few mouthfuls than she had consumed in her whole life. 'I mean will he live?'

'Haven't the slightest notion,' said Cheviot. 'Shall we go and ask him?'

'Do you know Mr Kean, Charles?' asked Mrs Randall.

'Yes indeed. Capital fellow. Somewhat wild and not at all the gentleman but always pleased to exchange a song or two (and a glass or two) with an amateur and dilettante, so long as he's not a lord. Hates the genuine aristocracy does our Edmund. Means I'm quite acceptable. Don't know about you, Mrs Rushworth, but however elevated your rank, I suspect he'll find something to admire in you. A very great deal, I should imagine.'

Cheviot scribbled a message, had it sent round to Kean's dressing-room, and shortly afterwards conducted the party to the back of the stage. They were respectfully greeted by the worried-looking man – Kean's secretary – and asked to wait a few minutes. Mr Kean was recovering from his performance and taking off his grease-paint, but would be delighted to receive Mr Cheviot and his friends as soon as he was presentable. From inside the dressing-room came the sounds of recovery and grease-paint removal, a rather noisier and more boisterous process than Maria had realised. Grunts, oaths, bellows of laughter, the clink of glasses, and the twang of furniture springs followed each other through the door, as the secretary tried to engage their attention by talking about the performance. There were other distractions too. Half-dressed actors shouting at each other, musicians quarrelling, scene shifters preparing for the next day's presentation. At last they were allowed into Kean's presence.

Maria wondered what had been going on, it was so untidy. There were clothes everywhere – on the floor, on chairs, over the screen. She had never seen so many clothes, nor so many bottles. A young woman – not one of Kean's earlier companions – was lying drowsily on a half-broken chaise-longue wearing only a dressing-gown which she had neglected to do up. Another was opening and closing the drawers of a tallboy, not apparently looking for anything specific so much as seeing what she could find. Naked to the waist and gleaming with sweat, the actor was standing before a large cracked looking-glass still removing his grease-paint. He was delighted to see Charles Cheviot and addressed him as 'My right honourable Pan – the only lord who's either right or honourable.'

'Not always honourable, seldom right, and never, alas, a lord,' disclaimed Cheviot, before introducing Maria and the Randalls.

An awkward silence ensued after the first compliments. It is always difficult to know what to say to an actor in his dressing-room. Considered dramatic criticism is the last thing required and flattery, disguised as judicious comment, too easily lapses into insincerity. Player and playgoer should both be too spent for serious talk.

'Thank you for the most enthralling evening of my life,' said Maria. 'If you are not unhinged you must be a genius.'

'Your servant ma'am. *Adulatio blanditiae, pessimum veri affectus venenum.*'

Neither the emptiness of the courtesy nor the ungraciousness of the Latin was entirely lost on Maria. She began to bridle but, noting that the actor was at least a head shorter than Mr Cheviot and perhaps an inch shorter than herself, decided to give him the benefit of the doubt.

'You were so realistic. By comparison, Mr Kemble is a wooden effigy or a figure in bas-relief.'

Kean looked at her with a spark of interest. 'A lady of perception, I see. Taste and discrimination, beauty and breeding – how seldom they coalesce. I am glad you were diverted by my humble efforts. *Varium et mutabile semper femina.* In my all too limited experience' (and here he glanced at the recumbent young woman) 'I have come to despise those cynics who claim that fashion and fortune are the sole preoccupations of the gentle sex.'

'Mrs Rushworth is a student of the drama,' interposed Cheviot, 'and might have become a skilled performer herself but for parental opposition.'

'It is most fortunate for us rogues and vagabonds that family disapprobation should withhold Mrs Rushworth's talents from public scrutiny.' Why, if Mrs Rushworth played Desdemona, who would notice Othello? Such beauty would attract all eyes. *Caveat actor.*'

Kean laughed loudly at his pun and continued complimenting Maria in this vein until it became tedious. Mr and Mrs Randall were plainly ill at ease and Maria was suddenly overcome by fatigue. Cheviot, on the other hand, seemed to relish every word that fell from the actor's lips and was reluctant to leave. At last Randall took the lead and, bowing stiffly, ushered the ladies out of what he subsequently called the presence. Cheviot followed them, with a meaningful shrug.

'*Sic noctem patera, sic ducam carmine, donec injiciat radios in mea vina dies,*' shouted Kean through the door.

Chapter Ten

They passed the night accordingly – Kean, Cheviot, and an all-Liverpool tragedian calling himself Wellesley Nelson – with cup and with song until the light of day at length did, indeed, shed its rays into their wine and brandy.

Awash with the actor's liquor, if not illuminated by his Latin, Charles Cheviot stumbled to bed still dressed, lost consciousness for an hour or two, and then awoke with burning throat and aching head. He closed his eyes and sought further oblivion but the pounding behind his forehead insisted on his full attention. Further sleep was out of the question and he lay panting on the bed, a helpless victim of the torturers within. As the pain increased, images and memories flitted across his mind: a woman who was going to New York; Kean's trousers flying through the air; Wellesley Nelson's claim to be king of the Liverpool underworld; the words of a most improper song . . . Suddenly the nausea returned. Realising that he must on no account violate his cousin Kate's second-best bedroom, he struggled to his feet and in less than a minute was clear of the house, round the corner into Duke Street, and retching in comparative seclusion.

When he was done, he felt slightly better but the fire in his head raged still and he set off at a brisk trot to see if healthful exercise – something he normally shunned – would help. At the end of the road he found the duke's dock and without hesitation dived into the inviting water. It was soothingly cool and he swam to the sluice where part of the dock connected to the Bridgwater Canal. A small slipway enabled him to regain dry land, shivering but beginning to think that he might, just possibly, survive. The canal led inland past warehouses and sawmills to open country by means of a wide towpath. For the next hour he walked, ran and swam alternately, indifferent to public gaze (one or two people were now astir). It was tiring but recuperative. Eventually he turned back and began to think seriously about the woman going to New York.

Who was the lovely Mrs Rushworth? What was sending her to America? Where was her husband? Dead perhaps. Why had she made such an impression on him? When would he see her again? On a lonely stretch of towpath some way ahead he saw a figure which he could tell, even from this distance, was a beggarwoman. There was no way of avoiding her. Either he would have to give her money or he would have to refuse to give her money. Poor as he was since his mother's death, he realised that refusing would take more courage than giving. He felt surreptitiously in his breeches pocket. The night before had been paid for by Kean, so his small store of coins was undisturbed. Perhaps if he gave her a few pence it would bring him luck with Mrs Rushworth.

As he came up to her he saw that the woman was a gipsy and that a ramshackle caravan was half-concealed behind the hedgerow in a neighbouring field. Though dirty and bedraggled, she was quite young and her dark blue eyes caught the young man's attention. Behind her piteous look there was just a hint of mockery.

'Buy a sprig of heather, sir. You have a lucky face.'

'If I have a lucky face, perhaps I don't need any heather.'

'Better safe than sorry,' said the girl darkly.

'How much is it?'

'Same as always, sir. The bigger the money the bigger the luck.'

'I see. Shall we say a penny?'

'For a penny you may only get bad luck,' she warned.

'Make it a shilling.'

'My good woman, you can see I have been swimming. One does not go swimming with one's pockets bulging with silver. I have only a few pence.' With a dramatic gesture he plunged a hand into his wet pocket, deciding on impulse to give her as much or as little as came out with it. 'Here, this is all I have.'

He opened his hand. Of the seven coins it contained, six were gold. Bewildered, he dropped rather more than his monthly income into the gipsy's waiting hands and, cursing his impulse, walked on almost forgetting the heather.

'Here you are, sir,' she called out after him. 'Good luck, sir.'

How such a large sum came to be in his breeches pocket was a mystery. Normally he carried as little as possible for

101

fear of spending it, though he tried to have something for contingencies such as this. He had a superstition that so long as he gave beggars something, however little, he would never become a beggar himself. Charity prompted by self-preservation rather than compassion, or so it had always seemed to him. As soon as he was out of earshot, he shouted an oath and kicked a broken crate into the canal so violently that he hurt his toe. He remembered now that Kean had started throwing money around (more or less literally) some time after midnight. Most of his largesse had been distributed among whores and spongers, but a few precious sovereigns had been his remuneration for a bawdy song.

A windfall wasted on a whim.

He could only hope that as far as Providence was concerned his unintended generosity would count as the genuine article, and bring him a commensurate amount of luck, as foretold by the gipsy.

Personable, gifted, and amusing, Charles Cheviot had lived five and twenty years on this earth without gaining any very intimate experience of the opposite sex. He had enjoyed superficial flirtations with the daughters of a few present-able families, been loved himself with innocent passion and romantic despair by a plain young woman, visited a *bagnio* while a student in Italy, and been briefly initiated into the disciplines of adultery à la mode by a shameless but very respectable first cousin once removed (who considered such initiations a duty). He remained, however, urbanely innocent, more chaste than chasing. His flamboyant manner masked lack of confidence which derived from an ambiguous social and financial position. In London's caste-ridden society, the Cheviots – northerners of no great antiquity – counted for little. They were neither rich enough for birth to be overlooked, nor gentle enough for lack of riches to be no handicap, but having some money and some breeding they were tolerated. A good marriage would improve Charles no end, meanwhile he could be received into the better London houses on approval, subject to reasonable conduct, and in return for his musical and artistic abilities. That was while his mother lived. With her death, Charles's income dropped to a derisory £100 per year and at a time when ostentation was more than ever before accepted as the true proof of merit. Like most young men in his position he began to acquire debts and look, ever more earnestly, for an heiress. Native caution staved off the inevitable crisis but eventually his creditors foreclosed. By selling shares and relinquishing rights in a family trust, he was able to settle or make provision for most of his debts and avoid public exposure or bankruptcy; now he had retired to lick his wounds on only £50 per annum in the company of affluent (but on one side not very grand) relations, and consider his next step.

'Kean offered me a job last night,' he said at breakfast. 'Thinks I would be a bad actor but good company. Wouldn't provide any competition for his genius, unlike the – to Kean – dangerous Mrs Rushworth. Wants me to do the singing.'

'Oh Charlie, you couldn't. Think of your position,' said Mrs Randall.

'I am.'

'I know things are difficult for you since your mother . . . but — '

'Cheviots and gentlemen – in so far as they are gentlemen – don't go on the boards, eh? Is that what you mean?'

'Yes, I suppose it is.'

'Garrick was accepted by all the best people. Mr Kemble and Mr Mayne Young are quite the thing, I believe. Even Kean claims to be the son of a duke.'

'But without foundation,' said Mr Randall. 'The Duke of Norfolk has publicly refuted the claim. Says he would be the first to admit it if it were true.'

'However that may be, I have to find remunerative employment. Can you suggest an alternative to the stage, cousin Kate? I can sing and play music. I suppose I can act and dance. I can draw pretty pictures and write verse of a sort. Little wonder my father disowns me. He only acknowledges three possible occupations for a gentleman, the army, the law, and the church.'

'With your gift of the gab you should have taken up the law. Why, oh why, did your mother send you to Bologna instead of Cambridge or Lincoln's Inn?'

'Because I insisted. Besides she never intended I should want for money.'

'It will have to be commerce, Charles,' said Mr Randall. 'No harm in that. Most of your London dandies are dependent on some commercial cove these days. You can add two and two, I suppose?'

'Possibly, sir, haven't tried lately. I have more experience of subtraction and division, unfortunately, than of addition or multiplication.'

'There is a position I could give you.'

'Most kind, sir. Nepotism is the one mercantile virtue which has my unqualified approbation. For the future prosperity of your house, however, I advise you seek out merit and application.'

'We need a new man in New York.'

'New York? It is true I was contemplating the abroad. An opportunity in India or China . . . New York, you say . . . in America?'

Mr Randall lifted his guileless face and looked thoughtfully at the ceiling, as if trying to puzzle what its function might be. 'Yes, our agent there intends to retire. You might go as his assistant and take over as soon as you have learnt the job.'

'But my commercial knowledge is of the scantiest; not but what this requires most careful consideration. You are most kind, sir.'

'Come to my study and we will talk it over.'

As a result of the discussion which ensued, Charles Cheviot took himself to the office of Messrs Cropper, Benson & Co., shipping agents, the following afternoon. Nothing had been decided about the New York position, but sufficient interest was felt for the availability of passages to be ascertained. And there were other reasons for the visit – artistic reasons.

The office was thronged with people. Many looked like passengers or potential passengers; others had clearly come for news of ships and cargoes, schedules of arrivals and departures, details relating to freightage, or for positions in ships' companies. All was commotion and it would clearly be some time before Cheviot's enquiries would be answered. He resigned himself to a long wait and began to study the crowd.

In Italy, he had received instruction in classical painting and in England had formed a lively appreciation of the natural, neo-classical and romantic schools, but his own taste and style inclined to caricature. Rowlandson was his model rather than Gillray or Hogarth: the quick, witty, uncommitted comment came easily to him, but he lacked private concern, political or moral. His drawings pleased but seldom probed, and the assorted humanity in the shipping office was very much his kind of subject. As he prepared to sketch, two gentlemen standing apart amid all the hubbub attracted his attention, and he decided to make them the focus of his picture. Half-pay naval officers seeking commissions on merchantmen, he surmised. Though aloof from his surroundings and talking animatedly to his companion, one of them was continuously casting his eyes around as if looking for some third person, and the sketcher caught his abstracted manner cleverly. The rough picture had him eyeing the front door of the office which stood empty towards the foreground. Almost without thinking Cheviot sketched a female figure into the empty doorway, drawing from memory the woman who was on her way to New York. It was a fair likeness except that Maria was dressed as a shepherdess. At this point he began to admit that half his reason for coming to the shipping office had been the hope that his mysterious Mrs Rushworth might also have business to transact there. She was, however, nowhere to be seen. Outwardly languid but inwardly impatient, he scanned the crowd without reward until it was his turn to enquire about possible boats and passages.

It appeared that sailings to New York had been delayed by weather and other hazards and that the next one would not depart for a month or more, though originally planned for the end of the week. He made a booking in the name of Mr Randall's company, and was put on the list. It was a busy time and all the berths had been reserved, but the clerk thought it likely that room would be found for someone representing so important a client as Randall & Co. The young man left the office more disappointed than he cared to confess by the non-appearance of Maria Rushworth.

A few minutes later, two well-dressed ladies entered the premises of Cropper, Benson & Co. The older one gave a contemptuous look at the crowd, strode to the counter, and successfully demanded instant attention. She, too, discovered that all New York sailings were postponed for at least one month.

'This is most inconvenient. They assured me there was a departure at the end of the week, and accepted my money, that is our money. We travelled all the way here, at great personal discomfort, expressly for that purpose. And now you say the sailing is delayed for several weeks? Outrageous. I cannot accept the weather as any excuse at all. This is the nineteenth century, and if your boats are coppered and copper-fastened, as I have been led to understand, there can be no reason for not sailing punctually, as advertised. How do I know there have been storms in the Caribbean? As for taking advance payment and then neglecting to carry out your contract, that amounts to false pretence. The law is most particular on that point. I shall take the matter up with your directors and unless I receive satisfaction, remove my custom elsewhere. As for you, young man, a little more consideration for your elders and betters would not come amiss. I am seriously displeased. Good day.'

She spun on her heel and stalked out of the office, followed by the younger woman (who seemed unmoved) and by glances of silent sympathy from all the others who were waiting in the office. Young William Price was too far away to recognise his relatives, but not so preoccupied that he did not admire his cousin's figure.

Chapter Eleven

In her liberated, even exalted, state the evening before any personable young gentleman might have attracted Maria's interest. Charles Cheviot just happened to be the young man she met. It was not, therefore, Mr Cheviot as such that engaged her thoughts, it was Mr Cheviot as a representative of the opposite sex in general, Mr Cheviot as a signpost pointing the way towards a reconstructable life. Or would he prove another Mr Fanthorpe; would all men become Fanthorpes once they knew her secret? Possibly, but her Leamington adventure seemed to matter less and less. It had happened to a different person. More consciously than unconsciously she decided, without committing herself in any way, to give the new young man any opportunity the next month might afford to fall in love with her.

To her aunt she only mentioned the externals of the theatre visit. Mrs Norris made some show of vicarious gratification but in reality was discomposed. She was irked at having missed the Randalls' hospitality, jealous that Maria had watched and met the great Kean, and instinctively suspicious of Charles Cheviot whom Maria, not choosing to mention his voice, represented as a conventional-looking gentleman with a somewhat small head.

'Cheviot, you say? Never heard of the family. Where do they come from?'

'I really do not know. Does it matter? A border family, I think.'

'An obscure one. Cattle-thieves and raiders, I daresay.'

Maria laughed forbearingly. 'I cannot imagine Mr Cheviot stealing cattle or even lambs. Do not condemn him before you have even met him.'

'Of course I shall not. I am the most tolerant of creatures – "tolerant to a fault" as Norris used to say – I was merely mentioning that Cheviot is not a name of any standing. They may be a highly respectable family, but if they do come from the border country, the chances are that they have a rude and turbulent background. I shall say no more on the subject. Idle speculation is not one of my vices. Not another word. Mr Cheviot may be a gentleman of refined taste, elegant manners, and artistic propensities – or he may be an adventurer without two farthings to rub together; it is not for me to conjecture. No doubt his intimacy with Mr Kean whose own private life, I understand, is scandalous, admits of a perfectly honourable explanation. What it might be escapes me for the moment, but that is beside the point. Mr Randall seems a most deserving person, and his wife, I understand, is connected with the Stanleys, or is it the Molyneux family?, and if they accept young Cheviot, who am I to question it?'

Before long the two families met again, and Mrs Norris had a chance of finding fault with the young man at first hand. His elegance, affability, and good breeding confirmed her most gratifying suspicions. He was another Henry Crawford, taller and better-looking but with the same engaging air. There could be little doubt that given the opportunity her niece might become attached to him. Mr Cheviot gave polished but evasive replies to the subtle questioning she put to him as regards his family, his future, and his fortune. That the first was intermixed, the second indeterminate, and the third inexistent was soon as clear as she could hope, and she was mindful once again of how much the family needed her perspicacious protection. Confirmation was provided by the disingenuous Mrs Randall when the two ladies took a turn in the garden.

'Dear Charles,' she volunteered, 'he is so charming and talented, but what is to become of him now his mother is dead, I really do not know. If only he wasn't so proud I am sure he could make it up with his father. We all must learn to suffer fools gladly, don't you agree? Besides, in this case, they are both so uncompromising. Father and son seem to enjoy the family feud.'

'Was Mr Cheviot very close to his mother?'

'Too close. He was the apple of her eye, and that makes it all the worse now that she is no more. Colonel Cheviot always resented the intimacy, but she was a strong-willed woman with her own resources. As long as she was alive there was someone to keep the peace between Charles and his father, though they were always as chalk and cheese.'

'No other children?'

'An elder brother and two sisters.'

'And can they not intercede with the father?'

'I do not think they want to. They were jealous of Charles's influence on their mother and the current estrangement suits their book. The Cheviot estate was never large and it has been badly managed, Mr Randall says, for many years. By cutting out Charles the other three will receive more in due course.'

'So poor Mr Cheviot is excluded from the estate.'

'Unless somebody has a change of heart, yes.'

'What an unsatisfactory state of affairs. I have always maintained that family fortunes should be shared evenly between the offspring concerned, as in France. Our English system allows gross injustices and creates family feeling. It is perfectly true that where the estate is modest and the family immodest, equal division among the heirs inevitably leads to decline of the property, but no one is forced to have a large family. Two or three children should be the maximum for families with less than £5000 per annum. My own father, the wisest of men, was most scrupulous in his dispositions, providing a fair dowry for the daughter who married Sir Thomas Bertram, and a token annuity – at once chastening and compassionate – to the daughter who injudiciously married a penniless lieutenant of marines and had nine children. The bulk of the estate went to the elder daughter and was devoted to the welfare of my husband and his parish.'

If Mrs Randall noted any disparity between her new friend's theoretical support of the Napoleonic Code and her simultaneous endorsement of primogeniture, she did not reveal it. The two ladies parted with protestations of mutual respect.

110

Over the next weeks the Randalls introduced the Mansfield Park ladies to Liverpool's burgeoning institutions and London-defying social life. They went to a reception in the Town Hall and listened to Mr Cheviot's well-informed assessment of Mr Wyatt's reconstruction work; they took advantage of the Lyceum, home of Europe's first proprietary circulating library (a hazard which gave them happily unfounded mis-givings); and they duly attended the draughty Wellington Rooms. The latter had been erected by public subscription soon after Waterloo and looked like a circular Greek temple, the portico as open to the elements as any in Attica itself. The weather, too, had become almost Grecian.

As for Charles and Maria, they were unsuccessful in their efforts to avoid each other's company. A series of inexplicable coincidences threw them together (to their continued astonishment, it is to be presumed), often without the benefit of older and wiser companions. Great town that it was becoming, Liverpool seemed surprisingly small and they met by accident when studying playbills, browsing in the music shop, taking cups of chocolate, and other improbable pursuits. That they accepted these juxtapositions with more than ordinary good grace was due, no doubt, to a shared knowledge that one of them was shortly to sail away from any chance of entanglement. It may also be that both felt they were receiving more pleasure than they were giving, a form of generosity they could safely afford. Subjects such as her past and his future were tacitly avoided; music and the theatre were recurrent topics.

'When I went to the lycée (that is the *liceo*) at Bologna, I immediately made friends with a fellow student who had already been there some years. He was precisely the same age as myself, we were both born on February 29th. Our ambition was to write operas like Mozart's, but we had to compose sacred cantatas instead. Like many Italians, my

111

friend professed a passion for 'Guglielmo' Shakespeare, despite abominable ignorance of the plays themselves. At my suggestion we took those two young men of nearby Verona as an operatic subject, and were just starting to work on it together when he received a genuine operatic commission from Venice. Off he went for a few weeks – and never came back. His name was Rossini, and but for that commission, I would have been his first collaborator . . . '

'Was the opera a great success?'

'No, but it established his name. Since then he has written about ninety-seven operas – good, bad, and brilliant. I have written none, but I am still tempted by the *Two Gentlemen.*'

'When are you going to commence?'

'Now, if you will help. How well do you know Shakepeare's songs? There is seldom more than one in each play, sometimes none at all. For example, only "O Mistress Mine" in *Twelfth Night*, only "Tell me where is fancy bred" in, I think, *All's Well that Ends Well*, only "Blow, blow thou — " '.

'You mean *The Merchant of Venice.* "Tell me where is fancy bred" comes in the casket scene.'

'So it does. I knew it, your knowledge of the bard is profound. You must be my new collaborator.'

Maria laughed and felt pleased. She was not deceived by the compliment but flattered by the teasing. 'I had to sing and play at home, but I am no musician, certainly no composer.'

'So much the better. You will bring no prejudices to the venture. A little knowledge is a useful thing. Let us assemble all the best songs and fit them into the story of those two young men, one so virtuous (the tenor) and one so reprehensible (the bass). A ballad opera to delight the *cognoscenti* for whom Liverpool is justly celebrated. Mr Randall's fine house shall be our theatre and we shall be stars of the season's most elegant, refined, and artistic reception.

112

'Twill be accomplished in a trice, for Shakespeare himself has already done the hard work and many of the songs have been set by acceptable composers such as the late Mr Arne. For the rest, I have this moment thought of the perfect tune for "It was a lover and his lass", and you shall sing it.'

Maria coloured. 'I can hardly do that. It must be sung by a man or it will make no sense.'

'A valid objection, Mrs Rushworth, but soon overcome. We shall change it to "It was a lover and her lad". Come, let us start without more (let alone much) ado.'

They did. The composition proved just as straightforward as Mr Cheviot had predicted and the inclusion of a few local references gave the entertainment topicality. The not too discriminating audience pronounced *Two Gentlemen of Warrington* a great success. Maria's beauty compensated for her vocal shortcomings and she revealed a pretty sense of comedy when disguised as the page; Mr Cheviot excelled with the voice and overacted engagingly. No one enjoyed the two-man performance more than the performers. Uninterrupted by any visitation from Sir Thomas Bertram, the rehearsals had been more enjoyable still.

At first Mrs Norris affected an aloof and patronising attitude to these provincial junketings, at least when she was alone with Maria. She was, after all, the sister of Lady Bertram. The assiduous respect shown her by Mr and Mrs Randall, however, and the unquestionable gentility of most of their circle, gradually disarmed her. To Maria's half-acknowledged dismay, she began to make herself officiously useful. Indeed she would positively have enjoyed it all had it not been for the presence of Mr Cheviot whose growing intimacy with Maria soon began to take on the dimensions of a threat. Mrs Norris did not think it desirable for Maria to form any serious attachment whatever, let alone an attachment to someone without means. From

113

time to time, she admitted to herself the possibility in the distant future of a second marriage for her niece, but only to a gentleman of her own choosing and on the strict understanding that she would remain Maria's guide, philosopher and friend. She knew better than to criticise the young man directly, however, and relied on innuendo and faint praise to counteract his influence.

'Such an estimable young man. What a pity he had to leave London. Really it is monstrous that in this day and age someone of accomplishments and taste should be unacceptable in the best places merely for want of a few hundred pounds a year. I have never been able to understand those who put wealth before character, or ostentation before true worth. Still, I have little doubt that his devoted cousins will find some satisfactory solution up here in the north without forcing him into trade. I understand he is painting the portrait of some cotton-master's only daughter. No doubt she will jump at the chance of being connected to a landed family, albeit minor and parvenu, and overlook his indigence.'

Maria had never known poverty and was disenchanted with wealth. She had married a very rich young man and run off with a fairly rich one. Neither liaison had inspired her with unalloyed respect for money and she endowed Mr Cheviot's straitened circumstances with romance. He was the first of her admirers who had a material need which she could meet. She was grateful to Mrs Norris for making her realise that.

Besides, he was taking her likeness too.

After the musical evening, Mrs Norris became selfless and indefatigable in her efforts to protect the young people from themselves. By various stratagems she managed to keep Maria and Charles out of each other's company for several days and to fabricate a number of petty misunderstandings – molehills which refused, however, to turn into mountains. Usually critical and quick-tempered, her niece seemed to have acquired a new equilibrium; the headstrong impulsiveness of the past giving way, temporarily at least, to wistful patience. She did not seem to need her aunt's counsel as much as she used to and the latter became more and more alarmed.

On the day Charles was due to finish Maria's likeness, Mrs Norris decided on a supreme sacrifice in the interest of them all. She arranged for the artist to be left alone in the hotel room which was being used for the sitting while she helped Maria with her hair and gown. As he went in, Charles's eye was immediately caught by a book lying open on the sofa table. He strolled over and looked at it casually. The names Maria and Rushworth jumped out of the page. With quickening interest he picked up the volume, looked at the title, and skimmed through the leaves: Bertram, Norris, Rushworth – the names were familiar; their juxtaposition in a book purporting to be fiction could not be coincidental. Perhaps this was the key to the mystery of Maria's background and the question none of them had liked to ask her about her husband and marriage. Hearing voices in the corridor outside, he hurriedly looked at the fly-leaf again, and put down the book. Maria and Mrs Norris found him in his favourite position standing at the window, but the aunt saw that *Mansfield Park* was lying closed on the sofa table and congratulated herself on having found a sure way of saving two young people from a grave mistake.

Maria sat down and composed herself for being painted, happily aware that Charles would look at her, as soon as Mrs Norris had retired, with the ardour of a young man as well as the detachment of an artist. This was the fourth sitting and she had prepared herself with unusual attention. She looked almost the same as on previous occasions, yet her colour was a trifle higher, her gown a fraction lower, the carelessness of her hair style had been achieved with even greater care. Conscious that she had seldom looked better she found herself thinking the strangest thoughts – thoughts certainly at variance with her intention of avoiding personal commitment. If the artist had suggested that they fly to the moon together she would have declined but without total conviction, and steered the conversation round to the services recently introduced at Gretna Green. He made no such suggestion; he nearly told her about his possible appointment in New York but decided it was not in his interest to do so yet. He must read that book first. Across the room the tell-tale volume, hidden from Maria by its familiarity, lay upon the sofa table, a poisoned cup.

'Charles could be the best portrait painter since Mr Romney, if only he would apply himself to the task,' said Mrs Randall, admiring the finished picture. 'The likenesses he achieves are extraordinary, and with such a simple technique. What an artist the age is losing by his refusal to paint seriously. He has too much talent, that is his trouble. Of course, I know nothing about art,' she concluded truthfully.

'I have always maintained that the artist's calling is nothing to be ashamed of,' said Mrs Norris.

'Likenesses are the caricaturist's stock in trade, cousin. *Tricks* of the trade, and not to be confused with proper art. I know my limitations.'

'Perhaps caricature will be recognised as art one day,' said Maria.

'I don't think so. It is too ephemeral.'

'Yes this picture has little of the caricature,' persisted Mrs Randall. 'Here is no exaggeration; here is no distortion of one particular characteristic; here is a genuine, balanced likeness.'

'For that you must give credit to the subject not to the painter. How can one exaggerate perfection? If all sitters were as Mrs Rushworth I might indeed take to the brush seriously, but as it is I shall stick to my last and daub for amusement only.'

Charles begged Maria to accept the picture with his humble devotion. She offered instead to buy it and an altercation ensued in which each of them spoke with more feeling than truthfulness. Finally the combined pleas of both Randalls along with Maria's own won the day, and Charles gracefully accepted twenty-five guineas, muttering something (which no one believed) about donating it to charity.

'Accepting pecuniary reward from one's personal acquaintance is not in itself discreditable,' Mrs Norris kindly reassured him.

After they had gone, Charles traced his steps to the library, acquired *Mansfield Park*, and, returning home, closeted himself in his room for several hours. Silent and preoccupied, he joined the company briefly in the evening only to retire again, pleading a headache. By the small hours he had mastered all three volumes and possessed himself of Maria Rushworth's secret.

Meanwhile in London one of the principal protagonists of *Mansfield Park*, Mr Henry Crawford (formerly of the 15th Hussars), announced his engagement to Louisa (*née* Musgrove), the rich and pretty widow of Captain Benwick, R.N.

Chapter Twelve

Sleep now came to Maria more easily than at any time since she had trapped herself into becoming Mrs Rushworth. She was very far from certain, however, that she wanted to change her name to Cheviot. Charles was delightful company but left a mixed after-impression: out of sight he was quite often out of mind. Suspended between past and future, she saw everything in Liverpool as slightly unreal and felt free to encourage his attachment (even at some personal risk to her peace of mind) since its duration must be so brief. Happily muddled, she was content to be borne along on the tide for a few more days.

At four in the morning her new-found peace received a rude jolt. She had been dreaming of the portrait session: the sunlight pouring through the window; the painter saying 'Keep your head still'; the objects which met her fixed gaze. Suddenly she noticed the sofa table. What was that volume, that too, too familiar little book? Dream, subconscious memory, half-assimilated impression, she was fully awake now and in the grip of a fearful apprehension. If Charles should read that book, all hope would be lost; Mr Cheviot's attachment would be destroyed for ever. She jumped from her bed, fumbled for something to throw over her shoulders, and groped her way to the door. The passage outside was well enough lit for her to run to the stairs and down to the portrait room. She hesitated, listened. All was silent. Then she took a deep breath and entered. But on the polished surface of the sofa table there was nothing, only the pale moon's light.

'It must have been my imagination,' she said to Mrs Norris after breakfast.

Her aunt had listened to the story with grave attention and momentary disquiet. The riskiest aspect of her design had been that Maria would notice the book at once and secure it the moment the sitting was finished. Then some explaining would have had to be done. She had a plausible story, of course, which she could put across with conviction (and if necessary with outraged innocence) but she was glad she had not had to use it.

'It is better that no one associate us – you – with a book so partial in its details and so false in its conclusion, but we

118

shall only be in Liverpool a few more days and it does not signify all that much what people say after we have gone. The London tittle-tattle hardly touches us here; how much less will Liverpool gossip hurt us in the New World.'

'All the same Mr Cheviot is the last person I should wish to read that book.'

'Are you afraid that his regard is so superficial as to be influenced by a tissue of lies?'

'Yes. I don't know. They're libels not lies. The facts are accurate. It's the depiction of character which is so unfair and wounding.'

'If Mr Cheviot is a man of discernment and sensibility — '

'Then he will be scandalised. He must be. Oh, I do hope he never sees it. Later on he might reconsider but his first reaction must be condemnation. If he later sees the other side, it will be too late.'

'As you wish, Maria. Far be it from me to question the propriety of your allowing a young man's attentions while taking steps to encourage his delusions.'

'What do you mean by that? Are you implying that I should tell him all? Besides, I'm not allowing his attentions.'

'I am implying nothing. My only concern is for your peace of mind. It would indeed be disturbing if Mr Cheviot learnt about your divorce now; might it not be even more awkward if he learnt about it after his attachment, and perhaps yours too, had grown?'

'It might. But we must risk that. Really, aunt, you talk about my peace of mind but keep sowing seeds of doubt. If one were to be strictly logical one could argue that no respectable gentleman would have anything to do with me if he knew about my past, and therefore that anyone, knowing my past, who continued to talk, let alone "pay attentions" to me, must, *ipso facto*, be a shameless scoundrel. So, either way, my position is hopeless. But I do not believe that to be true. I shall leave matters as they are and hang the consequences. And I shall thank you not to interfere.'

'I never interfere,' snapped Mrs Norris as Maria left the room.

Yes, Charles Cheviot was scandalised but not exactly as Maria imagined. His first reaction was bitter disappointment that a woman with £1000 a year – spirited, beautiful, and attachable? – should turn out to have a past. Obviously he could have no more to do with her; it was most vexing. He felt personally cheated by her rash and immoral behaviour. Why, she was no better than his cousin Pamela, society's epitome of adulterous rectitude. No, that was untrue; he began to see a glimmer of hope. Pamela was deceitful as well as (beguilingly) depraved, faithless even in her infidelities. Maria, on the other hand, had been openly unchaste, honourable almost in her dishonour. That much (or that little) could be said in her favour. If society were not corrupt, it would condemn Pamela and condone Maria; instead it did the opposite. Why should he, an artist, a friend of the great Kean, an admirer of Lord Byron and Mr Shelley, conform to convention's dictatorship? Why should he not make his own moral judgements, choose his own companions, snap his fingers at London (it had rusticated him anyway)? Where society was mean and revengeful, he would be magnanimous, for £1000 per annum.

Charles laughed, picked up the book, and refreshed his memory of an important passage in the last chapter. 'As a daughter, he (Sir Thomas Bertram) hoped a penitent one, she should be protected by him, and secured *in every comfort.*' Whatever the exact state of her fortune, Mrs Rushworth was agreeably talented and suitably beautiful. She needed more than the financial protection which was all her pious, narrow-minded father was prepared to supply. She needed comfort and moral support which he, Charles, could afford in plenty, whatever the world might think. Instead of being shocked by her behaviour, instead of taking base advantage of her disgrace, he would be honourable and magnanimous, heedless of his own good name. He would marry her. Thus interest and chivalry for once pulled in the same direction. He might even decide to fall in love with her.

Outside it continued hot. At the end of a cool, bleak summer, the winds had dropped and the clouds had disappeared. The weather could not last, but while it did, the ladies wore their flimsiest dresses, the gentlemen their reddest faces, and the River Mersey its most Venetian aspect. Indeed, Liverpool offered one attraction which not even Venice could boast, Mr Coglan's floating-bath.

At breakfast in Abercrombie Street, it was agreed that an expedition to the bath should be mounted that very day, and that Mrs Randall should entreat the ladies at the hotel to join the party. Neither Mrs Rushworth nor Mrs Norris had any experience of swimming, but both were feeling the oppressive heat. They welcomed the chance of refreshing themselves on the river. For Mrs Norris the expedition had the added benefit of giving her a chance to see how Mr Cheviot was reacting to his recent literary research.

Soon after midday the party presented itself at the pier on Princes Dock where Mr Randall had bespoken a boat. When they were all seated, Mr Randall apologised for the humble nature of their vessel.

'I had hoped to procure a steamboat for our hazardous journey to the middle of the river, but none was available. Alas, Mrs Norris, I must perforce entrust us all to the waywardness of tide and the fickleness of oarsmen. But look, there's the Runcorn ferry now. Ah, steam! What a sight, what a vision of the future: it walks water like a giant, reducing waves to the certainty and steadiness of Mr Macadam's highways.'

'Filthy, noisy, malodorous thing,' said Mrs Norris graciously. 'A nine days' wonder.'

'And when, sir,' put in Charles, 'do you anticipate that passengers and merchandise will cross the Atlantic Ocean by steam?'

'Not in my lifetime, I trust. I am a partner in three of Liverpool's fastest transatlantic sailing ships.' He laughed, then continued in more serious vein. 'With the speed of progress these days it is folly to predict the future. By the way, Charles, I forgot to give you this letter which came for you this morning.'

Charles glanced at the superscription and then, seeing they were fast approaching a ship-like construction, thrust it into an inner pocket.

Mr Thomas Coglan's floating-bath was built very much like an ordinary ship but it had a flat bottom and double sides. The central portion formed a large bath for swimming. The tide flowed through this bath, entering at the stem of the vessel and passing out through the stern. There were also dressing-rooms, a pleasant saloon, and two decks which visitors could use as a promenade and lookout. Moored in mid-stream, the floating-bath was cooler than Liverpool but still warm enough to tempt most of the party into the water. Bathing-dresses and towels were supplied by Mr Coglan.

To her delight Maria found that she had no difficulty in swimming. Charles explained the rudiments but the moment she was immersed she seemed not to need his help. She propelled herself through the water as if by instinct, soon out-swimming all. Hitherto unaware of this affinity with the watery element, she indulged it to the full, and long after the others had changed back into dry clothes she was still in the bath, laughing and exultant. Count was lost of how many lengths she swam, but when she finally emerged she was exhausted and very cold.

'Your lips are quite blue,' said Mrs Norris (who had declined to bathe herself). 'It will serve you right if you have caught your death of cold. When I was your age, I am sure I could swim like a fish, but I exercised a proper restraint out of consideration for others. In fact I abstained altogether lest I should become a burden to my family by contracting pneumonia. I cannot understand why your generation is so thoughtless. Summer colds are much more dangerous than winter colds, I always say. You will only have yourself to blame if . . . ' To everyone's disappointment she stopped in mid-sentence as Mr Cheviot reappeared along with a short, plump man in nautical attire.

'Mr Thomas Coglan,' announced Charles before introducing the floating-bath's proprietor to individual members of the party. Mr Coglan bowed and smiled to each in turn but perserved his considerable eloquence for Maria alone.

'Never, dear madam, have I beheld an aquatic performance which combined skill and grace in such exquisite perfection as yours. You put the very mermaids to shame. Can I believe my ears when I hear that which my eyes refute, viz. that you are the merest tyro and have never swum before today? It is impossible yet believe it perforce I must, for my informant is clearly a gentleman of impeccable credibility. But, you are shivering. Is Thetis then fatigued? Is the Nereid numb? Despair not. Coglan's cordial will induce calefaction in a trice.'

He left abruptly but reappeared in seconds bearing a hot drink for Maria and followed by a waiter with a tray of wine for the others.

Coglan's cordial was warming and very strong. Maria felt a flush coming to her cheeks and a glow suffusing her body after the first few sips. The glass was soon empty and soon replenished. After the second gill and a half, calefaction had

123

been so effectively induced as to bring with it a certain dizziness and immoderation. She held out her glass yet again and Mr Coglan, raising his eyebrows, poured a smaller measure. Maria drank it as thirstily as before.

'How are you feeling now?' asked Mrs Norris.

'Wonderful. I have never felt better. That cordial, sir, I must have the receipt, but first, perhaps, yes I think I would like another little swim. Now where do I go to . . . '

The combined remonstrances of her friends fell on deaf ears, however, for Maria had fallen asleep.

It was not until much later that Charles Cheviot remembered the letter Mr Randall had given him on the way to the floating-bath. It brought disastrous news. His London lawyers begged to inform him that following the failure of Messrs S — in the City (a firm of which they had warned him to be wary), the arrangements which had been agreed for the repayment of his outstanding creditors could no longer be honoured. His further instructions were awaited and the lawyers remained his obedient servants.

As Charles had no other resources beyond his personal goods and chattels, his first reaction to the calamity was absolute dismay. The day before he had chafed at the restrictions of £50 per annum, now such an income seemed comfortable wealth; previously he had resented the need to erode his puny estate by paying his creditors – now he saw the Marshalsea prison as a grim alternative.

What could he do? It was certain that no one in his immediate family would raise a finger to help him. His friends were either as poor as he or so callously affluent as to discard without a pang anyone who had the bad taste to lose out to (let alone pay) his creditors. Mr Randall had already helped him several times and had made it clear that the last time was the last. To ask him again, Charles realised, would only mean jeopardising the New York post, and that New York post was fast becoming imperative. If he could only leave England before his embarrassment became public, all could be well. He would formally accept the assignment now and make no reference to his financial collapse. If necessary, he would invent some fictive correspondent to explain away the letter he had received so publicly. It would be months, perhaps a year, before the law caught up with him again if he went to America, and when it did he could protest his ignorance of the calamity which had befallen Messrs S — . By then he would, no doubt, be in a position to start paying off his debts. The posts between London and Liverpool were unreliable, and if he could only set sail within two or three weeks . . .

He spent most of the night working on the plan and thinking up possible snags. In the early hours, however, he changed his mind and committed himself urgently to falling in love with Maria Rushworth. Up till that moment, he realised he had been passive, awaiting events but not leading them. Had he any strategy it was to use his abilities and charm to make her love him. It had been enough that he should let himself be loved. Now he felt that if he did sincerely fall in love with her, his passion would soon carry all before it. Some day he would have to fall in love, why not today, and why not with a woman as playful, audacious, and unusual as Maria? The jump from a prudent match to a love match was at once logical and cynical, calculated and binding, but there was no point in it unless it resulted in marriage as soon as possible. Unless already betrothed he would have to sail to New York by the next vessel and stake his chance on a shipboard romance. Ideally, she would save them both

125

the trouble and tedium of a long sea voyage by agreeing to make him the happiest man in Liverpool within the next few days.

Should fortune be on his side, he would ask her at the Wellington Rooms assembly the next evening.

Chapter Thirteen

The Indian summer came to an abrupt end. Maria woke up with an irritation in the throat and the premonition of a cold in the head. Outside a brisk wind and scudding clouds, harbingers of rain and autumn, seemed to be nature's interest on the borrowed heat of the previous weeks. Maria sneezed. In the middle of the Mersey, Mr Thomas Coglan realised there would be no further swimming parties until the following year.

'Did you sleep badly?' asked Mrs Norris at breakfast. 'You look positively ill.'

'I have never felt better.'

'So much for my powers of observation. I could have sworn you were feeling the effects of yesterday's imprudence. Of course when I was your age I had the energy of ten and never spared myself (nor, indeed, do I spare myself today), but under no circumstances would I have spent all afternoon swimming – no matter how much I liked it – lest the cooling properties of the water, to say nothing of riverborne infection, would lead me to my sick bed and make me a burden to others. The indisposition itself could be tolerated with fortitude but the trouble and anxiety which it must inspire in one's family, that would have been insupportable.'

'I hope I shall put you to no such inconvenience.'

'Oh, I do not mind inconvenience. It is not myself I am considering.'

'I was going to say, the question of what you would have done in my place is surely academic, since you have never swum a stroke in your life.'

'Precisely. I had too much consideration. There is no doubt in my mind that I could have been a most proficient swimmer, had I been prepared to sacrifice my family's peace of mind. It was much the same sensibility made me abandon my violoncello studies, though all agreed that I showed quite extraordinary promise. My father – deeply musical like all his line – was possessed of such acute auditory senses that the sound of a child, no matter how talented, practising the violoncello was physically painful to him. Seeing the distress of which I was the innocent cause, I therefore abandoned my musical studies, despite the — '

Maria sneezed again and Mrs Norris looked triumphant. 'I was right after all, I see. I told you it would come to this if you stayed in that water too long. It's bed for you my girl and no reception this evening. We cannot have you travelling to America with double pneumonia.'

'Two sneezes do not inevitably denote pneumonia, aunt. I shall be perfectly all right. And I have every intention of going to tonight's reception.'

Maria stood up abruptly and, muttering her intention of making a few purchases in connection with the evening ahead, left the room. A third sneeze shook her as she closed the door.

Left alone, Mrs Norris applied her mind afresh to the problem of keeping Maria and Charles Cheviot apart. Her niece was becoming more independent each day and might well be able to hold her own in a conflict of wills. A more subtle approach would be necessary. Mr Cheviot's financial plight would have to be demonstrated unambiguously and, if possible, publicly.

A knock on the door was followed by the hotel porter with

127

an urgent letter. It was addressed to Mrs Rushworth but Mrs Norris judged it best, in both their interests, to open it – waiting only for the porter to withdraw. Half-fearing, half-hoping it would be a letter from Mr Cheviot, she discovered with mixed feelings that it was instead a communication from the shipping office, to the effect that the delayed vessel had now arrived in Liverpool and that embarkation for the passage to New York would take place at the end of the week, on Saturday. Unaware that Mr Cheviot was booked on the same boat, Mrs Norris realised that the American visit was a heaven-sent avenue of escape from Maria's possible entanglement.

As the Tuesday wore on both weather and niece deteriorated. A threatening morning became a filthy night; a sore throat and three sneezes became an undeniable chill. Maria spent the afternoon in bed dosing herself with brandy and hot water, and each mouthful of that particular medicine made her more determined to attend the reception. By the evening she was thoroughly determined and would brook no argument. Mrs Norris shrugged her shoulders. Liverpool society accorded her adequate respect and all things considered she was quite happy to spend an hour or two giving the uncouth northerners the benefit of her views. The important thing was to keep an eye on Maria, prevent her from doing anything which might seriously undermine her health, and see that she went home early. It would suit her very well if her niece were then confined to bed for a couple of days, provided only she were well enough to board the ship at the end of the week.

The Wellington Rooms on Mount Pleasant were the very height of elegance and fashion but suffered from a serious design fault. The colonnaded portico was incurably draughty and the draught seemed to reach every part of the building. When Maria and Mrs Norris arrived the place was already crowded with shivering citizens (up till a few hours before it had seemed that no heating would be necessary) and it was difficult to move about at will. At first they could see no sign of their friends and before they knew what was happening they were being drawn by the jostling crowd towards the ballroom. For a moment Maria found herself face to face with a man struggling to go in the opposite direction, his height and strength alone enabling him to move against the tide. As their eyes crossed paths both of them gave a start of near recognition. Maria turned away casually, the gentleman frowned, and the currents of humanity parted them. Thinking furiously, it took Maria two or three minutes to retrieve his name from her memory, and when she did so she nearly fainted. It was her cousin William Price, Fanny's brother, the one who went into the Royal Navy. Probably on half pay now that the wars were over, what was he doing here? Had he been sent by the family? Had he recognised her? When had they last met?

There had been a ball for him and Fanny, Maria remembered, at Mansfield Park shortly after her wedding, a ball given by her father partly as a gesture to William and partly to encourage Henry Crawford in his pursuit of Fanny. She had not been there but it had been variously described to her by Sir Thomas, Lady Bertram, and Crawford. That would have been four or five years ago. It must therefore have been some six years since she herself had seen her cousin. It was hard to reconcile the awkward fifteen or sixteen-year-old midshipman she remembered with the powerful young man she had just seen, except for a certain family likeness between him and Fanny.

Maria had no wish to take up with William nor to have any other contact with her family on the eve of her departure for America. She thought it likely that he might have recognised her and decided to leave the reception as soon as she had spoken to Mr Cheviot. In the randomly surging crush she had meanwhile become separated from Mrs Norris.

Several minutes of indecision later, Maria reached the entrance to the ballroom. Here the crowd was somewhat less dense and she soon found a niche whence she could survey the scene and watch out for her aunt. A splendid chamber met her eyes but clearly something was wrong. No one was dancing though would-be dancers thronged the floor, and the stage – furnished with chairs and music stands for the orchestra – was empty. Maria was aware of expressions of indignation, boredom, and sardonic amusement on the faces of those nearest her, and in the middle distance a distraught-looking official who was gesticulating, as if to acquit himself of any possible blame, to Mr Randall. She remembered that Mr Randall, whose anger and embarrassment were plain, was on the Wellington Rooms committee. After a few minutes, Charles Cheviot joined the two men and started what seemed to be a more constructive conversation. This led to the official shrugging his shoulders acquiescently, Mr Randall nodding his head in relief, and the younger man making his way through the parting waves of Liverpool society up to the pianoforte on the stage. A stir of expectation swept the ballroom.

He began with a series of tremendous chords, lingering at first but soon tumbling over each other, as it were, to reach the audience.

'Music should be loud and fast,' Maria recalled Charles declaring, 'while beverages should be strong and effervescent.'

A flunkey placed champagne on the piano and poured a glass for the player. Several gentlemen raised a hearty cheer to which Charles responded by repeating the same chord several times in succession and then breaking it into its component parts so that the bass formed a first beat and

130

the treble second and third – identical – beats. An ingratiating melody followed and gradually the onlookers realised that they were being invited to divide into pairs for the dance which had shocked – and captivated – all the wickedest capitals of Europe, but had never before been heard in Liverpool. After some hesitation a few of the braver spirits took to the floor, the ostentatiously respectable left the ball-room, and the remainder fell into the attitudes of strained nonchalance naturally adopted by the upper-middle classes in moments of social uncertainty. Charles raised his eyebrows, looked directly at Maria, and began to sing:

Be far from thee and thine
The name (the name) of prude
Mocked yet triumphant, sneered at
Sneered at but unsubdued.
Muse of the many-twinkling feet!
Thy legs must conquer as they fly
(If but thy skirts be reason'bly high)
Thy breast, though bare, requires no shield
Dance forth: sans armour take the field
And own, quite safe from most assaults
Thy not too lawfully begotten waltz
The waltz, thy waltz, thy wicked, wanton Waltz

The singer took a draught of wine and raised his glass to toast the dancers, while continuing the waltz beat with his other hand. A few more couples hastily departed, some – Maria wished she were one – went on to the floor experimentally, to attempt the unfamiliar but much discussed steps.

What Charles's performance lacked in subtlety it made up for in audibility. Several young women surreptitiously attempted to hitch their skirts higher in the hope of winning the singer's approval, but none attempted

131

to bare her breast. Maria sensed that he was singing only for her.

An elderly young man bowed and asked her to dance with him.

'Thank you, sir, I prefer otherwise,' she said stiffly, not deigning to look at him or give any reason. Suddenly she coloured in confusion. That cold, indifferent tone of voice was the one she had invariably used when speaking to Mr Rushworth. It had been her sword and shield from the church steps to the marriage bed. Whatever the pathetic Rushworth had wanted, she had preferred otherwise. And she had always prevailed, negating her way from pyrrhic victory to pyrrhic victory, transforming a foolish wedding into a disastrous marriage. For the first time, she seemed to hear herself as others – as Rushworth – must have heard her. The stranger, meanwhile was bowing, about to withdraw.

'I didn't mean that,' she said quickly, 'at least not like that. I'm sorry. I – I'm indisposed. It must be the change in the weather, and those terrible draughts, and all the bathing I did yesterday. If I did not have to retire I should have liked to dance. Please excuse me.'

A few minutes before she had thought that she wanted to waltz; now she realised that she only wanted to dance with Charles.

'My dear madam, can I be of any assistance? I am at your command. Do you want a carriage, a doctor, a cordial?'

'Ah, there you are Maria – wherever have you been?' broke in Mrs Norris, suddenly appearing.

'Aunt, this gentleman is being very kind. Truly I am not feeling well and must return to the hotel. If you want to stay here — '

'Stay here? How should I wish to stay here when I only ventured out on this horrible night to keep you company? Besides, I never take my own wants into account: even if

I did wish to stay, I should go. As it is, I have spoken to all the people I wanted to see and am only too ready to remove myself from the noise and the crowd. What perfectly atrocious music. Oh, it's Mr Cheviot. Well, well . . . trying to turn an honest penny, I suppose. Surely the Wellington Rooms can afford an orchestra?'

Maria threw a final glance at the pianist, shook her head resignedly, and followed her aunt. There would be no chance of a private word with him after his public triumph. They escaped without seeing William Price again.

When he realised that Maria had left, Charles regretted the impulse which made him offer his services as stand-in for the absent orchestra. At the time it had seemed a good opportunity for helping Mr Randall, his benefactor, and simultaneously impressing Mrs Rushworth. With her declared fondness for acting, Maria could not but respond to an histrionic solo performance and must surely be the more likely to say yes to the proposal he intended to lay at her feet later in the evening. Her premature departure was therefore a grave setback to his hopes of an early, affirmative decision.

He was relieved when, soon after she had left the ballroom, the appearance of a scratch orchestra gave him an opportunity to follow her. Without noticing the loud applause and shouts of 'encore', he abruptly strode from the ballroom.

The new musicians, some of them unsteady on their feet, sat down awkwardly and began to tune up. They had been found in a tavern near the Theatre Royal, refreshing themselves after their evening's operatic stint, and had been unable to resist inducements from Wellington Room emissaries further to display their talents. There being as yet no director, the first violin held up his bow and proceeded to lead the players in an excruciating quadrille.

After the first few bars a semblance of order came to the music and dancers were tempted back on to the floor. Soon, however, the leader, who had turned over two pages at once, started playing quite different music from the rest of the band. Noticing that something was wrong, he stopped. At this the others stopped, too, only to be told 'Play on, damn you.' The dancers also stopped, or slowed down, or looked bemused. Trying to find the right place, the leader knocked his music stand to the ground and, trying to retrieve it, fell over himself. Some of the onlookers laughed, others scowled.

'He's drunk. They're all drunk,' cried a number of voices. This was too much for the principal violinist. He picked himself up with great dignity and thought of a withering retort.

'You think *we're* drunk?' he said. 'Just wait till you see the conductor.'

Charles meanwhile frantically searched the other rooms for Maria. He soon became certain she had left altogether and made his way to her hotel. Here he learnt that Mrs Norris and Mrs Rushworth had returned not ten minutes before and had gone up to their rooms. Having no further interest in the reception he decided to go back to his cousins' house and think things over. His way led him past the Wellington Rooms, however, and as he drew level with the scene of the ball, he heard a babel of voices.

'There he is!'

'Hey, wait! Mr Cheviot!'

'Come back . . . '

He walked briskly on but soon he was surrounded by flunkeys, officials, and a group of gentlemen guests. They asked him to return and play, but he declined. They explained that the band was incapable, but he remained adamant. They offered him money and champagne – still he refused. But when Mr Randall came up and personally implored him to return he reluctantly agreed. With heavy heart and troubled mind he went back to the ballroom, amid a chorus of 'bravos'.

Nobody noticed that the star of the night was the saddest guest at the ball; nor did the saddest guest at the ball admit that he was the star of the night. He may have suspected it, however.

Chapter Fourteen

On Wednesday morning he came to terms with the fact that there was only half a week remaining before the ship sailed. He would be ruined unless he either sailed to America or married Mrs Rushworth. Clearly it would be reckless to stake all on winning Maria within three days – and he had never been a betting man. Accordingly, after a businesslike conversation with Mr Randall, he directed his steps to the shipping office and confirmed his passage to New York. He could always cancel it at the last moment. As the clerk completed the necessary entries in ledger and daybook, Charles had a leisurely perusal of the passenger list. Mrs Rushworth and Mrs Norris were on it sure enough. It would not be the end of the world if he had to continue his courtship afloat and it would be interesting to see America.

Two hours later he was sure that he had acted wisely. A frustrating call at the hotel had informed him that Maria was ill in bed but granted him – after an appropriately prolonged delay – an interview with Mrs Norris. The good lady told him that her niece, though far from well, was not seriously indisposed. Provided she were sensible there was no reason why they should not sail on Saturday.

'Fortunately, I have no small experience in medical matters. I was in constant attendance on the late Mr Norris during his final illness, and our physician conceded that I had very possibly protracted his life by my skill at bleeding. There may be division among today's doctors about the efficacy of bleeding but I for one have not the slightest doubt about its therapeutic qualities. The old, well-tried remedies are best. I do not hold with the new notions we hear about these days. No good will ever come from interfering with nature.'

'Very true,' said Charles diplomatically, 'yet I trust that Mrs Rushworth's condition is not serious enough to warrant even so natural and well-tried a specific as bleeding?'

'It would seem not, Mr Cheviot, but I shall not hesitate to use it should the need arise. There is no cause for concern, I assure you. The patient is in excellent hands. My experience makes it a certainty that she will sail to the New World on Saturday.'

Mrs Norris gave one of her pleasantest smiles, as if to say how happy she was that in a few days' time she would be taking Maria out of Charles's reach. There was no mockery or challenge in the smile, only avuncular satisfaction. Relieved that he had still said nothing about his own travel plans, Charles departed promising that Mrs Randall would call the next day.

Later, flowers and a letter for Mrs Rushworth were delivered to the hotel, but intercepted by Mrs Norris before they reached the sufferer. The unsealed letter was soon steamed open; it was a pictorial epistle designed to amuse but also perhaps to warn, consisting of largely captionless drawings. Several of Maria's acquaintances were shown in attitudes of anxiety, Liverpool townsfolk offered up prayers to heaven, and the patient herself was shown swallowing an enormous spoonful of medicine from Mrs Norris who was also holding a jar marked 'leeches' behind her back. The text contained nothing of significance. Mrs Norris was not amused and wondered whether she should withhold it from her patient in the interests of her health. After a moment's reflection she decided to deliver the flowers, which would not only speed Maria's recovery but save a certain amount of trouble and expense, and overlook the letter, which could do no possible good and might do harm. She arranged the flowers in a vase and took them along the corridor, walking carefully so as not to slip on the just polished boards.

As she entered, Maria was composing herself in bed and the window, which had been closed, was wide open. Mrs Norris looked at it reproachfully.

'I couldn't breathe,' said Maria. 'It was so stuffy in here.'

'The reason you cannot breathe is that you have a cold in the head. This is a large room and not at all stuffy. Indeed it is just the opposite.'

'I felt like some fresh air.'

'Fresh air is all very well at the right time and place. Just now warmth is much more important. Besides, the only kind of air which Liverpool provides on a day like this is cold sea mist, and that's the last thing you need at the moment. You're shivering already. Here are some flowers from the Randalls and Mr Cheviot. Is that not civil? I shall now close the window and stir the fire.'

Maria turned on her side, drew her knees up to her chest, pulled the bedclothes over her, and closed her eyes as if to block out sound as well as sight. But she continued to shiver for a long time.

Her aunt had been right: she was not particularly ill, and so long as she kept to her room for a couple of days, she would be fit to sail on Saturday. Normally she would not have fretted at the enforced inactivity, would even have enjoyed it. She was quite prepared to leave the tedious, last-minute preparations for the voyage to her aunt. Yet now she felt trapped and cheated – compelled to leave England with her emotions in a tangle of uncertainty. That matters would have come to a head between herself and Charles, had they been given more time, was very probable, though in what way they would or should have been concluded was far from clear. In his company her feelings were very different from when she was alone. Lying in bed her doubts multiplied: that extrovert charm, so similar to Crawford's, had already been her downfall; that apparent attachment, so mistrusted by Mrs Norris, might only be inspired by pecuniary interest; that artistic repertoire, so complementary to her own taste, might mask serious shortcomings and weaknesses. On her own side, there were equal sources of scepticism: was she sufficiently recovered from the double disaster of her marriage and love affair; was she too anxious to escape from the increasingly comfortless solicitude of her aunt; above all had she known him long enough to accept or reject an offer from him, should he make one? Instinctive recklessness conflicted with painfully acquired circumspection. Yes, she needed time. Since that strange young mother had unknowingly planted seeds of self-knowledge, since that baby's first cry had awoken its reluctant midwife, everything had happened too quickly. If only the ship were delayed again; if only she did not have to sail with it – but to cancel the passages now would be to invite intervention from Mrs Norris. It was this train of thought which had prompted her to open her window half an hour before and force herself to sit night-shirted in the cool, dank breeze until she heard her aunt's footsteps in the passage. Becoming too sick to sail would give her the respite she needed. Now, as she lay once more between the sheets, the fundamental problem returned. Could she agree to marry again without telling her future husband about her past conduct? Would any possible husband still want to marry her if he knew about that past? More to the point, would Charles Cheviot? If so, what sort of man did that make him? What kind of man would be prepared to marry the kind of woman she must appear to be (though the appearance in this case was misleading)? A saint, perhaps, or a desperate sinner – and Charles Cheviot was no saint. And finally, did she, the real Maria (who was still very much a stranger to herself) want to marry the kind of man who was prepared to marry the kind of woman which her outward and published behaviour advertised her to be? These thoughts were as dampening as the autumn wind and did her just as much harm.

Next day brought a combined visit from both Randalls and Charles. Mrs Norris was the quintessence of civility, refusing most gracefully and considerately to allow anyone other than herself to risk contagion by seeing the patient. She gave no hint at all that a noticeable decline in Maria's condition now made postponement of the voyage a distinct possibility. The sudden change had taken Mrs Norris by surprise, and it was the new mental state as much as the physical state which worried her. Previously Maria, impatient to make the most of her last few days, had chaffed at her illness and made light of it. Now she seemed to have swung to the opposite extreme. Mrs Norris was loath to call in a local physician lest he forbid Maria to travel on Saturday – a stranger might have difficulty in understanding that the need for a prompt departure must take priority over any temporary ailment. Besides, her experience insisted that an equally fast improvement was probable in someone as young and strong as Maria. To aid the improvement she began to season Maria's scanty needs with laudanum, a panacea which she held in even greater esteem than bleeding.

So all the visitors got for their pains was a short note from Maria thanking them for the flowers.

'Do Mrs Rushworth and Mrs Norris know that you are to be their fellow-passenger, Charles?' asked Mrs Randall when they were alone.

'No. I haven't, that is . . . I thought — '

'You thought it would be a pleasant surprise.'

139

'Yes. Partly that.'

'A very pleasant surprise. For one of them.'

'Only one?'

'Only one. I do not think Mrs Norris will be particularly pleased.'

'She dislikes me?'

'She's wary of you. Perhaps she would be wary of any personable young man who might attach himself to her niece. I have been meaning to let you know, Charles, that Mr Randall and I think very highly of Maria Rushworth. We suspect that she has suffered a good deal and borne misfortune with courage. I wish I knew her full story. Then one might be able to help.'

Charles coloured. Never before had his cousin been so forthright. Normally their conversation was conducted in terms of affectionate banter which, though founded on genuine concern, reflected an unspoken agreement to respect each other's privacy. It was still open to him to ignore the drift of her remarks, or make some facetious return which would politely tell her to stop trespassing, but he was in no mood for badinage or pretence. For some seconds he remained morosely silent.

'What should I do then? What would you do?'

'I think I should tell Mrs Rushworth that you have taken a position in New York and hope to travel on the same ship as herself and Mrs Norris.'

'Why?'

'Because I suspect that Mrs Norris was being less than frank this morning. There was something about her manner which made me think that their journey might be in doubt, possibly because Mrs Rushworth's illness is worse than she makes out. If I read the signs correctly, the knowledge that you intend to sail too might prove remedial while the belief that you are to remain in Liverpool could have the reverse

140

effect, providing, as it were, an incentive for postponing the voyage. At least I should feel like that if I were in Maria Rushworth's shoes.'

'That's devilish perspicacious of you, Cousin Kate. But what about the aunt? If I come out in the open and say I'm going to New York, won't Mrs Norris try to keep Maria in Liverpool?'

'I don't think so. That would reveal her hand too obviously. In a straight battle of wills over a simple decision, Mrs Rushworth, assuming she is financially independent, would win. No, Mrs Norris would have to accept with as good grace as she could muster.'

'What a good schemer you make, cousin; thank you.'

Charles pondered. The showman in him had looked forward to the 'unexpected' meeting on the bridge, the delighted surprise (on one side), but he had to admit the pre-eminent importance of ensuring that Maria did, in fact, join the ship. Surprise or no surprise, the excitement of a long sea voyage, the opportunities for daily meetings, and the freedom from conventional restraints reportedly provided by a life on the ocean wave would be enjoyed just as much, and would still favour his plans, so long as Maria was not left languishing on shore. He therefore wrote a second letter to Maria announcing that he had accepted Mr Randall's agency in New York and expressing his satisfaction at the prospect of being the fellow-passenger of Mrs Rushworth and Mrs Norris. At the same time, he hinted that his decision to go to America was not unconnected with the knowledge that he would have at least one friend on that strange and unknown continent. Although his first letter and flowers had apparently been acknowledged by Maria without being seen by Mrs Norris, he decided to seal the new one as a precaution. He even considered bribing a hotel servant to deliver it, but rejected the idea partly out of diffidence, partly because

141

he felt it would lay him open to accusations of improper behaviour, but mainly because he surmised that Mrs Norris was keeping her charge strictly incommunicado and only the most devious scheme could hope to succeed.

Mrs Norris hesitated before breaking the seal and reading the letter, but not for very long.

'There is no immediate danger,' said Dr Gossage. 'Your niece has that inflammation of the bronchia which my colleagues Frank and Bodham have recently penetrated (thereby rendering inestimable service to mankind) and is also, if I am not mistaken, in the secondary stage of Italian influenza, a scourge of which no great port can ever be said entirely to be free. Warmth, rest, and a linctus I shall prescribe, should soon put her to rights. I have told the patient that sailing to America on Saturday is quite out of the question. Such a course, even with the skilled attention which I am sure you could provide, would certainly prolong the illness, exacerbate it, and might well prove fatal.'

Somewhat to the doctor's surprise Mrs Norris beamed her pleasure.

'I have no doubt your prognosis is correct, doctor, and shall see that your advice is followed to the letter. Postponement of the journey, though irksome, is a small price to pay for my niece's health.'

The fire crackled in the grate reassuringly. It was two hours since it had obliged by consuming Charles Cheviot's letter and watched Mrs Norris send for the physician. Now it was to be rewarded, it seemed, with prolonged and sympathetic employment by these two same gentle guests, instead of suffering the usual Merseyside winter of unreasonable

142

demands by cold, impatient strangers alternating with periods of clammy neglect.

After the first shock Mrs Norris had been delighted to learn that Charles was booked as a passenger on the *Nestor*. She had begun to see the voyage as a means of testing the young people's attachment or, more probably, preventing them from an entanglement which could bring neither any good in the long run, but she had no particular wish, at her age, to start a new life in America. It was much more suitable that the young man himself should be the one who put all those miles of sea between the two parties. Her course of action was clear. Maria, already wavering in her determination to sail, should herself make the decision to postpone the trip, and do so on impartial medical advice. It was virtually certain that no prudent physician would recommend a patient in Maria's condition to undertake a sea voyage, and it was the work of a few minutes to find the name of a doctor with a reputation for caution. She and Maria could take Dr Gossage's advice without explanations being required or offered on either side. Everyone would have behaved with utmost scruple. In all probability Maria would never learn about that burnt letter and she would certainly not learn about Charles's departure until he was beyond recall. From now on it was going to be plain sailing.

Shortly after the doctor's departure, a minor problem occurred to Mrs Norris. If the shipping office, even at this late hour, were told about their inability to use their cabins, there was every prospect that their fares would be refunded, for Mrs Norris knew that there was always a waiting list of would-be passengers. On the other hand, it was just possible that word of a last-minute cancellation would come to the ears of young Cheviot and prompt him into a corresponding post-ponement. Sharp enough to suspect that he had financial as well as tender considerations behind his sudden departure, she had no means of knowing that the urgency of his plight was such as to make it impossible for him to stay behind. It was probable that a discreet word and a discreet sovereign at the shipping office would safely quash that risk, though, anxious to save others from temptation, Mrs Norris did not approve the purchase of favours from social inferiors. Putting the personal considerations aside, however, she prepared to go to the shipping office without more ado, when a commotion in the street outside made her go to the window. Several coaches were being relieved of what seemed an inordinate number of boxes, while two groups of passengers looked on. Mrs Norris had a better idea.

There was no great number of reputable hotels in Liverpool – inns and rooming houses of dubious character abounded – and the establishment selected by Mrs Norris and her niece was the one normally used by the better class of Atlantic passenger. It was very probable that potential successors to the cabins they had bespoken were already sharing a roof with them. And so it proved. At the first inkling of Maria being unfit to travel, the hotel proprietor showed the liveliest interest. Apparently shipboard accommodation, particularly good accommodation, invariably became at a premium as the day of departure approached. Cabins changed hands at twice their normal cost. Mrs Norris had only to say the word and the proprietor could be of service to her; he could promise eminently satisfactory arrangements in strict confidence and gold coin; and the ship's owners need not be informed until the hour of embarkation. Mrs Norris said the word.

The hotel proprietor was practised and adroit at persuading his guests to bid against each other without their knowing it. In effect, he auctioned the tickets and eventually knocked them down to two representatives of Mr Rothschild's banking house, authorised, owing to the extreme urgency of their business in America, to pay a very handsome sum for an immediate berth. Also a student of character, the proprietor knew when and with whom to be honest. Accordingly, he told Mrs Norris exactly how much the bankers had paid and came to a very amicable agreement as to how the profit should be divided between them. It was agreed that bothering the bedridden patient with details of this transaction would not be beneficial to her health.

Friday brought no answer to Charles's letter and as the day wore on he became increasingly despondent. A visit to the shipping office told him that Mrs Rushworth and Mrs Norris were still listed as passengers, and a visit to the hotel confirmed the story. The two ladies were not receiving guests, but it was understood the younger one was making progress. The proprietor was polite and sympathetic but he had received strict instructions from the parties that they were not to be disturbed, and he was bound to comply.

Charles felt there was nothing more he could do. Everything pointed to Maria being on board tomorrow and her silence should no doubt be ascribed to the knowledge that they were shortly to be thrown together for a month or more. Besides, she might well think it inappropriate to express pleasure (or any other sentiment) at the prospect of his companionship, when so little of their mutual regard had been acknowledged. Nor had his letter positively demanded an answer; it had asked no direct questions. Everything was in order. It must be.

Had he merely been in love, he might have allayed his fears; since he was also in need, he soon became doubly convinced that something was wrong. Custom might not enjoin an immediate acknowledgement but attachment compelled the unnecessary. What could have happened?

Supposing she had, in fact, replied but Mrs Norris had prevented the reply from reaching its destination? That would be consistent with Mrs Norris's hostility, but, no, the hypothesis was untenable since Mrs Norris would undoubtedly foresee that her niece must discover the trick as soon as she and Charles met on board ship. He pursued the hypothesis a stage further back. Suppose Mrs Norris had read *his* letter before it reached Maria? She would then have learnt that he was bound for America on the same ship as them. Therefore it would be in her interest to prevent him from sailing or, more feasibly, persuade Maria to postpone their own departure. Maria's ill health, combined, Charles fancied, with her own wish to settle one way or another certain personal matters in Liverpool, would make the persuasion relatively easy. All Mrs Norris would have to do then was keep him in ignorance of the decision and allow him to sail off – alone. Charles had no means of proving or disproving the hypothesis – reason told him that it was the unreasoning figment of a mind distorted by love – but everything that had happened, and more particularly not happened, since his second letter was consistent with it. He determined to put it to the test, if necessary as late as Saturday morning. But how?

Charles walked round the hotel, studying it from every angle, and quickly dismissed the possibility of climbing into Maria's room. With his theatrical instincts, disguise was his element but, without more information, it was impossible to know what kind of disguise to assume. If he pretended to be a doctor, for example, and they were already being attended by a real doctor, his disguise would be penetrated immediately. Finally he decided that the back door, by which he saw the occasional hotel servant leaving or entering, offered him the best chance. The vestige of a plan began to form in his mind.

He went to the tavern near the stage door of the Theatre Royal and, as expected, found Kean's dubious friend Wellesley Nelson, drinking brandy-and-water. A native of Liverpool, Nelson (his real name was Higgins) played middling rôles at the theatre, and augmented his income by a number of more or less equivocal activities. Charles explained his problem . . .

Two hours later a hotel servant who owed Mr Nelson a good turn provided Charles with a sketch plan of the hotel, a key to the back door, and a suit in the hotel livery. Further, he undertook to engage Mrs Norris's attention for at least three minutes at ten o'clock the next day. The rest was up to Charles.

Meanwhile, in Northamptonshire, Fanny learnt that her elder brother had been commissioned as first mate on a privateer and was about to sail for one of the South American wars. The simultaneous intelligence of substantial improvement in the family's Antiguan affairs (unrest among the slaves having in their own interests, been quelled) helped to reconcile her to William's departure and its attendant dangers.

Chapter Fifteen

Despite her illness Maria was more content than at any time since the swimming episode. Another weight had been lifted from her shoulders. No longer had she to sail away from the possibility of happiness and a second marriage. Separation from Charles at this delicate stage of their relationship – so much had been signalled, so little spoken – would have been tantamount to re-embracing the passionless half-life she was just beginning to throw off. The impulsive side of her nature told her to place herself in his hands, in his arms rather, but her head kept warning that impulse had already been her undoing. Besides he had not even bothered to write during her illness. Oh yes, she had received some flowers, but she was not especially fond of flowers. Now that the voyage was postponed, she had several weeks to discover her real state of mind. And his.

The clock struck ten. It was time to take the physick prescribed by Dr Gossage. As she eased herself up into a sitting position, she smiled wryly at the thought of how red-nosed, hollow-eyed, and dishevelled she must look. She reached for a spoon and then, without hearing any knock, saw one of her doors swiftly open. A hotel servant plunged into the room, shutting the door behind him quickly and surreptitiously. Maria stared at him in horrified amazement – she had seen no one except Mrs Norris and the doctor for several days.

'What do you bead by this?' she said through her thick cold, instinctively clutching at the sheet to cover her half-exposed bosom. 'Rebove yourself this bobent.'

'Mrs Rushworth – Maria – I – it's me!' Charles was struck speechless by her beauty.

'Gracious heavens, Mr Cheviot!' She relaxed her clutch on the sheet.

'Yes. My profound apologies. I was worried about your health. How are you?'

'Bore or less better, I suppose, but what is this bystification?'

'It seemed the only way I could get to see you. Look, we haven't much time. Are you packed? Are you ready for the voyage? You don't seem — '

'Dough, sir. We are dot sailing after all. By doctor forbids it.'

'Oh no!' Charles collapsed into a chair and his head slumped into his hands. For a moment there was complete silence.

'Are you so anxious to be rid of me?'

'I knew it,' continued Charles, ignoring her question. 'I knew something was awry when you did not answer

148

those letters. Oh, I realise they did not absolutely require an answer, but — '

'What letters? I received dough letters.'

'You didn't? But I delivered them in person. Are you sure?'

'Dough. Dot one word. I did think it a little strange but then our acquaintance is of the shortest, add the barigolds were bery dice.'

'Damnation take the marigolds. Did you not hear that I am to travel on the same ship as you?'

'The *Destor?* Oh dough. This is awful. I would never have agreed. By aunt – two days ago – when she brought the doctor – if I'd doe'd – oh, bust you go?'

'Yes I must. I am irrevocably committed to sailing this afternoon.'

'Why did you dot tell me before?'

'A variety of reasons. At first, why should you be interested? And then, well, I didn't know for certain when or whether I was to go. The final decision was only made on Monday. I was going to tell you at the reception, but you disappeared like Cinderella.'

They looked at each other desolately.

'Where are you going to?'

'New York. Like you. I thought.'

'At least we shall meet in due course. Perhaps in two or three months.'

'Yes.'

Should she tell him? Should she say she had made herself iller on purpose in order to stay in Liverpool? Should she admit how eagerly, if secretly, she had agreed to take Doctor Gossage's advice? Should she go further and tell him the truth about herself and *Mansfield Park*, and risk losing him for ever? She longed to do so, but with the same longing that had betrayed her into trusting Henry Crawford.

'Is it impossible for you to postpone your voyage? Can

149

a few weeks make any difference? It would so relieve the tedium of the voyage if — '

'Out of the question, alas. Completely out of the question.'

Should he tell her why? Should he explain that his personal affairs were desperate and that he would be ruined if he stayed behind? Could he ask her for money and marriage in the same breath – and risk losing both?

'I wrote explaining all this the day before yesterday. Perhaps you were too ill to read. Then Mrs Norris refused to see me. I sensed something might be wrong. I . . . '

He lapsed into silence. A silence haunted by a prison called the Marshalsea and a park called Mansfield.

'Why are you wearing those clothes?'

She was crying; large, silent, baffled tears. He sensed that she was not interested in the question she had asked, or that it meant something else, but he answered it nevertheless.

'It seemed the only sure way I could see you. Your aunt guards you as a lioness guards her cub. I managed to arrange for her to be distracted at exactly ten o'clock. That was how I knew I could walk straight in. Do you think they suit me, these clothes? How's the fit? Quite an elegant cut, would you say?'

She smiled bravely. Silence returned. There was nothing to say except the unsayable. Both hoped the other would speak it. Both kept their own secret. It was almost a relief when Mrs Norris's voice was heard in the next room.

'No, I shall not disturb my niece now. She is resting. But when I take her her mid-morning cordial I shall give her your kind messages from the staff, not but what I fully apprehend that in giving voice to these, my good man, you have the scale of your ultimate gratuities in mind.'

150

For a moment Charles considered staying and facing the lioness, but Maria seemed to motion him to the other door. Besides he had promised to avoid at all costs being discovered, since doing so would have cost the servant who had helped him his position. With an impotent last look he tiptoed out into despair.

At first fury, frustration, and misery made thought impossible. Maria buried her tears in the bedclothes and wished she were dead. Peeping into the room her aunt saw that the patient was asleep. Gradually, resentment of Mrs Norris's interference developed into suspicion of her motives, and thence to almost total distrust. She would confront the woman with her treachery and send her packing. Maria seethed. But could she? Spoilt child and favourite niece that she was, all her life she had deferred to Mrs Norris. Furthermore it was her aunt, and only her aunt, who had stood by her after the Crawford débâcle. What would she have done without her during those terrible months (stretching into years) of rejection by family, friends and lover? And in any duel of wills between them, who would be the winner? Mrs Norris might not have a heart of gold, but she had a will of iron. Maria quailed; she knew she was not strong enough or sure enough to fight. Not on this issue, not now. She would be content to see Charles in America some time after Christmas and she would be on her guard against further interference. Forewarned was forearmed. The waiting would be painful but salutary. It would help her make up her mind. Thus head consoled heart but heart had only to conjure up Charles's last, speechless, irrefutable look for her hard-won common sense to falter.

'I have received the money refunded from our tickets and put it away safely,' said Norris, when she brought Maria

151

a light luncheon. Keeping her word to the hotel proprietor, she made no mention of the personal profit arising from the transaction.

Maria smiled wanly. She had long been secretly amused by her aunt's 'carefulness'. All monies, however small, were dutifully locked in a miniature strongbox whose key was then deposited in one of a dozen different hiding places. After shopping expeditions, even coppers would be safeguarded in this way rather than left in purse or reticule. 'Take care of the pence and the pounds will take care of themselves' had been one of the favourite axioms of the late lamented Reverend Norris – that unworldly gentleman being oblivious to the inconvenience of always having to rely on others for petty disbursements to which a conscientious interpretation of his principle condemned first his wife then his widow.

'The next ship,' continued Mrs Norris, 'is the *Orbit* under Captain Tinkham. She is a somewhat smaller vessel than the *Nestor* but reported to be more comfortable. If we wait until January, which is what the agents advise, we shall be able to sail on the *Canada*. She is 540 tons and the largest packet on the Atlantic service.'

Charles spent his last afternoon on English soil composing a letter to Maria:

> I cannot quit these shores without some further explanation
> of my reasons, and I am determined to make a clean breast of
> the whole, sorry business. Frankly, madam, my affairs are in
> a state of financial embarrassment. I am, in short, insolvent.
> Until a short while ago I was still a man of means, modest
> and inadequate means, to be sure but means nevertheless.
> Intelligence has now reached me, however, that the concern

152

to which I had entrusted my remaining assets, Messrs S —, has failed. Accordingly, I have lost everything. But that is not the worst of it. Arrangements I had made for the settlement of my outstanding debts – yes, I have debts, too, so trite and commonplace is my story, debts commensurate, I must plead, with my former means – those arrangements can no longer be honoured. I have no alternative, therefore, but to take the position offered by Mr Randall. By doing so I shall be able, in due course, to discharge my liabilities honourably and in full. Should I linger here, on the other hand, it is certain that my creditors will attempt to foreclose on me and finding that my property is gone have me consigned to the debtors' prison.

So behold that most ungentlemanly and inconsiderate of God's creatures, a pauper. This particular pauper has still some respectable clothes; he has never suffered the pangs of hunger – but he is a pauper for all that. You will understand now why he could not say that which his whole being longed to say this morning.

Nor is the catalogue of the pauper's transgressions complete. Know, for example, that very early in his acquaintance with a certain young woman, as he thought a well-to-do widow, he saw the possibility of reprieve from the reduced circumstances to which his mother's untimely demise had sentenced him. After their first meeting he decided to win her heart with whatever charm – or guile – he could command. At the time he had no plans to surrender his own heart. Indeed his own feelings in the matter were scarcely considered, though it may be noted that while it is always possible for a poor man to become genuinely attached to a woman of means, attachment is positively probable if the woman concerned be young and beautiful. In seeking to captivate her he enslaved himself!

The rest you know.

Ah, if only you did. I have promised myself to tell you

the truth, and tell the truth I shall. Madam, I know your secret! I know the story of your marriage and the events which led to its termination. A volume of a book which I need not name was left open upon the sofa table when I was painting your portrait. Waiting for you, I glanced at it, saw your name, and – suffice it to say that the Lyceum library had the work on its shelves. I read it immediately. At first, beguiled I presume by the elegant assurance, moral certitude, and, I concede, the occasional wit of the anonymous author, I was inclined to believe it an objective and accurate account. A few hours' thought, however, convinced me that it was a travesty. It was clear that you were more sinned against than sinning and that your family, having diligently and uncritically instructed you in false social values (I would almost say vices), betrayed you – no less – the moment you fell victim to those values, and deserted you moreover with expressions of moral indignation which are the purest humbug it has ever been my misfortune to encounter. However, it is not your family's conduct (let alone your own) which is on trial now, but mine. The only correct course was for me to admit that I had read that book, and with all my heart I wish I had had the courage to do so. Unable to predict the consequences of such an admission, I felt that the knowledge which the book gave me was a form of power which could be used to forward my own ends. The well-deserved collapse of all my plans shows how wrong I was.

By the time you read these words I shall be on the high seas. I cannot delude myself that we are likely to meet again. New York will no longer beckon you, even supposing you could overcome Mrs Norris's opposition. Lies and mendacity have destroyed my one chance of happiness in this life; I only hope my behaviour has not destroyed yours. Good bye, and may Gods and Angels smile on you.

Charles hoped he had not overdone it. Everything in

the letter was true, but who can ever know the whole truth? Written as a confession of guilt, it had a chance, he felt, of being read as a plea of innocence. He loved her too much not to try. The letter was handed to Mrs Randall with strict instructions for it to be given to Maria in person. After a fond but not too prolonged farewell, Charles departed for his ship accompanied by Mr Randall who had some last-minute instructions and messages in connection with the New York business.

The bustle and excitement of a ship about to leave had no interest for him now; the furniture and hangings of Francis and Jeremiah's new vessel, so admired by the Liverpool crowd, went unnoticed by Charles. Nor did the burning question as to the length of voyage – average passage forty days but the shorter ones little more than half that duration – have any significance for him. It was as cruel to be a hundred miles from Liverpool as a thousand. He now saw that it was entirely his fault he had lost Maria, a just reward for his attempted treachery. Every minute made him feel it more. Two people destroyed by the greed of one. And the supreme irony was that he would now be wild with joy to marry Maria even if she had not a penny in the world. He might even prefer her penniless. Yes, in seeking to trap her affections he had only ensnared himself.

Settled in his cabin at last, he gave himself up to self-pity and brandy. The latter gradually overtook the former, and in due course blotted out consciousness altogether.

Chapter Sixteen

Not until the second morning out did Charles emerge from his cabin. Despite the mild weather and the slow but smooth passage which the boat was making, he looked

155

distinctly green. They were sailing gently southwards down the Irish Sea before the gentlest of winds.

'Mr Cheviot, isn't it?'

Captain Simes had been asked to make Mr Randall's cousin as comfortable as possible, Mr Randall being an important customer of the company. Charles nodded discouragingly.

'Glad to see you are finding your sea legs, sir,' continued the captain, blind to the contrary evidence. Charles gave a liverish smile.

A taciturn young man, thought the captain. Must try to bring him out. Could be an asset in the ward room if only he would cheer up. Wonder what would interest him. Try the usual repertoire on him. Here goes . . .

It was very heavy going indeed. Hardly a flicker of response came from Charles beyond the demands of minimal politeness. The captain was on the point of giving up, and took out his watch preparatory to a bluff, businesslike departure.

'How long will this weather last?' asked Charles with no particular interest.

'Could last another forty-eight hours,' said the captain, grasping at straws. 'Very slow progress, I'm afraid. We shan't be in New York for six weeks at this rate. Confounded nuisance for those with urgent business in America like our surprise passengers from Rothschild's bank. Still, it makes it easier for the poor wretches down there.' He indicated the steerage quarters which were thronged with emigrants. 'They're the ones who really suffer when it rolls and pitches, poor wretches.'

Charles followed the pointing finger.

'Looks like too many people for that amount of space. Herd 'em in like cattle do you?' He pretended to be more indignant than he was.

'No sir,' said the captain with asperity. 'We try to limit the

156

numbers but they insist on coming: herd themselves in – and we can't stop 'em. We turn hundreds away every voyage as it is. They seem to think America's the promised land. Little do they know. My dear sir, you would not believe the competition there is for steerage passages, or the prices paid. It's the same story with cabin accommodation.' He shook his head in disbelief. Charles said nothing.

'You won't credit this,' persisted the master mariner, 'but two days ago steerage passages were changing hands at 20 guineas each. Why your own cabin only costs £30. But that's not the end of it. In the evening, just before we weighed anchor and when we'd been turning people away for three or four hours, an Irishwoman appears from nowhere (must have bribed her way on board) and offered £50 to anyone who would give up a steerage birth! Fifty pounds – that's ten times the going rate. She got her berth alright and I wouldn't mind betting that someone's been dead drunk in Liverpool ever since. But the strangest part about it is that she paid all that money just for the privilege of dying at sea, it would seem. Valhalla or something. Must be in the final stages of consumption. White as a sheet, coughing continuously . . . wonder what made her do it. Ah well, if I worried about every lost soul we carry, I'd soon have *Nestor* on the rocks with all hands lost. Glad you've found your sea legs, Mr Cheviot. See you in the saloon.'

Charles remained on deck a long time. The sea air gradually made him feel better and he began to look around with mild interest. He had never been on a large ship. Passengers, crew, shrouds, hatches, mast – all seemed to lose their individual functions and become part of a single entity. It was as if the ship were a miniature planet orbiting through the sky. Not but what the component parts of the planet were colourful and various. It suddenly occurred to Charles that a portfolio of 'scenes from shipboard life' by the celebrated

157

English artist Mr Cheviot might find a lucrative sale in New York. The shipping company, for example, might purchase the pictures for advertising purposes. Alternatively, he could hold an exhibition. Yes, that would be better than rotting in his cabin, he would make rough sketches and notes during the passage and turn them into finished water-colours, in the style of Mr Rowlandson, as soon as he was settled in New York. Impatient to begin he went below for paper and pencil.

The place had been aired and tidied, the empty bottles removed, but he hardly noticed this as he searched for his sketching things. Where had he put them? He tried two boxes without success and was about to tackle a third when he was startled to hear, close behind him, somebody cough. On the instant he spun round but could see no one. A quick look told him there were only two places of concealment – the wardrobe and the bunk. He strode to the latter, pulled back the curtain, and saw a blanket-wrapped figure face to the wall, apparently asleep.

'Who the devil are you, sir, and what are you doing in my cabin?' he demanded, shaking the recumbent body by what appeared to be the shoulder.

The figure slowly turned on its back and two large brown eyes looked up at him. 'Sure, that's no way to handle a lady, Mr Cheviot,' said a nasal voice with an Irish accent as Maria Rushworth sat up and blinked unsmilingly into his eyes. Then she sneezed. The effect on Charles was most peculiar, for he dropped down on to his knees, bent forward, and touched her on the mouth with his lips. *It was almost as if he wanted to catch her infection.*

It is fair to draw a discreet veil over the next several minutes. The dialogue was neither elevating nor original, the sentiments were banal, the doings private and repetitious. Yet together they seemed to do Maria more good than all Mr Gossage's physick and all Mrs Norris's solicitude. Nor, in spite of recurrent imprudences, did Charles pick up her contagion either now or later. At length the patient declared herself completely cured from her recent indisposition. This brought cautious disagreement from her new physician, however. He said that a possibly fatal relapse would occur unless she changed her name from Rushworth to Cheviot in the very near future.

Her eyes assented, but after a frowning pause she said, 'I cannot do that.'

'Why not?'

'Because you do not know who I am or what I am.'

'But I love you. What else matters? I have loved you since — '

'Then you love a falsehood. No, don't speak. I must tell you my story. Please do not interrupt until I have made a clean breast of it. Promise?'

Charles shrugged his assent and Maria sat down on the opposite side of the cabin.

'I shall begin at the end. After our last talk at the hotel I decided to follow you on to this ship and induce you to marry me.'

'But that's splendid. I accept.'

'Don't interrupt, please. I had, of course, been seeking to ensnare you from the first moment we met. Oh, it was quite deliberate even when I did not know I was doing it.'

'I'm sure I do not care, and I do not think I even believe you.'

'Please hear me out. You promised. As I say I decided there and then to marry you, and from base, selfish motives. True I was feverish, but I was also furious – furious that the designs on you – which I had been formulating over the weeks – had been thwarted by the hand of another, and before their time. Born of loneliness, family estrangement, and the lie I was being forced to live, that design assumed even greater importance when I had to acknowledge the treachery of my aunt. I decided therefore to quit Liverpool, board the *Nestor* (at any cost) and bring matters to a head. I saw marriage as a revenge – revenge on my aunt, revenge on society, revenge against the male sex.' Here she struck a pose worthy of Mrs Siddons herself. 'Revenge, you may ask, for what? Yes, look at me, sir, look carefully. You behold that platitude of our times, the fallen woman. I am an abandoned adulteress – abandoned in both senses of the word. You took me for a genteel widow, but no, Mr Rushworth lives and is now remarried. My lover lives and is betrothed to an eligible and virtuous woman – but Maria Rushworth, divorced and cast out, merely exists. She is condemned for the errors of all three. Sometimes, as just now, she forgets the prison she has built for herself and glimpses the sun again, but only for a moment. She had hoped, by marriage, to share or evade the burden of guilt but now she sees that matrimony would only add to it – and some unsuspected vestige of good feeling holds her back on the very brink of success.'

'Vestige of good feeling? Could it not be love, Maria?'

'The more sincere my regard, the more impossible for me to marry . . . but now you must let me go back to the beginning. Please don't interrupt and please – please don't attempt to touch me. Don't make it more difficult. Some five years ago, shortly after my nineteenth birthday, I allowed myself to become betrothed to Mr Rushworth, subject to my father's consent. He was in the West Indies at the time and not expected back for several months. I had been brought up to contract just such a marriage; my family expected me to consent to Rushworth's proposal; my aunt actively promoted the match – yet I need not have agreed to it, and I blame myself bitterly for doing so. Like the rest I was blinded by his twelve thousand a year. What are you doing? I asked you not to – what's this? Oh.'

160

Charles had taken the first volume of *Mansfield Park* from one of his boxes and placed it in Maria's lap. She picked it up, glanced at the title, and dropped it. '*Ave* Maria Bertram,' he said.

'So you know?'

'Yes, I tried to tell you.'

'I'm sorry Charles. I'm sorry I am not the person who, for your sake, I would like to be.'

'But you are, except that you exaggerate your fallen womanhood. Maria Rushworth the actress is forcing you to paint Maria Rushworth the woman in too lurid a light. You have been unwise, unlucky and wrong – and you have atoned with three years of your life. As far as I am concerned that is enough. My proposal stands. I made it when I was in full possession of the pertinent facts. But I too have a confession, and you must hear it before you answer the proposal. I assume, by the way, that you did not see my cousin before you boarded the ship on Saturday? Because I wrote my confession before leaving England. No? Well, it's soon said: I'm afraid I'm penniless; my debts exceed my assets, and I am running away from my creditors.'

Maria laughed in relief. 'Is that all? It does not surprise me in the least. Aunt Norris guessed as much from the start. She has a nose for such things.'

'She has a nose for adventurers, yes. If I marry you, people will say it's for your money. I don't know whether they are right or wrong.'

'Let them say what they please. But I must warn you, I haven't got all that much money.'

'I haven't all that many debts. Just enough to put me away in the Marshalsea. I had reduced my debts to £600 and arranged to pay them off in quarterly instalments, but the company in which I entrusted my minuscule capital failed last month, as I was warned it might, and I have defaulted on

161

my first repayment. I told you all this in my letter. I need a fairly small amount of money badly, but I would want to marry you even if you were destitute. I realised that as soon as I boarded this ship.'

There was a long silence during which the two schemers looked at each other and thought much the same thoughts as each other.

'My rapid recovery seems to have faltered,' said Maria at length, 'but I think it could be started up again without too much difficulty. Am I correct in thinking that ships' captains are allowed to conduct marriages?'

'*Ave* Maria Cheviot,' he said.

It is for the reader, not the narrator, to evaluate the sincerity of these declarations. Some may be distressed that love and marriage are so easily defiled by guilt; others may consider that the guilt had been expiated by mutual and unprompted confessions; still others, the cynical and worldly wise, may detect a glibness on either side which implies a lack of spontaneity – as if they sought to evade the truth by overstating it. Be that as it may. Captain Simes married the happy couple as *Nestor* passed the Fastnet lighthouse, and took them without further incident to New York.

The profits from Mrs Norris's ticket dealing, inadvertently removed from their hiding place by Maria, went a long way towards paying Charles's debts. I hope he will deserve his good fortune.

ENTR'ACTE

Nature abhors and wherever possible frustrates a void. Similarly, people whose lives are dedicated to helping others, quickly find new cares and obligations when the former objects of their solicitude are able to stand on their own two feet. At least it was thus with Mrs Norris. Rather than indulge in private comforts (though she did not altogether deny herself the luxury of hurt feelings), she very soon decided to put her services at the disposal of her other niece, Julia, and proposed a lengthy visit to the Yates establishment in Hampshire.

The loss of her trading surplus on the Atlantic passage transaction was certainly an irritant but once the first, natural chagrin had subsided, Mrs Norris acknowledged that she had been living very largely at Maria's expense for some years and had allowed her niece to pay for both the original tickets. A letter from Cork announcing that Charles and Maria were man and wife removed the last of her resentment: the money to which Maria had helped herself could serve as a wedding present, and a most handsome one too.

In that it did not positively decline her aunt's offer, Julia's reply was perfectly hospitable, but it reported that Lady Bertram herself was unwell and therefore in greater need of solicitous attention than the writer. Sir Thomas, Julia believed, would be reconciled readily enough to Mrs Norris's return providing the matter were approached tactfully. Never one to let personal feelings come before family duty, Mrs Norris set about writing the kind of letter which her brother-in-law would appreciate. After one or two false starts she soon struck the right note of humility, rectitude, loyalty, and thrift. An extensive opening passage of flattery disguised as general enquiry about Mansfield and the family led her by degrees to the once-painful subject of Maria:

I apprehend [she wrote] that none of us, perhaps, was entirely blameless for what befell, but accept that mine was the major fault. All stemmed from a marriage which was injudicious in everything except its *convenance*. Had you, sir, been in England when Mr Rushworth began paying his respects to Maria you would have discouraged the match. Your knowledge of the world, to say nothing of your paternal instinct, would have warned you that the young people were incompatible. In your absence it was I who had to guide them and my judgement – I admit it frankly – was imperfect. Accordingly, I felt it my bounden duty, after the débâcle, to forsake the pleasures and privileges of Mansfield (together with the subsidiary but no less satisfying rewards of my much loved White House), and help undo the damage to which I had been an accessory. To some extent, and with at least partial success, I have now achieved that end.

As you know – for I understand Maria has apprised you of her changed circumstances – your elder daughter is now married to Mr Charles Cheviot (formerly of Seaforth Grange, Northumberland). Her husband comes from a landed Border family and is a young gentleman of accomplishment and address. It is true that his means are limited but he has good prospects, well-placed connections, and a respectable position in New York. All things considered, Maria might have done very much worse. Your daughter's unhappy first marriage must surely cast doubt on the benefits of substantial independence and wealth in her case. Nor can I believe that the disciplines of economy and thrift, in which it has been my

166

constant aim to instruct her, will prejudice their chances of a union which will bring satisfaction to the young couple and credit to the family. Thus it will, in some measure, atone for past indiscretions.

I should add that I have not come hastily to these conclusions. Far from abetting Mr Cheviot's aspirations, I felt it my duty (as much to yourself as to Maria) to discourage them, so far as it was proper, and to test the depth and sincerity of their mutual attachment. In my zeal for their best interests I may have appeared at times almost obstructive but, chastened by my part in one ill-considered match, I was resolved to prevent any repetition, and have always behaved similarly towards any of those I love, asking no credit and accepting the probability of being misunderstood. In this case I cannot but admit that I have certain reservations about Mr Cheviot: he is not, perhaps, as serious as one might wish, though the responsibilities of marriage may well improve him in that respect. However, there can be little doubt as to the sincerity of his attachment or his suitability as a son-in-law. The family, in short, need feel no shame in its connection with the Cheviots, particularly in view of Maria's personal circumstances (of which her husband is cognizant).

May I now, dear Sir Thomas, solicit your advice as to my own affairs? Maria's marriage and departure bring to a conclusion my self-imposed period *in loco avuncularis*. My natural inclination, now strengthened by anxiety about my sister's health, is to return to the White House, but I could not take up residence there again – whatever my legal title to the property – without your compliance. I appreciate, of course, that much has changed in the last three or four years: Edmund has his own establishment; my little Fanny has grown up and married; Susan is now a young woman, no doubt – and I am an elderly one. All these circumstances suggest that if I return it should be as a retired and retiring relative. That I might sometimes meet with the family, at my own home if not at the Park, would be my hope, but I am well aware that the office I once fulfilled in your councils, albeit informally, has been superseded by events and time. I should therefore keep myself to myself, lead my own life in my own house with my own friends (for whom I shall, as before, always keep a room in readiness), subject only to my sister's need for help, companionship, or medical assistance. Before I begin to make any preparations, however, I seek your views on this proposal.

Mrs Norris concluded the letter with further oblique promises of good behaviour and unobtrusive usefulness. Reaching Sir Thomas at a period when his wife's health was giving concern, the letter reminded him of his sister-in-law's family allegiance. Time and distance had tempered disenchantment as to her officiousness and mistrust as to her judgement. Accordingly, he wrote back in accents of fitting condescension which betokened a qualified welcome.

At first, the prospect of Mrs Norris's rehabilitation was alarming to Fanny. However, the move from Thornton Lacey to Mansfield Parsonage, and the birth of a daughter, Cassandra, had brought sufficient new confidence into her life for even Fanny to put aside most of her doubts. Susan Price had moments of anxiety stemming from fear of the unknown, but her natural high spirits combined with Tom Bertram's increasingly protective interest soon allayed them. Lady Bertram genuinely looked forward to her sister's return.

Within a few weeks, Mrs Norris's new position was understood. She spent less time than before at the big house (though more than her letter had foreshadowed) and relied on it less for life's little perquisites. Appreciating the strength of Fanny's position, she soon saw that Susan Price's star was also in the ascendant. Accordingly, she befriended the latter and propitiated the former. Though suspicious at first, Fanny was not impervious to the flattering deference of her former oppressor, and found common cause with her aunt in the comfortable fear that no lasting good would come of Maria's second marriage. They became allies, if never friends. Lady Bertram recovered, and began making the quarter-mile journey to or from her sister's house, weather permitting, on foot; and Sir Thomas himself started calling for occasional advice on family matters.

The room which Mrs Norris held at the disposal of her particular friends was not for the time being pressed into service, but the good lady found plenty to occupy her energies. In particular she soon decided that a marriage between her spirited new favourite, Susan, and the heir to Mansfield Park was not to be discouraged. Her open espousal of their union made Tom hesitate at least a twelvemonth before seeking his cousin's hand.

<hr>

New York, meanwhile, took to the Cheviots and the Cheviots took to New York. Maria's first child was born in the first summer after their arrival, her second in their second autumn. Between these two events, she nearly died of the yellow fever which was still endemic in the town, though Manhattan's swamps were being drained and its valleys filled wondrously fast. The first signs of illness came when the little boy was three weeks old. Maria's face became flushed, her tongue scarlet, her eyes congested and ferrety, but after two feverish days her temperature fell and her skin turned lemon. Dr Macarthur knew the signs all too well and watched for the blood which had given the fever its dreaded appellation 'vomito negro'. The blood came but not too much of it, and after a week prostrated between life and death, Maria began to pull round. Macarthur was the best, and most expensive, surgeon in New York.

Though appropriately distraught, Charles found time to make some attractive sketches of his well-nursed first-born

169

to send back to relatives in England. He also found time to wonder what financial arrangements, if any, Sir Thomas Bertram would make for his grandson should Maria not survive. Ashamed, he put the thought aside; it returned, unbidden, once or twice during the crisis.

Maria's illness had several direct and indirect consequences: it increased her dependence on and devotion to Charles; it brought the first lines to her face; it separated her from her child. At the same time, it left her even happier than she had been before and more determined to make her husband happy. The barrier between herself and young Bertram was almost a relief since, unless she were to tie herself down to the nursery for years to come, it must have been erected sooner or later. Preferable surely to cut the final cord of reciprocal need before either was aware of the loss it might involve?

It is doubtful whether Maria would have developed very strong maternal feelings if she had been spared the yellow fever. She had not wanted a child so soon. The birth itself had been painful, and acute morning sickness, which with Maria started earlier and continued longer than with any of Dr Macarthur's previous patients, had marred her preparation for the *accouchement*. The doctor privately suspected that the sickness was a symptom of her reluctance to become a mother as yet. Charles made no such speculation but noticed that it regularly took place just after seven o'clock. Accordingly, he declared that he had married the prettiest alarum in Christendom. Though hating the sickness, Maria felt more concern on Charles's behalf than on her own, and became intermittently resentful, though never actively hostile, towards the new life within her. Impatience and exasperation were the strongest symptoms of her unreadiness: disinterest her usual feeling.

Even during the slow, tearing parturition a certain

170

detachment never quite deserted her. Inevitably, the pain demanded attention, but without producing the emotional impact which binds many young wives to their first-born. As soon as labour started, part of Maria's mind went back to the little girl she had brought into the world almost exactly a year before, and to the mysterious mother. She even copied the woman's pain-relieving movements and found that the light panting and stomach-stroking seemed to bring relief. Unknown mother and child returned to her again during the illness which followed so quickly, haunting lucidity and delirium alike. As soon as she was recovered she tried to work out what the date had been when she stayed in that inn on the border of Staffordshire and Cheshire.

'I don't think I ever told you, Charles, but back in England, just before I met you, I helped a young woman give birth to a child, and so far as I can make out, Bertram was born on the same date a year later. I may be a day or two out, but I think it was the self-same day. We shall never know for certain, unless you can remember. Such a pity neither of us keeps a diary.'

Charles expressed surprise. How should he remember?

'It happened at about three o'clock in the morning of that day last year when we all went to see Edmund Kean in the evening, and it was quite as dramatic, in its way, as the play itself.' Maria struck an attitude. 'There was I at some Staffordshire coaching inn, about to retire for the night, when a stranger appeared at my door. At first I was very angry. A perfectly common young woman, how dare she? I reached for the bell, but something held me back. She had authority above her station. What did she want? Money or money's worth? To send her packing, I offered her a hideous opal brooch, valueless to me since it came from Mr Rushworth. Still she stayed. Then she seemed almost to swoon. "Sweet heaven," she said, "my time has

171

come." Having been a married woman (albeit not a very respectable one), I guessed what that meant: we must send for the midwife. But she forbade it. I offered to pay, but she was adamant. If God was merciful, He would put an end to her sufferings that night. Very well, I returned, kill yourself and your child, and lay the blame on God. It is no concern of mine. And I stalked out of the room. End of Act One.'

'What a drama. Is it true or is it one of your own private theatricals?' Charles seemed irritated by these revelations.

'Entirely veracious. Act Two . . . There was an empty room opposite in which I composed myself for slumber. Impossible! I kept hearing the girl's moans, or imagining them. Ringless and unmarried she was merely some country girl lured into vice like thousands before her, and paying the inevitable price. I, too, had fallen into temptation, had lost and suffered infinitely more than this red-haired trollop – what right had she to impose on my unending misery? The moans increased but they came not from the room opposite, they came from my own heart. I would have to give her one more chance to be sensible and send for help. Back I went and,' Maria coloured, 'and gave her a good talking to and, well, to cut a long story short, she still would not hear of my telling the landlady, so I stayed and delivered the baby with my own two hands.' Maria was pleased with her performance.

The story was so incredible that Charles believed it. 'How did you deliver the child? By womanly instinct? Or had the percipient Mrs Norris included obstetrics among your many accomplishments?'

'Hardly that. The girl was superior in that she was a farmer's daughter and knew what to expect. Knew all about lambing and had helped at her sisters' confinements. At first it was – objectionably personal, but by degrees it became quite exciting. And when it was over, oh Charles, what rapture! It was like escaping from a dungeon into freedom and sunshine.

A few hours later, I met you. Sometimes I think God sent that woman, whoever she was, to my room that night, and sent you as my reward. Not that I deserved you.'

Maria wept with joy on Charles's breast. Although he responded with a cool caress, he felt more jealousy and embarrassment than sympathetic pride. Retrospectively he was insulted that his wife had had to perform so menial a rôle, and hurt that she had not told him about it earlier. They, or at least she, should have no secrets. Accepting the Rushworth and Crawford episodes in Maria's past, and never holding them against her, he resented other concealments and unorthodoxies, however creditable. It would take time for him to assimilate the news and incorporate it into his life.

His sullen reaction produced the nearest approach the couple had yet had to a serious row. Neither of them knew how to cope with it, and for some days they were distant and shy with each other. Eventually Charles returned to the subject of his own accord. 'That parturition affair, it does you credit, now I have absorbed it, great credit. And it explains something that has always puzzled me. You were so bright – incandescent rather – that evening that I was too dazzled to see you properly, and next day I could not have said whether you were plain or pretty, handsome or beautiful, young or old. It was days before I dared look at you properly.'

'What a shock it must have been when you did.' Apology and compliment were more than sufficient for Maria, who nevertheless decided that it would be best to forget, or at least not refer to, the midwife episode henceforth. That evening they made up the disagreement so conscientiously that Leonora was conceived.

The years passed quickly. Already beginning a reluctant love affair with the English upper classes, American society responded with enthusiasm to a free-spending couple who combined style and talent with a welcome lack of condescension. Equally at home in the Park Theatre (where they attended the American première of a delightful opera by Charles's former friend, Signor Rossini) or in Mayor Cadwallader D. Colden's parlour, they won golden opinions wherever they went. Even after an illness which removed the last traces of girlhood from her looks, Maria had half New York at her feet. Charles's virtuosity and versatility, standing out against a still embryonic artistic life, won him the other half. Their mutual contentment protected them from the suspicions of husbands or the jealousy of wives. A little mad, amusingly bad, they were perfectly safe to know.

And these were boom years, particularly for New York and Liverpool. In half a decade, the merchant tonnage between the two ports trebled, leaving a wake of fortunes and warehouses on both sides of the Atlantic. Charles took to trade so diligently that he all but justified his salary. Under his relaxed guidance, Randall and Company became a civilising example to the eager expansionism and cut-throat competition which otherwise dominated the commercial scene. He became especially popular with his closest rivals and was swept along profitably but unacquisitively on the current of their success.

Playing the businessman seemed easy enough to Charles even if the rôle were tedious and unrewarding. Playing father was more to his liking. In contrast to Maria, he spent hours romping, reading, and singing with Bertram and, as soon as she could crawl, Leonora.

The boy had been baptised Bertram against his mother's first inclination. Charles felt that his own family feud was quite enough and that an olive branch should be offered to

Sir Thomas. Maria, happily married and a thousand leagues from Mansfield Park, still thought her father a pompous old autocrat who should be ignored, but her attitude to the family was more indifferent than hostile. She fell in with Charles's wishes in the end, even to the point of embarking on a dutiful if desultory correspondence with the family in Northamptonshire. Out of punctilious respect for her aunt's privacy, Maria made a point of not including Mrs Norris in her occasional greetings. This courtesy was much appreciated at the White House – and never forgotten.

BOOK TWO

Chapter One

The Cheviots returned to England after seven years in New York. Mr Randall, privately aware that Charles lacked commercial ambition and professionally in need of capital for a new venture (proposed by his businesslike son), accepted a Yankee offer for his American interests. Charles was rewarded for his modest efforts with a modest sinecure in Liverpool. After a decent show of hesitation he accepted a very junior partnership in the cause of prudence and a growing family, though his enthusiasms lay elsewhere.

'Are you sure you are not wasting your talents by staying with Randalls?' asked Maria. 'Why not make the break and concentrate on music?'

'If I have any talents, yes, then I must be wasting them, I presume. My hands are tied, however.'

'Are they? How do you mean?'

'I still have no other resources. If I were to do what my instincts suggest, we should all starve.'

'But I have my allowance.'

'Hardly sufficient. Even assuming I could overcome a natural disinclination – indeed repugnance – at the prospect of relying solely on your money for support, we should very soon find ourselves in Queer Street. The arts are the easiest place in the world to lose money. Look at poor Sheridan (and he was a genius).'

'I was not proposing that we should lease Drury Lane. Surely we have enough to take a small house and pay our keep until you have made your name as the great new English musician? You can sing, you can compose, you can act: you should have all London at your feet.'

'How little you know of the London theatre, or the world. Money and influence rule everything; mere talent is the last consideration.'

'Your cynicism may be justified, at the same time it may be an excuse for inaction. Nothing ventured nothing gained. As to money, surely we have more than most artists? As to influence, surely Mr Kean would help? Of all the world, Mr Kean is in the best position to give you a start.'

'Perhaps, but one has one's pride. I would never try to take advantage of friendship in that way. Besides, Kean is insanely jealous of other people and surrounds himself with mediocrity for fear of rivals.'

Maria was silent. She could never decide what Charles wanted. Sometimes he seemed quite content to swim with the current, demanding little more than the admiration and particularity which his many accomplishments usually won him. At other times he seemed a man apart, frustratedly at odds with his ability, blaming others for a self-waste of which he was ashamed, and taking refuge, all too often, in a lofty, comprehensive contempt.

'If you are quite happy to be a provincial businessman and amateur of the arts, so much the better. I am very content with Liverpool, for sentimental reasons. But is that what you really want, Charles?'

'Yes, in a way. No, of course not. If only I knew. How lucky are those who know exactly what they want, or can only do one thing anyhow, or have no choice in the matter.'

'Most of them would think you, who have so many possibilities, the fortunate one.'

'Little do they know. Singing and drawing are what I find easiest, but I suppose I should write music. Competent vocal-

180

ists and caricaturists are two a penny; good composers are very scarce. England has produced none for a hundred years.'

'High time we did. You could be the man, Charles, I'm sure of it. You write such lovely, witty, tuneful music; so fluently, so—'

'You flatter me. I know a few party tricks and can toss off a piece in the manner of Gluck or Mozart, but to do anything original is another matter. I'm good enough to know how bad, or at least inadequate, I am. Serious composition is a labour of Hercules. I doubt if I have the strength, the dedication, or the talent.'

'But you may have. You cannot know until you've tried.'

'I do try. Sometimes I sit at the piano for hours.'

'And then you give up! Oh, I'm not saying it's easy and I'm not saying you ought to be a Gluck or a Mozart, though I do think you should compose for the theatre. If only you'd made a start back in New York. I'm sure the Park Theatre would have given you a chance.'

'They did. Surely I told you? Well, I meant to. They offered to give me a free hand in all their musical matters, but the remuneration was inadequate and the company little better than amateur, so I declined.'

'Might it not have been a good way of starting?'

'I judged not. They were trying to get something for nothing.'

'I wish you had told me at the time.'

'I'm sorry, but it would not have worked, Maria. I'm sure of it. Anyway, it is over and done with now.'

'And you don't want to talk about it? I must not become a scold. So long as you consider the problem yourself, Charles. Don't just hide your talents under a bushel and hope that something miraculous will happen, or you will end by despising yourself – and perhaps blaming me.'

'Never! My dear Maria, I have been thinking about

181

it a lot recently. I am convinced that a comparatively comfortable and civilised existence in Liverpool will give me just as much opportunity to further my musical ambitions as any more conventional form of artistic indigence in the back streets of Covent Garden – and it will be much more suitable for the children.'

So they leased an expensive but appropriate house in Rodney Street and considered it just as modish as anything in Bath. Charles still had enough work to justify a Randall salary which covered about half their expenditure, and carried it out with charming, gentlemanlike incompetence. The company could afford a passenger or two. He had plenty of time for his own devices and spent part of it thinking about the problems of writing an English answer to *Der Freischütz* or *The Barber of Seville*. For weeks on end he remained at the point of choosing a theme. No music was written but, as he told Maria, the initial conception was half the battle.

During their absence, Liverpool had grown in size, wealth, and fashionable pretension. Maria and Charles were very soon assimilated into the social whirl, and, as in New York, moved easily between the upper echelons of society itself and the growing, but less exclusive, artistic circles. They lived beyond their means, but not too seriously. Charles blamed Maria for their extravagance, with some reason; Maria blamed Charles, with less reason – but for the most part they kept these views to themselves and enjoyed the results. A family visit to Mansfield Park was mooted several times but always, by some intuitive collusion, deferred.

It was a visit from Edmund Kean that reopened the question of Charles's aspirations in connection with the musical stage. Maria had formed a more favourable impression of the actor in America than when she had been back-stage at the Theatre Royal on her first day in Liverpool.

On his American tour Kean had behaved in every way

as a player should, until the fiasco at Boston. Temperate offstage and tempestuous on, he had adorned their New York drawing-room several times without disgracing himself once. Maria sensed that her own attractions were not wholly lost on the demonic little man but was confident, too, that her husband's comradeship and talents were at least an equal magnet. The two complemented each other. On Charles's side there was admiration almost amounting to devotion; on Kean's, the rare pleasure of finding a boon companion who was not a sponger, a gentleman who behaved like an equal, and an artist who was not a threat.

After the Boston incident (in which Kean was held to have insulted the Massachusetts intelligentsia), Charles had been the only person to defend the actor, arguing that the abject humility traditionally demanded by playgoers of their entertainers was arrogant nonsense. Actors were not slaves and an actor of Kean's eminence was entitled to go back to his hotel rather than play to an empty house.

'But was the house empty?' Maria had asked, as Kean sailed back to England. 'I understand there were only a few people there at first but that it filled up quite well later, and even then Mr Kean refused to play.'

'That's only what the Boston papers claim. And even if it were partially true, surely a man can make a mistake without being branded a misshapen villain?'

'If he had apologised all would have been forgiven.'

'Kean would not be a genius if he were the kind of man who apologised to self-important nonentities for imaginary slights.'

'No, but it does seem a terrible pity, and so unnecessary.'

The genius had other battles on his hands now – with Elliston, the lessee of Drury Lane, with Macready the rising (impeccably behaved) tragedian, and with Mrs Cox, the mistress who was threatening to expose his own peccability.

'Devil take 'em all. I'm on my way to Scotland. *Ego meorum solus sum meus.*'

'But we are your friends, too,' said Maria, whose Latin was fair.

Kean happened to be sober and neither his self-pity nor his anger was all-consuming. 'So you are. And I only wish I could repay you for your kindness and support in America. How can I when you hide yourselves away in Liverpool, this wretched town whose every brick is cemented – as my late friend Cooke was wont to remark – by the blood of a negro? Your talents need a larger stage, my lordly Pan.'

'But my pocket rules my talents (such as they are). Here I have a job and an income; in London I do not. Besides, Liverpool is as good a place as any to write an opera, I suppose.'

Kean pricked up his ears. 'An opera, eh? So that's what you are about. Elliston claims that opera is all the thing these days. Opera and melodrama are meant to be ousting legitimate tragedy. A passing fad largely accounted for by my absence in America and Macready's attempted usurpation of the throne. I like a good song but opera will never succeed in Drury Lane, not while Kean's in England.'

'I would not aspire to Drury Lane, not even with Kean in Scotland,' Charles lied.

'The King's is the only theatre suitable for opera. In the person of the new manager, the King's may—'

'Do you know Mr Ebers?'

'Mr Ebers makes it his business to know me.'

'Yes, of course. What can you tell us about him?'

'Less of a villain than Elliston, less of a fool than Charles Kemble. Should take somewhat longer to bankrupt himself. I can speak to him about your opera if you wish. What is the subject?'

Charles hummed and hawed for a little before admitting that he had not finally decided on the exact subject. He was thinking of Shakespeare.

'Keep off Hamlet, Othello, Macbeth, Richard, and Shylock. They are my parts. And Lear now that the old king is dead. I suggest *Coriolanus*, one of Macready's favourites.'

'Years ago Maria and I worked up a ballad burletta based on songs from several of the plays set to the story of *Two Gentlemen of Verona*. I was considering something along that line.'

'No sir. Ballad opera is dead. Why animate a corpse?'

'The alternative might be to try an opera like *Der Freischütz* but on an English theme.'

'Or Queen Elizabeth,' suggested Maria.

'Alas, no. Already appropriated by Signor Crescendo himself, my old companion in arms, Rossini: *Elisabetta, Regina d'Inghilterre*,' said Charles. What do you think, Kean? Comedy, tragedy, or history?'

'*Nihil motum ex antiquo probabile est*, but I would suggest that a patriotic theme would stand a good chance. *Henry V!* Let young Hal be your muse and give plenty of rousing choruses to the rival armies.'

Charles began to improvise variations on 'The British Grenadier' and the 'Marseillaise' at the piano. Gradually the French tune became a caricature of all the charges and taunts made by the English against their neighbours over the centuries; gradually the Grenadiers grew louder, bolder, more patriotic, and when the music was at its most confident, Kean began to recite. He spoke quietly, as if his voice were 400 years away, but with such purity that every syllable was engraved on the music and such passion that the piano became no more than an echo to the poetry.

185

'Then imitate the action of the Tyger
Stiffen the sinews, summon up the blood
Disguise faire Nature with hard-favour'd Rage.
Then lend – lend

lend what, confound it? Never played Harry, but the part has its moments. Just right for a good strong tenor, eh Charles? And there's the Crispian speech. That must be the great aria; that will have them either showing their scars or thinking themselves accurst they were not there, poor devils; have 'em cheering and weeping at the same time, and heaven help any Frenchman in the house.'

The opera's triumph was soon an agreed thing between the three of them. Kean engaged to speak to John Ebers at the King's Theatre and undertook to pay for the production if necessary. By that time, however, he was not sober, and his memory of the later stages of the discussion proved hazy.

Chapter Two

Legal privateering under letters of marque made up part of the income Liverpool had lost with the slave trade's abolition. After the defeat of Napoleon and the cutting back of the Royal Navy, junior officers on half pay were attracted to the foreign navies which became Liverpool's new customers. In search of a commission, Lieutenant Price had gone to the town while his cousin Maria was waiting for her passage to America, and had half recognised her at the Wellington Rooms assembly. Shortly afterwards he had been appointed third officer on a Randall-owned privateer and become a sailor of fortune in South American waters. In the next seven years (with but one spell back in England) he had become a very successful mercenary, as was attested by unfamiliar affluence in the

Price household at Portsmouth and a four-figure bank account with Messrs Hoare in Fleet Street. His ship was now back in Liverpool and it was Charles Cheviot's lot to entertain him.

Neither man was aware of the family connection. William Price had heard of Maria's second marriage but had never known her new name since his mother (when she wrote) had forgotten it and Fanny (his regular correspondent) did not acknowledge Maria's existence if she could avoid it. Equally, Maria seldom spoke to Charles about her own siblings and never about her Price cousins, apart from Fanny. So the existence and name of Fanny's elder brother had dwindled in Charles's mind, an unconsidered detail in a book he no longer thought about very often. Such was the position of reciprocal ignorance when he ushered the tall, ungainly, self-assured sailor into the Rodney Street house. 'Maria, this is Captain Price.'

'Price? Cousin William? Surely I cannot be mistaken?'

'Not – if you are my cousin Maria.'

'That settles it.' They looked at each other in awkward silence until Maria thought of a cousinly rejoinder. 'You cut me dead, the last time you saw me. At the Wellington Rooms, do you remember?'

'Yes,' he replied with pleasing directness, 'but I did not recognise you until it was too late.'

'It wasn't because I was in disgrace?'

This time he did hesitate, as if trying to decide how to answer the question. Then he gave a broad apologetic smile. 'Yes, I was under captain's orders, from my uncle, to cut you dead should I ever have the misfortune to meet you.'

Maria laughed. 'Just as well. It was better that we did not recognise each other. Aunt Norris would have been odious and I should have been terrified.'

'I, too. Still am. I had much rather be outgunned by an enemy man-of-war than a *femme fatale*. We sailors are simple, upright souls with no experience of the gentler sex from one year's end to the next.'

'No need to worry now, William. I am a respectable, married matron. And you, if one is to go by the style of your banter, are by no means the innocent man of action you pretend. I suspect you may be your father's son as well as your sister's brother.'

William bowed without attempting to deny it, and with an abruptness that was almost deft brought his host into the conversation. 'So you are my cousin, sir, as well as my employer. A case of nepotism *malgré vous*.'

Beneath the badinage, all three were disconcerted. For Charles and Maria it was the encounter so long and so willingly delayed with her disapproving family. For Captain Price it was unsought intercourse with someone he had resented as a midshipman (on his rare visits to Mansfield Park he had been ignored or patronised by the arrogant Bertram girls), and deplored as a just-commissioned lieutenant – at the time of the scandal. All three realised that family and business considerations meant that they would have now to acknowledge and see each other so long as William remained in Liverpool. They could not pretend that this meeting had never happened. In short, Maria and her family would have to admit that each other existed. The predicament called for Charles's best wine.

As the evening progressed, the initial embarrassment subsided and points of mutual interest emerged. The sailor found himself looking at his cousin with unpredictable admiration. Beauty he might have expected – cold, scheming, conceited beauty put to the service of selfish, amoral ends. Instead, he discerned warmth and softness, wifeliness and wit, vivacity and vulnerability – and was quite disarmed. It was not difficult to imagine Maria doing something mischievous, but hard to see her a four-square sinner.

William himself was bronzed and lean; his ears stuck out, his hair was thinning, his eyes were almost dangerous. Maria wondered how closely Montevideo and Buenos Aires, free of the Spanish yoke, still chaperoned their daughters. Charles decided that the newcomer was an amiable ass. A few questions established that William had no knowledge of the arts and that his views were conventional. Physical gaucherie reinforced an impression of intellectual mediocrity and Charles would have had no patience with him had not his own jokes and sallies been greeted with unaffected enjoyment. The guest liked the host, so the host condescended to return the compliment, and make him a foil rather than a butt. Yet William had good sense and fair sensibility.

'Did you ever hear,' asked Maria, when she felt brave enough 'who wrote that book, about Fanny and, well, all of us?'

'*Mansfield Park?* The late Miss Austen. There is no longer any secret about the authorship.' William looked apprehensive.

'Miss Austen? I am not sorry to hear that she is "late". The book was true and yet so false. It had everything wrong except mere facts.'

'It was ridiculously wrong about my wife,' agreed Charles, 'condemned her roundly, but missed all her really bad points.'

'How did she obtain her facts? That is what I have always wanted to know. Have you any idea, William? I see by your face that you have.'

'I wish I had not.'

'Why, it wasn't you who told her?'

'No. Certainly not. I never met Miss Austen.'

'Then what are you hiding? It is nine or ten years since the book appeared, and the truth can no longer hurt me. I should dearly like to know who told the author.'

William looked away guiltily. 'Very well, I shall tell you

all I know. First, let me confess that indirectly I may be one of those responsible. If so, I apologise, but I could not have known. The late Miss Austen had two brothers in the navy. One of them, Francis William Austen, was a friend of Admiral Crawford and it was through his good offices that I was made up to lieutenant just after your marriage.'

'I thought it was Henry Crawford who helped you. In the book—'

'Yes, Henry Crawford spoke to his uncle, the admiral on my behalf, and the admiral spoke to Captain Austen. By the by, I am the first to acknowledge that I owe my advancement to Henry Crawford and I do not like the way Miss Austen ascribes all Crawford's generosity to base self-interest. Be that as it may, in my first appointment I found that my immediate superior was the other brother, Charles Austen, and that he, in turn, knew my father in Portsmouth. Another despicable thing about that book, incidentally, is the way it condemns my poor father – who had an honourable career as an officer of Marines, before he was wounded in the defence of his country. He is despised by Miss Austen, because he is poor, has only two servants, and likes his rum. That damns him in her eyes, but he remained a friend of Charles Austen, now an admiral.' William paused to collect his thoughts.

'At the time of your matrimonial mishap, or whatever we are going to call it, both the Austen brothers were in contact with one or more of the characters involved in Mansfield Park affairs. Much of the story already being public knowledge, thanks to newspaper reports, it was natural that we should talk about it from time to time in the ward room – the whole of London was doing the same thing. I have no doubt that the lady was given the facts by her brothers and then embroidered them into the somewhat partial reconstruction which was subsequently published. Though prejudiced, it is accurate and does have a deal of feminine insight, if I may say so. I am very sorry about my small part in the business, but do not believe I was seriously at fault.'

'No more you were. I forgive you William. As you say, the more scandalous parts of the story were already public knowledge. You are not to blame. I only hope that you were not harmed by having such a notorious cousin.'

'By no means. One or two of my mess mates envied me.'

'What about your superior offficer?'

'Charles Austen? Much as he respected his sister's talent, he did not share all her views. He did not see eye to eye with her on amateur theatricals or frolics in Sotherton Park, for example. Nor was Miss Austen herself always so stern, it appears. He once told me that her youthful spirits were very high but gradually gave way to impossibly strict standards of propriety as a result of disappointed love. The portrait of Fanny is her ideal of womanhood towards the end of her life. Charles Austen used to hope his sister would not hear anything about his own escapades. He was heart-broken when she died, but just a little relieved, for she would have been shocked at the way sailors sometimes make up for the time spent at sea. Incidentally, her earlier books are more lively. I could lend you one if you like' (here Maria coloured and looked away), 'but best not, of course.'

So the evening turned out better than any of them had a right to expect, and by the end of it all three were singing sea shanties lustily. Though unable to keep in tune, at least not at will, William had a rollicking voice and knew the words. In fact, he knew some words which would have surprised his relatives at Mansfield Parsonage, words he had originally learnt from Miss Austen's brother.

Eventually Maria decided to signal an end to the evening by calling for a different kind of beverage and singing a different kind of song. She leafed through the newly arrived *Musical and Vocal Cabinet*, found what she wanted, and placed it in front of Charles at the piano. Reading over his shoulder, she sang

> Let topers drain the flowing bowl
> And tipsy get for me,
> I ne'er their orgies shall control
> So I've a bowl of tea
> And let them jest and drink and smoke
> And stir up mirth and glee.
> I'll stir up pleasure to provoke
> A smoking cup of tea.

Charles cast aspersions on both beverage and song writer but William accepted the hint. He thew back a bowl of tea and started making his departure. Maria detained him.

'You must stay with us while you are in Liverpool, little coz. That would be properly familial. We owe it to Fanny.'

'I would not dream of trespassing on your—'

'Nonsense,' said Charles, exuding bonhomie. 'Of course you must stay. Come tomorrow. Or tonight. The house is at your service.'

'But the inconvenience to you!'

'Don't you want to stay with us? Are you worried that the rest of the family might object?'

'No. I should love to stay with you, but I do not want to put you to any trouble.' William was weakening.

'Well, stop beating about the bush and say yes. It is too late in the evening to go through motions of saying one thing when you really mean the opposite.'

William shrugged his shoulders with good-natured acquiescence.

'That's settled then. Now you know your way back to the hotel, do you not? It is but five minutes away and our new gas lighting makes the walk perfectly safe . . .'

So saying Maria took her cousin by the arm and led him to the front door, cutting short his adieus and thanks, but not resisting when he kissed her hand.

'Your room will be ready tomorrow. We shall expect you when we see you. Consider Rodney Street your Liverpool home.'

'The appellation is entirely suitable,' murmured the sea captain.

When Maria returned to the drawing-room, Charles was replaying one of the sea shanties.

'Might work this into the Harfleur scene. I must say, you showed young William the door with almost indecent haste, my love.'

'I thought he would never go, Charles. The fact is I have been having some quite other indecent thoughts for the last hour. Sea shanties seem to have a most improper effect on me.'

'But they have the opposite effect on me,' said Charles, resigning himself to being pulled upstairs. 'I'm sure it's only the manly presence of your cousin which . . . oh all right, I'm coming.'

The night's repose produced further indecent inclinations in Maria but a headache and bad temper in Charles.

'Must we have that fellow to stay?'

'No, dear, but he is a relative and he seemed good company in a simple sort of way.'

'He's a philistine oaf. Why did you ask him?'

'You asked him too. You said "the house is yours".'

'Rubbish. Did I really? Well, you asked him first.'

'Of course. As mistress of the house it is my province to do so.'

'In consultation with me. Please remove your hand.'

'How could I consult with you last night? This is too silly. It will only be for a few days, I expect.'

'But we have done all we need. Why can you never leave well alone? This is meant to be a home not a hotel.'

'Hotel indeed. We have been married eight years and—'

'What has that to do with it?'

'Please don't interrupt. We have been married eight years and the first time I ask a relative to stay you make a ridiculous song and dance about turning the house into an hotel. You should be glad to meet my family at last. William is no genius but he is quite engaging and would even be handsome if his ears were not so prominent. Family connection dictated that the offer had to be made. Look at the way we stayed with the Randalls before we found this house.'

'That was different. The Randalls are close friends as well as relatives. You hardly know William Price.'

'All the more reason for getting to know him. He is my oldest cousin and may help us towards a family reconciliation. You are always saying I should take more trouble about my family.'

After a dignified silence, Charles, anxious to have the last word, said, 'I concede victory to you, as usual' and magnanimously arose from the bed. As with previous differences of opinion, Maria soon forgot all about it, while her husband brooded for a good deal of the morning.

Two days later, William Price removed his bags from the hotel to Rodney Street. Notwithstanding the host's initial reserve, he soon became a popular member of the household, particularly with Bertram and Leonora. The children adored his sailor's tricks with rope and string, his tales of derring-do, and the gentle muscularity with which he fought them both for many an hour. Both parents were softened by this cousinly bond, Maria feeling that it compensated, in some sense, for

194

her comparative neglect, Charles finding common cause with his guest despite their evident dissimilarities. Accordingly, William's proposed visits to his sister at Mansfield and the rest of his family in Portsmouth were deferred – to general acclamation. All too soon, however, events in Northampton-shire intervened.

Chapter Three

Approaching the birthday which completed his allotted span, Sir Thomas Bertram had inspired varying degrees of anxiety in his family by becoming seriously ill. During several weeks his life was in the balance; the anniversary came and went; prayers were said; the servants padded around the house in muffled silence; and two physicians were in constant attend-ance. Gradually Sir Thomas began to improve and the day came when he was pronounced to be out of danger. Better still, he should live another ten years! The doctors' accounts fully reflected the skills they had devoted to affecting so remarkable a cure, though Mrs Norris made it clear that her nursing had been the crucial factor in Sir Thomas's recovery. She had a shrewd idea, however, that his return to vigour might be short-lived.

'I perfectly know the signs,' she confided to Mrs Tom Bertram with looks of gloom. 'During my husband's first illness, the surgeon declared that Mr Norris might not pull through, but I was adamant that he would. The surgeon even advised against bleeding (far too many of them have irresponsible prejudices, these days, against tried and trusted remedies) but I ignored the advice and sure enough Mr Norris lived another twelvemonth. Unfortunately something in his illness had fatally debilitated him, though he was still less than sixty years of age. Of course, he had never spared himself, poor man, and towards the end of his life had become skin and bone. He sometimes suggested that we should have a richer and more varied diet, but I knew that would have been the death of him. His constitution demanded gruel. Sir Thomas, though appreciably stouter, has something of the same look. Had I been permitted to bleed him, too, it might have been a different story. But no one ever listens to the voice of experience, except you, my dear Susan.'

Susan expressed suitable concern. She had expressed suitable concern throughout her father-in-law's illness, and felt it too. Hoping that he would recover, she had found time also to pray that he would be granted a speedy and painless release when his time was finally come. Unlike her sister Fanny, it was not the loss only of a severe but benevolent uncle for which Susan had to prepare herself. She would have the additional burden of becoming the new Lady Bertram with all the anxieties attached to large estates and an income to match. Happily her husband was facing the prospect with his usual bluff fortitude.

'Things being as they are,' pursued Mrs Norris, 'I really think Sir Thomas ought to look at his will again. I understand he has not materially altered it for nearly ten years, or at least since Edmund's marriage. You and Tom have a particular duty to make sure that his final will reflects his views now rather than his views of a decade ago. After all, much has happened in the interval. His elder son has married and his elder daughter has *remarried*' (this last with an emphasis partly lost on Susan).

'Does the will signify all that much, aunt? Does not the elder son inherit come what may?'

'He inherits the title, of course, and the entailed part of the estate; Mansfield Park and its farms. But Sir Thomas has considerable property besides. There is the house in London, part of the estate in Antigua, and a substantial sum in 3% Consols all free of the entail. Naturally, he must leave something to Edmund and Julia, but the new head of the family will need—'

'And to Maria, too, I trust, even though she was so very indiscreet. I must say I should like to meet my wicked cousin some day.'

'And, as you say, to Maria. I have always supported the principle of equality between siblings in so far as it is compatible with the maintenance of family estates. It follows that the head of the family must – in the interests of all the others – be left with the wherewithal to maintain and improve the estate. For if he is kept short then the estate must be neglected and as a result of neglect eventually, piece by piece, fall under the hammer. I have seen it happen time and time again. The upshot is that the whole family suffers – *and the poorer members suffer most.* Thus the principle of primogeniture serves the interests of the whole family and is therefore essentially egalitarian.'

'Is there any reason to suppose that Sir Thomas's present dispositions are less than prudent?'

'That is a question for his, and the family's, legal advisers. I do recall, however' – here Mrs Norris perhaps coloured a little and most certainly walked to the window – 'that at the time of, er, Maria's – not to put too fine a point on it – scandalous behaviour, your father-in-law in his kindness, made a particularly liberal provision for her. Indeed, with disinterested concern for both parties, I played some small part in those deliberations, I seem to recall. Sir Thomas's generosity (which must have reduced what he could do for Julia and Edmund) was prompted by circumstances which, following Maria's second marriage, no longer obtain. If he were to review the will now he might perhaps consider that it was unfair to the other children and, possibly, prejudicial to the future of the estate. It is not for me to say. Nothing on earth

197

would have made me allude to the will but an old-fashioned belief that justice should be done to all, and a recollection that Tom himself was still unwell (though convalescent) at the time of Maria's divorce. As I say, it is not my business (and clearly I have no personal interest in the matter), but if Sir Thomas's attorney were to suggest a review of the will's main provisions at their next meeting that would at least verify whether or not it still reflects his wishes.'

In her guileless way Susan reported this conversation to her husband who dutifully passed it on to the attorney who professionally alluded to the matter at his regular monthly visit to Sir Thomas.

'My word is my bond,' said the baronet.

'Quite,' said the man of business.

'A gentleman cannot, in honour, go back on responsibilities voluntarily assumed and undertaken after due consideration.'

'That would be unthinkable.'

'My commitment to my elder daughter's support is morally binding. It was and is my intention that she be maintained as becomes her station in life. That she erred cannot be gainsaid, that she merited harsher punishment than any she received is not in question, but a father is not a judge.'

'Very true. Paternal love knows its own . . .'

'Precisely. I flatter myself that the thoughts and feeling behind my commitment are just as important to my daughter as the financial support itself.'

'Without any doubt. More so in all probability. She knows that in her hour of need her family, more particularly her father . . .'

'Her family stood by her. Exactly. Of course her hour of need has long passed. I fancy that my support played no small part in helping her through to calmer waters.'

'She could hardly deny it.'

198

'Hardly indeed. Though now I consider she has never acknowledged it in so many words.'

'Has she not?'

'No, I am positive she has not. Gratitude – not that one expects or requires it – was never one of her particular attributes.'

'Perhaps she is waiting to express her thanks in person. After all she has been in America and only just . . .'

'On the contrary, my dear Jefferies, she has been back in England the best part of a year and made no move to come and see us.'

'Astonishing.'

'One has to get used to such treatment,' said Sir Thomas, picking up the will. He read certain passages thoughtfully.

'You instructed us,' said Mr Jefferies at length, 'to make such testamentary arrangements as would secure Mrs Rushworth (as she then was) an income for life of not less than £750 per annum. On her death without issue the capital sum – approximately £17,000 – to return to the estate . . . Her second marriage has materially altered matters. As things now stand, Mrs Cheviot continues to receive the income she has enjoyed these past nine years. If she dies, her husband has a life interest in the income which ultimately passes to her children. On your own demise, Sir Thomas, the capital goes in trust to the children with Mrs Cheviot retaining an interest for life. At the time such an arrangement seemed to correspond to your requirements. The question is whether it still meets your personal wishes, your family responsibilities, and your moral commitment to Mrs Cheviot.'

'I have never believed that my duty to Maria extended, without the possibility of amendment, beyond the grave. But I will not countenance changes while I am alive. The matter is over and done with. I haven't the patience to make some

199

new disposition, and have given my word. I shall do what I promised Mrs Norris.'

'The other principal objects of your will are, of course, to secure the future of the estate and to provide – supposing you predecease Lady Bertram – for your widow's independence.'

'Indeed. Those remain prior charges under all circumstances.'

'Naturally. The effect of the present arrangements is to commit £20,000 of the free estate (you cannot exercise any discretion over the entail, of course) to providing Lady Bertram's income and £17,000 to providing Mrs Cheviot's. A further £9000 is divided equally between Mr Tom Bertram, Mr Edmund, and Mrs Yates who thus receive £3000 each, while Mrs Edmund and Mrs Tom Bertram, you will recall, both receive £1000 outright. Apart from small legacies, including by codicil a recently restored legacy to Mrs Norris, that completes the will. I have taken the liberty of assuming that something more nearly approaching parity might now be worth consideration.'

'Edmund, certainly, might be thought hard done by at present, and Julia too. Even Tom will have appreciably less than I to run the estate. What are your suggestions, Jefferies?'

'If all four siblings were to receive an equal share of the free estate they would receive some £7000 (or £350 per annum) each. Alternatively, if Mr Tom's inheritance from the free estate is left at the present £3000 and the remaining three are treated equally, the latter receive rather more than £8000 each. Further possibilities exist: for example, Mr Edmund Bertram's portion could be increased to, say, £10,000 with commensurate reductions for Mrs Cheviot and Mrs Yates. It should also be borne in mind that Lady Bertram's £20,000 is in trust and will be divided up in due course.'

Sir Thomas pondered for a little time, asked some more questions, did a few sums, and decided to do what the lawyer had intended him to do. Maria's settlement was revoked, and equal portions (viz £7000) of the free estate were allotted to the four Bertram children. The £20,000 life settlement on Lady Bertram would be disposed of, on her death, so that Tom (or his heir) received one half, Edmund one quarter, and Sir Thomas's grandchildren by Mrs Cheviot and Mrs Yates the remaining quarter between them.

'The new disposition is certainly within the spirit of my commitment to Maria. It is, after all, the thought and feeling behind it which really matter. Restored to full parity with her siblings, she cannot expect more than Edmund or Julia. She is Cheviot's responsibility now. I shall write and tell her my decision. Perhaps after that she will deign to visit her elderly father . . . Let us hope that she has been prudent, over the years, with the inequitably large income she has enjoyed from the estate.'

If Charles Cheviot resented the amount of time Maria and her cousin spent discussing family matters, he did not show it. His occasional taciturnity could be ascribed to financial and creative preoccupations. He was mildly surprised, however, at the bond which seemed to develop between them, since, apart from shared grandparents, they had little in common.

'I really think we must visit Mansfield and introduce you to my father,' said Maria.

'I have no insurmountable objection,' replied Charles. 'Indeed I shall be happy to go, provided you remind me what subjects, amateur theatricals apart, have to be avoided.'

'Julia declares that Sir Thomas has mellowed quite extraordinarily. He is almost tolerant, it seems. However, it will

201

be best to assume a certain gravity, Charles. Pretend to be conventional. Make William Price (the William you will find at Mansfield) your model – a challenge to your acting abilities. And remember my father has been sick and may not have fully recovered.'

'Are you suggesting we should coincide our visit with William's?'

'I am not sure. Perhaps we should send a suitable letter by William's hand, and follow him a week or two later. William could, as it were, prepare the ground. I confess that I do not relish the prospect, after such a long separation, but go we must, I fear.'

They were spared the choice. Shortly after signing his new will, and without telling Maria its contents, Sir William had a sudden and fatal relapse. This time Susan's prayer was answered: the release was as quick as it was painless. The Cheviots and William Price travelled together to the funeral.

Chapter Four

It was the best part of a decade since Maria had seen any of them at Mansfield Park, except Mrs Norris. Tom, the new Sir Thomas, greeted his sister with bluff and knowing heartiness – the reformed rake saluting the blemished lady; Edmund and Fanny were apprehensive and self-conscious but made an effort to seem welcoming; Julia put on a show of sisterly affection, each question and compliment carrying a sting; Mrs Norris was noncommittally verbose . . . it was left to the dowager Lady Bertram to be unaffectedly pleased.

'So nice, so very comfortable to have the whole family together at a time like this. Sit here Maria and tell me all about yourself. For instance, how do you like this new black muslin of mine? Webster made it during Sir Thomas's previous illness, just in case. By the by, you have put on a little weight. It becomes you. I wish Julia would do the same, she's a regular beanpole.'

Mrs Yates looked round sharply and sniffed.

'Not living in Liverpool, I can dispense with the extra pounds madam. Hampshire must be ten degrees warmer. In the New Forest we like to be *en bon ton* rather than *embonpoint*.'

The contrast between Maria and Julia was startling. The younger now looked the older of the two by several years. Julia was still handsome but her face seemed smaller and thinner, her eyes closer together. The bloom of youth had given way to the loom of fashion, and lines – not of laughter but of discontent – were already, at twenty-nine, well established. Maria, on the other hand, had grown into full and glowing beauty, and was enhanced by mourning. Her lines only reflected the happiness which she gave and sought.

Their husbands presented an equal contrast: the honourable John Yates, though affability itself, was already stout, bald, and middle-aged; his face and figure suggested indolence in everything but field sports and good living, and his conversation had lost none of its inconsequentiality after eight years of marriage to Sir Thomas Bertram's daughter. Charles Cheviot remained as slim, youthful, and pleasing as the day he met Maria.

All these comparisons had flashed through Julia's mind before the Cheviots had been a minute at Mansfield Park.

'You must meet my new pug,' said Lady Bertram. 'Susan my dear . . .'

'Perhaps Mrs Cheviot would like to pay her last respects to my uncle,' suggested Fanny softly but with authority.

'Oh to be sure, I was forgetting. How sad it all is; surely I must be the most miserable woman alive? Such a considerate husband.' (Here Lady Bertram dabbed her eyes; Fanny seemed to expect it.) 'The coffin . . . Edmund you show her, dear . . . Oh, how I dread the funeral tomorrow.'

Maria suffered herself to be led through to the chamber where Sir Thomas's mortal remains were awaiting the morrow. There being a cushion beside the coffin, she knelt down, clasped her hands together, and closed her eyes. Edmund's presence positively demanded prayer. First she said, 'Goodbye father, I'm sorry I was such a disappointing daughter,' then she thought about heaven and death, then she wondered whether it had not been easier for Jesus Christ to be good than for other people, then she asked herself whether it was better to enjoy doing good works or to dislike doing good works but do them (just a few) all the same. Finally she counted slowly up to seventy-five. Touched by her unexpected piety, Edmund, who had been timing her prayers, put a forgiving and brotherly hand on her shoulder and led her back to the wintry drawing-room, as she dabbed her eyes with a handkerchief.

'I have endeavoured to make certain that the flowers will befit the occasion,' Mrs Norris was reassuring the company, 'but at this time of year there is little one can do. Some of the tenants, I regret to say, have been less than helpful. Mrs Oakes has made a nice enough little wreath but really it is no bigger than the one she made when Mr Norris died, and I could not help remarking that she still had at least two dozen of chrysanthemums in her garden. When I chanced to mention the fact to her, she naturally cut them at once – and they now look well enough as part of my own spray – but it would have been much more respectful if I had not had to drop the hint. Mrs Oakes has the most protected garden in the whole village, I should say, but you would never suspect it from the size of her wreath. If my own little garden had been less exposed there is nothing I would not have spared from it, but those autumn winds have wrought such havoc . . . I cannot recall when winter has arrived so early as this year. However, by taking the trouble to find out which gardens and which corners of the Park itself still have a little colour, I venture to think that my own floral tribute will not be unworthy. Now that Jackson family, who owe Sir Thomas—'

'Did I not see some late dahlias in your border?' put in Lady Bertram mildly.

'Yes, I still have a few. They are the ones I bought last year, that is the ones which were supernumerary to the Park's requirements and which Sir Thomas let me have, or rather, which I agreed to take rather than have them transplanted – thrown away, I should say – to the almshouses (where they would have been neglected; I cannot abide waste in any form). As they are only in their first year, it would be unwise to cut them just yet, and they look most appropriately dignified, of course, in that *particular* station. Since the cortège will be passing so very near the White House, almost within sight of it, I felt it would be quite wrong, disloyal as well as disrespectful, wilfully to remove that last blaze of colour. Besides Sir Thomas did not care overmuch for dahlias. But as I was saying Mrs Jackson and that son of hers—'

'How touchingly considerate . . . Impeccable sensibility as always,' Charles could not help muttering, *sotto voce*, to Maria.

Mr Yates, who was standing near by, began to snigger but hastily cleared his throat and made play with his pocket handkerchief.

Despite a fire, the room was draughty and chill. Charles looked about him with disfavour. The furniture was neither comfortable nor elegant, the pictures devoid of intrinsic merit, the walls and curtains sombre. A room of gravity and submission. His spirits sank and he began to

205

wonder how soon after the funeral he could decently make his departure.

'I must go and see to the final preparations for tomorrow's ceremony,' said Edmund. 'Laymen often imagine that the conduct of funeral services is the clergyman's most melancholy duty. Quite the contrary! In practice, the reality of everlasting life, the certainty of forgiveness, and the relief from fleshly burdens and temptations, as testified in the Order of Burial, invariably combine to strengthen him in his ministry. How much more so when the dear departed is one's own flesh and blood.'

'Yes, I am sure you will take the service very nicely, Edmund dear,' said Lady Bertram. 'You always do. But I wish it were all over. Must it last very long? I am certain your father would prefer the shortest possible service.'

Edmund and Fanny returned to the parsonage taking William Price, who was naturally *their* guest, along with them. The disconsolate widow led the remainder of the family in a solemn and copious dinner. Afterwards the new baronet enlisted Yates's and Cheviot's views as to the relative merits of the 1780, 1793, 1807, and 1812 vintages of port wine. The youngest was duly voted the best, and four empty bottles bore witness to the conscientious yet restrained manner in which the three gentlemen discharged their judicial responsibilities.

'And how do you like our new – for he is new to us – brother, Fanny?' asked Edmund next morning.

'Mr Cheviot seemed very agreeable, if a little strained.'

'It must have been an ordeal for him to meet Maria's family for the first time under any circumstances, let alone at the present time.'

'Yes, indeed. A certain awkwardness was only to be

expected. Too much composure would have been inappropriate and insensible. He comported himself with credit on the whole.'

'Maria, in short, might have done a good deal worse. I am heartily relieved to have it confirmed that our sister is respectably married to a gentleman we can acknowledge without reservation. It marks an unexpectedly happy ending to a long and troubled chapter in our lives. The only pity is that Sir Thomas did not live to rejoice with the rest of us.'

Fanny sighed. 'That my dear, kind uncle was denied the felicity was no fault of his,' was her delayed and thoughtful rejoinder.

'Very true. Here is yet another example of God's inscrutable way. He giveth and he taketh away.'

'All the same, it is perhaps a pity that Mr and Mrs Cheviot did not choose to come and pay their respects soon after their return from America. That showed a want of consideration, and Sir Thomas felt it. I agree with Aunt Norris that it clouded his last days. By no means would I suggest that it may have hastened his end, but it was a source of displeasure and disappointment that cannot have been beneficial.'

'I understand from William that they were on the point of proposing a visit when my father died.'

'So I hear. William seems to have taken to Mr Cheviot,' continued Fanny in the same mild voice. 'I cannot believe they have much in common.'

'It is quite normal for people to admire in others what they lack in themselves. William is the best fellow in the world, but no one would call him a musician or artist; Cheviot, it would seem, is most versatile and accomplished, but may lack that firmness of purpose which so distinguishes the man of action. Given goodwill on both sides these differences form a basis for mutual friendship and benefit.'

'Yes. I cannot think that Mr Cheviot is a very serious young man. He is most unlike the William we love so much. If anything he reminds me of—' she stopped short, coloured, and tried to turn the conversation. 'But it does not signify. I perceive the wind has dropped. Does that mean the first snow do you think, or a return to milder weather?'

'Hardly snow, I think. But of whom does Cheviot remind you, Fanny? He puts me in mind of somebody too, but I cannot find the name. It has been worrying me.'

Fanny hesitated. 'There was something about his manner, about his attitude which made me think, just for a moment, of—' she took a deep breath, 'Mr Henry Crawford.'

'I cannot agree,' cried Edmund quickly. 'No, I was thinking of someone quite different. Blessed if I can say who, but no one was further from my mind than . . . I sincerely trust that Maria has not tied herself to another rascal.' Now it was Edmund's turn to feel disconcerted. He had never managed to forget Mary Crawford completely. Hardly a month went by without his thinking about her at least once, if only to reassure himself that he was disabused about his former love and that he now had the best wife in the world. He repeatedly told himself that Mary, with her wit, beauty, harp-playing liveliness and mischievous irreverence would have been quite out of place in a parsonage. The ministry was a vocation for the serious-minded.

'No, no,' he continued. 'Once bitten twice shy. There is no similarity between Cheviot and Crawford.'

'I expect you are perfectly right, Edmund. I hope so. Mr Cheviot is much better-looking and probably more intelligent. I doubt if he is so bent on shallow gratification, but I did happen to overhear a disparaging jest he made to Maria (it was about Aunt Norris and would have been justified, even amusing, on a less solemn occasion) which put me in mind of the Crawfords' irreverent humour.'

208

'Such coincidences are not unusual. Only the other day I found myself thinking of poor Rushworth and his two and forty speeches! Crawford . . . what a name from the past. I had all but forgotten it.'

William's appearance for breakfast, occurring at this point, put an end to the conversation.

Over at the big house Tom was reading his morning's post, occasionally commenting on it to his wife and sisters. The final letter made him whistle with astonishment.

'God bless my soul! What have we here? The heartfelt and sincere condolences of Mary Crawford, no less. And all her news to boot. Listen to this:

> You will be relieved to hear that I finally acquired the title which my £20,000 so richly deserved. As a result I am translated into Lady Roscommon and, when not in town (where we live on decidedly the wrong side of the Park), am usually to be found riding to hounds with the Galway Blazers. It was my horsemanship which won Roscommon's heart (though my fortune had already captured his head) and for that, and for much else beside, I have my friends at Mansfield Park to thank. Pray remember me particularly to Mr Edmund Bertram and Fanny.

Well, well, well – what a voice from the past, eh Maria?'

'And long may it remain there,' returned his sister with a finality which persuaded Sir Tom not to indulge the heavy banter which he would normally have considered the privilege of an elder brother.

Maria's presence ensured a full house of God at the funeral service. The village turned out in force, the neighbouring gentry in greater numbers than had been expected in view of the old baronet's comparative seclusion. All were anxious to see what time and tribulation had done to his once proud and beautiful daughter. When it was found that they had punished her with brilliant looks and a tall, upstanding husband, indignation was widespread both among those who had themselves behaved like her but not been found out and those who had wanted to behave like her but had been too cautious or too ill-looking. Those, like Fanny, whose private inclinations corresponded exactly with public imperatives and had prayed for Maria's reform and repentance, felt that the forgiveness meted out was excessive. Pondering the doctrine of right and wrong, none of the congregation appreciated the dire organ-playing except Charles Cheviot who enjoyed every excruciating note.

Edmund conducted the service at funereal pace as if hell-bent on delaying his father's accession to eternal bliss. He sang or chanted most of the office and soon demonstrated that his voice was little better than William's. At last he arrived at the *Domine, refugium*, a psalm which Charles happened to know word for word.

'*Lord thou hast been our refuge*:' began Edmund quaveringly if not altogether convincingly . . .

'*From one generation to another*,' responded a strong, clear tenor. '*Before the mountains were brought forth, or ever the earth and the world were made: thou art God from everlasting and world without end / Thou turnest man to destruction: again thou sayest, Come again ye children of men . . .*'

Unaware that he was the only member of the congregation singing and that he at first drowned then extinguished Edmund, Charles filled the church with a voice which must have reached half-way up to heaven. Gentry, tenantry, and villagers were so affected by the unforeseen cultural treat that their mouths fell open and their eyes grew wider and wider, while Edmund at first looked stunned, then embarrassed, and finally angry. Though loud the singing was pure, restrained, and tolerably devotional. It was not until 'As it was in the beginning' that the stranger at the funeral allowed himself enough rubato to produce a secular effect. By that time he must surely have realised he was performing solo (but he insisted otherwise).

The ensuing silence was punctuated by Mrs Edmund's sniffing suppression of the brave, unobtrusive tears so often admired by the late Sir Thomas.

The remainder of the ceremony passed without interruption. In the churchyard, just before the interment, Maria found time for a brief altercation with her husband.

'You should not have used my father's funeral for showing off your vocal powers.'

'How do you mean? Was no one else singing? I did not realise.'

'They never do at funerals. Not at Mansfield. Only the parson.'

'How odd. Wanting in respect, I should say, but it is no business of mine.'

'Edmund is very cross and Fanny thinks you did it on purpose to make her husband look foolish.'

'Fiddlesticks! It is not my fault if your brother is tone deaf. But I shall apologise, if you want me to, as handsomely as I can.'

'Ssh . . .'

'Man that is born of woman hath but a short time to live and is full of misery,' said the Reverend Mr Bertram with instinctive approval, still looking in the Cheviots' direction.

During the concluding passages Maria found herself wondering whether Charles had made a serious or just a trivial mistake. Edmund and Fanny were affronted, but with Sir Thomas dead, their family influence was likely to wane. Her mother and Tom himself would scarcely have noticed the gaffe, and would soon forget it. Mrs Norris could be relied on to use it to their disadvantage should the opportunity occur, but that was all. In sum, it was a pity, but no lasting damage had been done. Charles had been making such a good impression.

'Always remember, dear, that in church very good singing is very bad taste,' she whispered at the next opportunity.

In spite of the occasion, Maria found herself unexpectedly content to be at home. The absence of a feared and unloved father was itself an improvement and Julia's reluctant envy by no means unacceptable. It was amusing to be with genial old Tom again – 'We all have to pop off some time' had been his only philosophical contribution – and to meet his pretty little wife. Susan had neither the soft expressions nor iron will of her sister, and her even spirits and twinkling eyes suggested that Mansfield Park must surely become a more relaxed and happier place. Maria could look ahead to family visits with a succession of balls, parties and concerts, if not theatricals. Should Edmund and Fanny disapprove, well, Tom was head of the family now, and Edmund, she supposed could always go away and become a bishop. Her own children might well find a second home with their Uncle and Aunt Bertram . . . and all these benefits would cost the Cheviots very little money. Yes, it was important that Charles should make a good impression and that she should resume her rightful place in the family.

The will was explained by Mr Jefferies soon after the local gentry, tenantry, and villagers, suitably refreshed in separate chambers, had departed.

'As some of you know, the late Sir Thomas reviewed his will a few weeks ago, after a lapse of many years. There can be no doubt that the document I have here is indeed his *last* will and testament or that it reflects his wishes at the time of his death. However, it cannot be denied that he was expecting to live for several more years and that in one respect at least his premature decease has created a partial anomaly. Of that more anon.

'It is unnecessary, in my opinion, for me to read the document out word for word. The will is inevitably quite simple for the bulk of the estate passes by entail to the elder son. Sir Thomas's free estate – the only part over which he had personal discretion – amounts to some £50,000. Naturally, he believed that his first duty was to provide an independent income for his widow. Accordingly, the will sets up a £20,000 settlement in which Lady Bertram has a life interest. That guarantees her an income of £1000 per annum in addition to monies she enjoys from her own marriage portion.'

He paused so that Lady Bertram could voice an appropriate comment. She made some word-like but inarticulate noises that were taken to convey grief, gratitude, and resignation in equal parts – and reached for her spiced vinegar.

'Apart from a few legacies, the remainder of the free estate is divided equally between Sir Thomas's four children. This decision – the new element in the will – was arrived at only after much deliberation. Clearly it provides parity between all the children as far as the free estate is concerned, but it leaves the new Sir Thomas with appreciably less to run the estate than his father, and it means a significant reduction in income for, er, Mrs and Mr Cheviot. Obviously the special claims of elder son and elder daughter (if they be admitted as special) could not be reconciled with the personal interests of younger son and daughter. Under the previous will, Mr Edmund and Mrs Yates received next to nothing, at least during Lady Bertram's life.

'I know that Sir Thomas discussed with his heir the effect of the will on the running of the estate and that certain economies and policies have been agreed. It had

213

been his intention to warn Mrs Cheviot of her unavoidably reduced expectations, and to explain the reasons. He hoped that this would enable her to put money aside from current income over the next several years. But that was not to be. In the circumstances, it would have been his wish, I believe, that Mrs Cheviot's situation and comfort should be borne in mind with particular sympathy. It will be for the head of the family to decide whether some *ex gratia* consideration would be in order.'

'How much money does each of us receive from the free estate?' asked Maria urgently.

'It will be not less than £7000, nearer £8000 perhaps. There are incidentally, a number of legacies: £1000 to Mrs Edmund Bertram; £250 to Captain Price; £100 each to Mrs Norris and Mrs Price; and several legacies of £25 or £50 to family retainers and estate workers.'

'That all sounds very fair and satisfactory,' said Julia with a broad smirk. 'I confess it is more than I had expected. Now at least we can redecorate the dining-room in town and engage Mr Elliott as cabinet-maker.' The honourable John Yates nodded his head responsibly. He was rich enough to ensure that the money was not frittered away on mere necessities.

'Dear Sir Thomas,' said Fanny, trying (unsuccessfully) not to weep.

'Very sound, very just. No less than I would have expected from my father,' said Edmund, putting his hand consolingly on his wife's shoulder. 'I shall be able to give my indefatigable curate an extra £50 a year. But can the estate afford this egalitarian munificence? Jefferies? Tom?'

'I can only repeat,' said the lawyer, 'that your father went into it all most carefully. He was convinced that if his successor continued with the present, sensible policies all would be well.'

'Don't worry, Edmund,' said Sir Tom, 'if I get into deep

water I can always call on you. Why, with two livings – one of them worth a good £700 – and an unencumbered £8000 on top of your marriage settlement, and a wife who turns out to be a positive heiress, you will soon be able to procure an arch-deaconry. And why stop there? Soon as I've found my way in Parliament, damned if I won't get you a bishopric!'

'My own legacy is, of course, entirely at your disposal, Tom,' said Mrs Norris. 'It was as unexpected as it was considerate. I have never sought pecuniary reward for my small services to the family, nor counted the cost of my poor efforts. If the late Sir Thomas assessed them at precisely the same level as my sister Price (whom he met but once in his life and that on his wedding day), it is not for me to question his judgement. My own attitude to capital has always been that any I have is held in trust for the younger generation. As to whether you make use of it now, Tom, or wait – it cannot be for very long – until my own will is read between these four walls, that must be your own decision. I only urge that such considerations as the repair work seriously needed at White House or the comfort of my declining years be set aside entirely. They are of no consequence whatever.'

'I shall move in to the west wing like Sir Thomas's mother when we were first married,' said the widow. 'The views are very nice and the rooms smaller and warmer than here. But what will I do about pug? I fear she will pine. She is used to such large rooms and plenty of brocade. I must build her a pretty new kennel as a reward for being a good girl.'

Maria sat in glum silence. She and Charles had both realised that the new dispositions would reduce their already overstrained income by nearly £500 a year.

'You are very silent,' said Julia with a hint of sisterly challenge (and triumph) in her voice. 'Are you not pleased that my father has seen fit to give the same share of his free estate to his poor, weak daughters as to his male heirs?

215

Is it not a "vindication of the rights of women" from a most improbable quarter?'

'On the contrary, the will is a clear breach of faith with one daughter, if not a breach of contract. The financial protection I was promised has been taken away.'

'All legal obligations have been honoured to the letter,' counselled Mrs Norris helpfully. It was her first chance of giving Maria useful advice since their Liverpool days together.

'I was not addressing you, aunt. Would you kindly—'

'Nevertheless, it was I who acted on your behalf in the original arrangements. As a result, I know better than anyone else, with the exception of Mr Jefferies, of course, what was intended and what was legally undertaken.'

'Very well. Was it not intended that I should have at least £750 a year?'

'I cannot recall the exact figure but—'

'Yet you are claiming to know all about the business.'

'I was going to say that the final figure was nearer £850 per annum. A handsome income – and a most decided drain on the estate – which you have enjoyed for nearly ten years.'

'It is misleading to call it a drain on the estate. What is an estate for if it may not be used for the benefit of the family which owns it?'

'It is not for the exclusive or privileged use of daughters. But let that pass. What cannot be denied is that you have received a generous and substantial income while—'

'It was an adequate income granted my father's circumstances. I am not complaining. At the same time it was not overgenerous, and certainly did not enable me to live in the same style as the rest of you. It was never intended to, since my father – understandably – felt little love for me at the time, only responsibility.'

'You would have had even less but for my intercedence.'

216

'That's as may be. The point I am trying to make is that he intended I should have the security of that income for life. I recall you telling me as much.'

'Not so. Legally he only committed himself—'

'I am not questioning the letter of the law. Mr Jefferies will advise me on that. It is the spirit that matters. What did my father intend? He cannot have thought that if I needed £850 a year while he lived, I would only require £350 after his death.'

Mrs Norris smiled commiseratingly, and looked in Charles's direction.

'Yes, dear. I remember discussing the matter with you, and saying I thought you could rely on Sir Thomas's help even after his death. But I also told you that he was fully entitled to change his will. It would have been indelicate, not to say cruel, to have mentioned the possibility of a second marriage at that time, but it is universally acknowledged that a daughter's change of marital status also changes and reduces paternal obligation. The arrangements he had made could not without great difficulty be changed in his own lifetime, but it was only to be expected, only right and proper, that his will would prescribe a more equal division of his free estate. As Sir Thomas said, when we were discussing it the other week, "You are Mr Cheviot's responsibility now."'

'Quite true,' said Charles. 'My dearest, I think you should accept the inevitable. There is nothing to be gained by challenging what cannot be altered. Your father's will is clear and fair.'

'You know very well,' proceeded Maria, ignoring her husband's interjection, 'that Charles is not wealthy, like John Yates. Marriage has not reduced my financial needs, quite the reverse.'

Whatever her private sympathies, Mrs Norris could not but heed the wider family interest. 'The choice was yours,

217

Maria,' she explained patiently. 'You cannot claim that anyone made the match. Not with your *second* marriage. It is most unlike you to cavil at what is surely an equitable arrangement. Sir Thomas's issue are treated as equals which is most à la mode, and so it should be. Anything else might produce family ill-will – something I deplore above all else.'

'But the effects of that equitable treatment! Do you not see that the results will be the exact opposite? I shall be very poor and the others will be rich. Tom inherits a prosperous estate. Julia is already married to a wealthy man, and simply becomes a little wealthier. The same goes for Edmund who, as Tom says, is already one of the best beneficed clergymen (entirely through family connection, mark you) in the diocese. But in the name of equality, the poorest of the four children shall become poorer still. It is monstrously unfair.'

'Unto him that hath shall be given, unto him that hath not shall be taken away even that which he hath,' said Edmund to no one in particular.

'I do not believe that even my father subscribed to that harsh, uncharitable creed, Edmund. It does credit to neither your heart nor your cloth.'

'I stand corrected,' responded the theologian meekly.

'The will is evidently of recent date,' pursued Maria. 'Who suggested that the previous one should be discarded? Whose idea was it for my father to compose a new one? Was it yours, Aunt Norris?'

'I was no longer his confidante,' she replied evasively. 'Sir Thomas would hardly have heeded my advice on such a matter even had I presumed to proffer it.' Mrs Norris walked away to the window, her overplayed unconcern suggesting guilt to Maria. All the more surprising therefore, that after a short, embarrassed silence a voice said,

'It was I – I think.'

'You?' Maria rounded on Susan, suddenly losing all control of her temper. 'You little upstart! What business was it of yours? I was in that will before you were born. Why did you have to interfere? Haven't you got enough already? Oh, of course, I see it all! You're another Fanny. A penniless schemer just out for number one. Just trying to feather your own nest. Is it not enough that you've trapped poor old Tom? Must you have my money too? What have I ever done to you, Susan Price, I'd like to know. Or were you put up to it by the others? By Julia or Fanny – Or Holy St Edmund over there?'

'Really, Maria, you go too far' – exclamations of warning and protest came simultaneously from Tom, Edmund, Charles, and William. They fell on deaf ears.

'Yes, I warrant it was you and Fanny in league. The fortune-hunting Price sisters wheedling their way into the old man's favour and all the time behaving as if butter would not melt in their mouths. I can see it all.'

'Fanny and Susan not only did their duty by Sir Thomas, they also gave him their love,' said Mrs Norris in all justice. 'It cannot, with the best will in the world, be said that you did either.'

'Cupboard love and canting hypocritical duty. At least I was honest. We all know my father was a pompous, sanctimonious, bigoted old despot. And you'll go the same way, Edmund, if you listen to that little prig of a wife of yours.'

'How dare you talk like that, you of all people? You who besmirched the family name, who broke your sacred marriage vows, who – hold your tongue, madam.' Further words failed Edmund, his anger being tinged by satisfaction.

'Spoken like a true clergyman! Trust you to bring that up, Edmund, the professional forgiver of trespasses. You know very well that I did no harm to any of you. I am the only one

219

that suffered, and still do, still must, it seems. Thanks to my pietistic, charitable, Christian family . . . Thanks to the two creatures who now control the Bertram fortune. For that's what it has come to, hasn't it? The Price sisters effectively own the whole lot, since they clearly control their husbands – and controlled my father too. Pah!' Suddenly (far too late) Maria realised the danger and futility of her words. Her rage subsided as quickly as it had arisen and she threw her arms despairingly round her husband.

Silence descended.

'Look here,' said Tom at length, 'I move we all take a glass of Madeira. No sense in having a family row. Nothing like a good malmsey to, er . . .'

'Susan dear, see if you can find my smelling salts. I hate it when people have words, and so does poor little puggy,' said Lady Bertram.

'If Maria is quite finished, I for one am prepared to forgive and forget,' said Edmund. 'We owe my father no less.'

'With Sir Thomas not yet cold in his grave it would be most unseemly to prolong the quarrel,' agreed Mrs Norris. 'Let us forget anything untoward ever happened. Maria's temper, as I well know, has always been quick. When she has one of her tantrums she says things she does not mean, or does not intend others to hear. She cannot help herself. Fanny must surely be familiar with the trait and will accordingly discount the wild and baseless accusations which have been hurled against her. But it has been a sorry trial for poor Susan. We must all assure her that none of us think her the upstart or schemer which Maria asserts, and that we all rejoice in her – and Tom's – married happiness. No one who actually knew dear Susan would credit for one minute the possibility of her plotting to gain control of the Bertram fortune. The very idea is laughable and I, for one, shall erase the slander from my mind for ever.'

220

'I'm sorry. I apologise,' said Maria expressionlessly. She left the room, followed after some hesitation by Charles.

'That was a very foolish and regrettable episode,' he said when they were out of earshot.

'Yes, I suppose I overstepped the mark.'

'What on earth did you do it for?'

'I've said I'm sorry.'

'Do you realise that you have succeeded in antagonising your whole family?'

'I cannot help that. Please don't—'

'What do you mean you can't help it? You are a rational being, are you not? Honestly, you return here after nearly ten years and proceed to insult virtually every relative you possess. Just when we were all getting along pretty well. I am ashamed of you, Maria.'

'All right, I lost my temper. I am sorry. Now forget about it. Like Edmund.'

'Losing one's temper is no excuse for saying what you said. To call your father a sanctimonious bigot not two hours after you've buried him—'

'Well, it is true. And it is also true that Fanny is a prig and Edmund a pious humbug. Surely you can see that?'

'I can see that you are behaving like a spoilt child. Besides, I disagree. They are all perfectly agreeable, apart from your aunt. Fanny is certainly demure but there is no harm in her. Susan seems a charming little thing. In future, please remember that and try to comport yourself with at least a modicum of dignity, even if you—'

'Don't lecture me, Charles. I do not like it. Anyone can lose their temper. It's over now.'

'Is it? I wonder. Well, don't lose your temper again. It is gross self-indulgence.'

'You speak as if one can help it.'

'One can,' said Charles frigidly.

221

'I don't think you understand at all. You don't feel things as much as me. You are too cold. When I realised that all those people with their long, reverential faces had been plotting to steal the money intended for me, for us, my head seemed to explode. Little Susan was the last straw. I could no more stop myself saying those things than I could stop a sneeze. They don't signify.'

'Oh no, they don't mean a thing! They have cost us hundreds of pounds but are of no significance whatever.'

'What do you mean?'

'Simply that the result of your little "sneeze" will be that we get exactly what is specified in your father's will and not one penny more, whereas if you had restrained yourself—'

'We might have been allowed a little extra? A little more fraternal largesse. Would you have me grovel to those Price girls for a handful of my father's silver?'

'It is not a question of grovelling. Normal social behaviour would have been quite adequate. The lawyer as good as said that some arrangement ought to be made to tide us over. He implied that your quarterly allowance should be continued for a while (at Tom's discretion). Not a chance now, I would say.'

'So that's it. Now the cat is out of the bag. All that moral indignation was purely mercenary.'

'Far from it. Not but what the continuation of your allowance for a further year, say, would make it much easier for me to finish my opera and finalise other plans for replacing our income.'

'Yes, it would be useful, but it is not so indispensable that one has to humiliate oneself. If the worst comes to the worst we can always use a little of the £7000. We may be poor but we are not penniless. I am sorry I have not brought you a fortune Charles, but £7000 is better than nothing. Please kiss me.'

Charles walked away sulkily. After a cold silence he said, 'As it happens I can stop myself sneezing if I wish.'

'Then why do you not do so? You sneeze frequently.'

'Because I enjoy it. And I suspect that you enjoy losing your temper and shouting.'

The remainder of the visit passed off with some awkwardness but without any renewal of hostilities. A further apology was offered and, with varying levels of conviction, accepted. Tom, Susan, and Lady Bertram were genuinely unconcerned; Edmund applied his professional skills to an act of forgiveness; Fanny prayed that reduced circumstances would increase Maria's prudence; and Mrs Norris constantly reminded them all that it was their duty to forget all the unkind things Maria had said about them. Nothing further was mentioned about the possibility of Maria's previous allowance not being terminated too abruptly until both the Cheviots and the Yateses had departed.

'I say,' said Tom to his wife, 'we never went back to the question of Maria's money. Fact was I did not like to bring it up in case there was another scene. Do you think I ought to do something about it?'

'Yes,' said Susan. 'After all, in a way Maria is right. She *is* the only one who is poorer as a result of your father's death, even if you are all receiving equal shares. If you can do something to ease the transition for her, poor thing, I am sure it would be appreciated.'

'I think so too. I shall have a word with Edmund about how much to give her and for how long. You liked your cousin, eh, in spite of what she—?'

'Apart from the time she turned on me, yes. She is charming and very beautiful, but not so worldly wise as she thinks.'

223

'Bit self-centred though. Always was.'

'We all are. Fanny says your sister was spoilt outrageously as a child.'

'Shouldn't be surprised. I say, old Yates was in pretty poor shape!'

'He has never been prepossessing, but he is amiable enough.'

'And the artistic Mr Cheviot, what did you make of him?'

'Quite a welcome addition to the family. He did not talk to me very much.'

'Too clever in some ways. But I liked him. Must be a good man to have at a party. Sings and plays like a professional, I understand.'

Notwithstanding Maria's accusations, when consulted Edmund and Fanny readily agreed that the Cheviots should be given help beyond the call of testamentary obligation.

'Jefferies evidently discussed the matter with my father,' said Edmund, 'and if he thinks something should be done, I feel we can do no less.'

'It is tantamount to a dying request,' added Fanny, 'and therefore binding.'

'The only question is, how much?' said Tom.

'And for how long?' added Fanny.

'And in what form?' put in Edmund.

'Suppose I maintain Maria's allowance for a further year or two? The estate revenues could manage that, I imagine, particularly if the rains reach Antigua in good time.'

'That would be most generous,' said Edmund. 'Yet I question whether that is really the kind of arrangement my father had in mind. After all, that is not so much giving money to Maria as taking it away from the estate. Your first duty – for the sake of the whole family – must be to the estate. To deprive it of, say £1000 or £1500 *at this particular time* could be something you would live to regret.'

224

'The estate must come first, I see that. Well, suppose we shorten the time to nine months or six?'

Mr and Mrs Edmund Bertram considered the new suggestion. 'Certainly that seems more realistic. However a payment of, say, £500 in a year when the estate's expenses are bound to be heavier than usual thanks to the funeral, the legal costs, the legacies, and so forth, would probably exceed anything my father had in mind.'

'I had rather, in a case such as this, do too much than too little.'

'To be sure. Yet there is a point beyond which generosity does harm both to the donor and to the receiver. It becomes a form of self-indulgence which leads to pride and the expectation of gratitude on the one side and humiliating dependence on the other.'

'Besides,' said Fanny, 'any funds which are taken from family revenues and sent to Liverpool are lost for ever. They will be spent (prudently or imprudently as the case may be), whereas retained here they are invested in the estate for the good of the whole family, including Maria.'

'Perhaps then, it would be better for all if the sum were diminished to a level which the estate would scarcely notice but which would still represent a useful increase, by comparison, in Mrs Cheviot's new income. She will have £350 to £400 a year from my father's will. A further £150 or even £100 a year from the estate should meet my father's wishes (as hinted at by Jefferies) and Maria's expectations.'

'There is no knowing but that she may be expecting very much less than that,' said Edmund, thoughtfully. 'In effect you are proposing an annuity, albeit a relatively small one. Yet if Maria lives twenty years – and she may well live thirty or forty – the cost will add up to several thousands.'

'The annuity would be an annual drain on the estate such as Sir Thomas, had he thought it necessary, would

225

surely himself have included in his will,' said Fanny. 'It is not for us to know better than Maria's father, the most just and thoughtful of men in the eyes of many, if not those of his elder daughter.'

'Yet Jefferies definitely thinks that support of some kind is a moral obligation. I feel it too.'

'So do we all,' said Edmund. 'Moral support is incumbent upon us. We must welcome Maria back into the fold unconditionally, even if she sometimes behaves more like a wolf than a lamb. Finance is a different matter.'

'Let us consider,' said Fanny. 'She has, shall we say £350 per annum from her father. That alone is enough to support a family in comfort. Many stainless clergymen make do on very much less. Then too, as Mrs Norris mentioned the other day, she has £100 per annum arising from Mr Henry Crawford's "conscience money". And Mr Cheviot himself has a position for which the remuneration, I daresay, is on a par with at least one of Edmund's livings. All in all, I do not think their income can be much below ours.'

'If at all,' agreed Edmund. 'Not significantly. Jefferies surely meant that Maria should be afforded the perquisites of her family connection: extended visits to the house (occasionally); presents of game and fish (in season): perhaps a piece of furniture or a picture to remind her of Mansfield and her father. I see no call to insult her by offering money. To patronise her now might open up old wounds. However, you must decide for yourself. Far be it from me to have the final word.'

Susan was less sanguine when the conversation was reported to her. She insisted that Mr Jefferies had had money in his mind, and she persuaded her easy-going husband to send his sister an unconditional £100 together with a good copy of Downman's portrait of Sir Thomas.

William Price remained at Mansfield. Before their departure, Maria and Charles had both noticed his silence at the ancestral home of the Bertrams. In Fanny's presence, particularly, he gave little hint of the intrepid sailor by whom they were half-amused and half-impressed in Liverpool. At Mansfield he was conventional almost to the point of invisibility.

'That is what Fanny likes and expects,' said Maria. 'She has always been devoted to him, and he to her.'

'His sister is the strongest character. Mrs Edmund is a most interesting study. She speaks very little and appears to defer to all and sundry, yet I suspect that she usually gets her way. Even Mrs Norris is afraid of her. Tom, Susan, and Edmund all dance to her tune, if they know it or not. Damned if I understand how she does it.'

'At a pinch, Susan would stand up to her. But in general you are right. More's the pity you antagonised her by singing in that way.'

'I see no reason why she should hold that against me. If an error at all it was involuntary. My subsequent apologies were decidedly handsome, if privately insincere.'

'She has convinced herself that you were trying to make a fool of her husband, and Aunt Norris encourages her belief. Those two have become allies, even if they will never be friends.'

'A pox on them both.'

At Mansfield Parsonage, meanwhile, William Price continued to behave as if butter would not melt in his mouth. He had always been very close to Fanny yet he found himself visiting his younger sister at the big house more often than might have been predicted. This was not only because Sir Tom kept a better table (and much better cellar) than Edmund but also because the new baronet manifested affectionate and unqualified solicitude for Maria. He was full of plans for entertaining the Cheviots as soon as a proper period of mourning was over; on one occasion he even resuscitated the idea of some private theatricals for their enjoyment. Susan, for her part, longed to meet Bertram and Leonora, her nephew and niece.

Where the big house forgot Maria's outburst, the parsonage forgave it again and again; where the big house looked forward with pleasure to a visit from the engaging Cheviots, the parsonage prayed for their moral rehabilitation. William did his best on behalf of Maria and on one occasion defended her with such warmth that Mrs Norris began to suspect yet another cousinly attachment between the Price and Bertram families. The thought was too horrid not to be cultivated. Fanny made no such deduction but was disappointed in her brother for the first time in her life. He remained the person she loved most in the world after her husband, but when the time came for his return to Liverpool, the parting was not as painful as it had been in the past. Mrs Norris asked if he would again be staying with his fair cousin and was more than satisfied by the offhand but agitated manner of his answer.

(I suppose the unanimous warmth of Uncle William's reception at Rodney Street might have confirmed his aunt's agreeable suspicion, but it seemed merely familial to Maria.)

Chapter Five

Soon after the return to Rodney Street, Charles had to attend another funeral. A cotton-master who had been in a regular way of business with Randall and Company for many years had died, and Mr Randall being himself on a protracted visit to London, Mr Cheviot was the partner who could best be spared from the office to represent the firm. He set off to Manchester with very bad grace, determined to sing as much and as loud as he pleased.

Next day he returned in high good humour with a story to unfold. 'I have never enjoyed a funeral so much in my life. Comedy, tragedy, farce, pathos – it was an education in the way of the world and the spirit of the times.'

'Tell me all about it,' said Maria obligingly.

He was only too happy to be equally obliging (having rehearsed some of the scenes of the way home). 'The funeral itself followed the same libretto (the esteemed Cranmer) as at Mansfield church last month, but there the resemblance ends. Not one of the cotton-master's numerous family was present, for example, and the front pews were empty apart from the widow, a gaunt, veiled figure in black. The rest of the church was thronged with the lower orders of society. Sam Clayton's mill workers had been given a half day's holiday, and their rendition of "O God our help in ages past" was so lusty I could not hear myself sing. A very good thing too, you will think, no doubt?' Maria merely smiled.

'After the interment it was back to t'mill for the mob and up to t'mansion for those with clean shirts or some pretensions to gentility. I found myself in a carriage with two other people, a middle-aged couple who seemed to be relishing the proceedings.

'"Poor old Sam," beamed the gentleman, "what a way to go!"

His wife cheerfully admonished him to show a proper respect for the dead, and as her husband only responded with a considerate chuckle, appealed to me for support. Was this how our common acquaintance should be remembered? I explained my presence as cousin and representative of Percy

Randall, and asked some conventional question about the sud-
denness and unexpectedness of the death.

'"Very sudden," said Mrs Farnes.

'"Not at all unexpected," said Mr Farnes. Then, with
unconcealed glee on his part and but perfunctory reluctance
on hers, they imparted the cotton-master's story. It seems
that after years as a widower he had recently married a
woman young enough to be his granddaughter. The match
had been opposed by his family on the grounds that the woman was beneath him. But Sam Clayton wanted her beneath
him, even if it proved his undoing – which, in fact, it did,
after three energetic months. Mr Farnes was positive that
his old friend had passed away *in flagrante delicto*, hence his
opening remark, "What a way to go". A spot of envy there I
fancy. The upshot is a young widow richly endowed with all
his worldly goods.

'"No offence," concluded Mr Farnes, "but if you are on
the catch, Mr Cheviot, better not waste too much time." I
assured him I would institute divorce proceedings as soon as
I returned to Liverpool.'

'Remind me to furnish you with suitable grounds, my
dearest.'

'To continue. We arrived at the mansion, newly built,
about twice the size of, say, Mansfield Park and three times
as ugly. The widow was waiting for our condolences. She was
still veiled but I could now see that she was slim rather than
gaunt, distraite rather than distraught. After uttering meaningless conventionalities we were told that rooms had been
prepared for those like myself who would not have time to
return home after the funeral baked meats. A cold collation
was spread in the dining-room and consumed with gusto. I
must say, the late Mr Clayton had a very good cook. His
choice of sherry wine likewise met with approbation, the
mourners without exception finding that it mitigated their

melancholy. It prompted Mr Farnes to make a speech. To his good wife's relief he made no reference to the immediate cause of death. Eventually the local inhabitants bowed to the widow and about six of us were shown to our rooms. It was now about four o'clock. We were warned that a further meal would be served in the evening.

'From my window I had a fine view of the Clayton cotton mills. Everyone was now back at work, physically and spiritually refreshed by the break. After a while, wearying of the prospect, I decided to explore the house.

'Though ugly it had every comfort, including a Turkish bath. There was a well-equipped gymnasium, a conservatory, an orangery as well. All had an unused look, as if waiting for house guests who never arrived. In one room only there were faint signs of human life. Four gentlemen were gravely playing at billiards in an atmosphere heavy with cigar smoke. They held the dead man's cues with all due reverence and exhibited only the most doleful satisfaction on the potting of any ball. I was not asked to join in the fun.

'At last I came to the music room. Here I was presented with a choice of instrument: a small organ; an Erard harp; or a curious six-pedalled keyboard affair. Impressively hideous, the latter was some nine feet tall and I soon decided that it must be the Dutch giraffe piano which I had heard of but never seen. I sat down and tried the effects of different pedals. One gave a bassoon-like resonance, another produced the sound of bells. Two seemed not to be working, the fifth was a damper, the sixth a sustaining pedal. Having mastered these details, I played a funeral march, a dirge, and a *dies irae* in slow, gloomy succession. The piano had an easy action and immense volume. It was loud enough to raise Mrs Clayton from her repose, if not Mr Clayton from his, for suddenly I heard a voice.

'"Please play something a little more cheerful, if play you must."

'I jumped up guiltily but she brushed my apologies aside. "No further funeral marches. I am sad my husband is dead but not so hypocritical as to pretend that I am inconsolably wretched. Pray continue in a lighter style."

'I do not think she appreciated – as I suddenly did – that my musical lamentations, because satirical and insincere, were in the worst possible taste.'

'I did, however,' put in Maria.

'I made sure you would. Since she wanted cheerful music, I provided excerpts from *The Barber of Seville*. Though I say so myself, I played quite well, considering it was all done from memory. Lost in admiration for Gioachino's genius, I forgot about my audience until the very end. When I looked around, Mrs Clayton was fast asleep. Later she told me she was not very musical.

'Our party at the evening meal was limited to the four billiards players, Mrs Clayton, and myself. Each course was copious, but billiards had whetted the appetite and the four gentlemen did them full justice. Never very lively, they became more and more somnolent as they ate, and when Mrs Clayton left us to our wine they became positively drowsy after a couple of glasses. I therefore joined my hostess in the drawing-room where she was taking tea.'

'You haven't yet described her, Charles. What is she like? Is she handsome? Is she – a lady?'

'She is not of gentle birth, as you will hear. She moves well, has regular features and chestnut hair. She also has £5000 a year. Any woman with chestnut tresses and £5000 a year is handsome, nay beautiful. That is a well-established fact.'

'Is she intelligent? Educated?'

'Nothing in particular. She has common sense and on occasion can be articulate and perceptive. Her manner is direct. It was very soon clear that something was preying on her mind and that she was going to honour me with her confidence, whether I wished it or no. All at once she said, "Two acres and a cow. That was what Sam Clayton started with; as did my own grandfather. They came from the same village and we are the same stock. So his daughters have no right to look down on me."

'It seems that Sam Clayton had two daughters by his first wife. Both were married more for their father's mills than their personal attributes. Their husbands soon tried to force the old man into retirement, but he knew his *King Lear* and told them to wait. They resigned themselves, hoping that their father-in-law would be civil enough to pop off before he became a burden to others. So when Mr Clayton announced his intention to marry again, they were horrified. He was a virile septuagenarian – suppose he had a son! They bullied him, tried to prevent the marriage, claimed he was senile, demanded that he hand over the business lock, stock, and barrel to them. At first, Clayton still intended that his daughters should be the principal heirs, but he insisted on making some provision for his bride-to-be. The daughters and their husbands resented any diminution of inheritance and declared that the business could not afford to support fortune-hunting trollops. They wanted everything for themselves and in the end got nothing. Sam Clayton threw them out of his house and out of his will.'

'I do not blame him. The daughters are greedy little fools and their husbands are worse. So the second Mrs Clayton inherits the business too. Does she want it?'

'Hard to say. She insists that her needs are modest in the extreme, but when I ventured to suggest making peace with the family by handing over the mills, she refused. "That would be to defy my husband's last wishes. He made me promise."'

233

'How convenient. She is bound in honour not to deplete her wealth. What will happen now? She will marry again most probably and perhaps choose no better than her step-daughters. I suppose we shall never know.'

'But I have to keep in touch with her for a little while,' said Charles. 'The will names Percy Randall as executor, and while he's in London, I am his deputy. Rather a nuisance, but Simpson at the office will do all the donkey work. Or should it be mule work?'

He laughed as if at a joke. Maria looked blank and Charles kissed her. 'Without Crompton's mules, there would be no Sam Claytons, and calico would be twice as expensive. And what have you been doing while I was sampling the delights of Salford?'

Maria coloured. 'I have been entertaining a gentleman. Soon after you left, there was a knock on the door, and guess who it was? William! William Price summoned back to the shipyard earlier than expected. He wrote from Mansfield but arrived here before his letter. Fanny and Edmund implored him to delay his return, but I think – oh, here he is.'

William entered the room and shook hand with Charles. 'It is a relief to see you. On hearing that you were away in Manchester yesterday, I proposed, for appear-ances' sake, removing to an hotel, but Maria would not hear of it.'

'How very proper of you, William. I never knew you were such a dangerous guest. Do many people see you as the Don Giovanni of Rio Mersey?'

'Far from it, but you know how they talk. Mrs Cheviot's good name must be—'

'People would certainly talk did they know that I too spent the night under the roof of a married woman. To be sure she was a widow and was chaperoned by four elderly friends of her husband's, but that would be no

234

obstacle to any self-respecting scandalmonger. Opportunity turns the most trifling indiscretion into iniquity where anyone has a mind to it.'

The two acts of innocent impropriety were dismissed without further ado.

Chapter Six

It is unclear who first suggested holding a little hop at the Rodney Street house. It might have been Charles, in sturdy defiance of his debts; it could have been William in thankful discharge of the mourning enjoined by Sir Thomas's legacy; most likely it was Maria on guard against the reproach of being thought too prudent and house-proud. No more enjoyable way of compounding the Cheviots' pecuniary embarrassment could have been devised. Captain Price, aware of his cousin's circumstances, resolved to bear the costs himself, for the thing must be done in style or not at all; it was soon resolved to make it the talk of the season. The wheel of fortune thwarted his intentions, however. He took Maria to her first race meeting and with beginner's luck, or perhaps an eye for a horse, she won enough money to pay for the ball. The sensible course would still have been to accept William's offer in return for the hospitality he had been given, but sensible people do not throw good parties, win at the races, or have books written about them. Maria not only insisted on footing all bills but also rearranged the evening on even more extravagant lines.

Charles's contribution was to be artistic. What more opportune occasion for trying out the music of his opera than a ball? Some half of *Henry V* was already composed. The opera, in fact, was proceeding apace and since it included an English square dance (for Hal's army), a quadrille and

235

a minuet (for court scenes), a waltz (for Bardolph) and a mazurka (for Fluellen and Gower), the guests could all join in without learning the words or music. Inspired by the challenge, Charles added a stirring patriotic song for the young king, a coloratura air for Kate, and a love duet, working half-way through the night more than once. Maria, for her part, decided to augment the customary violins by all the other instruments in the Theatre Royal's orchestra, an expedient which led in turn to the employment of every music copyist in Liverpool. A group of singers had been engaged, too, before it was appreciated that the chamber which constituted a fine gallery at Rodney Street was yet not so magnificent that it could do service as concert hall and ballroom for band, chorus, and two hundred guests – including perhaps a Molyneux or Stanley. There was nothing for it but to take the Wellington Rooms instead.

'It will be well worth the extra expense, for I am sure (and so is Mr Barrington) your music will sound much better in a space designed for concerts and recitals.' As well as the respectable rich, who were rising to propertied gentility, and the indigent gentry, who were falling unless prepared to marry trade, the guest list included Mr Barrington, proprietor of the Theatre Royal, and such Liverpool Bohemians as had claims to elegance, talent, or wit.

Satisfied with these arrangements, Maria purchased a new pianoforte for her husband. It is truly astonishing how far a sum from the turf will stretch when a determined woman wishes to turn money into harmony.

Though it lasted scarcely above eight hours or fifty dozens of champagne, the ball was considered a fair success. Musical offerings, it is true, interfered with serious gaming, but were fast enough and noisy enough for the auditors simultaneously to eat, drink, and be merry without spoiling the general effect. Mr Barrington, all too

236

used to vociferous audiences, so appreciated the music that he promised before witnesses to stage the opera as soon as it was ready. Everyone remarked that Maria was the most beautiful woman in Liverpool, but few of them held it against her after eating the lobster salmagundy. The gallant Captain Price danced – gallantly. Although his ears stuck out, he was never in want of a fair partner, and several young women marked him out as a possible source of prize money.

In short, everyone agreed that it was a good little hop, even if no Stanley, in the event, honoured it with his presence. Only Maria ever knew how much it cost. She continued to decline any contribution from William and, as the accounts came in after his departure, regretted it. She did accept the five other books by Miss Austen which he had suggested she read. His mind on his muse, Charles neither interfered nor criticised. He left the financial side to his wife and she left the musical side to him. Captain Price sailed off, not to South America this time, but to Portugal, where Dom Miguel must be taught a lesson.

'It seems too easy,' said Charles, who was, on the contrary, finding it very difficult to resume work. 'Those songs and dances I dashed off just before the ball were not particularly good, you know. Two of them were just tunes I wrote years ago dressed up to sound new. Yet everyone cheered. The public seems very gullible or incredibly polite. Of course, they were drinking our champagne.'

'The tunes are better than you think. I love your music and I love you too. But sometimes you do not work hard enough (as regards either of us).'

'You are prejudiced in my favour. But do you suppose anyone at the party was able to judge the music on its merits? Barrington, for example, is a musical ignoramus. He may have a shrewd notion of how to fill a theatre, but he neither knows nor cares anything about art. The party

237

success proves nothing. I need an informed, critical assessment of what I have done so far and constructive advice on how to proceed. Had I finished my musical studies in Bologna, I might be able to finish the opera instead of being caught in a quandary. I feel as if I am composing in the dark, writing little numbers without seeing the work as a whole.'

'I expect all composers feel like that sometimes, even that friend of yours in Italy who has written so much.'

By an extraordinary coincidence, Gioachino Rossini had arrived in London that same day. He was still feeling seasick and was confined to lodgings at number 90 Regent Street with his wife and parrot. A month later, Charles Cheviot read in the newspapers that 'Signor Crescendo' had been received by the king at Brighton Pavilion. He decided to visit his old friend, and wrote to him at once. That evening he showed Bertram and Leonora the portfolio he had kept from his Bologna days. They were unimpressed by scurrilous sketches of Padre Mattei and the *liceo* staff, but laughed and laughed at a series entitled Orchestral Macaroni.

Rossini took his time to respond, but when he did so he was cordiality itself. England, he declared, was the most liberal country it had ever been his pleasure to visit, the king was affable and discriminating, London society had taken him – at fifty guineas a night – to its bosom, and all that he lacked for total felicity was the company of his *caro* Carlo. Engagements, however, were numerous and he had to finish the first act of *Ugo, Re d'Italia* for delivery to Mr Ebers at the King's Theatre. How charming that his old friend was also composing an opera of regal theme. He longed to hear the music but must wait until the spring.

238

Resigning himself to a wait, Charles requested and obtained leave of absence from his duties with Randall & Co. His cousin had returned to Liverpool and wanted to know about Sam Clayton's funeral and will. Charles obliged with an abbreviated version of the recital he had devised for Maria.

'Mrs Clayton used her power of appointment to make me the executor while you were away. Briefly, the will leaves almost everything to her. As a result Mr Clayton's family, particularly his two daughters, are hopping mad. The lawyer and I suggested that Mrs Clayton should give half the estate back, and after a certain amount of resistance, she reluctantly agreed to do so.'

'Handsome of her, and possibly foolish.'

'She does not need all that money and would not know what to do with it. All she wants is a modicum of security and comfort. However, that is beside the point, for the family turned her down flat. They demand the whole lot and have decided to contest the will.'

'On what grounds?'

'They claim their father was of unsound mind when he wrote it, that Mrs Clayton deliberately enticed a dying man, that their exclusion from the will goes against natural justice – and much else beside. They would appear to be in the hands of an unscrupulous lawyer.'

'It may just be a stratagem to frighten Mrs Clayton into increasing her offer.'

'If so it has failed. Her response was most spirited. She has withdrawn the offer altogether and decided to run the mills herself. If they do take her to court, she will fight them tooth and nail.'

'With a good chance of winning, I should imagine.'

'Her lawyer seems to think so. There is no real doubt as to Sam Clayton's sanity and plenty of evidence that it was only his daughters' greed and malice that excluded them from the will. Everyone knows that their husbands are on the make and only married them for their expectations.'

'And Mrs Clayton herself, is she, in fact, a penniless adventuress? (I almost hope she is, in view of the daughters' treatment of my old friend.)'

'She is something of an enigma. It's possible she may have been on the stage at one time. Her family used to live in the same area as Mr Clayton's – smallholders, yeoman stock. I think she went up to London. Yes, she could be called an adventuress, I suppose, but she also seems respectable. Of course, I hardly know her. I have only met her the once. Most of our intercourse has been conducted through the lawyer by letter.'

'Much younger than Clayton, I believe?'

'And probably younger than his daughters. About thirty or, to be gallant, twenty-nine. And handsome to boot.'

'No doubt she will find a second husband before you can say Jack Robinson.'

'True. Incidentally, it would be her third marriage. Mrs Clayton has a daughter who receives a substantial legacy from the will when she is eighteen. The Clayton family are contesting that too. It seems the old fellow was fond of the little girl, intended to adopt her, and wanted to make her independent even if her mother's fortune fell into other hands.'

After a pause Mr Randall concluded, 'The only cause for concern is the prospect of Mrs Clayton trying to run a group of cotton mills. Our own company has no small interest in the efficiency of the Clayton operation. 'I hope she has got some good advice.'

'She knows she can always consult me.'

'That's all right then.' Mr Randall raised his eyebrows slightly.

'And I shall consult you,' said Charles, with a deprecating smile. 'Unless you wish to take the whole thing over, as originally intended.'

'That is the last thing I want to do. Let us leave well alone, but please let me know about the lawsuit. I take it that nothing will happen until after your return from London? The law always grinds exceeding slow.'

With some trepidation Maria consented to accompany Charles on the London visit. It was ten years and ten hundred scandals since her indiscretion; none of the main participants lived in town; Mrs Rushworth was forgotten and Mrs Cheviot unknown. Yet she was nervous. Charles promised they would go to the opera and the drama and to concerts at Almack's, but let the past alone, leave no cards on former acquaintance. For a day or two after their arrival, Maria, fearful of recognition, saw accusatory eyes wherever she went, but she soon realised that as in Liverpool and New York she only attracted admiration (or envy).

No one admired her more than Signor Rossini, who, at their first meeting, and in the presence of Madame Colbran-Rossini, declared himself her slave. Latins, Charles later explained, are given to exaggeration. In fact, the susceptible Italian's gallantries were deliberately overpitched to allay the suspicions of his wife. His heart (only a philanderer's heart) was at once attached by Maria, and his bland passion persisted for several weeks. He soon became resigned to her unattainability, however, and his attentions never exceeded the bounds of flirtatious propriety. The great composer consummated his love magnanimously, by helping the loved one's husband. For his part, Charles won the friendship and support of La Colbran by making a most

241

flattering likeness of her at their second meeting. The singer compared her flabby husband with her charming portraitist and decided not to be jealous of Maria. Thus they formed an harmonious quartette.

Rossini was indeed in benevolent and generous mood. He was earning more money in London than he had ever earned in Italy, and doing very little for it. He tinkled at the piano while his wife sang; occasionally he sang too; sometimes he was joined by his compatriots Buzzi (horn) and Dragonetti (double bass) but all they had to do was improvise, and bow to the applause. At first he had conducted two or three of his operas at the King's Theatre, but Mr Ebers had not paid him, nor had he paid, as contracted, for the first act of *Ugo, Re d'Italia*. This was Rossini's only real quarrel with London, but since he was already putting by £1000 a month where he had never before saved one farthing, and since it meant that he could in all conscience abandon work on the new opera, it did not worry him unduly. It was rumoured that Mr Ebers was losing £250 a week at the King's Theatre and that he would not be able to renew the lease.

For these reasons the maestro was happy to place a good deal of time at Charles's disposal. He studied the score of *Henry V*, noting all the signs of inexperience but also finding plenty to admire. Despite its shortcomings, the music made him want to sing, and sing it he did (improving it as he went along). Soon he was suggesting significant changes and extravagant embellishments. Charles was astonished at the speed with which the corpulent, indolent sybarite seemed to work, the effortless spontaneity with which he overcame problems of continuity and recitative, and the endless supply of new tunes which he dispensed to his protégé as if pouring wine. Later Charles realised that most of this help was borrowed from the first act of *Ugo, Re d'Italia*, but when he hinted as much, by dubbing his own opera *Enrico, Re*

242

d'Inghilterra, Rossini denied it with a lofty wink. After extensive revisions had been made, La Colbran was persuaded to sing two of the airs to Prince Leopold of Saxe-Coburg and his guests. Nobody noticed that the music was not entirely Rossini's, nor that the words were by Shakespeare and sung in English.

After five or six weeks, they returned to Liverpool with the opera still unfinished but essentially composed. Charles's original notions had been augmented, his mistakes rectified, his technical problems resolved. Mere industry was required now to fulfil the joint inspiration. The result would be no *Barber of Seville*, perhaps, but perfectly presentable 'school of Rossini' such as never before achieved in England. Mr Barrington perceived enough to become greedily enthusiastic and urge Charles to finish the opera as soon as possible, even proffering a second £25 advance.

A few weeks later, Rossini left England for good, taking a post at the Paris Opera. Elsewhere, his successor in Naples, one Gaetano Donizetti, was working on his new opera. It was called *Emilia di – Liverpool*.

Chapter Seven

Unfortunately, business and domestic affairs now claimed Charles's prior attention. Mr Randall, his cousin and protector, was preparing for the day when he would take a less active part in the company's affairs, and David Randall, his only son, had moved to Liverpool, along with someone known to all as Mr Hugh. The latter was an ambitious but unpopular young man who worked sixteen hours a day for the glorification of the house of Randall. Though still in his early twenties his effect on the fortunes of the company had already been beneficial, and all its members were resigned to him exerting influence due far more to industry and merit than to family connection (he was, in fact, some kind of cousin, rumoured to be illegitimate) for decades to come. In return for unswerving loyalty to both Randall and Son, Mr Hugh was permitted to make more and more of the important decisions. He soon made it clear that family sinecures played no part in his vision of the company's future, and Charles realised that his job was no longer as safe as it had been. More than ever aware of mounting debts at home, he now found it expedient to devote several hours a day to business matters and to control his instinctive dislike of the earnest young merchant. He very soon stopped making jokes at Mr Hugh's expense, therefore, though perhaps not quite soon enough, and his newly discovered entrepreneurial zeal prompted him to write to Sir Tom Bertram about the possibility of Randall & Co becoming involved in the management of the family estate in Antigua.

At this time too, executorship of the Clayton will again devolved on Charles. As foreseen, comparatively little had happened in his absence. Mr Randall hinted that the long-standing business links between his company and the Clayton undertaking might now be reviewed to everyone's advantage. The hint was not lost on Charles (who little realised, however, that his cousin had deliberately abstained from personal initiative in order to give Charles the opportunity of earning credit), and he decided on an early visit to Manchester.

At home the Cheviots were soon reminded of matters they had put aside in London. Debts had piled up and income, thanks to capital expenditure, had declined. This necessitated further capital expenditure, justified as before by the prospect of Charles's future earnings. As a concession to thrift Maria reduced the Rodney Street staff by three, the chief result of which was a marked decline in household comfort and efficiency without –

since wages were low – any significant saving. Though an excellent hostess on the important occasion, Maria had little interest in the day-to-day running of the house and made few demands on the remaining staff. She did not mind untidiness. Charles, on the other hand, both noticed and minded it. Neat and orderly in many ways – his handwriting, for instance, was meticulous – he chafed at the increasing slovenliness in Rodney Street, only to be told that the servant problem was worse than it had ever been owing to all the new employment possibilities in the area.

'There are no bad servants, only bad mistresses,' he replied with satisfaction.

'Or bad masters. You instruct them if you think I am so incompetent. I claim no pride of office.'

'That is ridiculous. It would be quite wrong and you know it. My position . . . it is not my job to—'

'There you are, you see. You are very quick to criticise but when it comes to doing anything constructive you refuse to help.'

'You know very well that I haven't enough time as it is. I am out half the day and when at home I should be working on the opera in order to keep the wolf from our unwashed doorstep. How can I supervise the servants as well?'

'We have been back more than a month and you have not written another note.'

'Certainly I have. The fact that I have produced comparatively little does not mean that I have been idle. And I am making progress, too, not but what the filthy mess in this house is far from inspiring.'

'I do not believe the mess (as you call it) has any bearing. You just use it as a convenient excuse. If anything, I blame the children as you spend more time in the nursery

245

than in the music room. That is no way to write an opera, oh laudable parent!'

'And what, pray, do you know about musical composition? It is not like working in a counting house, you know.'

'I never said it was, but now you mention it, I do not see all that much difference. Like any kind of work unless you spend time actually doing it you achieve nothing. Unless you go hunting, you kill no foxes.'

'What the devil has hunting to do with—'

'Unless you sit down and compose even when you feel uninspired, inspiration will not return. It won't come out of thin air.'

'If you know so much about it, perhaps you would like to try. "Hunt" away, madam, to your heart's content.'

'That is as unhelpful as it is silly.'

'It is precisely what you were suggesting when you asked me to take charge of the servants.'

'No. That was different. Ordering servants about requires no special gift, it is just a nasty, boring job which should be left to officious people like Aunt Norris. Oh Charles, why do we have to quarrel like this? Is it my fault? My dearest, you have the talent, I am only trying to help you use it. Please say you love me.'

'Oh, is that what you are trying to do? Many thanks.'

Squabbles of this nature gradually became a regular part of their domestic life. Without enjoying them, each brought a certain relish to these childlike duels and each, on occasion, seemed deliberately to court another confrontation. In so far as either emerged victor or vanquished, righteous indignation or sullen resentment were the commonest after-effects. Maria soon forgot but Charles brooded, and it was after several such tilts that he paid his second visit to Mrs Clayton, combining it with some other Randall business in the Manchester area.

The Mosley Arms, Wednesday, 6 o'clock

My dearest Maria

It is now six and thirty hours since I took a cool, distant leave of you, and every minute has been a reproach to me. You are the best and loveliest of wives and I the most wretched of husbands, not worthy so much as to gather up the crumbs from under thy table. Sometimes, it is true, there are rather too many crumbs under thy table, but that is one thousandfold preferable to the crumbless immaculacy of the house I visited yesterday.

I hasten to continue the saga of Mrs Clayton, though I cannot decide whether yesterday's exchanges cleared up or deepened the mystery of who she is and what she was. Whatever the truth, she is now running the mills herself and not without success. 'I would have made a good shop-keeper,' she remarked soon after my arrival. 'Money is not so difficult as your sex pretends.' To which I responded, 'It is a profound mystery to me, madam, and always has been. As your executor, I applaud your acumen in all except your choice of executor. The one thing I advise is that you never take my advice, especially on matters financial.' Pithy and succinct, as always.

Pretty soon she turned the subject to matters matrimonial. Should she marry again? How soon? Whom? I put on my wisest countenance, said she should indeed remarry, opined that the customary year of celibacy after a spouse's death need not apply in her case since her husband's relatives were already irremediably affronted, but urged her to choose with extreme caution. She suggested that a woman could accept or decline but scarcely choose.

'Cynics down the ages' (I pontificated) 'have claimed that it is always the female who chooses, except in certain arranged or dynastic marriages. It must undeniably be the case where the woman is handsome, independent, and well-endowed with worldly goods. In all such cases the

247

choice is the woman's and the field is wide.' She wanted to know if I was a cynic.

'Only as your counsellor and executor. What I say is sensible. One must always give sensible advice. My private view is that mutual affection, preferably love at first sight, is the best ground for marriage, but as your executor it is my duty to warn you that such a view is dangerous error.'

She has had several proposals already. Most are animated by her fortune, though one was from a wealthy, elderly man who desired what Sam Clayton desired, and one was from a suitable and blameless young man whom she does not fancy. 'I am not capable of love at first sight,' she lamented, 'but I am capable of some spark of interest. I know I could never be interested in Mr Holdsworth. Yet it would be so convenient. The mills are a heavy responsibility, the house is far too large, both need a man even if I do not.'

I told her to sell the house and hire a manager rather than make a hasty, reluctant marriage. To my surprise she agreed. I suspect that was the first time in my life anyone has ever taken my advice. It was soon settled that the house would be sold through the good offices of Randall & Co. To which end I was given the grand tour so that I could make notes and sketches of the principal rooms.

I have never seen such a tidy or such a gloomy place. Everything is new, spotlessly clean, and polished. Nothing looks as if it has been used, no chair seems to have been sat on, no book has been cut, no portrait has any function beyond the provision of extra surfaces to be dusted each day. Only the schoolroom showed signs of use by a human being, with a pair of dolls negligently bestriding a stool. 'My daughter must be having her riding lesson,' said Mrs Clayton, unconsciously rearranging the dolls. She said her servants cleaned the house from top to bottom every day and after that were free to go about their own business. She seems embarrassed by having servants.

248

Sam Clayton's bedroom had a telescope mounted in the window bay facing the mills. When the cotton-master was feeling too tired to go down to his spindles in person, he inspected them by telescope. It invariably revived him! The magnification was astonishing: I could see every detail of the cramped conditions, mean clothes and wretched bearing of the workers of the mightiest nation on earth, and as I pondered the lot of my fellow-men, Mrs Clayton moved on.

I went into the adjoining room and finding it empty was just leaving when I caught sight of her in a glass. She was half-undressed and striking the attitude of some lovesick but wanton Arcadian shepherdess awaiting her divinity lesson from a goatish immortal. I blinked my embarrassed incredulity and the image obliged by reassembling itself into a competent painting in the manner of François Boucher, but the auburn-haired nymph still bore a startling resemblance to Mrs Clayton. It was a charming thing, immodesty posing as innocence, painted, I surmise, fifty years before its double was even born. I envied the artist's technique, admired his model, and studied both as a humble fellow-craftsman. When my hostess came in, I ventured to presume that Mr Clayton had bought the picture because the nymph looked somewhat like Mrs Clayton, there was something about the eyes and hair.

'No, Sir, he bought me because I looked like the picture, my eyes and hair.' As I could think of no response, she continued, choosing her words with care but speaking without expression. 'Do you want to see more, Mr Cheviot? On the whole I think you have seen enough, perhaps too much.' Here she paused and touched the spring of her lorgnette. 'Yes, you have made notes on all the main rooms, the others are of no consequence. Besides, it is the hour of my afternoon visit to the mills. On another occasion perhaps we may have a rubber of piquet. I have had no one to play with since my husband died. It would be a nice change from solitaire.'

249

I bowed, was honoured, would prove but a poor opponent, must proceed on my way. 'Thank you for your advice, Mr Cheviot, and do find a buyer for my little nest.'

On the road into Manchester, I startled the coachmen by singing *Henry V* right through (as far as I have got) and giving several encores. You would have enjoyed the performance, my darling Maria, but I suppose Mrs Clayton would have found it soporific. (Perhaps she was an artist's model.)

My dearest, I long to return to Rodney Street, I long to resume work on the opera.

Believe me, Yr truly affec[te] husband,
C. Cheviot

Chapter Eight

Mr Charles Cheviot's business proposition reached Mansfield Park at an auspicious moment. Once again the Bertram estate in Antigua was more productive of anxiety than sugar. Revenue was down, costs were up, the plantation manager – too long in the job or too fond of a liquid end product of his crop – was far from well. To cap it all, the island had suffered its worst drought for many years. Accordingly, the suggestion that Sir Tom should conclude a deal with Randall & Co. seemed a good one. The Liverpool concern already managed one estate in Antigua and had other interests in the Leeward Islands. Professional management should be able to reduce costs and increase production, and further economies would be effected by combining the two estates into one. In due course, other plantations might be taken over too. Antigua would become a Randall-Bertram preserve, with the Bertrams not only sharing the profits but being guaranteed a generous dividend in bad years as well as good. Tom pondered the outline proposal and the more he thought about it the more he liked it. To be spared the worry of the estate while enjoying increased benefit from it seemed an opportunity not to be missed. The alternative would be for him to go out to Antigua again himself, but in his married state he had no wish to repeat such a lengthy venture, nor was he sanguine that his own presence would yield tangible improvements. There seemed only one obstacle to the Randall proposal.

'Your brother Edmund would mislike it,' said Susan. 'And so would Fanny. I know they would, Tom, I sense it – but I am not sure why.'

'You may be right. Perhaps there is no need to mention it to them. They have an interest in the family trust but no personal shares in the enterprise so far as I know.'

'But Aunt Norris has. She told me that for years your father used to let her invest £50 per annum in the family business.'

'So he did, I remember. He used to pretend that it was a useful contribution when, in fact, it was a great nuisance.'

'Do you think Aunt Norris would approve of her precious shares being looked after by Mr Cheviot?'

Tom Bertram laughed nervously. 'No, I suppose not. But, of course, it would not be by Cheviot himself. Frankly I think Charles is no more the man of business than I am, but he's a good sort of chap. I like him and want to help him. Randall and Company are a sound concern, I believe, and would give my aunt, as well as the rest of us, an improved return on capital.'

'In other circumstances, that would be welcome to her, but I question whether the increase in income will be sufficient to overcome her suspicions of Mr Cheviot.'

'You may be correct. However, my aunt has such an insignificant share-holding that I am under no obligation to inform her of any changes. The best plan is to say nothing to anyone until I have discussed the matter with old Jefferies.'

Susan was surprised that her husband should take such an independent line. Though head of the family he normally treated his serious-minded brother as an equal partner, if anything deferring to Edmund's views. Of a sunny and uncritical disposition, Susan had cordial relations with all her relatives, but she was well aware that in a battle of wills her husband was no match for the Edmund Bertrams and Mrs Norris. However, she realised that Tom still felt uneasy about the effects of Sir Thomas's will on the Cheviots and about his own, weak agreement to the family interpretation of how Maria should be compensated. Going through with the Randall proposal would indirectly atone.

Accordingly, Sir Tom consulted Mr Jefferies. The family lawyer did very little work on behalf of the West Indian property and therefore had no pecuniary interest in maintaining the *status quo*. On the other hand, the transfer of management to another company and the proper protection of the Bertram interest would, no doubt, involve substantial fees.

'I see merit in the scheme. Worry about Antigua almost certainly contributed to your father's untimely death, and your own visit to that pestilential tropic so undermined your health as to lead to protracted illness. Further visits, which will surely be required of you from time to time, may have similar, or worse, effects. I am confident that a contract with Randall and Company, if carefully considered and professionally executed, would be beneficial, and shall therefore draft out heads of agreement for your consideration.'

Tom baulked at the idea of enjoining Mr Jefferies to keep the project secret from his brother. Even if the two should meet in the next few weeks, itself unlikely, the normal canons of confidentiality would surely be observed. It never occurred to Mr Jefferies, however, that this was anything but a family

252

decision as he rightly believed that the brother, and to a lesser extent Mrs Norris, were Tom's normal counsellors. Certainly he saw no reason for discussing the Antigua proposals with the others, nor did he see any for not doing so. In practice, he had no occasion to talk to Mr Edmund but he did have a meeting, some two weeks later, with Mrs Norris.

On her husband's death, Mrs Norris had been granted a life tenancy on the White House by Sir Thomas on generous but vague terms. A nominal rent was fixed, for the punctilious payment of which she expected regular gratitude, but it was unclear to what extent it covered the repairs, maintenance and improvements which were periodically effected. At first, Mrs Norris had successfully argued that all of them should be borne by the estate since the estate would benefit in due course, but after her departure with Maria and subsequent return she had deemed it prudent to pay for minor improvements, such as a new bedspread for the spare room, herself. It was to broach a capital investment of little use to her but of great value to the estate in the long run that she sought a meeting with Mr Jefferies.

'As you know, I never consider my own comfort. Self-denial is second nature to me. However, I do feel it my duty to ensure that the White House shall be in better condition when I quit it than it was when I first took up residence in it. To this end I have made improvements, too numerous to mention, entirely at my own expense. The money means nothing to me. So long as others may benefit, my efforts on behalf of the property (which I regard as a family trust rather than a properly rented abode) shall be without stint. The particular improvement which I want to discuss with you, Mr Jefferies, is one which, inured as I am to the severities of our climate, has no special appeal to me personally. It would, however, increase the value of the property and be an asset to the estate. I wish to install a bath and hot-water system.'

'I am sure that Sir Tom – all of us – appreciate your concern for the White House, Mrs Norris, but is not the installation you seek something of an extravagance, if you do not require it for your own use?'

'Mr Thomas Crapper of London estimates the cost to be little more than an hundred guineas. Extravagance indeed – it would be money well spent.'

'Even Mansfield Park has no bath chamber.'

'The Park does not need one. The Park has adequate staff. It is no trouble for the maids there to fill tubs whenever the family requires. My own household, however, is modest, and my only maid has quite enough on her hands without fetching and carrying hot water. Indeed, it is to save work for poor Edith that I am principally resolved on this course. I may seem old-fashioned, but I cannot bear the ill-treatment of servants. We have obligations to them just as much as they have duties towards us. I would be prepared to pay for the work myself if it were not for the fact that investments of this kind are, by the agreement I made with Sir Thomas, the estate's responsibility. Once undertaken, I honour all agreements absolutely.'

'It could be argued that the estate itself should make such decisions. With the new regime in Antigua, however, it should be able to manage something next year if not this.'

Mrs Norris pricked up her ears. 'The new regime in Antigua? Ah yes, to be sure.' She was loath to acknowledge that she knew nothing about any new regime. 'You approve of the – the new broom, do you, Mr Jefferies?'

'Why certainly. The management out there has been unsatisfactory for far too long. Randall and Company have an excellent reputation. Yes, I think it would be advisable to wait until after transfer has been effected before proceeding with your project, Mrs Norris, but I see no objection in principle . . .'

254

It took Mrs Norris a very few minutes to divine that Tom Bertram intended to put the management of the family plantation into the hands of Randall and Company. Further thought convinced her that, whatever Mr Jefferies might imply, her own house improvement plans were not dependent on or related to a deal being concluded with – specifically – the house of Randall. A change on Antigua might be overdue, but the new broom could be any of a dozen West Indian trading concerns. A company which employed such an unbusinesslike dilettante as Mr Cheviot, however charitable, was not the safest concern to which the estate could entrust its affairs. Others no doubt had better judgement. Mansfield Park's copy of the Annual Register soon gave her the names of several companies and enough information to sustain arguments in their favour as opposed to Randall's.

'It would be so much more convenient to deal with a London firm,' she said to Edmund and Fanny, having called at the parsonage for the first time in weeks. 'The post to Liverpool is most unreliable, and no one ever *goes* there – whereas the family has a house in town. Oh, I am sure Mr Cheviot would do his best, but he is a musician – perhaps I should say a *singer* – rather than a businessman. It is just like Tom to want to help Mr Cheviot (indeed we all do; I hold nothing against him myself) but the estate should not be put at risk out of kindness. It would appear that there are several London concerns better qualified to handle our West Indian affairs than Randall and Company.'

'One has overlooked, nay forgotten, Mr Cheviot's unfortunate conduct in the matter of Psalm 90,' said Edmund. 'Fanny and I both wish him well. For that very reason I cannot endorse my brother's plan. I cannot be accessory to a scheme which will give Mr Cheviot a direct interest in the exploitation of slaves. As you know, I abhor slavery from the bottom of my soul and have always had grave

255

reservations about the family plantation. For that reason I decline to have personal shares in the enterprise and only accept a modest, and in effect unavoidable, share in dividends from the trust. The latter – and, if I am pressed on the point, the consumption of sugar at all – I justify by the conviction that, unlike others, the Bertram plantation is ultimately being developed in the interest of the estate workers. As I understand it, the Bertrams are custodians charged with the husbandry and improvement of the plantation until such time as the negroes themselves are, with God's help, able to run their own affairs in a civilised, Christian way. That time will surely come, though it may take hundreds of years. Meanwhile, Liverpool remains a slave town at heart and is the last place on earth I would look to as a source of progress for Antigua. I agree with you, aunt, we should look to London. Only there shall we find a concern which believes that the complete emancipation of slaves (in God's good time) is compatible with agricultural efficiency.'

Sir Tom put up very little defence against the altruism and compassion of his brother. He already felt that he had behaved in a slightly underhand manner and gladly accepted the chance of changing heart without losing face. In Liverpool, where the prospect of the deal had added to Charles's standing, the Bertram decision brought sarcastic comment from Mr Hugh and imprudent but ineffective correspondence from Maria.

Chapter Nine

As if to compensate for the Antigua disappointment, Charles was offered a post at the Theatre Royal. Unexpected by Maria, the offer did not come as a complete surprise to her husband. Over the months he had had several meetings about *Henry V* with the owner-manager, Mr Barrington. Discussions had largely centred on the opera's progress and the likely date of its completion, but from time to time there had been hints about the possibility of an official contract. Without committing himself, Charles had encouraged Mr Barrington to believe that he would welcome a link with the theatre if suitable terms could be agreed.

Everything hinged on the terms. Deficient in musicianship himself, Mr Barrington believed there might be commercial advantage in improving the company's singing and playing, but he was determined to hazard as little as he need on an experiment which might not pay. Charles, on the other hand, was interested in augmenting his funds and hoped to do so at no more personal effort than that involved in periodic advice and criticism. Both wanted something for nothing.

Maria read the terms suggested by Mr Barrington with growing excitement. She saw the chance as a turning point in her husband's life. 'This is a wonderful opening, Charles. You must take it whatever the cost. It is your vocation.'

'Barrington drives a hard bargain. The remuneration is less than my Randall salary and the duties will be much more time-consuming. I cannot do both jobs.'

'Mr Barrington implies that your income will be made up to its present level and more by a share in the profits, and by increments if you sing or act yourself.'

'That is his way of making a miserable pittance look respectable. Very possibly there will never be any profits. Barrington and his book-keeper need only declare one when it is in their interest.'

'Perhaps he could be persuaded to improve the terms.'

'Let us hope so. It will have to be a significant improvement.'

Maria sighed and wondered to what extent her enthusiasm was merely naïve. 'I still have enough money for our needs. Even without Mr Barrington's pittance we would be better off than most of the theatrical profession. All that I have is yours.'

'I cannot allow – besides, if I take on this new work I shall never finish the opera.'

'Why not? Practical experience in the theatre should help the opera. And Mr Barrington says you will receive at least one "benefit" each season, probably two.'

'That means I shall receive a little more money if I do a great deal more work, viz. if I become actor and singer as well as composer and director of music.'

'Does it matter how hard you work if you are doing what you really want to do? Surely you are not afraid of hard—'

'I have never been afraid of work,' said Charles inaccurately, 'and I ask no favours of anyone, but I resent being exploited.'

'Apart from the remuneration, do you think you could make a success of it? Would you like to be a musical Kean or Garrick? That is more important than the money side.'

He replied in the affirmative but neither of them was sure he meant it. Behind the bravura of his salon personality, Charles had his share of self-doubt. It was easy to scoff at poor performances on the provincial stage but something quite else to expose one's own talents to the test of public approbation. Could he, in fact, raise the theatre's musical standards sufficiently for anyone to notice, and was his own signing significantly better than that of the company's principal tenor? He was reluctant to put himself to the test unless he was very well paid. In addition, did he, in fact, want to throw in his lot with rogues and vagabonds? Actors were good company in green room or tavern; Kean was a genius; Garrick had mingled with the highest circles in the land, but the Liverpool theatre was not the place for a gentleman to make his home. Writing plays or operas was compatible with his station in life but joining Barrington as an artistic mercenary meant complete dependence on personal merit. If the classless freemasonry of the stage had its appeal, so did the privileges, however eroded in his case, of birth.

Mr Barrington improved his offer and Charles reduced his demands, but the gap remained and in the end it was decided to wait until *Henry V* was finished. Time enough to consider a new arrangement in the light of the opera's fortunes. Charles meanwhile would be free to devote all his artistic energies to composition. Piqued at the postponement of an interesting and inexpensive experiment, Mr Barrington decided substantially to re-write the proposed contract in his own favour. At first he had been in danger of uncharacteristic generosity in consideration of Mr Cheviot's social status.

Maria was disappointed. Less gifted than Charles, she had a greater respect for the arts which came so easily to him. Originally more secure in her family background, she had become indifferent to it. Already wounded by convention, the lost star of *Lovers' Vows* was attracted by the nonconformity of the acting profession, and she secretly hoped that if Charles joined the Theatre Royal, sooner or later she might do so herself. Success on the stage would justify her past, extenuate retrospectively her deviations from the straight and narrow.

For once she held back when her arguments failed and her wishes were ignored and Charles, reacting to Maria's muted dismay and half-conscious that he might have repudiated some tacit aim of their married life, tried to atone by love and work. He locked himself away and composed for hours on end. In Maria's company he was warm, tolerant, and affectionate. On the surface harmony reigned in the rest of the house as well as the music room. Bertram exhibited scant interest in music, but little Leonora

259

listened in unseen rapture (peeping through the keyhole) as her father worked at the piano.

Frequently left alone for long periods while her husband composed and her children were occupied by nurse or governess, Maria started visiting a ladies' card club of an afternoon. Trying to be sensible, she only gamed for low stakes and had enough luck to convince herself that the diversion was harmless. Sometimes she finished with a small surplus, other times with a deficit, but over the weeks deficits outnumbered surpluses and before long she started dipping into capital to pay debts. Unlike Maria, Charles had no interest in gaming and could not understand its allure. It seemed, as he said, a stupid way of losing money and a sordid way of making it.

Mrs Clayton's affairs, meanwhile, continued to occupy some of Charles's time. 'I am having to do more than I bargained for, what with the sale of the house and the lawsuit, but it should be finished quite soon. I think we have disposed of the mansion already. Considering that the wealth needed to sustain that scale of living is seldom accompanied by such poverty of taste as finds the style of Château Clayton acceptable, I think we have done well. They say my pictures made the place look more elegant than it really is. Anyway, some new parvenu has been persuaded to take it complete with unread books, unnamed ancestors, and most of the unwanted servants. Mrs Clayton and her daughter are planning to move to a rustic villa within walking distance of the mills.'

'What about the naked nymph?' asked Maria. 'Does she go to the villa or stay in the mansion?'

'She is being sent to a picture restorer to have her
bosom covered and her bodice more securely tied.' This
was said with a straight face, but may have been a joke.
'The lawsuit now looks like being settled out of court, since
the daughters have been advised by counsel that they have a
poor case. Mrs Clayton still wants to make a gesture, though
we have warned her that charity may only exacerbate the
family feud. The largest mill is physically apart from the
other three and could be made over to the daughters as
an independent going concern. It seems they may now
accept the offer, though without surrendering their right
to continued ill-will. They have been very badly advised
in the past. Whether Mrs Clayton will live to regret her
magnanimity remains to be seen.'

'I hope not. The offer does her credit. She has behaved
well in my opinion, whatever her background. Did you find
a manager for her?'

'Yes, but it is too early to tell how good he is.
Unfortunately he is married. The ideal would have been
an industrious bachelor who could have married the owner
as soon as he had proved his ability. She is still pursued by
men more enamoured of her property than her other assets.
I suspect she enjoys the luxury of saying no but pretends to
find it merely tedious.'

'Meaning that she is secretly flattered by these attentions.
How like a man.'

'She doth protest too much. If she mentions the matter
again I shall advise her to play the giddy widow, engage
in silken dalliance with militia officers, or entrap some
lusty young fellow of two and twenty. What do you say
to that, Maria?'

'The third suggestion may be wiser than you suppose.
A malleable young beau, fresh from Cambridge, would be
my choice if I were in her shoes. Who wants some worn out

261

man of the world? But has Mrs Clayton sufficient courage? She sounds too conventional, with her spotless house and her tightly-laced bodices. Would I like her Charles? Have we anything in common?'

'No,' he replied emphatically, striding to the piano.

Chapter Ten

At last the opera was finished.

'Finished enough to go into rehearsal,' Charles told Mr Barrington. 'It may need some final polishing here and there.'

He played through the score, singing all the parts himself, and to the not very musical impresario it sounded fine: tuneful, martial, and patriotic. Liverpool was no Venice or Milan but its concerts were usually well attended and it boasted enough music lovers to ensure houses of £300 or more for several nights, particularly if some of the town's favourite players took part.

'Opera has never done very well at the Theatre Royal and an unknown piece by a little known composer, as yet little known I should say, is unlikely to take more than £200, at most £250, a night,' said Mr Barrington carefully. 'In such cases it is customary for the financial risks to be shared by composer as well as the Theatre Royal.' Mr Barrington was not a man to take unnecessary risks and saw no reason for not driving a hard bargain with the superior Mr Cheviot who had been so unaccommodating when his services would have been really useful to the theatre.

Charles frowned. 'Are you suggesting I should pay to have *Henry V* performed – as if I were some amateur or nobody? Surely you are aware that the intelligentsia of Liverpool has already acclaimed excerpts from the opera and that it is agog to see the finished work?'

'To be sure, to be sure. The auguries are excellent. But public opinion is notoriously fickle. Is it fair that all the risk should be mine? The cost of staging a new opera is not inconsiderable. All I ask from you is a partial guarantee against losses.'

'I have no knowledge of theatrical finance,' said Charles, 'and have always heard that it is full of trickery. For all I know, you may make losses on half your productions. I cannot guarantee you against them.'

'There is no question of it. My dear Mr Cheviot, your suspicions, though in this case unjustified, do credit to your perspicacity. Rest assured your liability will be restricted to performances of *Henry V* and, in the event of losses being incurred, you will have the right to call off further performances. The cost of rehearsals, the cost of production shall be my sole responsibility. Only if takings fall below, let us say, £200 shall I ask for some small contribution and even then I shall share the loss with you equally.'

'Pray explain in more detail.'

'Certainly. It is really quite simple. Suppose that instead of taking the expected £250 or more – and remember that the house can take as much as £500 – suppose we take £150. In such a case the difference between £150 and £200 would be borne by yourself and myself equally. In short you would stand to lose £25. A paltry sum. Naturally you may show the contract I shall draw up to your legal advisers.'

'I most certainly shall. However, I have not written the opera in order to lose money, but rather to make it.'

'Precisely. And that is my reason for staging it. And to show my faith in the work, I shall pay you fifty guineas the day we start rehearsals. That will be an advance in respect of your share in the profits. Furthermore, if you personally sing the part of Henry you shall be paid the same as my principals, even though you are as yet untried. But let us leave

263

the sordid details. My lawyer will draft a contract and yours will alter it as he thinks fit.'

'Very well. As to the cast, I confess that the tenor rôle is suited to my voice, but would it not be better to have a well-known opera singer? Garcia has been my model and would be my first choice.'

'Garcia is the highest-paid singer in the world. To bring him to Liverpool would ensure a financial deficit. Besides, it is most unlikely he would deign to come here even if he were free of engagements.'

'Mr Barrington, none of your stock company is a better than competent vocalist. To have a fair chance we must call upon real singers with experience of opera. I thought that was understood.'

'So it is. I have it in mind particularly to use singers who are well-known in Liverpool. Many of those who have enjoyed popular success at, for example, Mr Kalkbrenner's concerts have operatic experience and are already favourites here. You shall have your pick of these. I have already engaged Mrs Quick who is positively adulated after her triumphs last year.'

'Have you indeed? For the part of Kate. Well, she may not be Madam Pasta but by all accounts she can sing a bit. *Presta ma non Pasta* as one might say.'

Mr Barrington looked blank.

Mrs Polly Quick had made a small talent stretch a long way. Good-looking and strong-willed, she had early recognised her limitations, quitting the London stage as soon as she had played a few operatic serving-maids. Helped by the reflected lustre of the capital and, some said, a catholic appetite for provincial managers, she soon established a good connection outside London on both the concert platform and the musical stage. Charles knew her by reputation only, but he was satisfied with

264

Mr Barrington's choice. A local favourite could do his opera no harm.

An adequate cast was duly assembled. Most of the Theatre Royal's stock company had to sing in burletta as part of their normal employment, and some were fairly musical. The better singers were given minor rôles, the remainder, augmented by members of a local choral society, formed the military choruses; half a dozen singers with local successes to their credit were found for the principal rôles; and Charles himself, after wanting to conduct, agreed to play Harry. He was also to direct rehearsals, with help from Mr Barrington.

Apart from Mrs Quick, everyone seemed to learn the music without difficulty and to enjoy singing it. Even the motley orchestra began to make a fair stab at a score which really required twice its number of players. Singing well within himself, Charles noted that his own voice stood up well in comparison with the professionals and was satisfied he would be able to make some stirring effects. Rehearsals were easier and more enjoyable than he had expected.

The only problem was Mrs Quick. It soon became apparent that she considered herself the principal attraction and, as such, a prima donna above direction, licensed to come and go as she pleased. As a result, she rarely attended rehearsals and when she did, not knowing her music, reduced the proceedings to disorder. Though restive in her presence, the cast seemed strangely in awe of the leading lady. It took Charles some little while to realise that for the duration of her present contract at least, Quick was enjoying the special protection of Mr Barrington. No wonder protests about her behaviour were met by indifference.

'Despair not. Polly will be fine on the night,' said Mr Barrington. 'Your fears arise solely from inexperience with

265

artistes. Do you suppose your friend Mr Kean bothers to turn up at every rehearsal?'

'Yes. For a new play, certainly. Not for *Othello* or *Macbeth* maybe. Besides, Mrs Quick is no Kean.'

'Believe me, she could be the making of your opera, my boy. The public adores her.'

'I cannot think why. Her voice is unremarkable, what little I have heard of it.'

'She has presence. Fear not. I shall see that she has her part.'

As the days went by, Mr Barrington's attitude began to change. Confident of his support, Mrs Quick's manner became more and more high-handed, even towards her protector. Rumours about her behaviour began to circulate. One evening she threw an inkwell at Mr Barrington's head (missing the target but breaking a window) after he had mildly drawn her attention to the terms of her contract. Then for three days she disappeared altogether and Charles insisted on appointing an understudy. The best of the company's young actresses had already started learning the part of Kate.

When Mrs Quick returned it transpired that she had been to Manchester to take part in a concert engagement with Mr Kalkbrenner. All Manchester was raving about her rendition of songs by Arnold, Dibdin and Shield, and she intended to repeat her success, at public demand, the very next week, contract with Mr Barrington or no. Meanwhile she was prepared to have another look at Mr Cheviot's silly opera and see what she could do to make it worthy of her skills. Airs by Dibdin or Arnold should certainly be incorporated. Her Manchester programme had consisted mainly of songs which she had adapted to her own vocal style; if she did the same for *Henry V*, it might stand some chance of success.

Much incensed, Charles demanded that her contract be

revoked. Barrington was annoyed and insisted she should be given another chance. Her commercial value to the opera was unaffected by her improper behaviour.

'Is she contracted to you or to Kalkbrenner? I have never heard anything to equal it. Really, it is becoming impossible to work under these conditions,' Charles protested.

'Believe me, I appreciate your difficulties, but to act precipitately now would do more harm than good.'

'She is in flagrant breach of her contract.'

'I know.'

'And you do nothing about it. What is a contract for? You will make yourself a laughing-stock. The whole company will despise you.'

'I think not (and care less). However, I shall take disciplinary action. The contract makes provision for the imposition of fines for certain misdemeanours. I shall fine Mrs Quick – and teach her a lesson. I shall fine her, let me see, yes, I shall withhold three pounds from her money.'

Charles lifted his eyes to heaven, temporarily speechless. 'God give me patience,' he said at length. 'And in the opera I am supposed to make love to this frightful woman.'

It was not to be. Mrs Quick refused to pay the fine and flounced out of the theatre convinced that Mr Barrington would come to her, grovelling on his knees, in order to save the production. Instead he confirmed the understudy in the rôle of Kate, summoned his lawyer, and vowed, not for the first (or last) time, to give up actresses. Rehearsals were resumed in a much happier atmosphere.

Mrs Quick soon reappeared, apparently penitent. She had thought the whole episode over, decided she had acted

267

hastily, and was prepared to let bygones be bygones. She would even pay the fine, if Mr Barrington would lend her the money. The olive branch was scornfully rejected by Charles and she was ordered to leave the premises. Instructions were given that she should not be readmitted under any circumstances. Hearing that his temperamental Pol had transferred her affection to his opposite number in Manchester, Mr Barrington made no attempt to mediate between them. On reflection, he considered her departure good riddance, and began to exhibit an interest in the young understudy. Assuming that his attentions were inspired by the pretty progress Miss Stradling was making with her part, Mr Barrington may have been more musical than Mr Cheviot believed.

And so the rehearsals proceeded towards their climax. Maria began to attend them and, despite fears that the production was being mounted too hastily, was pleased with the way it was taking shape. It was probably too long, she thought, and there were certainly some passages which lacked real drama or relevance, but Charles himself seemed to improve each day. All in all, Maria suspected that the present version of the opera should be considered essentially an experimental first run but she kept these views to herself.

It was heartening that even in its present state the opera should represent Charles's first earnings from music. Their lawyer had succeeded in wringing better terms than Mr Barrington had offered, despite the latter's insistence on a number of indemnity clauses which, he maintained, though of no practical significance were invariably included in such contracts to safeguard both parties.

Shortly before the opening night, a heart-breaking notice appeared in the *Liverpool Mercury*:

Mrs Quick presents her compliments to all those citizens of Liverpool who appreciate the musical and theatrical arts, and unhappily informs them that their most devoted and unstinting servant has been prohibited from appearing, as advertised, in an operatic presentation entitled *Henry V* at the Theatre Royal owing to the infamous and unprecedented behaviour of the manager, Mr Barrington, and his creature, Mr Cheviot, the so-called composer.

In defiance of natural justice, theatrical custom, and contractual obligation, and despite being billed as the prima donna of the opera, she has now been debarred the Theatre Royal, erased from the cast list, and supplanted in the character of Princess Katherine by an untried, unknown, and inferior artiste, and for no other reason than her appearance at a charitable morning concert with Mr Kalkbrenner. For this offence, for succouring orphans and thereby being the innocent instrument of some slight inconvenience during rehearsals at the Theatre Royal, Mrs Quick is now dismissed, and Liverpool is deprived of a performer it has invariably (if undeservedly) acclaimed hitherto. Yet, an orphan herself, without brother or protector, widowed while still a bride, she would not hesitate before committing the same heinous error again if it meant relief for the weak and suffering.

With oppressed feelings, heart-rending to her friends and triumphant to her enemies (though mayhap they be but two), she now appeals to that town famed for its justice and hospitality. If she has erred surely it is but equitable that she be allowed to make reparation? If her act be merely venial surely she should be reinstated for the sake of her fellow artistes and musical followers?

No stranger herself to hardship and toil, Mrs Quick is dependent on theatrical engagements for her entire subsistence. Is she to be deprived of her own livelihood for seeking to improve the life of others? Is she to be fined (for even that indignity has not been spared) for adding to the widow's

269

mite? Is Liverpool to stand idly by while a helpless artiste is curtly and wrongfully silenced?

Mr Barrington was inclined immediately to refute the appeal.

'A tissue of falsehood, an edifice of fabrication. If the public knew how she was behaving, it would appreciate that we had no alternative.'

Charles, Maria, and most of the company, deeply engrossed in final preparations for the opera, made light of it. They felt that a reply would be undignified and that the storm would soon blow itself out.

'*Qui s'excuse, s'accuse*,' said Charles. 'No sense in drawing attention to the wretched woman. Much better to ignore her. Besides if that concert really was a charity we have chosen an unfortunate pretext for—'

'Charity my foot! Polly charged her normal fee, always does. She told me as much herself. Kalkbrenner may have made some small donation.'

'Even so, it will hardly do to engage in a public duel with her.'

'On the other hand, silence might be construed as a confession of guilt,' said Mr Barrington. 'I must at least publish a notice to the effect that Mrs Quick repeatedly infringed the terms of her contract. If she disputes that she should seek legal redress through the courts.'

Charles shrugged and went back to the rehearsal. Next morning a dignified advertisement from Mr Barrington appeared and as this elicited no further move from the prima donna, the matter seemed closed.

Torn between doubt and hope, Charles had other things on his mind as the rehearsals reached their climax. If only the first night were a success, everything else would follow. England, surely, was crying out for an English opera. Yet he knew that the band was second-rate, the singers were a scratch lot, the production and sets were being skimped, and the opera itself often seemed a mere tissue of musical compromise. Would Liverpool see the faults or the possibilities?

After a technically disastrous dress-rehearsal, Mr Barrington ordered last-minute changes and had his stage-hands hammering, shifting scenery, shouting and cursing far into the night. Charles watched with growing despair. Would they ever be ready? Each man had the work of two, except one, a burly Scot, who strolled around in the middle of it all doing nothing but whistle. An island of calm in a sea of activity, he was supposed to be the supervisor, Charles recalled indignantly. Why did he not control the chaos instead of adding to it with that infernal whistling? Well, it must be admitted that the fellow could hold a tune. In fact, it was really rather musical whistling, quite a virtuoso performance. Suddenly, with a tingling of the spine, Charles realised that he was listening to his own composition, hearing his music for the first time, as others would hear it tomorrow. At this, his doubts dissolved, he became calm, almost confident: if it was good enough to whistle, it must be good enough for public approbation.

Charles went home and slept for nine hours.

Chapter Eleven

The house filled up steadily as the evening's entertainment progressed. A short ballet, a dramatic recitation and a one-act farce all preceded *Henry V*. By the end of the farce the boxes were replete and resplendent with Liverpool's best-dressed theatregoers, many of whom had been at the Cheviot ball. These upper classes paid scant attention, for the moment, to the acrobat and tumbler who next came onto the stage; they were more concerned with each other – and with Maria who sat in the centre

271

of the centre box flanked by the Randall party. As to dress, jewellery, and animation the composer's wife was favourably appraised by some of the town's most acidulous critics.

Downstairs in the pit the middle orders of society were in hearty good spirits with one eye on the stage and the other on the main chance, while up in the gallery a motley and vociferous cross-section of humanity was out to enjoy its money's worth to the full, all six pence of it. Looking through his spyhole, Mr Barrington noted with satisfaction that there was well over £300 in the house and that the audience was no worse behaved than usual.

When the overture began Maria closed her eyes, crossed her fingers, and held her breath. Everything depended on the next three hours. The opera was the true offspring and purpose of her marriage. Oh, let it be successful, please. I promise to spend all my spare time helping the poor and the sick, if only it is a success. After praying for several minutes and hearing not a note, she opened her eyes. Thereafter she listened attentively – to the audience.

The audience seemed to like it. Opening with the tennis-ball scene, it gave Charles an early chance to show his mettle as actor and singer. He exploded into Kean-like fury when the balls were nonchalantly bounced at him by the French ambassador; the stirring call to arms which ensued won applause and only a few half-hearted catcalls. The first patriotic chorus, 'Now all the youth of England is on fire' was cheered heartily, and – to Maria's surprise – even the Eastcheap badinage between Nym, Bardolph and Pistol raised some laughs. Xenophobic jeers greeted the French court on its first appearance, but the mocking parody of effete Gallic manners (the

Dauphin being played by a female contralto) won gleeful approval. The penultimate scene, an ensemble and
chorus based on 'Cry God for Harry, England, and
St George!' received an ovation. Maria relaxed, relief
engulfed her. For Charles's sake, for both of them,
she hugged herself, and forgot about helping the poor
and the sick.

The second act was an even greater success. Every
aria was cheered to the echo except one. Maria was now
listening to the music and almost enjoying it. She was
puzzled by the one failure, since Katherine's half-French
song about the difficulties of learning English had always
seemed a clever adaptation and was prettily delivered by
Miss Stradling but the gallery did not agree. It punctuated
the number with jeers. At the end there was sufficient
applause from boxes and pit for Miss Stradling to take
her bow, but she could not turn a deaf ear to the
concurrent boos.

Act Three contained the best music, including a tender
love duet and multi-dialect trio (which Rossini subsequently
re-used in *William Tell*). All went well until the duet, but as
soon as Katherine opened her mouth the operatic criticism
from the gallery began in earnest. The jeers were now
continuous and it was becoming clear that they were
also planned and organised. Poor Miss Stradling could
hardly make herself heard. Charles rose to the occasion
by determining to out-sing the gallery. He had a naturally
powerful voice, though the quality of his fortissimo was
harsh, and it had the effect of magnifying the soprano's
powers too. What followed was a veritable duel between
stage and gallery, and it was just about won by the
singers, heavily outnumbered as they were. The claque
subsided into comparative silence, licking its wounds. At
the end a storm of applause broke out, three-quarters of

273

the house by now being passionately partisan on behalf of brave Miss Stradling and heroic Mr Cheviot. For the first time in his life, Charles felt the joy of a standing ovation, a joy above all others to the performing artiste, the equivalent of victory in battle. Maria almost fainted in pride and ecstasy.

But the claque was only biding its time. Unhappily the duet was followed by King Harry's exit and Katherine's (solo) cavatina. The gallery now had her at its mercy, and though Miss Stradling began with some confidence this only spurred it on. Soon the boos and catcalls were accompanied by ripe fruit and rotten eggs. The rest of the audience quickly became involved too – boxes cheering encouragement to the singer, the pit demanding silence at the top of its collective voice. Some of its armoury of vegetables was now directed by the gallery at the boxes. Miss Stradling was inaudible and in tears, and when a half-eaten mutton pie scored a direct hit ran off the stage. The claque hurrahed its approval and the orchestra faltered into silence.

Maria closed her eyes and prayed that Charles would return to overcome the claque by sheer force of singing. Instead, Mr Barrington appeared and began the obsequious speech he kept in readiness for high-spirited audiences. He was heard with amused tolerance until interrupted by a cloaked and behatted figure which ran on to the stage to a roll of drums. Loud cheers from the claque as the figure revealed itself to be – Mrs Quick.

She acknowledged her reception with smiles, bows and curtseys, and after several moments of triumph held up her hand for silence. Then, still smiling sweetly, she broke into song with her popular version of Shield's 'The Thorn':

274

From the white blossom'd sloe, I my lover requested
A sprig my poor breast to adorn
No, by heaven, he exclaimed, May I perish if ever
I plant in that bosom a thorn

Apposite as they were to Mrs Quick's position, the words made an immediate impression on her supporters, and fresh applause rent the air. Mr Barrington gesticulated for the singer to retire. Mrs Quick refused to budge, and instead launched into 'The Thorn's' next verse. At this the manager signalled to the wings. Two burly stage-hands (one of them the whistling Scot) came forth, charged the singer, and, taking one arm apiece, began to haul her off – though a vicious kick on the ankle made one of them let go long enough for Mrs Quick to punch the other on the neck. Fresh reserves of vegetable and ovarious ammunition were now brought into the fray. Aerial missiles flew in all directions hitting friend and foe, neutral and belligerent at random, as the curtain fell.

The blocking off of the stage at first brought little respite. With no performer to attack or support, sections of the audience turned on each other, while parties with less relish for the fray left the theatre. Mrs Quick's supporters, cheated of their favourite song, chanted demands for her return: 'We want Quick! We want Quick!' Gradually, however, the incipient riot began to subside. Backstage, Mr Barrington decided to gamble on continuing the opera with Katherine's remaining scenes excluded.

The curtain rose on a half-empty (but half-full) house. The rumbustious and catchy marching song soon won approval, and at the end only token booing greeted Fluellen, Macmorris, and Jamy when they strode to the front for their Welsh-Irish-Scotch trio. They were large, popular actors but, like all the cast, indignant at what had happened and nervous of what might be in store. As well they might, for Fluellen immediately skidded on some fruit and crashed to the boards, losing hat, sword, and leek. The audience expressed its sympathy by prolonged laughter. Grabbing the nearest property department cannonball, the fiery Welshman (true to the part he was playing) hurled it at the nearest of Mrs Quick's supporters. The shot was a bullseye, reducing the hired operaphobe to sudden silence. 'He's done for Tommy,' cried a colleague in tones of deep concern. Someone returned the cannonball and caught Macmorris in the midriff. At this the fiery Irishman, also acting in part, swung his mighty shillelagh at Tommy's friend. It missed its mark but hit a sailor and shattered a mirror. To enforce the peace, Fluellen unleashed another cannonball, while Jamy, in the interest of military discipline and fiery Scotland, tossed his caber-like spear at everyone in general and no one in particular, felling several at one throw.

The audience now turned to self-preservation, many of them endorsing the view that attack is the best form of defence. Seats and lamp brackets were requisitioned as projectiles; gilt from the walls and ceiling was hurled at the stage; the great chandelier was smashed, its smithereens quickly augmenting the broken bottles which were also pressed into service; ripped up floorboards became popular deterrents; a bench from the gallery crashed into the pit, while a number of patrons from the upper floor, unable to contain their excitement, discharged bodily fluid on those below.

Whatever philosophers may say, war can be more fun than art.

Watching Napoleonically through his spyhole, Mr Barrington waited until the fun reached a certain pitch, then hurried to his private room beside the prompter's box. He knew how to procure a cease-fire; Barrington's Box was the answer.

Four feet deep by two feet square, the metal box was stuffed with torn-up paper and card, some of it damp, and had round apertures at the front and back. Attached to the latter was a simple pair of bellows. Barrington put a candle to the paper, closed and positioned the box, and began to pump the bellows. Within seconds smoke was pouring into the auditorium. 'Fire!' bellowed the stage-manager, who also knew the signs and had rehearsed the procedure. 'Fire!' echoed all the stage-hands.

The belligerents to a man deserted their posts, turned tail, and ran for it. In very little time and with minimal loss of life (if indeed any) the theatre was empty. The outcome of the battle, therefore was inconclusive, but Mrs Quick and her friends were satisfied that they had made their point.

Chapter Twelve

As soon as the smoke dispersed, Mr Barrington's staff, assured of extra money (as usual on these occasions), began clearing up the mess and assessing the damage. They had seen it all before. Charles and Maria were much less stoical as they conducted a gloomy post-mortem in the Randalls' house.

If only Fluellen had kept his head, much would have been saved – such emerged as the Cheviots' view. Mrs Quick's supporters must have been a small minority compared with those who wanted to hear the opera through. It was probable that having expressed their sympathy for the banned singer and their hostility to her substitute, the demonstrators would have been content with little more than occasional barracking. Mrs Quick had neither the resources nor desire to organise a disturbance on the scale achieved; a riot was not in her interest. No doubt she had paid out a few pounds, rehearsed interruptions to the English-lesson scene, and relied on a modicum of support from ordinary theatregoers who thought she might have been ill-used (or who merely enjoyed audience participation). If the fiery provincials had not retaliated, disaster could have been averted.

Mr Barrington concurred without being particularly hard on the players, some of his most reliable and versatile performers. Sorely tried, they had lapsed excusably. Fluellen and Macmorris would be fined sufficient to replace lost cannonballs and shillelagh but should not be held responsible for the lively behaviour of the Liverpool crowd. If Mr Barrington seemed unruffled as the damage was totted up next day, it soon became evident why. According to his interpretation of the contract, Charles had indemnified him against just such trouble as had occurred. Therefore Charles must pay for the damage which the theatre had sustained, including the hundred-pound chandelier. There was also the question of lost revenue for the period during which the theatre would be out of commission. No doubt they could come to some amicable arrangement about that. It was all in a day's work as Mr Cheviot would realise when he was a little more experienced in the theatre.

Charles's heart sank and he hurried off, contract in hand, to consult the lawyer. 'I thought I was only liable if the house receipts fell below £200. Last night's receipts were over £300.'

'Alas no. There is at least a *prima facie* case for saying that these indemnity clauses give you an extra liability. We can seek counsel's opinion if you wish, but I would advise—'

'Surely you said those indemnity clauses were purely nominal?'

'So they are, so they would be, in ninety-nine cases out of a hundred. Yours, it seems, is the hundredth. If you will take my advice—'

278

'I shall not pay him a penny. It was no fault of mine that he quarrelled with that woman nor that the Liverpool mob ran amok in his theatre. Every theatre-owner takes that risk, that is their business.'

'But in the present instance the theatre-owner quite properly took steps to spread the risk. Such contracts are not uncommon, I understand, particularly with unknown – that is to say inexperienced – or rather, in short, with dramatists and composers who are still at the start of their careers. The established artist whose work is in demand can no doubt negotiate better terms. It is the same in many walks of life.'

'You told me nothing of this.'

'I believe I did, Mr Cheviot. I certainly drew your attention to the indemnity clauses. Of course, I could not possibly foresee . . . and besides you were so impatient, so insistent on signing the contract and starting rehearsals, as was Mrs Cheviot too, I recall. Mrs Cheviot felt you had already affronted Mr Barrington and must, as far as possible, try to co-operate with him.'

'What should we do now?'

'Let us find out how much the repairs will cost, and offer to pay one third. If he insists on one half – on, hem, his pound of flesh – then we shall have to think again.'

The negotiations with Mr Barrington were handled with such skill that Maria had to realise less than £1000 of her patrimony. 'This would never have happened if you had taken that position he offered you last summer,' she said.

'The lawyer considers you were largely to blame for being so anxious to placate Barrington,' said Charles, embroidering a little. Then he added, 'I feel as if one of my children had been smothered.'

279

Liverpool's Theatre Royal was not the only place to have trouble with its crowd that month. Following the verdict against Kean in the Court of the King's Bench, Drury Lane audiences rioted whenever the adulterous actor appeared. The proceedings in court had made Kean's private life public property, mercilessly exposing his behaviour towards Mr and especially Mrs Cox. As a man he was now reviled, as a tragedian he was a laughing-stock. Serious playgoers stayed away from Drury Lane rather than sully their ears, and for the first time, Mr Elliston, the lessee, found that the opera and ballet were more profitable than the drama.

'Poor Mr Kean,' said Maria, 'our troubles are nothing to his.'

'He has lost only £800, and he must still be a very rich man. The audiences will soon forgive or forget. How he could become entangled with that unspeakable Cox woman is a mystery. He has never been short of female companionship of the most seductive kind. To throw himself at that fat, common, middle-aged hussy is unworthy of him. I am sorry in a way, but he deserves what he has got. What have we done to deserve our fate?'

'I suppose he loved her, and could not help it.'

'Love is not like that, certainly not Kean's *amours*. Anyone would think we – you and I, Maria – had outraged society in some way. We have done nothing. Our lives are blameless and we are treated as if we were moral lepers. I wish I were dead.'

Charles relapsed into glum silence. The withdrawal of *Henry V*, the breakdown of relations with Mr Barrington, the crippling indemnity, had destroyed all his hopes and ambition. Profound depression enveloped him. He saw the episode as a direct, personal rejection. In vain did Maria argue that it was only a setback, that the audience had warmly approved of the opera, and that the disturbances had had nothing to do with the quality of his work. Charles could not feel it that way. All that effort for nothing, two years wasted. His spirit was as dead as the winter weather outside. It was as if the opera had never been. Even the newspapers had only reported the riot.

The weekly *Liverpool Mercury* carried a report of the disturbance but no review of the opera. The provincial press seldom criticised the arts and many papers, following the *Leeds Mercury*, banned all mention of the theatre. Certain musical and dramatic critics had, however, attended the première, and, unknown to Charles, favourable appreciation began to appear in the London press. The influential *London Magazine and Review* (which conscientiously kept an eye on provincial music) wrote in the following terms:

On the 23rd, a new English opera was performed at the King's Theatre in Liverpool with surprising effect. Mr Charles Cheviot's adaptation of *Henry V* furnished a single but brilliant exception to the musical indignities so often inflicted on the Bard. We have not for some time heard an indigenous opera so well written or so well sung. The composer himself gave a sonorous account of the stirring music allotted to King Hal, and Miss Stradling, as the French princess, sang with a delicacy and charm which delighted all except Messieurs les claqueurs (of whom more anon). The composer proved himself equally felicitous in transposing Shakespearean humour into the operatic idiom, while his use of traditional airs for Welsh, Scotch, and Irish soldiery was most resourceful. We have no hesitation in declaring the first two acts of *Henry V* the most accomplished operatic debut for many years. Mr Cheviot, it seems, studied musical composition in Italy and some of his ensemble writing is not unworthy of Signor Rossini himself, notably the finale of Act I and the sextet in Act II.

Act III, alas, was misappropriated by the notorious Liverpool mob. Numerous and determined claqueurs hissed the exemplary Miss Stradling to the rafters and had her replaced by the actress who, it must be supposed, had paid them. She attempted to sing 'The Thorn' but completed only one verse before she was ejected. (In singing she was unequal to the piece but in smiling she far exceeded it. A lady should not show her teeth to the public as she would show them to a dentist.) The battle which ensued led to an unhistorical defeat for Harry, England, and St George. We hope it will not deter the talented Mr Cheviot from turning his attention to *Henry IV* part 2 or *Henry VI* part 1.

Unaware of this and other silver linings to what appeared impenetrable cloud, Maria found that she had not only lost over £900 but also, it seemed, a husband. He kept to his room most of the day and all the night. Sometimes he went long, solitary walks in the rain. Occasionally he went to Randalls to pretend to work. When she did see him it was almost worse than when she did not. He seemed to blame her for encouraging his composition and for urging him to make the most of his musical talents. Morbid silence was his other form of companionship. All wifely attempts at diversion or consolation were repulsed.

In her loneliness, Maria tried to get closer to the children. Bertram and Leonora had a sensible governess and good manners. Polite and dutiful, they were never quite at ease with their mother, and treated her as they might a remote but lovely aunt. They were much more at home with the governess. Their respectful, awesome, startled reaction to the sudden interest of the goddess-like stranger made them

282

seem to Maria almost as unattainable as their father. She wished she had elected, back in New York, to bring them up herself, but it was too late to start now. Bertram would soon be eight. Did none of her family need her?

It was in this state of mind that she found herself wondering what that clever, opinionated writer, the late Miss Austen, would expect in circumstances such as hers. She turned, for the first time, to the set of books which William Price had left behind. Sometimes she would put reading aside and spend the afternoon gaming with a genteel circle of ladies in the Liverpool imitation of Almack's, sipping Sauternes and nibbling nuns-cake. As before, she lost more often than she won but whichever way the cards fell an extra glass was always needed, to celebrate a gain or allay a loss. Sometimes she stayed there until late but no one in Rodney Street seemed to notice. One evening she left at midnight having lost over fifty pounds. After that she kept away from the club and devoted herself guiltily but defensively to the five Austen books.

Charles seemed more engrossed than ever in his own misfortunes. He embraced despair with relish, took mordant satisfaction from infecting Maria with his own gloom, and twisted her attempted encouragement into further rebuffs.

There is a limit to how long people like Maria, even when trying to be the heroine of a romance, can sustain the rôle of understanding wife. At length she said, 'If you ask me, you are now being childish, self-indulgent, and cowardly. I have been sorry for you long enough. From now on you deserve everything you get. If you feel so suicidal, go and kill yourself, and be done with it. It will make no difference to me. Good riddance to bad rubbish. But you haven't the courage for real tragedy. Your misery is make-believe and your acting of it sham.'

It was not a pretty nor a spontaneous speech, but it had more effect than her sympathy. Charles continued to brood and sulk but in a more detached, self-mocking, superficial manner, as if he was acting rather than being. But the jesting entertainer continued to rehearse Hamlet and spurn Ophelia. His northern soul had a streak of Calvinism, usually well-controlled, but now abnormally active.

This unhappy chapter was terminated by interesting letters arriving for Charles on successive days.

Chapter Thirteen

The first letter was from Sir Henry Bishop of Drury Lane theatre.

Sir,

Our attention has been drawn to favourable reviews of your opera, *Henry V*, which have appeared in the London papers. Moreover, Mr Wm Hazlitt, who attended the performance in a private capacity, has assured us that your opera is worthy of its subject and in conception if not in execution displays the high musical standards which it is my endeavour to enforce at the Theatre Royal. He goes farther, declaring that he has not heard a first opera with more promise since the Lyceum production of my own *The Maniac* some fourteen years since.

It is my great pleasure, therefore, to invite you to work with us here at Drury Lane in the capacity of assistant to the composer and musical director (myself) for a period of three to six months. Mr Elliston, the lessee, supports this proposal and, like myself, is most eager to have the honour of your acquaintance. It is our fervent hope, I may add, that this temporary arrangement may lead not only to a salaried position in the company but also (in the fullness of time) to the commissioning of an opera from your own pen. Meanwhile

284

the composition of my new opera, *Aladdin*, is going forward apace, and the details of its preparation and production will provide the experience which your talents demand.

The assignment may commence at your convenience, but the sooner the better. I salute you, sir, as a brother votary of St Cecilia, and remain your most humble friend and colleague,

H. Bishop

Charles read the letter twice before tossing it over to Maria with an angry snort. 'Insult added to injury. Drury Lane now solicits my services but declines to pay for them. They want me to work for nothing now in the expectation of some future commission. The arrogance is as great as the impertinence. What they suggest is barefaced exploitation. No doubt Bishop has run out of ideas and wants me to give him mine.'

Maria saw the letter as a godsent second chance. Here was Charles's opportunity to show his true colours in an arena far more important than the Liverpool theatre. Remuneration or lack of it was of secondary importance. To work at Drury Lane or Covent Garden must be any young English composer's ambition.

'I beg you to consider the offer most carefully. It would be wrong of them not to pay you, but the letter does not say that in so many words. Since they have never met you, however, never heard your music or singing, know of you only through reports, it is probable that your remuneration would be modest. When you have proved your worth, made yourself indispensable, that will be the time to ask for better terms. It is the opportunity that matters, not the remuneration. The tone of this letter is arrogant but the burden is complimentary.'

Her manner was so sincere, so conciliatory, so reasonable that it infuriated Charles. Yet he kept all snubbing retorts to himself, and agreed to think it over. Next day another unexpected opportunity arose. A letter from Mrs Clayton to her

285

trustee contained the following paragraph:

> Once again may I solicit your advice? The villa is a
> considerable improvement on the big house, but is bleak
> and charmless, and deserves improvement. What it may
> perhaps call for is a scheme of decoration. I know
> nothing of such matters but when I was in London
> I heard that artists like Mr Wyatt could be persuaded
> to paint walls and even ceilings and in so doing could
> greatly improve the interior aspect of a house. If that
> be so, may I venture to ask whether you know of any
> competent artist in these parts who would be prepared,
> for a suitable fee, to undertake that sort of commission
> for me, and to take my daughter's likeness too? Forgive
> me for troubling you, but there is no one else whose
> taste I can trust.

'I have always wanted to undertake such a commission
myself,' said Charles, with his nearest approach to enthusiasm since the disaster.

'You would do it exceedingly well, but the Drury Lane
offer is by far the best.'

'Is it? In pecuniary terms, it is surely the worst.
Elliston is up to his ears in debt, while Mrs Clayton has
more money than she needs. The expenses of moving to
London would be considerable, not least because I would
forfeit my Randall pittance. Even if Drury Lane agreed to
pay me something, I should still be out of pocket, whereas
the Clayton commission would be lucrative. Within reason, I
daresay, I could name my terms.'

'Drury Lane is your destiny, Charles, for richer or
poorer.'

'That is more or less what you said when you tried to
make me accept the offer from Mr Barrington. What kind
of destiny is it to play second fiddle to Henry Bishop who
is as bankrupt of talent as Elliston is bankrupt of funds? Why

286

should I help him, no doubt anonymously, with his *Aladdin* or *Lamp Sweet Lamp* as he will probably call it?'

'You sneer, but at least he has written one song which everyone knows and likes. We both believe you can do better. The fact remains he is the most successful musician in London and offers you the chance to go there and displace him. Nothing could be more right, more challenging, more magnanimous on Sir Henry's part. It would be mere frivolity to paint pretty pictures in Prestwick instead of taking the offer – taking it "at the flood".'

Charles smiled sardonically. 'I fear you overrate my music and underrate my frivolity. A bird in the hand is worth two in Drury Lane. It is unthinkable for me to reject the chance of recouping some of our recent losses. But, very well, I will also bow to your wishes. I shall write, as obsequiously as you like, to Sir Henry Bishop expressing my gratification at the honour bestowed on me despite my unworthiness, and my ambition to be of service to music at the Theatre Royal. After suitable courtesies about the immortality of "Home Sweet Home", I shall explain that duties and commitments up here must delay my departure from Liverpool for a short (unspecified) period. Finally, I shall advert to the pecuniary losses I shall sustain and ask, as a family man, what terms they offer. By the time we have come to an agreement, I shall have finished painting pretty pictures in Prestwick and be at least one hundred guineas to the good.'

Charles wrote a procrastinating letter to Drury Lane and soon afterwards took up residence in comfortable lodgings procured and paid for by Mrs Clayton. William Price, meanwhile, had returned to England sooner than expected and was making a satisfactory recovery at Mansfield from wounds sustained gallantly and to good purpose in a skirmish at the mouth of the Tagus. Sight had been fully restored to one eye. Fanny thought that his black eye-shade made him look just as heroic as the victor of Copenhagen and Trafalgar. This intelligence was conveyed to Maria in a letter from young Lady Bertram, telling her not to worry.

Chapter Fourteen

It is a truth universally known that a married woman deprived of her husband is in want of good books. Maria applied herself diligently to the works of Miss Austen, accepting that, like *Mansfield Park* itself, they were compounded of fact and fancy, hearsay and harangue. She assumed that people like Mr Bennet, Mr Collins, Lady Catherine, Mr and Mrs Elton, Sir Walter Elliot, and General Tilney must certainly have existed, and was, on the whole, diverted by their proceedings. Of the heroines, she had some fellow-feeling for Emma and Elizabeth but less patience for the Dashwood girls or Anne Elliot. Not one of them, however, deserved the miserable fate which surely lay in store for her beyond the altar. What could be duller than to be Mrs Edward Ferrars, Mrs Brandon, Mrs George Knightley, or Mrs Darcy? On reflection, there might be some hope for young Mrs Henry Tilney and matronly Mrs Wentworth. Not one of Miss Austen's heroes was half as attractive as her own husband (or Henry Crawford) – and look how impossible Charles himself had become. The author's general observation of matrimony seemed to coincide with Maria's and to contradict the happy-ever-after implications of her final chapters. Was there, for example, a single 'happy marriage' of any significance among the older generations depicted in the books? Married life must have been wretched indeed for

Sir Lewis de Bourgh, for Lady Elliot, for Mrs Woodhouse, for the general's wife – all of whom, understandably, had found solace in an early grave; hardly less wretched for Mr Bennet, whose every utterance reflected the empty folly of his choice. And what of her own parents? Procreation apart, Sir Thomas and Lady Bertram's marriage had been as barren as the Bennets' – they had rubbed along without open disharmony because one was asleep half the time, the other all the time.

Maria was startled to realise that there was so much implicit criticism of marriage in Miss Austen's work, and found herself asking how far the partners had even been faithful to each other. This took her into a veritable Gomorrah. General Tilney, she knew for certain, had betrayed Mrs Tilney repeatedly. It was clear, too, that the supremely handsome Sir Walter was a practising ladies' man in every sense of the word. Sir Lewis de Bourgh was a shadowy figure but it must be presumed that, unless a natural celibate, he kept the mistress he deserved (and could well afford) in Richmond or Twickenham. Poor Mr Bennet could only have married Mrs Bennet to make her an honest woman but had probably remained faithful to her as long as she retained her looks. And Sir Thomas, her own father: while in this mood it was difficult for her to believe that his lengthy parliamentary visits to London and his protracted business in Antigua had been, against all fashion, innocent. She smiled at the thought of mulatto siblings in the Caribbee. Mr Woodhouse, however, could never, even in his youth (in so far as he may be said to have had a youth), have been anything but incapable. This meant, Maria realised with a gleeful chuckle, that Mrs Woodhouse must have erred at least once (probably with Mr Perry).

To find herself in the company of so many sinners, to find that she was not alone, gave Maria feelings of exhilaration and excitement which she did not altogether understand. Yet her amusement, even gratification, at penetrating these secrets gave way to alarm when she applied them to – Charles. If marriage vows meant so little to so many pillars of respectability, why should they mean more to the emancipated artist who admired Shelley and Byron? Why should they mean anything at all to a mysterious widow who had already exchanged virtue for a fortune? Her husband's letters, when read between the lines, seemed to confirm her fears.

'My first task,' he wrote, 'is a portrait of the lady herself. It depicts her wearing spectacles to symbolise a life of commerce and industry – the female of the future free from the shackles of man-made convention. I call it "The Cotton-mistress" (as opposed to cotton-master), and it's going ahead famously.' Reading between the lines, Maria decided that free from the shackles of convention Mrs Clayton was wearing nothing for her portrait except her spectacles. 'Nude with Lorgnette' would be a better title and would be only too characteristic of Charles's humour. His dubbing the conceit 'mistress' no doubt conveyed intention if not accomplished fact. She felt angry and frustrated at the discovery and pondered it long into the night as she lay sleepless in the bed which Charles had not visited since before the opera.

Next day she realised how groundless her suspicions had been. Of course Mrs Clayton had been clothed. Mrs Clayton was a prude. Mrs Clayton put bodices on goddesses. Charles was safe and trustworthy (and not unduly interested in that sort of thing). He should paint nobody in the nude – except herself. With a shock she realised that she would rather like him to do that, to portray her perhaps as an odalisque, but she would never dare to tell him. She wrote him a tender letter saying how empty the house felt and how much she missed him.

She also wrote to William Price, sympathetically and at some length. Containing a first full account of their operatic débâcle and some mention of the Clayton commission, the letter aroused wide interest in the family at Mansfield. Fanny and Edmund, strongly disapproving of everything theatrical, saw the riot as a Sign and hoped the appropriate lessons would be drawn; Sir Tom decided secretly to defray his sister's losses to the tune of £100; Mrs Norris, privately noting that Maria's husband was away from home, suggested that the Cheviot children should pay their long-awaited visit to Mansfield Park and that William Price, advancing his projected business in Liverpool, should escort them back himself. William, now sound of wind and limb except for one eye, agreed so eagerly that Mrs Norris had to suppress a smile.

Charles's next letter, however, rekindled Maria's impatience and disquiet. A second portrait was now required for hanging in Mrs Clayton's principal mill, the scheme of decoration for the villa – an allegory on the blessings of cotton – was becoming more and more ambitious, and a neighbouring magnate was eager to engage his services in connection with a newly established dye works. Charles could see himself earning more in a month by his brush than he earned in a twelvemonth with Randall & Co., and was convinced that a small fortune could be made by painting (as he put it pandering) the new money of Lancashire and Cheshire. They would all be despicably easy to please. In these circumstances, the Drury Lane opening (Mr Elliston now offered an honorarium of £50 payable in arrears) was hardly worth considering. The work might be more interesting in London, but it would be selfish and irresponsible to go to Drury Lane for less than £300 per annum, and even that would be a dangerous gamble. Out of regard for Maria's preference, however, he had again written to the Theatre Royal seeking better terms instead of declining the offer.

291

With the letter to his wife, Charles enclosed a telling caricature entitled 'Mr Cheviot Torn Between Two Worlds'. It
portrayed the artist as Siamese twins, one of them ill-dressed
and bedraggled, conducting an opera with broken fiddlestick
as a plump soprano was forced from the stage by aerial bom-
bardment; the other, elegant and complacent, was painting a
group of buxom deities beginning to adorn themselves with
the first batch of sprigged muslin to arrive in Elysium.

Maria was so enchanted by the drawing that she tore it
up and threw it into the fire, wishing she could do likewise to
the insolent expressions which, she was sure, Charles would
have used in his latest letter to the opera house. His pride, his
sloth, his envy, his greed (that is, his reaction to comparative
poverty) – which sin was animating him now? He claimed that
he would never accept favours from social, artistic, or intellectual inferiors, but if Henry Bishop and Robert Elliston were all
these things, so was Mrs Clayton. His attitude was but a pose
to dress up indolence as integrity. In practice, he was breaking faith, for music, not art, was his unique, God-given talent.
Infidelity to one's true vocation was worse, far worse, than
matrimonial infidelity. With application, Charles could be the
best national composer since Dr Arne or even Purcell, and
he was throwing it all away because he had also been given
a charming inconsequential facility with pencil and brush.

People in love are often uncritical and prone to over-
estimation.

It was Mrs Clayton's fault; she had seduced him with
her tainted silver. Was it only with silver? The woman
must have a pretty face and an elegant figure or she
would never have tempted old Mr Clayton into making
such a fool of himself. She had won a fortune by pleasing
another and now could afford to please herself. Very well, let
her set her cap at Charles, let her entangle him briefly, the
woman remained nobody, a philistine, a shopkeeper, nobody

at all. Maria told herself (and tried to believe it) that she would forgive misconduct with *nobody*, a temporary lapse on Charles's part, provided he afterwards accepted the Drury Lane position. She wondered whether he would extend the same degree of magnanimity to herself should the need or opportunity arise.

Our lonely, de-husbanded heroine led herself into this dangerous, compromising mood at least in part because she had no fear, experience, or conception of want. She had never felt the pinch, let alone come face to face with poverty. Her outburst at the will-reading had been inspired by her father's (and as she wrongly supposed, Susan's) treachery, not by fear of straitened circumstances. She could now see that Edmund, Fanny, and Mrs Norris had probably conspired against her but she still had no idea that their success could produce anything more burdensome than an irritating increase in the debts which were an accepted part of civilised life. Charles, however, while never lacking for bread, knew what it was like to be genuinely needy, had always felt hard up, understood that society can never forgive its paupers, and realised just how slender their (that is, Maria's) resources had become. Had he possessed a business sense, he would have made a prosperous living from Randall & Co., but family sinecures, though better than nothing, were ill-rewarded in these hard times. Therefore the chance of earning good money while indulging a pleasant pastime (he refused to paint ceilings) was more than tempting. It was something very close to necessity which kept him in Manchester and taught him to tolerate the undemanding monotony of Mrs Clayton's company without resorting to satire. He tried to explain as much to Maria but his own want of *gravitas* robbed his arguments of full conviction. Although Maria half-believed him she thought he might be protesting too much, particularly when he admitted that Mrs Clayton was very handsome but claimed her complexion was too high and her figure too slim. Maria examined herself critically in the glass. Her figure was a little fuller now but no one would call her fat.

No one would call her fat, least of all William Price who is on his way to Liverpool. Again he is unheralded, but this time it is because Mrs Norris has insisted that she be allowed to write the letter of invitation (since it was her idea) and by an altogether uncharacteristic oversight has forgotten to dispatch it.

Oh, keep him away. Let him turn back. Give him an accident on the road. Or make a distorting lens of that one good eye so that she does appear fat to the black-patched sailor with his devilishly Nelsonian look, the as yet unrewarded warrior.

Chapter Fifteen

Like Mrs Norris, the reader may have some inkling of what could befall in this short chapter. I make no excuses nor assign any blame, unless my very detachment be constructed as extenuation. Heroines, after all, deserve loyalty (not least from the writer), and minor characters must be kept in their place.

Very well then, as you have surmised, neither Maria nor William Price reposed entirely alone during the night which followed his unexpected arrival in Rodney Street, looking heroic but needing nurture. They retired to separate chambers but under cloak of darkness found themselves in each other's company again. I decline to speculate whether it was Maria who crept into William's bed or vice versa. Whoever it was met with little resistance. There was a saving decorum in the improprieties which then ensued. For one thing, the night was pitch black so neither of them saw anything which ought not be seen. In awkward surprise, moreover, neither said or declared anything which should not be declared or said. However, some slight adjustment of their night attire did, in due course, enable them tangibly to express the admiration which both had secretly felt from time to time without being able to put it into words. Yet their essential privacy remained intact even as those parts which are meant to be private made fleeting, not unenjoyable contact. And when it was over both fell asleep as soon as good manners allowed.

Thus wickedness and sin notwithstanding, very little indecency took place at Rodney Street that night, nor extravagant, licentious pleasure. A victor in battle enjoyed his traditional spoil and that was all. Maria soon realised that nothing would induce her to grant any further spoil, even if she continued to be suspicious of Charles or angry at his neglect. If, as she half-hoped, half-feared, Charles happened to be similarly circumstanced, she trusted he would be similarly untouched and unimpressed by the transaction. Perhaps it would bring him back. (William is only a minor character so he had only minor thoughts, of *bagnios* and such.)

Charles Cheviot, however, was asleep in his lodgings; Mrs Clayton was asleep in her villa; (God never sleeps).

Next morning they awoke in separate bedchambers. Maria had a slight feeling of nausea and a strong feeling of guilt. She dressed hurriedly and went to see the children. Bertram and Leonora were surprised by her sudden interest in their breakfast, their lessons, and their plans for the day, but answered her questions courteously, as was their duty. Neither of them noticed that their mother went pale when they asked if Papa was to return soon, or that she flushed pink when they asked how long Uncle William was staying.

When she could think of nothing more to say, she suggested taking the children for a walk, something she had never done in her life. They always took their walk after lessons, they reminded her, with Miss Harland. Tactfully, the governess asked if the walk could be deferred to the usual hour. Routine was important for the young.

Leaving the children, Maria tripped over a dustpan left negligently on the upstairs landing. The house, she saw in a flash, was a disgrace in its untidiness. Like a vengeful fury she descended to the kitchen and gave peremptory orders to maids and housekeeper. They were all idle good-for-nothings who had taken advantage of her kindness. The windows were dirty, the brasses were dull, the shelves were dusty, the woodwork was unpolished, the carpets were never swept, the cobwebs were left to grey and blacken. Everyone would be dismissed unless the house were straight and tidy, bright as a new pin, by evening. How dare they take so little pride in their work? Maria herself undertook to show them the standard she expected and spent the next five hours spring-cleaning her bedroom and powder closet. Then she tackled Charles's dressing-room. Preoccupied with the cleaning, she soon forgot about the walk she had promised the children. Bertram and Leonora accepted the omission with their usual dignity.

William woke late with a slight feeling of guilt and a strong wish to go back to sea. As a sailor of fortune, he had already discovered that respectable married women were sometimes fair game, but it would be deuced complicated if he was expected to continue this affair, and he could hardly accompany his cousin and her children half-way across England as if nothing had happened. A quick visit to his parents in Portsmouth seemed the best solution, since the other alternative – returning to Mansfield without any Cheviots – would lead to awkward questions, explanations and, perhaps, lies.

Accordingly, he made his room ship-shape, packed his bag, and wrote a carefully worded message to Maria claiming urgent family business. Rather than play the total coward, he decided to give her the letter by hand, but was unable to find her in any of the living-rooms (not that he tried very hard), and being unwilling to seek her upstairs by the broad light of day, he sealed the note, gave it to an unusually industrious maid, and left.

Maria was equally relieved when she broke the seal. William had done the right thing. The night before would make no difference to their cousinly friendship or her love for Charles; it would make no difference to anyone or anything ever. In a little while they would both forget it had happened. Meanwhile, if she could not face her husband and act as if nothing had happened, then she had no right to consider herself an actress or to yearn, as she still did, to be allowed on the stage. To prepare herself, to wash away the feelings of the morning and the promptings of the night, she ordered a hot bath in the middle of the afternoon. A new thought occurred to her in the tub but she dismissed it with a quiet laugh.

Thus far, Mrs Norris's manipulation has been successful beyond her dreams. For the one-eyed hero has not only done his duty with manliness but with fecundity. New life has sprung from the cousinly bond and it is not very long before Maria, abnormally intuitive through conscience, begins to fear the truth. Suspicion hardens with sickening haste, the sickness taking place, as before, at seven o'clock one morning, a mere fortnight after the fateful night. So what will our heroine, if heroine still, do now?

Should she be rather lucky or very cool-headed, virtue and Mrs Norris will be frustrated while vice and Maria

297

go unpunished. All she has to achieve is a restitution of conjugal rights before Charles learns about the early morning indisposition. The child will then be accepted as a Cheviot and no one, not even William Price, will know its true paternity. Very shocking but something which happens in all walks of life and often saves a great deal of unnecessary distress and pother.

Unaware that Maria has compounded sin with cynicism, Charles soon obliges by returning to the family home for a few days. Less morose, less self-pitying, less impoverished, his disposition now makes unwitting co-operation with his wife's subterfuge a distinct possibility.

Something was different. He sensed it as soon as he entered the Rodney Street house. The hall was immaculate, fires were blazing, floors and furniture gleamed with polish, a maid took his hat and coat as soon as he was through the door, and Maria was playing at three-handed cribbage with Bertram and Leonora. When Charles suggested he join them in four-handed crib, all agreed with alacrity. To the children's amusement their parents made a lot of silly mistakes and lost the game. However, they all enjoyed the strange new sensation of playing together as a family, enjoyed it despite a certain unreality and awkwardness. The children's bedtime came as a pity. Irresponsibly, Charles agreed to Leonora's suggestion that he read to them before their departure. Sweeping aside their mother's protests, he read a complete story from *German Popular Tales*, a newly translated book by the brothers Grimm in which the illustrations by George Cruikshank had already been hand-coloured by Bertram Cheviot.

Left alone with Charles, Maria took refuge in nervous gaiety. To his surprise, she eagerly agreed with all he said, laughed at the slightest provocation, and did everything she could to please him. The opinionated equal had become submissive at last. What had caused it? More amused than gratified, Charles did not pursue the question very far. No doubt the truth would emerge. Perhaps she wanted something from him; perhaps she was apologising for her headstrong behaviour in the past. In some ways he preferred the old Maria but it would be interesting to see how long the new one would last.

'You are uncommonly civil this evening, Maria, what have you been up to?' Strolling to the window, Charles did not notice his wife change colour.

'Nothing. I promise. What do you mean?'

'Have you been planning another ball, for example? The last time I was away from home you and William Price conceived a scheme which cost us a pretty penny at the Wellington Rooms, I seem to remember. At least, I have always suspected that the two of you hatched the notion while I was away. Did you not say that William was expected here, by the way? Has he arrived yet?'

'No – yes. He had a sudden change of plan. I think he went to Portsmouth.'

'And never came here at all?'

'No,' she hesitated. 'That is, for one night only. Poor William. Did I tell you that he lost an eye but won a medal and now looks like Lord Nelson? Shall we have some champagne to celebrate his safety and your homecoming?'

Maria hoped that wine would induce an amorous mood in her husband. At first it did. He put an arm round her waist, said how nice she was looking and how glad he was to be home again. He even gave her an improper and suggestive squeeze. Then he asked for another bottle. It seemed that no wine at all had been served at Charles's lodgings, and very little by Mrs Clayton.

'Her father was a strict Methodist. How do I know? Well, from certain discreet questions and certain acute

299

observations, I think I have solved the mystery of Mrs Clayton's former life. Her first husband must have been an artist who died young and left her penniless. She had been his model and I rather think she augmented their meagre income by presenting tableaux or attitudes, like Emma Hamilton, for there are drawings of her depicting Boadicea and Mary Queen of Scots. After the painter died, she went back to her father's two-acres-and-a-cow. Is this champagne making me too talkative, Maria? Are you sure? In practice, it was a sufficient smallholding of nearer ten acres, but within a couple of years her only brother died of consumption, the broken-hearted father followed him to the grave, and the mother had a seizure which left her dependent on the one remaining child. Mrs Clayton ran the farm herself and managed to provide for her mother and daughter, but occasionally had to sell off one of the pictures which were all she had retrieved from her former life in London. Are you sure I am not boring you, Maria? In due course, Sam Clayton bought the painting that I thought (wrongly) was by a contemporary copyist of Boucher. He quite fell in love with the face and form (lovingly delineated) of the shepherdess. Discovering how the model was circumstanced in real life, he married her or, as she puts it, bought her, soon after the mother's demise. I think that is the story in all essentials. Some of the details may be fanciful. As a matter of fact, I suspect that Mr Clayton purchased all her pictures and won her hand by paying inflated prices for them. Perhaps we should open another bottle, these monologues are thirsty work. When she was sitting for me, I noticed at once how relaxed and natural she was. She reminded me of the life classes I used to attend in Italy, not but what she was fully dressed and much less ample than those Roman matrons.

'So that's a little mystery explained. It's strange she should now be both prim and proper, despite having spent a good part of her youth posing nearly nude. No Emma Hamilton she, at least I do not think so, whereas you, my darling wife, who would never dream of being painted less than fully draped, sometimes look distinctly Hamiltonian. There are times, indeed, when I know just how Lord Nelson must have felt.'

Towards the end of the third bottle, Charles was so overcome by lewd desire that he fell into the arms of Morpheus.

Next morning Maria tried again. Before the house was stirring, she went to her husband's room and found him tired, grey, and ill-tempered. He had awoken downstairs with a feverish headache as the clock struck three, and had scarcely slept a wink since then. 'It must have been very poor champagne.'

Maria was all wifely sympathy. 'Then why did you drink so much of it?'

He answered with a groan, but generously made room for her in the bed. To distract his attention from the headache she tried to find out if he was equally afflicted elsewhere. He protested feebly and at first it seemed that the wine's enervating influence was all-pervasive but after a while there was some slight sign of recovery. It proved a ticklish business to enhance the rally but Maria handled it delicately and as the clock struck seven, began to feel that the point had been made. At that very moment, however, the familiar wave of nausea overcame her. She sprang from the bed and darted from the room before Charles could restrain her.

By the time she felt well enough to return, the day had begun and her husband was fully dressed.

'You were not the only one to have too much wine last night,' she said, by way of excuse.

'I hope you feel better than I do. The thought of spending all day at the office under the watchful eye of Master Hugh is daunting. But go there I must or questions will be asked.

301

Perhaps we can have another hand of cribbage when I return. I want my revenge.'

'The children will be glad to play, though Bertram only likes it when he wins.' Maria had a sudden idea. 'Perhaps he needs a brother,' she added. Charles winced.

Bertram was not a good loser. His failure at cribbage that evening almost made him forget his manners, and the game ended on a discordant note with both children squabbling. That was a pity since it took away half the satisfaction from Charles's well-deserved revenge.

'It is not a brother he needs,' said the father, 'but a school. That would knock some sense into him. A baby brother could have no possible influence on Bertram for years. He would merely be an extra mouth to feed. It is a blessing that we only have two children, for they are quite enough of a handful, to say nothing of the expense.'

It is usually wiser for a woman to pretend more agreement than she feels. Maria was not always wise but she refrained from contradicting her husband. The evening passed companionably. Charles was to spend at least a further week at home and at the Liverpool office before returning to complete his commission at Mrs Clayton's. He confirmed that the Drury Lane authorities had been unable to meet his demand in full but had made a slightly improved offer. If he earned sufficient money from Mrs Clayton and her peers, he might consider coming to an arrangement with Sir Henry Bishop later in the year, or maybe the following year. Again Maria stifled her disappointment and affected cheerful resignation. She was rewarded, in due course, with an equally companionable night.

It was, however, an unsatisfactory reward as far as her main objective was concerned. Charles established that while the gift of continency had indeed departed from him, he was still not prepared to give due consideration to the causes, especially the first cause, for which matrimony was ordained. On the contrary, he took Maria in hand unadvisedly, wantonly, and like some brute beast – after the manner, in short, of the late, often beastly, Lord Byron. Although Maria exclaimed loudly a few times, she was more thwarted than hurt, and might, at another time, have participated with some curiosity. Charles apologised before retiring to his own room.

Early next morning, feeling some obligation to elaborate on that apology and perhaps to stress the imprudence of having another child before their affairs were in order, he tiptoed back and softly opened the door. Maria should be half-awake by now, drowsing in that warm, languorous style which both of them had often found agreeable. Instead she was standing, back to the door, retching into a basin. Downstairs the grandfather clock began to strike. For a moment Charles thought he was back in New York, then drums, cellos, brass, and cymbals exploded in his head and a momentous chord told him what must have happened. Without thought he guessed everything. Still unobserved, he closed the door and plunged through the abyss which led back to his own room. So that was why she had prevaricated about William Price, that was why she wanted a brother for Bertram, that was why . . .

He dropped into a chair and wept. He had loved her, for all his aloofness at times, for all her recklessness and independence and temper, he had loved her. Since that night ten years before when in another inspired flash he had *decided* to fall in love, he had never wavered. Even

303

when having volcanic rows, they had been together, as one person. Now, in a single act, she had destroyed their common existence. A wave of nausea briefly overcame Charles too and he groped to a basin.

Slowly he started to think as well as to feel. His instinct was for revenge. He would destroy her, both of them, and good riddance. He had rescued her from shame and disgrace and look at the thanks he got! No punishment was bad enough. As for William, his career with Randall's was finished. No further commissions would come his way from anyone – and the precious family at Mansfield Parsonage should know all. William would be an outcast. Alive or dead, both would suffer the torments of hell. Or could his instinct be wrong? Had he jumped to a false conclusion? Those early morning harbingers of Bertram and Leonora in New York remained vivid – and the thought of his beautiful alarum brought another lump to his throat – but they might, just conceivably, be irrelevant. Yesterday Maria had eaten pork and it often disagreed with her; the weather had been upsettingly changeable; dysentery was endemic in Liverpool; a particularly infectious stomach disorder was abroad. In his heart he felt he was clutching at straws, but surely he owed that to Maria. He must give her the benefit of the doubt before colluding in the destruction of their world.

His head searched for explanations but his heart, and even more emphatically his stomach, denied them. What had he done to deserve it? Like most husbands he had been selfish and querulous and sarcastic from time to time, usually with at least a modicum of excuse. No, he did not claim to be perfect, never had, but his imperfections had always, he congratulated himself, been venial. And so had hers been heretofore. Until this overwhelming transgression. Adultery had never entered his head, and when it had he had always put it aside with resolution (for the time being). Adultery was a different order of fault from any infraction of his. It was sin and crime combined in a monstrous violation. The marriage itself had been murdered.

Or was she, despite all appearances, innocent?

He brooded all day, pretending to work. Next morning he arose just before seven and listened at her door. The tell-tale retching met his ears. The following day there was silence, and he began to hope again, but the day after that the retching was worse than ever. And the next.

'Good morning, Maria, I trust you are well.'

'Perfectly well, thank you, Charles.'

'You managed to wrest a few hours' merciful oblivion from the troubles of this mortal coil?'

'I slept as well as I ever do these days.'

'These days?'

Maria made no reply.

'How fortunate you are,' continued Charles. 'You sleep like a top. I envy you, always have.'

'If you must know, my lord and master, I no longer sleep so well.'

'How so? Since when? Perhaps you should see the doctor.'

'Since I have been a banished woman from my Harry's bed.'

'Is that the trouble? I see. As a matter of fact, I came to your room this morning.'

Maria looked up sharply. 'When?'

'About seven o'clock, five past maybe. It seemed to me you were not feeling quite your best, so I withdrew.'

'What do you mean? What on earth are you talking about?'

'I gathered you were being sick.'

'Sick? Oh yes, so I was, I had clean forgotten. I did have a touch of indigestion. It must have been something I ate yesterday.'

'But you are perfectly all right now?'

'Perfectly, thank you.'

'Do you often have stomach upsets these days? You never used to, but I hear there is a lot of infection around.'

'No. Why all these questions?'

'Husbandly concern about your health. You have been sick in the morning every day since my return, have you not? It is natural for me to be worried about you.'

'I have not. There was one day when – that is . . . you must have been spying.'

'Is it spying to go to one's wife's room in one's own house?'

'It is *my* house. My money bought the lease.'

'In my name; our house then. It has nothing to do with the question on hand. Madam, I suspect you are expecting a child and I know I cannot be the father. Tell me I am wrong and I abase myself at your feet and ask forgiveness for my prurient and unworthy suspicions, while in my heart singing with joy and relief.'

What should she do, bluff it out? There would be no physical sign of her condition for two or three months. Meanwhile she might miscarry. Or it might still prove a false alarm brought on by a bad conscience. Yet instinct told her it was true. Could she live a lie for weeks on end? And suppose he continued this self-imposed celibacy?

Suddenly the room spun round, sight faded from her eyes, and she swooned.

The hesitation and the fainting fit both confirmed Charles's worst fears. Grimly jealous yet furiously triumphant, he ordered a maid to send for the physician, and carried Maria to her room.

Chapter Sixteen

'It is too early to say for certain but Mr Gossage predicts a happy event around Christmas. He advises that you rest this morning and will prescribe a tonic. Would you like to give me your explanation now or after your rest?'

Maria looked at him in speechless fear. How calm he sounded, not a trace of emotion. It was no use lying any more, the truth was bound to emerge now. What a terrible mess she had made of the affair. All over the world, wives took lovers without being found out, but one brief indiscretion, and she was discovered at once. She was penitent, yes, but it was grossly unfair. Why did it have to happen to her? Why did it always happen to her? That business with Crawford, she had been the only one to suffer, had suffered, it felt, for all the other adulteries which went unpunished. In the new case, certainly she had been wrong and stupid but she had not been wicked, she had not meant to hurt Charles nor repudiate her marriage nor had she been unfaithful *in her heart*. The act had been cousinly kindness, temporary relief – taken too far – from private preoccupations; solace given when required, a hero's reward. How pitiless and cynical of fate to make such a paltry act the end of a marriage perhaps, but the beginning of a life. Creation and death should spring from momentous actions, not from faintly ridiculous improprieties. Besides, she had been thinking of Charles at the hardly about William at all. No infidelity was intended, she could see that now with blinding clarity. It had all been a frightful mistake.

The reader must judge how far these arguments amount to special pleading applied retrospectively and therefore worthless. For myself I hold that venial amorality is in reality inexcusable immorality as practised by those we love. In so far as I accept Maria's excuses, therefore, I am open to the charge of partiality.

'I love you Charles,' was all she said at first. 'There is nobody else. You are all I want. Believe me if you possibly can.'

Charles was surprised to find himself wanting to trust her and being moved by her simplicity. He considered saying 'I love you too', but it seemed lame in the context and he decided not to commit himself until Maria had finished her explanation.

'Trust me and forgive me. Yes, I am afraid something did happen, just once, between William and me. What came over us, I cannot imagine. I suppose he had been away at sea a long time, and then at Mansfield Parsonage, and needed, well – nurturing. And I was upset at your neglect. You had not been near me for months. And you were with another woman, innocently I am sure, but at times like that anything makes you jealous. It is no excuse, I know, but—' she paused, perhaps hoping for a response.

'Oh Charles, say you will forgive me. Please, please, please – I promise, I swear by Almighty God, I shall never do anything like it again. I never have (the Crawford business was quite different) and I never shall. I never for one moment meant to do it in the first place. It was a stupid, terrible accident. Give me another chance. Give our marriage another chance. I will do anything you say. It was just a momentary aberration. Forgive me. I do love you.'

Knowing how much he disliked tears (which he described as women's weapons, cheap as lies) she was determined not to weep. She looked at him in fearful doubt, and still Charles did not utter. 'I can say no more. I do not defend myself. I confess all. For the sake of the past ten years, for the children's sake – spare me. Forgive me, dearest Charles.'

'I forgive you,' he said and left the room without another word, without another look (in case he should wholly forgive her). Maria gave a sigh of relief and wept into the pillows.

Charles needed time to think. He was confused. Anger, pity, self-pity, and remorse jostled for dominance, though remorse did not jostle as hard as the others. He no longer wanted to kill them both. Even William's death sentence could be commuted to one of grievous bodily harm; for example, a permanently disabling kick in the regenerative organs. Yes, he would forgive, but did forgiveness preclude indignation?

Dammit, how dare she? Her morals belonged to some other century, to ancient Rome or some period yet to come. Had she learnt nothing from her first marriage or her affair with Crawford? Whether her behaviour was due to wanton depravity or casual promiscuity, it was equally inexcusable. Everything was soiled.

Mistake indeed! Accident forsooth! Yet it was possible; in some ways it was probable. She had always been a creature of impulse. She was reckless and headstrong, not vicious. She might indeed love him still, if you could call what she felt love. If that were the case and the brief, unsanctioned coupling meant nothing, then why all the fuss, why all the pain?

The child. It was all about the child. He would be a Cheviot in name without a drop of Cheviot blood. William's son but Charles must pretend to be the father. It would mean living a lie for the rest of his life. No man should be asked to do that. If only there were some vestige of doubt about the paternity.

They both knew there was none. The child must poison the whole family. How could he love Maria when she was bearing the child of another? Easier to love the child itself, at least it was innocent. By an act of magnanimity (itself creditable) he might indeed become fond of it, but the mother . . . One could forgive by an act of will, but not forget. And love was dead, it had to be, self-respect insisted on it.

Even if he ignored his self-respect, he could no longer love her. Were he to embrace her, he would only think of William's arms around her; if he kissed her, he would only imagine William's embristled mouth. While she would be making comparisons rather than love. That was it. She must be bored with him even if she did not admit it. She found him inadequate and longed for some foreign Casanova. William was British enough but might have picked up exotic amatory practices on his travels. Charles never claimed any special prowess in that sphere and had always been suspicious of those who did. William was probably much better at it. After ten years of marriage no one could be original all the time. Nor should it matter a jot. A banished woman from her Harry's bed, but only for a week or two, a month or two. A few weeks after ten years and she threw herself at a sailor like some animal in season. He would forgive her but it must mean an end to all that side of the marriage.

Anyone else would throw her out of the house.

It was not as if he had been cruel or unfaithful. For ten years he had never looked at another woman. Was this his reward? Nine men out of ten would have taken advantage, for example, of Mrs Clayton's approachability, but not him, not Charles Cheviot. Loving his wife, he had resisted temptation, only to have his loyalty thrown in his face. Well, that love was dead now and here was the chance to transfer his affections, with honour, to Mrs Clayton. No one could blame him. All would agree that he had no alternative but to take decisive action – his wife with child by another like some Old Testament sinner. Mrs Clayton would make a good mother for Bertram and Leonora (a better one than Maria herself) and her own child could be their sister. True she was not a gentlewoman but nor was Maria *now*. Mrs Clayton's background might be ambiguous but her money would ensure their acceptance almost everywhere. The Clayton fortune would enable the Cheviot talents to fructify.

No, it was a tempting thought but he would not entertain it. He owed it to himself, admittedly, but he owed something to Maria too. He would be noble. If he ran away at the first hint of trouble was he not lowering himself to Maria's level, betraying their marriage as she had done, albeit with more excuse? Two wrongs do not make a right. That first betrayal must be decisively worse than any consequent one, but did not absolve him from all responsibility. It just entitled him to a certain amount of guilt-free licence. The world might not blame him if he freed himself from his errant wife, but he would blame himself, even though love – his pride and manhood demanded it – was necessarily dead.

Yet if love were dead, why did he feel so jealous? Anger and humiliation were understandable in the circumstances, but could he be jealous if love were gone? Did his present turmoil mean that, given time, he could love her once more? Yes, Maria should have another chance, little as she deserved it, but she must be taught a lesson as well.

'It would be insufferably pompous in me to read you a lesson,' he began pompously. 'If your own heart has not told you how grossly you have dishonoured and betrayed our marriage, no words of mine will do so. I shall merely record that you have made me the most wretched man on earth. For ten years I have loved you, and this is my reward. How deep and lasting the wounds may prove, time alone will show. For the moment I am no longer your husband but his ghost. No,

311

hear me out. If I indulge in bitterness, it is out of protective grief rather than vindictive rage. My words cannot hurt you as much as your actions have hurt me.

'The issue is what should we do now? That which is past is past and cannot be undone. There are three possibilities. The first is that you now require your liberty in order to start a new life. From what you have already said I understand that is not the case. Rest assured, however, that I shall not stand in your way if, on reflection, you wish to throw in your lot with another man. The second—'

'Must you torture me, Charles. This sounds like a prepared speech. You know I could never—'

'The second is that I should denounce you and institute divorce proceedings. After all that has passed between us I cannot bring myself to do that unless you ask me. Wounded as I am, I shall not strike back, however unmanly that may seem. I shall therefore adopt the third course, if you agree, and take no action at all. No doubt it is very weak of me: my principles have never been very strong and this episode further exposes my lack of firm character (as well as my other marital shortcomings). In other words, I forgive you (as I said yesterday). For the sake of the children and for your family's good name (and mine) we had best continue as man and wife, if that is still agreeable to you.'

'Oh Charles, it is what I want more than anything in the world. Thank you.'

At this point Charles should have said no more. He had hit back with his tongue hard enough for honour to be satisfied and wife to be hurt. No permanent damage had been done. Further and sweeter revenge was unnecessary, but too tempting, especially when she tried to kiss him.

'Then it is settled.' He repulsed her embrace. 'Naturally I shall respect your personal privacy. I shall make no tedious conjugal demands, you may be quite sure on that score.'

312

This was a medicine which it would have been wise for Maria to take with a submissive shrug.

'What do you mean? I impose no such condition.'

'I should hope not. You are hardly in a position to name terms. Nevertheless, as a gentleman, I shall respect your clearly implied preference. It would be dastardly of me to thrust unwelcome advances on a defenceless woman.'

'Why should they be unwelcome?'

'I can hardly flatter myself that they would be welcome, whatever you may insist now, after such a pointed demonstration of where your true affections lie.'

'It is you I love, not William.'

'The avowal fills me with confidence, madam.'

'You don't mean that. You are being sarcastic. How many times must I tell you it was all a mistake? It was the unconsidered act of a moment, foolish and wicked, but nothing to do with you and me.'

'You have made that clear. That is why I have forgiven you, whereas most husbands . . .'

'You call this forgiveness?'

'What else? It will save our marriage, our home, and our children. It will save you from the stigma of a second divorce. I cannot help it if I sound grudging; it is better to be grudgingly magnanimous than not magnanimous at all. If you do not wish us to remain man and wife, you have only to say so.'

'Man and wife in name only. A hollow mockery of marriage.'

'Do you think so? Very well, but it is you who have made it a mockery, not I. The cuckold is merely turning the other horn. Perhaps I should say he is turning the blind eye (a metaphor which your seafaring admirer will recognise). Do not worry, your good name is safe. What more can you want?'

'A husband, Charles, a husband, not an iceberg.'

'There is no need to raise your voice. Surely we can talk this over calmly, without shouting?'

'Not if you distort everything I say, but I will try again. Very well, we both know what happened and who is at fault. The sin is mine and mine alone. That is not in dispute, but you keep raking it up in different ways and taunting me with it while pretending to be sweetly reasonable.'

Charles sighed, reasonably. 'I am sorry you find my patience annoying. Tell me what you wish and I shall endeavour to comply without further comment.'

'I want a little kindness for a start. A little help and understanding.'

'I shall try to be kinder and more helpful.'

'And a little love.'

'Love?' Their eyes met fleetingly, for the first time during the interview. Both turned away at the same moment. Charles walked angrily to the window. His wrath was genuine but overacted (as usual). The battle of words now mattered more to him than any conflict of aims.

'I love you, Charles. That is what matters – only love.'

'Is it? Yes, you keep saying you love me. Thank you. I shall try to be worthy of your continuing affection.'

With an effort, Maria choked back the retort which his reply deserved. 'Do you love me still, a little? A vestige? Or does nothing remain?' Maria spoke in a whisper and held her breath but the question was ill-timed.

'Just at the moment I only confess to anger, jealousy, and mortification. Perhaps they are hopeful signs, but it is hardly the time for such enquiries. Let us consider the facts and leave our feelings for a more opportune occasion.'

'Your evasion says everything,' said Maria blankly.

'Do not jump to conclusions, Maria.'

314

'That is the first time you have called me by my name. All right. Let us keep to facts. Assuming they can be separated from feelings. What are the facts?'

'The main one is that people change. A new feature has arisen in our marriage and has to be dealt with. It is not uncommon, I understand, for some kind of sea change to occur between husband and wife after the first few years. Often it happens after a few months. You and I have been more fortunate than most, but the halcyon days could not go on for ever, it seems. Sooner or later comes the time when, to some extent, the wife goes her way, the husband his. We appear to have reached that stage. As you see I have been thinking about it all. Angry and hurt as I am, I accept my share of the blame, but that is beside the point. There is no call for panic or melodrama. We merely have to adjust and try to develop a new *modus vivendi*, some form of friendship perhaps, not too demanding but accepting each other's human frailty.'

'Frailty. Another of your jibes. For the last time, I tell you William means nothing to me. If we were alone on a desert island for the rest of our lives my frailty would not allow him to touch one hair of my head.'

'Good. I take that with a pinch of salt, but the intention is laudable.'

'And what about your frailties?'

'They are legion, I confess, though the particular one to which, I take it, you are alluding is not among them. As yet.'

'As yet?'

'As yet. I have not, as yet, been anything but faithful.'

'Are you implying that you are now going to start? Do you plan to take a mistress?'

'That is my own affair. You have forfeited—'

'No, it is mine too. Answer, answer!'

315

'All right, but only because you shout. I can hardly afford the luxury of a mistress. They are usually very expensive, I understand. On the other hand, one cannot necessarily foresee all the consequences of a newly celibate domestic life.'

'Why must it be celibate? As far as I am concerned nothing is altered.'

'Delicacy suggests a certain monasticism . . .'

'Tump, sir! I do not believe in this delicacy of yours. Call it cruelty or hypocrisy or self-righteousness rather.'

'Call it whatever you choose, Mrs Cheviot. It cannot alter the fact that you are carrying another man's child. Delicacy, hypocrisy or plain distaste – it matters not which – makes it unacceptable for me to cohabit at this time with my lawful wedded wife.'

'So you claim the right to cohabit with someone else.'

'I am not aware that I have done so, but if I were to form some other attachment, I would expect your understanding. You are hardly in a position to object. Indeed, you should be grateful, for it would diminish – and share – your burden of guilt.'

'Thank you very much. You would only be taking a mistress to make me feel better. Is that what you mean? How very considerate.'

'Madam, for the sake of the children I am prepared to overlook and forgive your behaviour. For your own sake I decline to do what most husbands would be in honour bound to do. In return I have a right to certain freedom of action which I may or may not exercise. It was no wish of mine that you should abrogate your matrimonial rights and privileges.'

'I see. So it amounts to this: the price of your "forgiveness" is to turn our marriage into a travesty. We may share a roof and a name but not a bed. We shall lead separate existences in the same house for the sake of respectability and for the children – while you carry on like some Turk, no doubt starting with that Clayton woman.'

Charles flushed. 'I have no wish to behave like any Turk. Should the occasion arise, however, I claim dispensation from certain matrimonial restraints at least equal to those which you have already assumed. But you are putting far too much emphasis on—'

'In fact, you claim your pound and a half of flesh. *Quid pro quo* with a vengeance.'

'If you see it like that.'

'Well, I hope you enjoy your revenge, for that is what it is. My God, what a humbug you are, Charles! Pretending to forgive, you accuse, taunt, and humiliate me at every turn; pretending to be pure as driven snow, you claim the right to be as immoral as you wish; pretending to save our marriage, you cynically mock it. How could any self-respecting wife accept your terms?'

'Laying aside the fact that no self-respecting wife would have put herself into your position, the interpretation you put on my terms, as you call them, is characteristically melodramatic. Common sense should tell you that the *modus vivendi* I recommend is in the general interest, even if it has some trifling corollaries which may not be entirely to your liking.'

'Trifling! You call them trifling. Oh, I cannot talk to you any more when every sentence is some new sneer. We go round and round and always come back to the same point. Leave me alone, I can sustain this interview no further.'

Charles hesitated and shrugged. At the door he bowed and withdrew, lower in his own esteem. Yet he had at least done the decent and magnanimous thing even if he had done it in a shabby and censorious manner. In practice he was unlikely to exercise that *quid pro quo* and would probably return to his wicked wife's fourposter as soon as she had

317

eaten enough humble pie. Meanwhile she had received the lesson she deserved, even if it hurt him as much as it hurt her. It was settled that they should both seek increase in their wretchedness.

Humiliated, ground under, Maria could feel but not think. Better unmarried than submit to the fate Charles proposed. She would not stand for it. Rash and over-generous, she had meant no ill; proud and true to herself, she had done nothing wrong by her private standards; guilty, she felt no shame; remorse but not shame. Must she be treated like a leper for ever because of a moment's cousinly kindness? How sordid and squalid of the world to set such store on one particular act while condoning so many genuine betrayals. How stony-hearted and cunning of Charles to twist the knife so murderously while pretending forgiveness. Lethal forgiveness! Life on his terms would be a walking death. For the sake of two children she hardly knew and a family which had cut her off with a shilling, she was to be allowed to lock herself up in a grave. No, a thousand times over. Better the final sleep than a half-life on those terms; better the world's condemnation than eternal chastity.

She would kill herself, and serve him right. No, that would play into his hands. He would go straight to Mrs Clayton or some other woman. Suicide was not only wrong but difficult and required more courage than staying alive. Besides she was dead already. Charles had murdered her. There could be no return to the old warmth and trust, after this. Too much had been uncovered. If he had given one hint that he might in time forget, if he had only hit her or lost his temper or shown that he was out of his mind with rage and not responsible for his actions, then there could be hope. But that icy, inhuman control; that calculated indifference; that determination to hurt, had nothing to do with love, nor even hate. Where there was hate, love might return (at the moment she

318

hated Charles, it was the only alternative to loving him), but where there was only polite, malignant unconcern, love had surely fled for ever.

Arrogant, priggish, inadequate, grasping, sanctimonious sponger – let him rot in sterile gentility; lazy, pretentious, facile, superficial pasticheur – let him never sing or write another note, let him lose the use of pen and brush. His mean spirit and viper's tongue should not dominate her. She would make her own life. She would choose freedom, the freedom of the boards. She could always go to Edmund Kean. And if, despite appearances, Charles loved her still, he would seek her out. Else she would become a great actress, and be damned to him.

However, she could wait till next week. She would give him another chance.

Chapter Seventeen

Let others dwell on guilt and blame. For my part I acquit Maria and Charles Cheviot of the major charges they brought against each other, although events may seem to bear them out. Often a merciful fortune protects us from the effects of folly or weakness; at other times a malevolent hand exposes us to retribution out of all proportion to our fault. Charles was hurt and clever but not cruel; he only wanted a little revenge. Maria was proud and passionate, but not impenitent; she only needed a little mercy. Both had qualities of temperament which must lead to occasional friction and both had lessons to teach the other. Reconciliation was possible, but someone must be first to break the ice.

The following week was spent in hostile silence, acrimonious recapitulation, and futile negotiation. Each time they returned to the problem they found themselves repeating the same arguments, like actors locked in their parts. Their lines might change but the meaning remained the same. Every Othello has to smother his Desdemona; each Lady Macbeth must goad her husband to his downfall. One day when they had both acted the same old drama with even more exaggerated intensity than usual, Maria left home with black looks and her jewel case. Half-way to Birmingham she almost turned back but the thought of Charles's sardonic, implicitly victorious welcome fortified her determination.

In Birmingham she found Edmund Kean and asked him for theatrical work. The great actor had deteriorated horribly: pox and Cox had taken fearful toll and drink had reduced him to a physical wreck. To make matters worse, the Birmingham audiences were giving him a rough ride, every performance producing more or less riotous behaviour. London playgoers had taken similar action for a few weeks after the Cox trial but had later relented, admiring his persistence and courage as much as his declining powers. The provinces, however, seemed less easy-going and Kean had to atone nightly for the open scandal of his private life.

'*Magnus amator mulierum*, I bid you welcome Mrs Cheviot, though I have fallen on evil days.'

'No more than I have, Mr Kean,' said Maria.

'How so? Has Charles, my noble Pan, betrayed you? Heaven forfend.'

'He has cast me out. All but that.'

'Leontes and Hermione?'

'Except that this Hermione is at fault.'

Kean looked at her shrewdly with quick, black, penetrating eyes. 'I ask you nothing,' he said, 'only tell me why you have come here.'

'For work. I wish to support myself by acting. Please give me a chance.'

Her audition was brief. Kean gave her four or five Shake-spearean cues and a goblet of brandy. Maria responded as Juliet or Portia or Lady Anne, held out her goblet for more and, showing some familiarity and ability with the texts, was given her chance. The company was short of female players who could pass as gentlewomen and she was allowed to play royalty or aristocrats with small parts. At first she was awk-ward and frightened but she soon gained experience and, within a month, was acting confidently. On one occasion, playing Lady Allworth to Kean's Overreach in *A New Way to Pay Old Debts* (the first play in which she had ever watched Kean), she almost stole a scene, and was warned by the star's scowl not to do so again. For the most part, he treated her with marked consideration. Every night she hoped Charles would be in the audience.

The Cox scandal had made the great actor wary of wives. He made a few amorous advances in his cups but was easily resisted. Perhaps Maria would have given in had he tried harder or threatened to dispense with her acting services. Yet it was assumed by the company and the press that the new player was Mrs Cox's successor. The supposed affair was gleefully taken up by caricaturists, delighted that Kean was once more associating with a married woman, indeed a lady. The most popular cartoon depicted a trouserless Sir Giles Overreach saluting a decolletée Lady Allworth, while an irate passenger who has stepped off the Liverpool Mail impotently beats on their window with a baton. It was entitled 'His Old Way of Acquiring New Debts'.

Terrified of another lawsuit (and one in which his involuntary innocence would never be believed by judge or jury), Kean hurriedly passed Maria on to an old crony with a small touring company, persuading her that she would gain invaluable experience and be able to play many more parts than in his own company. The deal cost Kean hundreds of pounds less than the damages he feared would be awarded to Mr Cheviot.

Compared with Kean, the new actor-manager was quiet and kind. He even believed that players should act as a team and, to her surprise, Maria found that she did learn more than under Kean's virtuoso shadow. It was a modest company but knew its repertoire and enjoyed its work despite being in constant financial difficulties. The public appreciated stars more than teamwork. Often Maria had to go without her meagre salary and in time she was prevailed upon to lend some of her diminishing funds to keep the group together. After three months, she was pawning her jewellery to help; the show had to go on.

And one day it did. The company de-camped while Maria was seeing a physician about her pregnancy, now apparent to the close observer. She had seen them through the summer and given them most of her money. It would still be easy enough to search them out and demand compensation, but what good would it do her? If she was not wanted any more, she was not wanted, and that was it. There was no money for wages let alone compensation.

It was early November and the Scottish winter was descending on a solitary heavy Maria who still retained some pride. Since she had left Rodney Street, a few curt letters had been exchanged. At first a gesture of submission on one side or a hint of tenderness on the other might, probably *would* have led to the reconciliation which both wanted on their own terms but, as time passed and neither made the first move, both became more intransigent. Even the self-disgust which grew as her belly grew, took second place to the spirit which prevented Maria, deserted and destitute, from throwing herself upon her husband's mercy. She had used up all her capital but the Rodney Street lease had been purchased with Bertram funds. Charles could send her money if he wished but she would not beg from him, nor from William (wherever he might be), nor from the rest of her family. She might be alone but it was they who were on trial, for by now all at Mansfield must know about the rupture in Liverpool. Deciding to remain in Scotland, she sent Charles an address. If he cared remotely he would rescue her one way or another. Her few remaining pounds and trinkets would see her through until the child was born.

I draw a veil over the next few wretched, lonely weeks. The little girl was born in a cold Edinburgh attic on Christmas eve with the help of a midwife Maria had met in a tavern a few days before. Mother and nurse were both intoxicated when labour began but child and mother survived. It was an easier birth than Bertram's or Leonora's; more like the one Maria had assisted on the way to Liverpool. But no kindly aunt welcomed the child to the world with tears, and no fairy godmother left it a diamond brooch. Its first visitor was the landlord with a final demand for overdue rent. After paying what she could Maria was left with a few shillings and her wedding ring. Her pride quailed, her spirit capitulated. Removing the ring to pay the midwife, she wrote to her brother Tom at Mansfield Park.

Meanwhile, what of Charles? At first, though infuriated by the irresponsibility of Maria's flight, he saw it as one of her tantrums, recklessly over-indulged. She would soon return, chastened and penitent – and he would forgive her, with more right on his side than ever. The children and servants were told that she was visiting friends and only the Randalls were given some hint of the true state of affairs. When he heard that Maria had joined Edmund Kean, however, Charles's stomach turned and his heart stood still.

Part of him might hero-worship Kean but he knew, better than most, that off-stage the tragedian was an insatiable lecher. It was inconceivable that a man who used two or three whores during each performance should not make advances to a beautiful, would-be actress such as his wife. Moreover, Kean had never made any secret of his admiration of Maria. He would seize his chance for sure. And the result? – with a further spasm of nausea Charles remembered that Kean's venereal disease was public knowledge.

Yet he continued to hope and trust. Despite appearances, despite probability, he clung to the belief that the episode with William really had been an aberration and that Maria would not be unfaithful again. Irrationally and with agonising doubts he continued, on balance, to trust her. If only she would come back to him – but unless she came back of her own volition her motives for returning would be for ever suspect.

And then, some two months after Maria's departure, an unexpected parcel arrived just when Charles was beginning to give up hope. It had been most carefully wrapped and contained a tastefully mounted colour engraving entitled 'His Old Way of Acquiring New Debts'. The likenesses were not very good but the principal figures were immediately recognisable. Initially, Charles seemed paralysed, incapable of feeling or thought; then numbness gave way to utter desolation; in time (several full seconds), the misery deepened into righteous fury – before exploding into fearful elation and fatherly relief. So he had been gulled again, his innocent credulity had been misplaced, and the cynically obvious had indeed occurred. Yet suffering, he began to realise, sometimes liberates.

In pitying himself (and not forgetting to acknowledge his own small fraction of the blame), Charles did not at first notice where the parcel came from nor ask who sent it. Later he found that it had been franked in Northampton and that its superscription was in a hand similar to that in Maria's *Works of Spenser*, a confirmation present from her Aunt Norris.

The lawyer whose advice he now sought said he had no alternative to divorce proceedings; the Randalls supported him with unquestioning family loyalty; Mrs Clayton was sympathetic and understanding; Bertram and Leonora wept perfunctorily; everyone applauded him for keeping the home together and standing by the deserted children. He now considered himself morally free, yet total discretion continued to guide his conduct in relation to Mrs Clayton. For her diversion, however, he did re-enact the will-reading scene at Sir Thomas Bertram's funeral sooner and with more explicit financial detail than good taste or true artlessness permitted.

The pathetic letter, begging help, reached Mansfield Park just as its proprietor was considering his New Year resolutions. Sir Tom immediately consulted Edmund; Edmund broke the news to Fanny; Fanny confided tearfully in Susan; and Susan told Mrs Norris. Unnecessary to report the horror and indignation, the waspish comfort, and the complacent worry with which the story was greeted. Yet turmoil and upset were not as great as on the previous occasion. The truth was that William's complicity muted the general wrath, confused the censure, and inclined them to charity. Maria, of course, was accused and William excused, but it was soon agreed that the family had to close ranks, and act. A number of plans were discussed before Mrs Norris, casting her mind back more than twenty years, suggested that they should take charge of the child and bring it to Mansfield. Remembering her own unhappiness as a foster-child, Fanny began to protest, but found it impossible to articulate her objections without hurting

325

her new ally or criticising the dead. In any case, a newly born baby was different from a nine-year-old child.

'She need not be treated as one of *us*,' pursued Mrs Norris. 'She could be looked after by Nanny or, if Nanny is too old, be adopted by one of the tenants. The Marshalls, for example, are childless. Yes, the Marshalls will do very well, hard-working and thrifty as they are. They would require very little pecuniary inducement to take on the child. Indeed they should require none, since their own needs are so simple. I would take it amiss if we have to support her while she lives at the Marshalls, for I cannot abide meanness in any form. And when she is old enough she may carry out light duties for her elderly great-aunts, so long as she is grateful and well-disposed and remembers her place. I do hope she will appreciate her good fortune in coming to Mansfield. Yes, that is quite settled in my mind as the best solution for all concerned.'

The others shifted uncomfortably; at first no one spoke. Eyes turned to Fanny but she remained silent and pre-occupied. She was thinking less of her own childhood than her own child. She ought not to permit any solution which would put Maria's baby at Mrs Norris's mercy yet she could not bring herself to take it into her own house as a disturbing and perhaps dangerous little sister for Cassandra. And yet it was William's child too. Favourite brother William, how could he, how could he?

'If she comes here at all she comes as my niece twice over,' declared Susan stoutly. 'Whether as William's daughter or as Maria's she is innocent herself and has a claim on every one of us. You and I must adopt her Tom, unless Fanny claims her for the parsonage.'

'I agree, we all have a duty to the child,' said her elder sister. 'It is only Cassandra's extreme delicacy which prevents me from insisting she come to us. If you had not spoken first, Susan, I should certainly have made the offer.

Edmund and I could manage even if it meant disturbing ou[r] plans for Cassandra and turning the household upside down. The fact that Cassandra, just at the moment, needs such very special care . . . What do you think Edmund?'

'I concur with all you say, my dear. As head of the family, Tom must have first refusal. My dear brother, if you and Susan – unblessed as yet by children – prefer not to have her, then we shall be very, very happy to take her in, whatever the cost and inconvenience.'

'That settles it,' said Tom with unusual finality. 'She comes to us.'

And in the event, they went to Scotland and fetched her. Maria readily consented to the adoption and agreed to renounce all claims on the child. Young Lady Bertram loved her little daughter from the moment she saw her and gave her, within the year, a little brother as companion. Sir Tom had half a mind to thank Maria for his son and heir.

As for Maria herself, as soon as she was able to travel she went back to Liverpool hoping against hope for a reconciliation and prepared to accept any terms Charles might impose. She felt that the child's adoption by Mansfield Park had somehow finished and legitimised the episode. If Sir Tom was so kind and forgiving, why not Charles?

No one was at home, however, and the Rodney Street house was for sale. Not daring to face the Randalls, Maria betook herself to the family lawyer and learnt that she was all but divorced. The decree was a certainty since her letters had confessed adultery with Captain Price while her supposed infidelity with Edmund Kean was known to every gossip-monger and caricaturist in the country. In both cases 'opportunity by association' was not in question. The lawyer had some personal effects of Mrs Cheviot's in his strong room and was authorised to hand them over in return for a signature. As to the Rodney Street house, legally it was r Cheviot's but there was nothing to prevent her bringing an action if she thought she had a claim on it. On the other hand, it was his duty to warn her that his client had an undeniable counter claim against Mrs Cheviot and her paramours for 'criminal conversation'. In a common law suit, damages would normally be awarded to the husband according to the loss he was supposed to have suffered by the seduction and desertion of his wife. In the circumstances it would probably be wise to settle the two matters out of court and, if Mrs Cheviot's legal adviser approached him, he was sure that Mr Cheviot would be as accommodating and amicable as those same circumstances permitted. His client wanted to be as fair as possible.

Amicable, accommodating, fair – Maria knew it was all over. Final rejection was contained in the lawyer's passionless legalism, ultimate betrayal in Charles's uncaring, calculated correctness. Life, spirit, even anger ebbed. He had killed her. By letting her ruin herself, he had murdered her as surely as if he had given poison; by failing to stop her he had pushed her into the abyss; by bringing out her shortcomings and playing on her weaknesses, he had manipulated her destruction – while appearing to do more than was reasonable to save the marriage. And after it had all been so good for so long. After he had meant everything to her. After they had loved each other without condition, and thought themselves beloved.

She was finally dead and the cruellest part of her death was that the body had to go on living. How? Where?

Maria rotted a month or two in Liverpool before deciding, in numb defiance and despair, to try her luck in America once more. Tom and Susan had given her enough money for her passage. She let Charles have the Rodney Street house without a fight, and sailed on the first convenient boat. On the trip she took Shakespeare

as her reading matter and developed a special identificat
with Cleopatra.

As soon as he was free, Charles Cheviot married Mrs
Clayton. Bertram and Leonora were content with the arrangement though they would have preferred their father to marry
the governess. The only untoward incident on the wedding
day was when Mrs Clayton's daughter, known to everyone
as Moo, arrived at the breakfast wearing a brooch inscribed
with her real name. It was a superbly executed piece for a
mere child to wear and it must have cost a mint of money
to have 'Maria' picked out in such large diamonds. Charles
prayed that his own children would not associate it with their
mother. It never even occurred to them to do so.

Moo explained, 'It was a birthday present from my
fairy godmother.'

But Charles declined to entertain any ghosts that day.
He frowned for a moment when he learnt that Bertram
and Moo were born on the selfsame day one year apart but
dismissed as absurd the unbidden idea which knocked on his
memory. The door was soon bolted, the fact accepted, and
the idea forgotten.

Six months later they all moved to a comfortable
residence outside Manchester in the Pennine foothills.
During the move, for which Charles's furniture was tak-
en out of store, the second Mrs Cheviot happened upon
a portrait of the first Mrs Cheviot. Painted by Charles
on board the *Nestor*, it was the only souvenir of Maria
he had retained.

'I am sorry,' he said to his new wife. 'I could never
bring myself to part with it. Best thing I ever drew of
her or anyone else.'

quite understand,' she said after a very long pause. is beautiful. We must hang it.'

'My dear, I do not think we need go as far as that.'

'It is right that Bertram and Leonora should be reminded of their real mother. Let us put it in the nursery.'

The children thanked her with their usual good manners, but seldom gave the picture more than a passing glance. Only one person in that household paid any tribute to Charles's masterpiece. When she was alone she would steal into the nursery and kneel before it and weep. Sometimes the portrait wept too.

Time passed and the affairs of Clayton Mills began to slip. Ever-increasing competition and incompetent or dishonest managers produced a steady fall in profits. The sum of £10,000, intended to convert the weaving sheds from hand-looms to power-looms, disappeared in mysterious circumstances and could never be traced. Charles advised that they soldier on with hand-looms since the older method gave a better weave. The advice was taken, greatly to their competitors' advantage. Sam Clayton's heir seemed to lose her touch and her interest. Within two years she was forced to sell the business at a knock-down price and, by the time lawyers had finished their work, the Clayton fortune had been reduced from £5000 to £500 a year.

The second Mrs Clayton kept the house clean, the children tidy, the meals punctual. She saw no one socially except the parson and his wife. Business responsibilities gone, there was all the time in the world for Charles to revise his opera or compose new music, but he seldom went to the piano. With £500 a year there was no need. He settled into a placid way of life, gained weight and lost hair. He went short

330

walks, dreamt of recognition, drew pleasant little sketches, and taught all three children as much music as their modest talents could absorb. On Sundays, he played the organ in church. Sometimes he wondered why the former artist's model had become so stern and respectable. However it was more peaceful than being married to Maria. The new Mrs Cheviot never argued, never cajoled, never enthused, never laughed, never lost her temper, and never noticed if he was in a bad mood. Occasionally a news item, like the production of *Antony and Cleopatra* in Boston, Massachusetts, with an unknown English actress in the title rôle, reminded him of the old days, and he thought of them regretfully, but not for very long.

And Maria?

A certain Mrs Rushworth settled in Boston. She had not been there above six months when an advertisement in the newspaper advised her that if Maria Cheviot, sometime Rushworth, *née* Bertram would apply to the offices of Messrs Harris & Hardstaff, she would learn of something to her advantage. On doing so, and having proven her identity, she received a draft for the sum of £10,000, donor anonymous. Since this was the capital sum she had forfeited by her father's change of will, she always assumed that the gift (which helped to establish her on the stage) was a further example of a liberal act designed to erase a mean one.